SLANT OF THE WILD WIND

BOOKS BY *Garland Roark*

SLANT OF THE WILD WIND
RAINBOW IN THE ROYALS
FAIR WIND TO JAVA
WAKE OF THE RED WITCH

Garland Roark

SLANT OF THE
WILD WIND

SEARS READERS CLUB   CHICAGO

*The characters and the incidents in this book
are entirely the product of the author's imagination
and have no relation to any person or event in real life.*

Library of Congress Catalog Card Number: 52-5127

TO BRYAN C. BURK

Contents

Book one

[*THE GATHERING WINDS*

CHAPTER I

Captain Redd stood the poop, his eyes on the head yards abox, and topsails soon to fly. Jib sheets were hauled aft and ready for hoisting, and the tug brought the ship's head to wind and tide.

The *Lady of Glasgow* got her sheer in the right direction. Her jibs would fill now and he called for a hoist. She was easing along. Her sails were filling aft. The foreyard had to come around in a hurry, the jib sheets eased off, and spanker set.

Acres of sail were pouring down from aloft. She was on the wind—the full and by—all hands jumping to the stream of orders, "Haul taut! Mains'l haul!" Then, "Let go and haul!" The spanker eased off as the tacks were boarded. The quay was fast falling astern; the wake lengthened. The tug cut loose and she was on her own, driving for Bradley Head and the open sea.

The arms of the harbor slipped by as the sun clung to the edge of the sky.

Big water loomed up ahead, choppy and burning alive with sunset colors. Then the sun bedded down and the last shades of day faded into evening. The riding lights winked on, and stars glimpsed through a veil of flying mist, creating an illusion of a race in the heavens. The *Lady of Glasgow* rocked and strained ahead, cordage groaning, rigging whistling in the wind.

She was in the deep stream of the Tasman.

Captain Redd seemed reluctant to leave the weather side. He felt the ship under him, alive, running east, and tearing on, the wind's eye six points on the bow. He took in the position of land beyond the wake and ordered the helmsman to strike the warning for the change of the watch. A rough energy settled over him, as though it descended from the top-hamper even as it lifted from the rolling sea. He was at home. The sea was a consoling woman, never quibbling over right and wrong, demanding only one virtue in a mortal man: the strength to cope with her. Only that. If a man didn't possess it, he didn't belong.

He welcomed the flying spray striking at his face, and the tossing deck under him as the *Lady* split the starlit waters in a race to rising seas and winds. Now the sea owned him; the baptism was ended, the communion renewed. The practical man emerged.

"I haven't seen Mr. van Oren," he said to Mr. Hyde when eight bells struck.

"Below, sir, I'm sure. He asked me to send his bags down before we filled away. Shall I take over?"

"We're running against Untell and time, Mr. Hyde."

"Captain Untell?"

"He's got a big lead on us. I'm whistling for a beam wind, but by the looks of the weather I may get hard squalls."

Mr. Hyde had sailed under Redd for a decade. A big man with hooked nose and square jaw and a deceiving softness of eye, he had more than once risked his life for Redd. He was loyal, and he knew Redd was loyal to him. The bond was strong and unspoken. He shared a trust, and he knew that Redd charted a proposition as carefully and boldly as he charted a course, this one was no exception, whatever it was. And it must be a big one with the head of the firm aboard.

He looked at his captain again. The stamp of the sea was written all over him, in the stern eyes and clean pride of his face. Rippling muscles flowed down from his sea-bronzed neck to wide shoulders. There was a glimpse of brutality in his physical bearing. He towered over Mr. Hyde, who was wondering why Captain Redd and the shipowner were chasing a sister ship of the Van Oren line. Like Redd, it was something out of the ordinary.

Captain Redd was cracking on sail. The crew had the experience to know it took a seaman to do this at night. But every man aboard knew he had a knack for calling the turn of weather in total darkness, and they knew his sense of weather was keyed to the occasion when the freshening wind took on a rainy moan. All light sails came in, prudently, and let hang in their gear; upper topsail yards were lowered, and the helm was shifted so the ship would take it over the quarter. When the squall bore down on them in a wicked hiss, they were ready. Redd, calm, impatient, waited for the sea to go down. A little later he said:

"Mr. Hyde, the wind is shifting fair. We'll run under all she's got."

The steward appeared before he could order a trim. "Sir," he said, "I waited for Mr. van Oren so's I could serve his supper. Then I knocked at his stateroom. He ain't there. Nor in the saloon."

Redd ordered Mr. Hyde to take a look below and on the main and fore decks. If the steward was drinking again, he'd log him. He ordered the foresail reefed, for lifting effect, and headsails down. He would run before this sea. He was scudding under main lower topsail and reefed foresail when Mr. Hyde came aft, saying:

"The steward's right, sir. Neither head nor hair of him. Odd, I'd say."

Redd broke a growing silence between them with, "Very odd." Sheet lightning lit up his inscrutable face before he said, "Take over, mister."

The chief mate started. When Redd used the word "mister," something big was in the wind. There was an edge to his voice that alerted those who really knew him. Mr. Hyde watched him stalk off, unaware that he staggered under the weight of a serious proposition suddenly shifted to his shoulders.

Redd felt nothing but resentment; it flared high. And with it came a prodigious urge to toss the whole thing back at the shipowner in damn lively fashion. He was considering doing just that as he threw open the door to his quarters. His salient jaw clamped tightly as his gaze swept the room. He sat down and reached for a bottle and glass, saying:

"Easy as you go, Captain."

He drank slowly, thinking, looking for a way out, always returning to the deception practiced on him——

Sir George had come aboard with his bags about an hour before the ship sailed. A busy time for a captain when the last of the barrels rolled across decks and cargo slings swung aboard and a ship was in the process of divorcing land. He might have chosen that hour purposely, realizing that even a shipowner could not compete with ship for a master's full attention. However, Van Oren had come on an urgent mission.

Thinking back to their meeting on deck, Redd remembered clearly the worried look dominating Sir George's handsome face. A man in his fifties with shrewd gray eyes, he suggested by his bearing the power he commanded in Australian shipping circles. He was called Sir George, though he was not a baronet. All this ran through Redd's mind, as did the words of the owner:

"Another bank closed yesterday, Captain, with money in the vaults. It isn't necessary to explain the position it puts me in. You've got to overtake the *Castlereagh*."

Redd knew of the big bank failure. The Great Sydney Union was just another big bank that had gone under in this financial crisis of 1893. The Australian money panic emanated from the amount of capital locked in the banks that had failed. Before the crisis speculation had become so furious that banks of Australia had lent more than ninety million pounds sterling on mining schemes, land, cattle, wool, and sugar. The inevitable happened. And at a time when world trade was shaky. But what Redd didn't know was the *Castlereagh's* connection with all this. He soon learned:

Van Oren had shipped bullion to England, so, he said, he could draw on banks that would not fail. He had ordered Captain Untell to sail fast. And the ship had scarcely hit the open sea before the bottom fell out of Sydney. The bank failed. And Sir George wrapped up his problem in a few words:

"The gold Captain Untell carries is all that can save me."

Redd started; he remembered well this unpleasant surprise. His own fortunes were caught in the strangling web. Whatever happened to the great firm of Van Oren, Limited, would happen to him and all others under the house flag. Small wonder then that Sir George was impatient. With enough gold to save the firm somewhere out on the high seas, time was a factor.

Sir George talked on, about: how fast Captain Untell could drive a ship, and his one-day start on the *Lady of Glasgow;* how he was needed here at a time like this, though he must go along to effect a transfer of the gold.

That was when Redd asked why he didn't send a written order by Geoffrey Lipscomb-Grey, his business manager, for a quick return to Sydney with the gold. The question drew an answer: "There's more to it than appears on the surface, Captain Redd." With this remark he seemed to close up like a clam, as though afraid of revealing too much to his ship captain.

A little later he said it would require damn fast sailing to overtake Untell. And he smiled knowingly. He knew what lay behind the rivalry between his two famous captains, and the fact that it almost approached open animosity appealed to him now: the faster Redd drove the *Lady*, the quicker he would lessen the threat of ruin. Redd said it would be a pleasure to show Untell he could do it, and Van Oren smiled once more and talked about his daughter Martha who was due home from England soon; which was another reason for overtaking the *Castlereagh* in a hurry. This would please Geoffrey, he went on reminiscently, since Geoffrey, his logical successor, had waited for Martha to grow up.

Even then Redd wondered why Sir George was telling him this. He was thinking also of his many voyages under the Van Oren flag and that this one presented a rare opportunity for him to serve the shipowner and thereby himself. He said: "If you're needed here, why not send a written order to Untell by me? It's that simple."

Then Sir George frowned and rejected it, saying, "I want nothing in writing to connect me with the boxes."

So there was more than one box of gold! No. Sir George could no longer evade him, and he disclosed, hesitantly, certain facts: there were seven boxes, six of which contained Bendigo ore—he was refinancing the mining syndicate with British capital, if he could, before it collapsed, and using the ore as a cover for the gold; a precaution against loss in shipping, he said, adding with a humorless chuckle:

"However, Captain Untell thinks all the boxes contain ore."

Redd covered his surprise with a facetious reply. "Nothing like putting full trust in your shipmasters, Mr. van Oren."

A sudden intensity in Sir George's eyes fell away before a look of tolerance. "Perhaps I deserve it, Captain. But I can't be too careful. Just remember this: no man can serve me or my flag without being rewarded handsomely."

Then the ship demanded Redd and he left Van Oren, who was asking the chief mate to place his bags in his stateroom. Where he had gone from there, Redd could only imagine. Probably strolling along the quay in one moment and, seeing no one aboard ship watching him, streaking off toward Bridge Street and his offices the next.

Anger was justified, though he was wise enough to know it wasn't his best friend now. But it ran high in him as he saw Van Oren slinking away from any actual brush with the gold. And here he was driving at top speed to rectify the owner's mistake in shipping the boxes to England. Sir George van Oren was shrewd, and ruthless.

"Aye, mister, you're cunning as they come," he said aloud. "If I run into trouble serving you, I'm responsible, not you. If I fail to serve you, I'll lose my command."

2

All the while his ship ran on, cleaving the seas and spreading acres of foam out from her sides; on toward the *Castlereagh*, eating up the Sydney-Auckland track; ran on when it was in his power to turn about for Sydney. He wanted to do that. And yet the swishing of water down her sides and the roar of the rigging restrained him. The rhythm of the sea, his command of the great *Lady of Glasgow*, these rose up strong in him. Should he turn back now and lose them; or should he go ahead and risk losing his master's license, his right to sail under the red ensign?

The Board of Trade dealt severely with sea captains who violated rules of the stream. And getting the boxes from a man like Untell, who had no love for him whatever, was likely to provoke charges against him. If they were strong enough, a naval court would hear all evidence. On the other hand, Untell's position under Van Oren paralleled his. Sir George could handle Untell. In summation, he was perhaps imagining all sorts of trouble that didn't exist.

As for Van Oren—"No man can serve me or my flag without being rewarded handsomely." He had said that. And what service was more important to Sir George van Oren than saving his firm?

Redd's mind was made up. What had appeared to be a dirty trick was shaping into an opportunity for bettering his fortune. Van Oren would be more in his debt than if he had remained aboard ship. Aye, it was nothing short of a windfall.

With the big decision behind him, he looked ahead to a meeting with Untell; and beyond that to the worst that could come of it. A volume of British maritime law was opened and he read carefully the letter of the law dealing with piracy. It would be just that, since no captain would give up any portion of his cargo without sealed orders from his firm. Untell was a stickler for rules. But the law was one thing and conditions another; it was a matter of tying them together. And now was the time to begin.

He went straightway to the quarter-deck and, after a quick look at his sails and weather, said, "Mr. Hyde, you'll break out a search gang and cover the ship for Mr. van Oren."

"But, sir! He isn't aboard."

"I want it official, for the logbook. Now show lively."

Perplexed, Mr. Hyde obeyed. During the search Redd asked for a reading of the log, and when the men had combed the ship and returned with palms-up shrugs, he said for the benefit of the entire crew:

"Thirty miles out of Sydney." Then, almost in the same breath, he cried, "All hands abaft the mainmast."

They gathered, only the helmsman missing, a curious lot who couldn't understand how a shipowner could be lost. When full silence fell over the group, Redd commenced:

"Mr. van Oren boarded us in Sydney for this voyage. Did anyone see him depart?"

The bosun spoke up. "Aye, sir. I seen him walkin' along the quay before the order for takin' in moorin' lines. But I guessed he'd boarded us when we filled away."

After further questioning, Redd addressed them: "Seems we thought he was aboard and sailed off without him." Allowing a pause, in which he seemed to fathom every thought behind their faces, he said, "That's why I've assembled you here. I'll tell you this much: our destination isn't land. And since Mr. van Oren's absence is likely to cause me some embarrassment, I want every man of you to trim a sharp eye and remember all you see."

That was all. And not a member of the crew possessed the temerity to ask the question in every mind: where were they going and why? Captain Redd looked at them a few seconds then moved to the weather braces. Mr. Hyde's "To your stations" sent them forward, reluctant and unsatisfied.

Eyes of the crew shifted in the night from ship and weather to captain. He was piling on canvas, maneuvering the last stretch out of her sails. He ran through light squalls and gave her a lift above the attending high seas; he ran out studding booms and snared a following wind while it lasted. The men realized he was in a "billy-blue" hurry to reach destination, which wasn't land. They were by nature curious. Thus the puzzle of this run bounced back at them time and again during the night, unsolved. The majority gave it up as useless effort more tiring than wrestling with big sails high in a moist wind. It was all a little strange. But so was the personality of the ship, for that matter——

The *Lady of Glasgow* was a sailor's idea of a smart sailing vessel. She had fine lines. A double white stripe ran her black topsides and she showed a golden copper below. She was long and magnificently sparred, and a scroll of white and gold framed a big-breasted goddess at her bows. But she possessed a fault, a defect that wasn't built into her. It was in her name, which she flaunted in challenge to an inviolate tradition of the sea. There were thirteen letters in her name, which meant to sailors that she would come to a bad end.

But her gamble against tradition lay in the lap of the wind gods, who seemed to smile upon her master. The men believed that as

long as Captain Redd remained the favored son there was nothing
to worry about. He was captain of her destiny, and theirs.

He wore well with them; gave them credit for knowing their
work; expected no more of them than the next master. Where
he stood apart from other captains began nowhere and ended
there, as far as facts were concerned. However, there was something about him, his bearing, his sustained reserve, that lent him
that mark of total sureness which constituted the highest virtue
in the eyes of seamen.

And now in the predawn light he was sailing with less pru-
dence than he had ever before shown. As a consequence some
sail was blown. When the watch ended at four, he continued to
stand the poop, a trait uncommon to him.

The day came on slowly, painting the sea in soft colors. The
sky blossomed over the water full and clear. As they ran on under
all the canvas she could carry, the sea calmed and winds held fair.
Two lookouts were posted, and on through the day the *Lady*
continued to eat up the seas. The sun settled behind her wake
and stars peered down through the rigging. The second night out
was much the same as the first.

Just as the sun lifted above the rim of ocean next morning the
lookout sighted sails a few points off the starboard bow. Redd
studied them through the glass for a long time. He continued to
watch the ship after identifying her. She ran like a wild stallion
bent on showing a pair of heels to any pursuer. And there was a
rhythm about her that suggested the sureness and ease of a master
mariner on her poop. And Untell was just such a seaman.

Redd knew she would not be easily overtaken. By a careful
manipulation of sails and helm, a reef here and a bonnet there,
precise wisdom in the employ of wind and weather, he brought
the *Castlereagh's* hull up over horizon within a few hours. He
paced the long turbulent wake of Untell's ship for another hour,
gaining slowly, steadily, but not without taxing his skill and the
Lady's speed to the utmost. The rush of water down the sides
spread out into acres of foam, met the roil of the wake and ran
astern.

Ahead, Untell bared his mizzen of the last rag and took his lift
and fall just like the expert he was. But he ran heavy with cargo

and his hull was minus the dead rise of Redd's ship. Endurance and sail versus lines and maximum driving sail in the hands of a fox-sensed skipper soon gave Redd the advantage. Within five hours after sighting her, Redd was running almost abreast of the sister ship with a scant sea separating him from her long sleek portside.

Untell stood her, silent, watchful, waiting, and Redd raised his trumpet and spoke her, asking her to stand by. The *Castlereagh* tore on as if it suited her to ignore the *Lady*. Redd hailed Untell again, saying:

"Urgent business, Captain!"

A little later the ships sat still.

Captain Redd and Mr. Hyde made the crossing to the sister ship. The chief mate listened to his instructions and remained on deck of the *Castlereagh* with the oarsmen from the *Lady*.

Captain Untell met Redd on deck, a hostile look in his sharp blue eyes. From broad shoulders down he was a man of powerful build, and the set of his face certified him as a man who would not hesitate to use his muscular strength when driven too far. But Redd knew him to be a man who did not waste his force in anger. Behind his black brow was curiosity, which he contained as he invited Redd below.

When they were in his quarters with a bottle and two glasses before them, Untell poured and gulped his drink without waiting for his guest. His glance never left Redd's face; in it were questions—what sort of deviltry was Redd up to; did he think for a moment that the past between them was buried?

Redd knew he was thinking of the times their paths had crossed. It was written in the tightness of his mouth, in the co-ordination of his eyes. Their first meeting—both entering Manila Bay five years in the past, Redd's ship close-hauled on the port tack, Untell's just as close-hauled on the starboard, with neither wishing to give ground. In the light easterly wind, Redd deliberately crossed Untell's bows, forcing him to pay off, to collide with a Spanish merchantman. It was enough to stir up lasting enmity, though the girl in Melbourne sealed it. Her name didn't matter; her dual life did, since Untell fell in love with her. Redd didn't, and won. There followed a series of minor clashes in the employ of Van Oren, Limited, but ships that crossed in the stream and a woman under their eyes touched on things strong in a seaman's blood, violated the unwritten code—"Respect my ship and leave my private life alone."

"What's the tack?" Untell asked bluntly.

"Trouble in the firm. Financial."

"Yeah?" Untell was all interest now. "It must be very damned urgent to bring you in chase of me."

"Right. Mr. van Oren sent me. Another bank failed a few hours after you sailed."

"Why did he send you?"

"You're carrying seven boxes of ore, aren't you?"

"To England in a hurry."

"I could make something out of that," Redd smiled. "But I won't."

"Go ahead, and be damned! I sprung a mast at the hounds, or you'd be from here to Sydney under my stern."

"Mr. van Oren wants the boxes in Sydney. It's a matter of saving the firm. He boarded me to tell you in person, but I ran off and left him."

"Give that the deep six," Untell scoffed. "Just why are *you* here? Sir George knows how fond I am of you."

"I think a lot of you too," Redd smiled. He knew Untell's bluster and he liked it as much as he respected the man, which was considerable. But each thrived on open enmity; because it served the spirit of rivalry between them, he guessed, saying, "Someday I'm going to race you to England, just to show you I can beat you."

"I'm ready," Untell said, rising to the challenge. "Just like I'm ready and anxious to take you on with bare fists."

"We've got that to look forward to, all right," Redd admitted. "But down to business. Mr. van Oren wants the boxes in Sydney in a hurry. Now, if I were you, I'd return with them."

Untell knit his brows and leaned forward. "Just what have seven boxes of Bendigo ore got to do with the firm's salvation? Answer me that. I suppose Geoffrey Lipscomb-Grey can wave a wand over them and they'll turn into virgin gold."

"I hope so. But what the ore has to do with the firm's shaky position is none of my business; or yours. However, Mr. van Oren could want it back for the same reason he wanted you to get it to England."

Untell considered this. "Could be. But there's something strange about it. A little man came aboard and watched the boxes stowed. He reminded me of the Melbourne banker, Tysbee, whose picture was in the paper along with an account of his bank going under. But it's none of my business."

"No," Redd agreed. "Your business is to obey orders and release the boxes."

"Release them!" Untell was upon his feet. "Now I know there's something funny about this business." He sat down after failing to plumb Redd's calm face. "Since I'm running to England in a hurry with the boxes, it's odd as hell that *I'm* not ordered to return them to Sydney. However——" He stuck out a hand and said:

"Let's see the orders."

Redd thought quickly. "Let's see the boxes."

"Aye. They're handy," came the gruff reply. "In that locker room."

Redd finished off his drink with a lazy indifference before getting up and going to the locker. He opened the door and saw seven boxes, each about three feet long and two feet deep. A certain fascination fell over him; perhaps it was the enormous wealth inside one of the sealed boxes. He turned suddenly and found Untell's attention fixed on him, full and unguarded; a deep suspicion showed its brisk motion in his eyes.

Redd sat down. Feeling himself governed by circumstances he could neither avoid nor control any longer, he said before Untell could ask him, "I carry no written orders."

Untell started. His face slowly relaxed into a humorless smile. It was in a sense menacing. His eyes showed a little satisfaction; at being right in his judgment, Redd thought.

"What's your game, Redd?"

Redd tried to place conviction in his voice. "Hell, man, I'm not in the habit of playing chase with an expensive ship under me! Do you think Geoffrey would allow it? Be reasonable for once. I'm sailing a Van Oren ship. So are you."

There was hope in Redd that the other would turn ship and take the boxes to Van Oren. It was high and urgent. But he knew Untell to be a stubborn man who couldn't see past the missing written orders. Hope fell when Untell said:

"By the deep blue, I've never seen your equal. Now show me the kind of orders a shipowner would send or I'm raising sail for England, as I was instructed to do."

"Sorry," Redd answered easily. "Under the circumstances I can't so much as give you a receipt for the boxes."

Untell shook his head as if he were doing his best to assess the man before him and finding it impossible. "Captain," he said, "get a hold on your helm. She's wild. Why, not even a fool under his first command would give over his cargo without a written order. And what's more, Sir George wouldn't ask it of me. You can lay to that. Aye. Now my answer is just this, belay!"

Redd took his time in getting up. He shrugged lightly and said, "I'm sorry you can't see it. We'll all go under together, it seems." He stood motionless, looking for a way to convince the other. Then he tried to reason with Untell:

"Listen. What's between you and me is our business. But this is Sir George's business. Can't you see he's got a reason for not putting it in writing? Turn back and let him tell you so. Or are you too damn stubborn?"

Untell drew in his lower lip and rubbed his swarthy face. Then he said, "You may be right. But why didn't Sir George send me a written order to turn back?" Redd was unable to answer this, and Untell went on, "It would have been easy and simple, and the proper way to handle it. But he didn't."

Untell arose and said with finality, "So I'm holding my course."

Redd eyed him sharply for some time, asking, wondering, why Sir George had refused to put anything in writing, and looking for some plain path around the use of force in this awkward situation. But he had gone over the latter for two full days without any hope other than that he might persuade Untell, and very little of that. He knew now what he must do, and would do. He was committed to it.

He stuck out his hand and said, "Well, that's that."

Untell looked at the extended hand. "Stow it," he growled before raising his glance to Redd's face. What he saw flashed a warning through him; it was not a simple exchange of glances, but a look that was stripped bare of everything but raw purpose. In that swift moment Untell was off guard, and before he could collect his wits it was too late.

Redd's fist came up short and struck him below the ear with such force that his knees buckled. When he came to he was securely gagged. Standing over him was Mr. Hyde. And his cabin was filled with sailors from the *Lady of Glasgow* who strained at the boxes. He saw the first box of his entrusted cargo moving up the companion, then another and another. Redd was nowhere about, though he came in a little later and said:

"Mr. Hyde, there's an off-wind humor in the situation. The mates and crew of the *Castlereagh* are lending a lively hand on deck."

Mr. Hyde said nothing, and Redd looked at Untell, whose eyes blazed fury up at him. "Mr. Hyde," Redd smiled with perfect impunity, "this is a bit unusual, isn't it? Men have hanged for less."

Then the last box was on deck. It was lowered away to the raft affair atop three boats. A little later the hawsers from the *Lady* tightened and the boats were drawn slowly across the water. All was clear. Redd looked at Untell and said:

"Sorry it had to be this way."

In his voice and face there was unmistakable sincerity. Untell recognized it even as he plumbed the man for a note of apology which was not in evidence. Only purpose and strong conviction and the kind of poised vigilance expected of a big deep-water man.

After locking Untell in, Redd took his time, even pausing on deck to thank the mates of the *Castlereagh*. Mr. Hyde despaired of his unhurried manner at a time like this. The muffled shouts of the captain as well as the beating on the door were clearly audible now.

They were in the boat and riding up a swell when Untell's voice sounded from his deck. At the stern sheets, Redd stared straight ahead at his ship as if oblivious to the stream of oaths and threats that carried across the water. Only the final thrust, one Redd was sure he had purposely saved for the last, caused him to turn around slowly:

"Listen, you damned pirate! By the deep blue, I'm piling on canvas for Sydney and the Board of Trade!"

CHAPTER II

Excitement was high aboard the big sailing vessel *Endeavour* as she entered the mile-wide expanse of water separating the heads of Sydney Harbor. It had been a long, rough voyage and she was days late.

No one on deck was more pleased than Martha van Oren. She was wearing a blue dress, holding up the skirt with one hand as she made her way to the rail. A flush of color had enlivened her face. The shawl fell to her shoulders and in the sunlight dark brown hair took on a tawny gold sheen. Glancing ahead at long green fingers of land jutting out into the harbor, she opened her reticule. Finding a coin, she surprised the passengers crowding the rail when she tossed it into the water with an almost reckless gesture. Smiling, she watched it strike a wave and disappear.

Feeling herself under observation, she looked about her with an air of haughty detachment. Let them wonder why she did it, whether for thanks, luck, or out of sheer impulse. Any guess or all could be right.

She turned her face to Sydney again, wondering if her father was showing his years; and Geoffrey, who had written often; perhaps both of them would be at the quay to meet her. And how would they react to the woman of twenty-two whom they had last seen as a girl of seventeen? She was wondering herself what five years in a finishing school had done to her. She wasn't altogether prim and English. In England total reserve was an integral part of modesty; in Australia it wasn't.

Ahead Circular Quay sharpened in detail. A small crowd was there. And ships. She had never seen so many in the harbor at one time. Surprised, she looked closer, and when the ship drew nearer the quay, she thought the maze of square-riggers, barks, schooners, and steamships looked all but deserted. Then she knew they were. Sail rotted in harbor furl and cordage hung limp. Ships once white with salt to lower masts or snubbed funnels were brown with rust. Missing were the creaking of slings and the wail of derricks and the buzz of friction winches; the smells of hot metal, oil and steam and pungent cargoes. Something was wrong in the harbor. The life of trade was missing. But a more important event crowded this out of her mind: she was home at last.

The ship was gliding in to the quay. The jib boom was coming in above the forecastle head, and men stood ready to cast lines to the dock bollards. The crowd had enlarged on the quay and she searched for her father's face. Cries of excited joy from land and ship's rail added to the bedlam of shouts aboard ship as the vessel swung gently to a stop. The gangway was ashore now. She moved with the passengers, her chaperon forgotten, craning her neck and darting happy, expectant glances. He would appear out of the crowd suddenly, any moment now, to greet his daughter.

He didn't, however. She was standing on the quay when she saw Geoffrey. With a feeling of being drawn to him, she rushed forward with hands outstretched and gladness in her eyes and smile.

"Geoffrey!" she said, appraising him swiftly.

He looked no older. Though he was perhaps thirty-five now, he was the same tall, suave Englishman of years back. She knew he could be cold, reserved, or genial; and strange at times, as though he looked deep into one and mocked all he saw. Yet his engaging air always contradicted this impression. He was advancing with both hands extended, bright welcome in his face. His hands closed over hers and he said with possessive pride:

"By Jove, you've really grown up! Welcome home, Martha."

Geoffrey could not help admiring the full, slender body of a mature woman and a face he had dreamed about. Though her lips were a little full and too firmly set, suggesting willfulness, he saw in them a vigor to match the way she carried herself. Five years had given her voice a timbre that excited him.

"Geoffrey! I'm glad to see you! Aren't you going to kiss me?"

"Here?" he asked, lifting his brows.

"Here!" she replied, placing her hands at his neck and drawing him down to her. Before he knew it, her lips brushed his cheek at the parenthesis of his mouth. She laughed. "Always at embarkation and arrival," she said, pleased at the look of well-guarded interest that broke through his reserve. She was thinking of what fun it would be to penetrate the wall of a man so schooled against any show of emotion. Then she said:

"Where's Father?"

Instead of replying, he spoke to her chaperon, a little woman of small features and stiff bearing. Next he directed a man to their trunks. Martha had time in which to study him. She used it. This was the man her father wanted her to marry. A strong pride akin to arrogance showed in the fine set of his head and shoulders. His eyes and dignity were still a challenge to her judgment, even as she knew her independence was a challenge to him. But somewhere, something was missing. He did not stir her emotions.

"Now what were you saying, Martha?" he asked.

"You haven't forgotten," she accused. "Where is Father?"

"First, let's be off," he replied, pointing to the victoria. They were inside and moving off when he said, "Your father was detained at the office." He added slowly, carefully, "On a matter of urgent business. He sends his regrets and all that, of course, and promises to make up for this little inattention."

"At the office? It must be very important business, Geoffrey," she said, trying to hide her feelings.

"Yes. You wouldn't know about the bank crisis. It's even worse in Melbourne where we are heavily invested."

"Bank crisis! Is that why all the ships are tied up and deserted?"

"Yes."

"Is Mr. Tysbee's bank in trouble?" Geoffrey said it was. Remembering her father's close association with the banker, it wasn't difficult for her to imagine what was happening to Van Oren, Limited. Then she asked about the ship she had always claimed as her own.

"The *Lady of Glasgow* is at anchor here. But this business

is only temporary. Now let's talk about you, Martha. You've grown into a lovely lady. And seeing you home makes this just about the soundest day in my life."

"Take me to the office, Geoffrey," she demanded.

"By Jove, I'm entitled to a moment of jubilation. Suppose we drive on to Muirkirk Hall. I could do with a drop of something short, by way of celebrating the occasion."

"Geoffrey," she said, meeting his glance, "you are very engaging. And evasive. Now order the driver to Father's office."

"Very well," he said, resigned. "But really, you shouldn't subject yourself to the ordeal of waiting for him this afternoon."

"Wait for Father! Geoffrey, you amaze me. After five years do you think he would want that any more than I?"

"I suppose you're right," he said, though his voice was minus conviction.

With Geoffrey at her side, she entered the Van Oren Building. The countinghouse, ordinarily a busy place, was manned by only a small staff of clerks who seemed more interested in her than in their books, calendars, chandler's quotations, and shipping reports. Beyond long rows of desks, the business of mines, wheat, wool, sugar, hides, cattle and sheep stations in the brush country was carried on in large offices. Geoffrey's was the largest of these, other than her father's, and done in florid Victorian style. It was a big business house, and many bankers as well as Parliament members came and went. Though Van Oren, Limited, was listed as a maritime house, it owned more mines than ships. But the color of the firm and its owner lay in sails and house flag. The latter was as well known on the seas as the Union Jack. Martha missed nothing, paused often to refresh some memory, to connect a mere object with an event. At a large model of the *Castlereagh*, she said:

"I've loved all this, what it stands for, Geoffrey, since I was a child. Whatever it is now, the sea built it."

He knew her feeling for the sea and ships. While it seemed natural, in another sense it was strange, and he wondered if a subconscious salty fierceness flowed in her. There had been times in the past, as now, when the untold things in her dark-shadowed eyes stirred him deeper than usual. Stirred up warm passionate winds inside him. Then his practical side took over and scattered brief visions of a mystical woman with a simple truth: she was the result of environment.

Her mother had died when she was six or seven. Geoffrey could remember from his early days at Van Oren, Limited, the many times Sir George had taken Martha and the governess aboard one of his ships and sailed off to Melbourne or Dutch Java. For a girl she had a broad acquaintance with the sea. And now he was content to look at her for what she really was, the woman he meant to marry and not the spirit of a figurehead at the bows of a restless ship.

Even so, she had a fault that both challenged and irritated him. Her independence exceeded the standards he had always placed on a wife. Right now she was demonstrating it. Against his wishes and judgment, she was entering her father's outer office. He followed reluctantly, aware that she was listening in with natural curiosity on the business that kept her father from meeting her. Sir George was saying:

"Captain, I repeat I'm as surprised as you. Who could imagine that Untell would toss his command in my lap and go to the Board of Trade?"

"And I repeat, Mr. van Oren, my career is at stake. He's got to be stopped. How you do it, I don't care."

"What do you suggest?"

"Buy him off or have him shanghaied."

"Captain Redd, you suggest drastic measures which I——"

"Hold fast there," Redd interrupted. "Who left drastic measures up to who on the high seas? If you think a promise of increased shares above my quarter interest in the ship are enough, you're on the wrong tack. What good will they be if I lose my master's license?"

Martha turned a puzzled face to Geoffrey, who lifted his palms and smiled innocently. She was aware of trouble of a sort—never had she heard a captain address her father with anything but deference. She forgot it instantly, as she would some trivial matter; the desire to surprise her father surmounted all else. She said, stepping into view:

"Hello, Father."

As she walked inside, Van Oren halted in midsentence. He was on his feet instantly, the shrewd expression driven off his face by a look of strong pride and welcome. He carried them like a banner as he met her and held her at arm's length. Then he drew her to him and broke the silence that oftentimes rides the crest of emotions.

"Five years!" he said. "And look at you. Where's the girl of seventeen?" He said to Geoffrey, "So you brought her to me after all. Fine!"

"She brought me," came the reply.

"Like a fair wind, Geoffrey. Martha, I——"

A little-girl eagerness flickered across her face and she said with a gentle scolding on her lips, "After five years you're too busy to meet me!" She laughed with him until she felt alien eyes on her in strong appraisal.

Captain Redd stood apart from them, taking in the scene, but most of all the girl. He was looking her over carefully, as he would a disturbing turn of the weather at sea, when she glanced at him.

Meeting the steady scrutiny of his eyes was unlike anything she had ever experienced before or expected here. She was unable to break the glance and he would not. Something in his bold, sea-tanned face held her suspended among the unsaid things between them; things composed of strong attraction, physical and aesthetic, and a mutual admiration that admitted no satisfaction in letting this relationship remain as it was.

She was glad when her father introduced them. It broke the tension and released her from him. Nor did she dare look at him again until after he excused himself and walked to the door. And then her eyes fell to his strong back and lingered there with a mixed feeling of curiosity and injury.

"Captain Redd," Van Oren called after him. "I'll expect you at Muirkirk Hall tomorrow evening. There will be a great party to celebrate my daughter's return."

He faced them, silent and motionless for what seemed a long time before looking straight at her. "Thanks," he said.

Martha felt relieved. His going was like the departure of an unwelcome intrusion on her peace of mind.

Whirling suddenly, she said, "Father, who is that man?"

"Captain of the *Lady of Glasgow*, Martha."

"The *Lady!*" she exclaimed. "Of all things!"

"He's stood her poop for four profitable years," Van Oren said. "But you sound disappointed."

"I think I am, Father," she said, causing him to ask why. "I heard enough to suspect you are in trouble. And, somehow, that man reminds me of the meaning of the word trouble. Or," she went on, not missing the quick exchange of glances between Geoffrey and her father, "it could be that he's a twin of the thirteen letters in the ship's name—if one is to put any faith in superstition."

"Which I don't," Sir George smiled humoringly.

She knew the story, of how he lost heavily on a cargo of tea in his early shipping days because a superstitious captain refused to sail with it on a Friday, was blown on the reefs on Saturday. If tradition interfered with profit, practical George van Oren simply eliminated tradition. Perhaps it bolstered his ego to trample superstitions of the sea under his feet, to scoff at predictions that the *Lady* would come to a bad end.

His arm went about her shoulders and he said, "Perhaps you didn't hear me mention a party to celebrate your return, Martha. I've planned it for some time, though the date was vague. Imagine sending the governor an invitation reading, 'On the evening of the day following the *Endeavour's* arrival.' "

She brightened, forgetting captain, ship, and any shadow of trouble. He rolled these things aside, making her return a warm and wonderful experience. And in the true Van Oren manner he was richly icing the cake with the cream of Sydney's assorted social life. Excited and happy, she was unwilling to admit that her father's welcome was dominated by selfish schemes, however pardonable, when he said:

"Perhaps you and Geoffrey can make an occasion of it."

2

In the early evening of the next day, Martha walked in the garden. Lavender painted the stone walls of Muirkirk Hall and

the harbor dimmed over as the last upsurge of color faded. A
touch of England lingered in the quiet scene about her. The great
house was like a castle from the mother country. It stood majestically atop a tongue of land that jutted out and spilled down to
the long harbor of Sydney. Her father had built it when she was
ten and named it after the town in Scotland where he was born.
Sometimes she thought he had created all this to impress Sydney
and Australia. Perhaps he had. Australia was a land of liberated
ideas and ideals. It teemed with all the vigor of youth.

Martha was thinking of the evening ahead. The excitement of
coming events obscured all else. Carriages would soon roll through
the north gate. The viceregal party; and a baronet; and the Nizam,
or Raja—she couldn't remember which—of Jubbulpore. She had
laughed at Crippen's rehearsal in his precise English voice that
afternoon: "The Gaekwar of Baroda." It was fun to imagine the
Indian's absurd descent from a golden howdah. Her father's
friends, Kerry of the Royal Exchange, and blunt Finch of the
Bendigo Mine, as well as Milton Tysbee of the insolvent Bank of
Melbourne, would be there among other businessmen. In Australia
captains of industry didn't take a back seat to poets and peers.
Sea captains would join members of Parliament here, as equals,
each openly denouncing something each would fight to keep
alive: British imperialism. On the other hand, there was the snob-
bish element which could not reconcile any departure from severe
English customs. She thought Geoffrey belonged to this latter
class as much as to the former.

But Geoffrey never revealed himself in full.

She stopped short as she realized that he would no doubt propose to her this evening. Their relationship had been gently but
firmly shaped in this direction. A climax was due, and her father's
suggestion that they make an occasion of the party left little doubt
in her mind. As for herself, she would probably consent to become his wife. It would please her father. It would also please her
to have her social position assured.

Suddenly she wasn't thinking of Geoffrey at all, but of the tall
captain who had piqued her by his cold appraisal. Her pulse
quickened with the memory of this puzzling man, as it had that
morning while riding, and again at her piano in the afternoon.

Her mouth grew tight and she felt a sudden tensing of her facial muscles as small waves of spent anger raced through her. She dismissed him, drove him out of her mind, but not before admitting she was looking forward to another meeting with him; and with a sharp twinge of excitement entirely missing in her at the thought of Geoffrey's forthcoming proposal.

Something impelled her hurriedly toward the warm lights of Muirkirk Hall. She wished for Geoffrey then, hoping he would arrive early. He was a bulwark of the rational society to which she belonged.

Geoffrey was in the library with her father when she came downstairs. She had dressed for this event with such care and pleasure that time seemed a matter of no importance, and she stood under the wide arch with an awareness of the admiration she would evoke from him and others.

Her father had a troubled look on his face. He glanced from a newspaper to Geoffrey—both were handsome in evening clothes. Then Geoffrey felt her presence. A sudden intent glance, a smile of pleasure and admiration, and he was walking toward her, looking from her hair, done up in a chignon, to the satin of her rich emerald evening gown and the sapphire pendant pointing to the cleft of her bosom.

He said, "Were you in a great frame, Martha, I should say Gainsborough had done you in oil. Tonight you will brighten the ballroom with a beauty that says, 'Behold a finished lady of England.'"

She smiled teasingly. "You know better, Geoffrey. With Scotch and Dutch blood in an Australian wearing a Paris gown, I'm quite international, am I not?" Looking beyond him, she said, "Father looks worried."

Geoffrey remained attentive as he said, "Business, as usual. Van Oren, Limited, is a hard taskmaster."

"It doesn't seem to bother you."

"In this matter, no. I think I know the answer already."

"And I don't even know what the puzzle is," she said curiously.

"You're a much more interesting one, Martha. May I have the honor of drinking the first toast to you this evening? A very special one? And, let me see, I have four dances booked with you."

Before she could reply, a little man with iron-gray hair and energetic eyes moved toward them in somewhat of a hurry. The excited look on his face underwent a forced change, as though he had no time for the niceties demanded of him. Even as he greeted Martha and spoke to Geoffrey, he darted anxious glances toward Sir George. When he left them abruptly, Martha said:

"Mr. Tysbee is upset also, Geoffrey. The puzzle thickens. What is it?"

Taking her arm and moving toward the ballroom, he said easily, "Let us say that a man of responsible position under me is pushed too far. Isn't it natural that he will act in self-defense? If he is resourceful enough to win out, I have no cause for worry. If he loses, then I must get rid of him. It's very simple."

They were surrounded by servants, one of whom was pouring wine at Geoffrey's behest. She felt herself silenced, though determined not to let Geoffrey get away with it. When he lifted a goblet, and was about to launch a toast, she said, moving away:

"Who is this man you speak of?"

"He could be anyone," he replied, falling into step beside her.

As she looked at him a maze of questions formed and fell away unanswered before his look of strong interest.

"Now," he said, touching glasses. "To my success this evening when I ask a very important question of a very beautiful woman."

Puzzles slipped out of her mind unnoticed. Geoffrey held her glance, and his glass was poised at his lips. She could not deny his charm. She didn't try to. She could be proud of this politic Englishman schooled in business and behavior. A smile formed on her face and she lifted her glass. The taste of bubbling champagne was to his success.

She watched how well he contained his elation. There was no hint of boyish eagerness in him. Nor did he so much as mention the future during the next few hours when music and wine and lovely women in colorful fringes and flounces became one in kindling intimate and romantic conversations on the ballroom floor. He seemed content to dance with her in his accomplished manner, to say the things a woman liked to hear. He gave her up to her father, who continued to appear worried, and he waltzed with the governor's wife when the baronet and members of the viceregal party claimed her for dancing and talk over wineglasses. His friend and her father's, John Kerry, had one of Martha's dances booked, and so did several other prominent men, though he claimed her most of all.

As the evening advanced and wine loosened tongues, Martha began to feel an insidious undercurrent at work in the room. Once, while sitting with the governor's wife, part of a conversation behind her was overheard: "That's Milton Tysbee. I hear his name will sound at the hearing when Captain Untell gets up steam. He's too closely associated with Sir George, you know. His Melbourne bank took quite a buster." Another voice said something about Sir George being "shrewd enough to get by with it." Then Mr. Finch of the Bendigo Mine, which her father controlled, claimed his dance. He, too, seemed unduly preoccupied, and, being a poor dancer at his best, she was glad when Geoffrey came to her rescue.

She soon put aside what she had heard as Geoffrey swept her along to the strains of his favorite waltz. In the lilting swing of it she knew a pleasure that bubbled in her like champagne. Soft warm light fell from the great chandelier. The sparkle and tinkle of crystal, gay laughter, and couples gliding past and on like romantic dreams, a woman's long train, like burnished gold in a fleeting glance, then a wine-red dress, all these things lent the formal Victorian ballroom a provisional gaiety. Trouble was a difficult thing to harbor.

"I've never seen you so happy, Martha," Geoffrey said when they stood with glasses filled.

"And I don't know when I've felt so gay," she replied, her glance sweeping on to meet the advancing governor of New South Wales.

She and Geoffrey, together with the Indian prince and the governor, were sipping wine on the veranda when two men sauntered by, one of them saying, "You can place a bob or two on the seriousness of the case when a naval court is appointed. Doesn't Sir George's grave face prove it?"

Geoffrey looked up sharply and cleared his throat noisily, purposely, Martha thought, though she heard enough of what the other man said to astonish her: "If Captain Untell can make a piracy charge stand against Captain Redd——"

The governor was speaking to her. She smiled conformingly even as a word seemed to explode in her mind—piracy! A Van Oren, Limited, captain accused! What was worse, another of the firm's captains, Untell, was the accuser. Then the conversation in her father's office yesterday sounded again all too fresh in her mind: Redd was saying his career was at stake, that Untell had to be stopped; then—"Buy him off or have him shanghaied."

And now Geoffrey was adroitly turning a question the Indian prince had directed at her. He knew her mind and she was thankful. When they moved inside and she had him alone for a brief moment, she spoke with rising concern of the things she had overheard and felt. He admitted the presence of conflict in the firm, but no more, and turned his charming side again.

Smiling a little, she offered her face to him. Her expression was unyielding, however, and he had a faint idea of what was to come before she surprised him with:

"Geoffrey, you mentioned a man under you who was being pushed into self-defense. If he lost you should get rid of him. You said he could be anyone, but you had Captain Redd in mind, didn't you?"

His denial was very convincing and she wanted to believe him, but doubt wasn't easily dismissed. Her withdrawal of attention, to think, to draw estimates on her father's, and Geoffrey's, loyalty to those whom they demanded loyalty from, was suddenly arrested by a remark that reached her ears: "There's Van Oren's pirate! Captain Redd in person."

Martha looked quickly. Her glance stopped on him. Captain Redd stood a little distance away, dressed for a quarter-deck instead of a formal ball. The jaunty flare of his tie, the aloof calm of his face, and the square set of his shoulders gave him the bearing of a king.

3

Martha noticed these things about him, and more. At liberty to study him without any collision with his eyes, she did so, seeing in him a man at once stormy, soft, and mysterious. Here was a driver of sail, deep-water sail, in a deep-sea wind. Here was a man who challenged her emotions.

Fascinated, and resenting it, she placed her hand on Geoffrey's arm and applied a little pressure to her fingers. Geoffrey mistook her meaning when he saw a sharpening intensity come into her eyes. Observant, he found displeasure in her face and traced her gaze to Redd. Together they saw him make his way to where Sir George and Tysbee sat with Kerry and Finch, saw him refuse wine and say something to them that caused Van Oren and the little banker to excuse themselves and lead Redd into the library.

Geoffrey stood for a moment of indecision, his eyes speculating on what Redd was up to. Then he glanced at Martha and seemed to relax under a slight shrug. He said:

"Come, Martha. The bright moon outside is making demands."

How he could turn away from the drama and mystery and adventure she thought was blowing like a wind into the library, she didn't know. Geoffrey, who lived the business of Van Oren, Limited, seemed possessed with the amazing faculty of appearing immune to the shaping of events in the very shadow of its house flag. He offered no explanation as he led the way unhurriedly to a secluded part of the terrace.

Taking her hand in his, he moved into a circular arbor where trailing vines clung to round pillars and followed the open cross-work of ceiling. Patches of moonlight created shapes on the stone floor and seats, and nearby a night bird called.

"It's a perfect setting, Martha," he began slowly, sweeping the night in a glance that fell to her face and withstood a silence between them. When she half averted her face, he turned her to him, saying, "It isn't necessary to voice my sentiments, since you know my mind, Martha. However, I shall not miss the opportunity to do so. I've been in love with you for many years; or I thought I was. Waiting has not changed it. Not at all."

"Geoffrey!" she almost laughed. "Aren't you carrying it a bit far—saying you've loved me for years? You showed nothing of it when I left for England."

"It was a matter of a man of twenty-nine and a girl of seventeen. I wasn't sure I loved you, though I was sure I desired the heir to Van Oren, Limited."

"You are frank," she said. "Perhaps that's all you really want now."

"It's an advantage," he said, smiling urbanely. "A decided one. But such things are small by comparison. A man needs much more to complete his life. I'm sure you can understand this."

Martha could. And she admired him for the clever way he had eliminated the barrier of wealth and position. Also in his favor was his behavior of minutes ago. He had walked away from what was happening in Van Oren, Limited, in order to be with her. And his declaration of love seemed sincere; it was tinctured with frankness. Perhaps the flaw was in the way he went about it, so fully composed when the slightest trembling of his voice could do more than words to vouch for his feelings. He was saying:

"Martha, I knew my heart was asserting itself the moment I saw you on the quay yesterday. The only thing that could complete my life had just walked off the ship. Since then I have been hard put to hold the question in tow."

She was looking deep into and behind his eyes, searching for more than he realized; seeking long faith and assurances over the years; trying to adjust the harmony of their minds into a tenable adventure from the outset. And he appeared to be opening the way for her inspection, hiding nothing as she seemed to possess him for only that purpose. Out of it, he said:

"Martha, will you marry me?"

She had expected this question. But hearing it was something else, and she could not answer him at once.

"This comes as no surprise," she said at last, thinking of her father's wishes in the matter. "And I suppose I should be prepared to answer you right off." She turned away. "But I'm not."

"I understand," he said in a low voice. "It is a permanent thing." Her back was to him and his hands fell gently to her shoulders. "But you must know how your father feels about us. I think he would enjoy announcing our engagement tonight." She made no reply, and he went on:

"Certainly it would make me the happiest man in Sydney to hear you say yes, Martha."

"You haven't asked if I love you, Geoffrey. And somehow, you sound as though you are taking my answer for granted."

"With a deep and sincere hope for both," he said directly. "I would be a fool to approach you without confidence." He brought her around for a look into her face, saying when her dark eyes lifted to his, "Without confidence or love."

"Geoffrey, I am trying very hard to see more than just an ideal arrangement."

"So that's it," he said. "It stands in the way, doesn't it? The business manager of your father's firm is proposing marriage. Even your father's wishes are a handicap, I'm sure."

"You argue well, Geoffrey."

"Then your answer is yes?"

His hand found hers in search of a pledge from her, and his pulse beat a little higher, enough to cause a trembling at his finger-tips. She was thinking fast, of just the thing he was saying, that her father would be pleased to hear of the engagement; of the many advantages of the arrangement. Almost on impulse, she said:

"Very well, Geoffrey."

He looked at her closely, feeling in the co-ordination of her voice and eyes the suddenness of the decision. It was almost as if she had said, "Why not?" But the answer was in his favor, and it was enough for the present. Her upturned face invited him with all the curiosity of her sex. His arms went about her and his head tipped to kiss her.

Martha felt the touch of his lips, her mouth neither firm nor loose as she waited for him to warm her out of inertness into a state of eager response. But he was quite gentle and formal about it: there was a brief touch between them, like a pressure of his hand on hers. Then it was all over.

Disappointed in him, and wondering if he had struggled and won over his wants in that moment made for some show of them, she scarcely heard his correct and composed statements about the honor she had done him, and his eternal fidelity. He evinced pleasure now—of her words of acceptance!—directly after refusing a greater pleasure she had placed before him. He was leading her to the house when she said:

"Geoffrey, I'm not going inside just yet. I want to think."

He departed reluctantly. She watched him melt into the shadows. Alone, she felt a little small and depressed, and her calm was giving way to an overwhelming incertitude. She knew anything but the peace and enthusiasm she had expected with her engagement. There was much she did not understand.

As she looked out into the night, soft music from the ballroom seemed to fall from the stars above her, belittling her problems, and mocking them, as though some contact with infinity had overtaken her. Then the fleeting moment of peace was gone. In its place a mortal man appeared on the terrace and paused not a dozen yards away. Not knowing of her presence here, he looked straight ahead, lost in thought——

Captain Redd.

As she looked at him she experienced a feeling made up of many things. He appeared to be different now. Perhaps Geoffrey's passiveness had something to do with it; or there could be a rising sympathy at work in her for this captain who commanded the *Lady of Glasgow,* or the man who would soon face a charge of piracy. It was as instinctive as it was sudden, and it fought back and forth with the resentment she harbored for him. Then she seemed to know what prompted this softness of feeling.

It rose up out of Geoffrey's expression—"If he loses, then I must get rid of him. It's very simple."

It was also very callous-sounding. She wondered if Geoffrey and her father planned to use him; and if, failing in that, they intended to blind themselves to his years of service and toss him aside.

CHAPTER III

Redd was thinking of the new adventure that had overtaken him. It was touch and go, all sail loosed in a gale wind. Imprudent sail. But he was deep into it; in fact, the central figure; his past was up for examination and his future was a matter for five men of a naval court to decide. And all because he had served a ship-owner who wanted to put nothing in writing concerning seven boxes of "ore."

Only that afternoon the newspapers announced the appoint-ment of the naval court—"*And it shall be the object of this court to determine whether or not Captain Gordon Redd of the Van Oren, Limited, ship* Lady of Glasgow *is to be tried by a court of the land for piracy on the high seas.*"

Untell's threat had not been idle talk. And Untell would do all in his power to tie the charge fast to him. But that was to be expected. What had come out of the meeting short minutes before in Sir George's library hadn't been expected. There he met Tys-bee for the first time. A man of small stature who had skidded from lofty heights, he seemed to retain all the authority of his former position.

Gazing over the pale glare of the lawn, Redd felt again the quiet dignity of the library, heard the soft music behind closed doors, saw seated around a small table two men and himself, all expectant and watchful. Redd saw Tysbee again, and felt again that bleak appealing stare of a gambler fastening into him. And George van Oren's anxiousness began in the ballroom when Redd approached and came to the point, in the presence of Kerry and Finch, with:

"You've read the papers."

It might have been the way he said it, and meant it, that caused Van Oren to hurriedly lead him and Tysbee into the privacy of the library, to say when they were seated:

"We might as well face it." He drained a pony of brandy and remarked defensively, "I tried to stop him, but Untell was furious. Here, Captain, help yourself to drinks."

Redd ignored the invitation. "Mr. van Oren," he said, "you might as well face something else. I'm looking out for one man in this matter—myself."

"Now, Gordon"—*It was Gordon now*—"haven't we engaged the finest legal talent in Australia to defend you? Cailler Rise has no peer."

"That isn't enough," Redd told him directly. "From what I

gather, this case won't stop with the incident at sea. What's back of it will be dug at, and if there's more to it than appears on the surface, I'm caught in the halyard kink."

Tysbee's calm gave way to nervousness; brisk excitement flickered across his eyes. He was in it up to his neck, Redd thought, and all Untell had said about his being on hand when the boxes were stowed aboard the *Castlereagh* seemed to indict him now. And it was unlikely that Untell would forget him when the hearing opened.

Redd went on before either man could reply, "So I'm taking the safest way out. I'll tell exactly what happened and throw myself on the mercy of the court." He looked at Van Oren, adding:

"They'll say I'm a man guilty of an act of piracy. But I'm actually guilty of nothing more than a small error in judgment—loyalty to a shipowner."

Van Oren smiled, though his hands were raised in protest. And protest he did volubly, until Redd reminded him that he had failed to stop Untell.

"And since you've left me to walk the plank, Mr. van Oren, we'll see how well you can explain that box of bullion to a court."

"But, Gordon, don't you see I can't be involved in this? I——"

Redd's crisp voice stopped him with, "The hell you can't."

A moment of surprise and silence was broken by Van Oren. He lifted his palms and smiled shrewdly. "I asked for it, Gordon, didn't I?" Turning on Tysbee, he said, "If he tells all he knows, those boxes will become headlines in Sydney's newspapers."

Redd looked at Tysbee. "I don't know what this is all about, but Captain Untell recognized you when you came aboard his ship with the boxes."

The banker's eyes narrowed to mere slits and his hands gripped the chair until his fingers seemed a bloodless white. "Are you sure of that?" he asked. Redd stared coldly at him until he brought his gaze to bear on Sir George and said, "This comes as a most unexpected and unpleasant shock."

"Rubbish!" Van Oren scoffed. "There's a small chance of bringing you in on this."

"Don't be too sure of that." It came from Redd.

Van Oren arose and stood with hands behind him, looking

straight ahead. Once more he faced the problem by saying he had
no idea that Untell would do more than raise strong objections
upon his return to Sydney. Tysbee reminded him that Untell had
done more. Then Redd asked a question, a very pertinent one:

"What's back of all this, anyhow?"

Van Oren turned a piercing yet thoughtful gaze on Redd. It
fell on Tysbee at last. "Milton," he said, "We should acquaint
Gordon with a few facts, eh?"

"And let him spill it at the hearing?" Tysbee showed a poor
opinion of Sir George. "Don't make another big mistake in judg-
ing one of your captains."

"I?" Sir George said in a huff. "Wasn't it you who said every
man had a price?"

Tysbee scoffed, "Don't try to fob me off with that. Lay it on
the third partner, Geoffrey, and get on with your approach to
this man. Remember he's the important figure in the case."

They were snarling at each other now. It both pleased and
amused Redd, who listened to their arguments. They ended with
Sir George saying to Redd, "We're all in this, and we need each
other. Are you open to a proposition?"

"A man in a trap listens to anything."

"Then listen to this. The verdict will hang on what you say at
the hearing. If the charge against you stands up, we're all in
trouble. They'll dig deeper into the case, perhaps to the very bottom of it. If the charge doesn't stand up, the whole thing will be
dropped. Now instead of asking the mercy of the court, you can
be steadfast in denial of the charges and do as Cailler Rise sug-
gests: let the case rest on what the boxes contain. All seven will
be in court—full of Bendigo ore. Now who would pirate ore?
That's our case."

"Go on," Redd demanded.

"As you know, one box contained gold. Lots of it. Naturally
I don't want that mentioned at the hearing. First, it would estab-
lish a reason for piracy, which is not in your favor or mine. Next,
I would be called to the stand to disclose the source of the gold.
Do you follow me, Gordon?"

"Aye. Perfectly."

"What do you think of it?"

"Rise is smart, all right," Redd admitted. "But so is the Board of Trade's man, Lancefield. He may ask why we pirated ore."

"Rise isn't worried about that. The trump card is what the boxes contain. Who would steal ore?"

"Captain Redd of the *Lady of Glasgow*," Redd answered. "And Lancefield will prove it if he can."

Tysbee poured out a peg of whisky and said, "Captain, we could argue all night over a point. The question is, do you want to come out of this better off than you were before?"

With Redd's expected reply, Van Oren said, "Then here's our proposition. The bullion belongs to Milton, Geoffrey, and me. Play this thing our way and we'll take you in as a partner. A tenth of it is yours."

Tysbee said quickly, "If you are not indicted."

It was something to think about. Redd poured whisky and forgot he held the glass in his hand as his mind held up his future for examination. The mercy of the naval court was one thing, gold and strong alliance another. The former would brand him; he would be known as a man who threw a shipowner to the jackals, a squealer. And the reward of rightness and justification would be his inability to get a ship. In another year he'd be lucky to sign on as a second mate in any port of the world. Actually, he had little choice.

On the other hand, he was innocent now. The moment he accepted this proposition, he would become as guilty as the pair before him appeared to be. Lowering the untouched whisky to a table, he said:

"I'll think it over."

And now, on the terrace, he was still thinking it over. Behind that wall of music and gaiety they waited for his decision. They thought him resolute in his intent to tell the truth in court. He smiled wryly and took a few steps in the direction of a vine-covered arbor. They could not suspect that he was not one of their kind, that only as a last resort would he think of throwing the shipowner overboard. Why? He didn't know, unless loyalty was an entire thing with him. He expected it in full and he gave it that way. The sea bred in him qualities he didn't accept as virtues. But accepting Van Oren's and Tysbee's assumed guilt for a share in their loot when all he wanted was a clear name was something else. He wanted gold. Aye, he could use it. But he was afraid of the price he must pay to get it, afraid of what it would do to him. However—the sea ran strong in him and his ship sailed proud and free; he didn't want to lose that ship.

His mind was not quite made up when he was arrested by a movement under the arbor. A figure emerged into the open and stopped still, her dress in the moonlight shimmering like the emerald of a lagoon. He recognized her even before she said:

"Captain Redd, I wish to talk to you."

2

He moved to her, curious and not at all displeased by her intrusion upon his thoughts. She had been considerably in his mind since their meeting of the day before. He saw her now a woman more lovely than yesterday. With her full attention on him, he felt the clean pride and challenge in her eyes. What was in them now, in the turn of her head and the poise of her lips, was enough to strike a spark from a man's imagination.

When he stood near her, she said directly, "Captain, what's behind all this talk about you and my ship?"

He had no reply for this, and she went on, "You're the only master of the *Lady of Glasgow* who wasn't approved by me."

A humoring smile played on his face now.

"The *Lady* was father's first big ship, and I was only nine when I christened her. Since then she's been a fancy I've cherished."

"Then we've got something in common," he said.

"I wonder, Captain," she said, searching him for total sincerity. "I've always thought her the proudest thing afloat. And I don't want to see her abused."

She paused, a thinning energy coming into her eyes. He saw purpose and impulse at work in her as she said, "I was in England when gruff old Page died and you were placed in command. That was in '89, which makes me four years late in passing judgment on the present master."

"You picked a fine time for it," he said with humor.

"Yes, I suppose it is a little late for that. But just what is the trouble? What's back of it?"

"Just say it's likely to stir up a full gale wind in Sydney, Miss van Oren."

"I've overheard enough to believe that. But piracy sounds a little preposterous in these civilized times. And yet it is hard to imagine that Captain Untell would prefer such a charge unless he were justified in doing so."

He looked toward the lights of the house and back to her. "It's odd that you aren't in there dancing," he said. "Why aren't you?"

"I came out with Geoffrey, Captain. He had several duty dances and I wanted a few minutes to myself."

His heavy brows lifted. "And he just walked off and left you in the moonlight! Some men take a lot for granted."

She swept him with a quick sharp look and walked inside the arbor. He followed her to a carved seat and sat beside her. The moon through the vines painted her, and as she moved the glancing planes of her face moved. She said, her voice not quite masking her attempt to defend Geoffrey, "We became engaged here tonight, Captain."

"He didn't waste much time. I'm sure Sir George is tickled." He spoke with such unconcern that she glanced up in surprise. He added to her consternation when he said, "And Geoffrey remembers duty dances at such a time. I wish I had his faith in my fellow men."

"In Captain Untell, for example?" she said with an edge to her voice.

He laughed, and she reminded him that she had learned little about him or the trouble he was in. She tried to maneuver conversation toward the subject with a pertinent question: What had brought about the charge of piracy? He could not evade her altogether, so he said:

"The bank crisis, Miss van Oren. The *Castlereagh* sailed for England just before a big bank closed its doors here. Her cargo had to come back. I went after it. I got it."

"I don't quite understand. Both were Father's ships, so why should trouble come out of it?"

"Untell didn't want to give up the cargo."

"And so you took it?"

"And so I took it," he replied with perfect innocence.

She could not quite hide the consternation that crept into her eyes. She was thinking that he was a little too bold in a rash way to make an ideal master for the *Lady*; that he was born to be a blockade-runner or privateer, or pirate, all too late. He had the dash and bearing of a pirate. She said with uncertainty:

"I believe the *Lady* would fare better under an older and more cautious captain." Avoiding his accusing smile, she said, "Where are you from, Captain? Tell me something of your life at sea."

Briefly he sketched his life from birth aboard a Yankee clipper captained by his father, in '59, to his years in the American merchant service; and on to his first command under the British red ensign; his schooner days and his first command of a Van Oren ship. Then the *Lady of Glasgow*. She listened eagerly, and when he was finished she abruptly returned to the present with a hopeful question:

"Captain Redd, how could you be charged with piracy?"

"I didn't have the necessary papers."

"Why?"

"That's the prize question."

"It's all very confusing," she said.

"Aye," he grinned devilishly. "It's that, all right."

She stared at him, unable to reconcile him to what he represented. Captains of the sea were supposed to accept their trusts in honor-bound seriousness. But this man violated a tradition. She said, perplexed:

"You speak of it so lightly, so irresponsibly, for a man born to the sea. How can you?"

"Maybe you've forgotten that I'm the captain you're passing judgment on." He added facetiously, "I'm trying to impress the fair shipowner."

"You are," she returned firmly. "And rather unfavorably."

"Then we'd better start all over."

"I'm trying hard to understand all this. And you're not helping me, not at all."

"Why should you bother with it?"

"But I am," she said. "It's my ship and my name. Perhaps you'd answer this—are you guilty?"

"That, miss, is for the court to decide." Thinking of the proposition awaiting his answer, he said, "Right now I'm standing between guilt and innocence with one foot in and one out."

She got to her feet and said, "There is no such position." When he reminded her that there was, she said, "I'm trying hard to believe you innocent. And yet——" She turned away from him with a hopeless shrug. "I believe you are guilty."

"I hope the court is more lenient," he laughed.

"I can't bear to think of all the embarrassment you're causing Father," she said, turning on him.

"Neither can I," he said with mock seriousness. "Poor Sir George."

He was no more blind to the challenge in her than he was to the curve of her breasts. It ran strong and boiling in her now. He liked the way she stood up to him, and he liked the sparks of amber in her eyes and the defiant set of her lips. Then she was saying:

"Have you no defense to offer, nothing whatever to say for yourself?"

"At the right time and the right place," he said.

Her look told him he was the most baffling man she had ever met even as she said, "Since it is quite evident that my opinion in the matter is of no concern to you, I'll bid you good evening, Captain."

She had taken a step toward the house when his hand reached out to her arm. She stopped still, her glance dropping from his face to his hand and imperiously up at him again. He said nothing, though his dark, intent look held her. In his stern eyes she felt him commanding her to stay where she was. It infuriated her, and she lingered to return as much as he gave; she was telling herself this, disavowing anything in his favor, when he said:

"Your opinion of me is a matter of utmost concern."

"Then why don't you do something about it?" she burst out.

He favored her with a searching, instantaneous glance. It fell away and came on again, this time strong with purpose and warning as he said, "I'm going to."

His arms were about her, and in her state of shock and anger she was unable to offer resistance other than inertness. She stiffened when he tipped his head and, unmindful of what he saw in her eyes, found her mouth. Then she felt the heaviness of his passion and trembled all over before his rough handling. Her firm mouth dissolved under his and she felt herself responding to the burning fires he kindled in her. With hands clinging to his shoulders, she was returning all he gave with a pressing eagerness.

Geoffrey's kiss had been nothing like this; and this was like nothing she had ever expected. There was no end to her hunger. And suddenly there was no end to the shame she felt. She broke from him abruptly, her wants unsatisfied, her feeling of shame and anger rising like cresting waves. She stood there, still and confused, torn from her conventional roots.

"You're warm and deep," he was saying. He was big and he frightened her even as he attracted her, made her want to feel his brutal strength again. Then anger flared up, obscuring all else——

She slapped him, hard. She wanted to do it again. And then she wanted to escape from him, to find the quiet, tenable safety of lights and music and rational people, rational Geoffrey. She was moving away, toward these things, running almost, when his laugh sounded ahead of words she wouldn't soon forget:

"You'll sail far and wide to find another man who can kiss you like that."

3

He watched her hurried departure, his face tightening up under the impressions she had made upon him. There was a last glare of moonlight across the twin swell of her breasts and she was gone. Turning his face up to the wheeling stars and back to the house, he decided to put her out of his mind and take up Van Oren's proposition where he left off. But it wasn't that easy. His blood ran red and strong and warm. She had stirred up a hot tropical gale inside him. She could turn his parting words on him if she only knew it. Aye——

He had sailed far and wide, but never had a woman returned

as much as she, not in one brief kiss. She was his twin in spirit. There had been others who hadn't quite struck the note. They tried . . .

As Myra, of Melbourne. Fresh from Untell's noble proposals of marriage, she murmured wordlessly as she tried to stifle him with kisses. And when he responded and felt the warmth of her under his hands, she pretended to balk, provoking a laugh out of him, or a savage palm to her face, which she liked. But beyond her passion, she was empty. As empty and void as the French woman on Rue Catinat in Saigon. But they had nothing at all behind their lovely faces.

Martha van Oren had. It was not in her position and wealth, it was in her, the woman. And had he found her in a fancy house in Bombay in exchange for pound or rupee, it would not alter the fact that she possessed the rare golden note of accord.

But he was a practical man and he placed her back in her proper position in the scheme of things. Right now she appeared to be as inaccessible as his good reputation of yesterday. Only one day separated him from a hearing. Thinking of her father, who waited anxiously for his decision, he was able to take a sane view of her interest in the case.

The ship was more to her than she admitted. He saw this now. And the good name of Van Oren surpassed that. She had made a courageous approach, bidding, without asking in so many words, for his help. "I've always thought her the proudest thing afloat." She was also looking at the stainless house flag. "I believe the *Lady* would fare better under an older and more cautious captain." She was searching for smut on the flag. "I can't bear to think of all the embarrassment you're causing Father." She had found smut. From then on there was in her eyes a look that said only he could remove the stains. She was right in a way; and he longed to serve her. It was strong in him.

He moved slowly toward the marble terrace, and music, the grimmer aspects of the case weighing on his mind. Sir George was in trouble, bigger than he knew. So was Tysbee. And Sir George had bungled twice, once in not going after the boxes, again in misjudging Untell. And—Redd felt it strongly—he would make other mistakes. Hell! Van Oren needed him more than he needed Van

Oren. The girl needed some protection in this affair. A woman's mind was sensitive.

But again he was crowding on too much sail, overreaching. It was pure nonsense to deceive himself with pictures of his own gallantry when his forthcoming acceptance of Sir George's proposition was inspired by self-defense. However, she had something to do with his decision, if only that he was of a sudden touched with a secret desire to protect her from their mistakes.

He entered the ballroom smiling at the surprise he had in store for Sir George and his crony.

People made a way for him. He passed by the governor's party with the easy stride and independence of the Lord High Chancellor of Great Britain. Pretty women's eyes followed him with an awareness of his size and bearing. One of these was Martha.

She drew his glance and taunting smile. He saw her hand tighten on Geoffrey's arm as color flooded her pretty neck and face. Her head was high. He paused to accept and toss off a whisky before putting the music and gaiety of Muirkirk behind him.

Sir George looked up quickly when he opened the door. Tysbee seemed less anxious and more nervous. Both got to their feet with his approach, Sir George smiling in a most engaging manner as he said:

"Have you reached a decision, Gordon?"

Redd stood with hands in pockets, feet spread apart. "Sure," he said. "But you aren't going to like it."

Both men sat down slowly, open disbelief in their faces.

"I've decided to take what the court has to offer. When I get through with my story, I don't think I'll lose my right to sail the seas."

As Van Oren groped for words, Tysbee said something about another mistake. Red of face from too much brandy, Sir George flushed the deeper color of anger. He was turning on the diminutive ex-banker when Redd dropped a hint:

"You two must have a pretty small scheme afoot when you offer a paltry tenth share for my help."

They exchanged rapid glances and looked up at Redd, who was moving away.

"Captain Redd! Gordon——" Van Oren was on his feet again. Redd paused. "Gordon, that one tenth is a lot of money. More than you'll make aboard the *Lady* in years."

"Not interested. When I sell myself, I want a fair price. And when I sell myself into a partnership, it's going to be on even terms, even say."

Tysbee laughed. "He'll be wanting all the gold soon, didn't you know?"

A sharp chill edged Redd's reply. "It's your wind, mister, and you're caught aback in it. Know what I mean?" Tysbee didn't. "There's talk about the buster your bank took. Maybe the gold came out of it."

Tysbee paled and reached for brandy. It was all Redd wanted. He walked to the table, poured a pony around, and grinned. "I've got one foot in a whirlpool," he said. "Now do I remove it or put the other one in, Mr. Banker of Melbourne?"

Van Oren stared from one to the other, waiting out the passing seconds for Tysbee to make up his mind. Then it came, Tysbee's voice forced, his decision reluctant:

"One fourth." He gulped his drink and sat back, staring straight ahead.

"Now you, Mr. van Oren."

"One fourth," Sir George said with noticeable relief.

"Well, that's that," Redd shrugged. "I won't ask how much money I made in the raise. Instead I'll say this: there won't be as many mistakes made from now on."

"You sound deucedly important all of a sudden," Tysbee said.

Redd looked deep into him before replying, "And I feel guilty as all hell."

4

He had no sooner turned to the door than he saw another man in the room. How long Geoffrey had been there or how much he had overheard made little difference to Redd. Only his presence and watchful silence, these and flashing pictures of a stealthy entrance, seemed to matter. Then nothing but the half-hidden intensity in his eyes and the tensions of a subconscious duel between them. As their glance held, strong and unsettling, he could not suppress a little admiration for Tysbee and Sir George; they worked in the open.

Then Geoffrey's reserve thawed into geniality. Smiling suavely, he said, "Captain Redd, now that your course has been established, perhaps you'll join in a toast; to what Sir George will announce in the ballroom—my engagement to Miss van Oren."

CHAPTER IV

Captain Redd left his ship next morning and walked to Bridge Street for a meeting with the famous barrister and Sir George. He arrived at Van Oren, Limited, early and moved straightway to the shipowner's office. As he reached for a nautical gazette, a gruff voice attracted his attention. From his point of vantage he could not only hear all that was said in Geoffrey's office, he could look in as well. The man had just said:

"So Captain Redd has his aces back to back."

He was a big man. He wore a pith helmet with green puggree.

"We are taking no chances, Mr. Finch," Geoffrey replied.

Redd placed him now. Finch operated the Bendigo Mine in the colony of Victoria. How much weight Van Oren, Limited, exercised in the big syndicate Redd was soon to learn. Geoffrey was saying:

"We need cash *today*. In view of the hearing tomorrow, we must consolidate our position now. Today, Mr. Finch. If Captain Redd's weight before a naval court isn't enough, the minnows will eat the Van Oren whale. Now——

"Where can you raise five thousand pounds, on your own, Mr. Finch? Never mind. Just have it by noon, or the Bendigo Syndicate will collapse on you."

"Talk sense, Geoffrey. You know damn well nobody's got that much cash for any Van Oren enterprise today. Yesterday morning I could have raised it."

"We didn't need it until the papers carried the story last evening. Now the squeeze is on and the banks are powerless to help us."

"Or me!" Finch bellowed. "Damn you, Geoffrey! You and Sir George know what you're doing to me!"

Much to his surprise, and Redd's, Geoffrey offered him a cigar. A strange token to hand a man departing on a fool's errand.

Redd didn't know what to make of it. He was wondering why Geoffrey wasn't using the gold bars when he saw entering Geoffrey's office a tall man with a haggard expression on his face. He had seen the man at the party last night. The moment Geoffrey sounded his name he knew him to be John Kerry, often called the Wool King of Sydney.

"I need money," he said bluntly, drawing from Geoffrey a laugh and, "Who doesn't?"

He sat down wearily. "The market is away, Geoffrey, and I'm facing a buster. I paid off two thousand bales yesterday at eighteen pounds each for Sir George—before the papers carried the story about this beastly ship captain of yours. Thirty-six thousand pounds—cash!

"Now half of Sydney thinks Van Oren, Limited, can't pay its way out. The other half thinks it can—with gold taken from one of its own ships."

Redd started; he could see it now, as plain as the nose on one's face. The gold he had returned to Sir George was too hot to turn into the cash that would save the firm. It explained why Geoffrey was eating the minnows: to keep them from devouring the whale. And Kerry, a little frantic now, was speaking for all of Sydney, saying:

"I was told at the New South Wales Bank that unless this Captain Redd blows Untell's story to hell, Van Oren credit won't be worth a damn in Australia. And if Van Oren goes under, God help Sydney."

Redd scarcely heard Geoffrey say, "We can't pay you a shilling of the thirty-six thousand pounds." And the picture of Kerry just standing there shaking with disbelief as he stared at his own ruin was vague. Instead he looked at and measured the weight that had fallen on his shoulders. "If Van Oren goes under, God help Sydney!" rang in his ears. If the firm folded, confidence would be shaken; not because of the firm's wealth or power, which in no way compared to that of the banks, but because it stood solvent and firm in the weather of insolvency. With public confidence low, any new catastrophe could bring disaster to the remaining banks. And he, Captain Redd, by an amazing twist of fortune, could be holding the economy of a colony in the palm of his hand.

He smiled wryly. It was, of course, a preposterous thought, though it made him think of all that had happened in the wake of piracy on the high seas. During the next few hours, as he sat with Sir George and Cailler Rise, he paid little heed to Van Oren's decision to hide out during the hearing in order to escape any personal brush with the case, or to the barrister's sudden shift in preliminary strategy, or to what he seemed to know was continuing mercilessly on in Geoffrey's office.

But his thinking mind was suddenly alert; maybe Geoffrey was responsible. He wasn't sure. He crossed swords with Rise over the strategy to be employed and held firm. Rise could still hold the contents of the boxes up for his ace in the hole, but there was no need of dealing out a pack of lies in the approach to it. He didn't wish to be charged with perjury later on. They gave in to him at last; they had to.

He returned to his ship in a trance, and he saw her a thing apart, at once a haven and a cruel master of men and destinies. In the seclusion of his quarters, he poured out a peg of whisky, and another, and another. He continued to drink, and remained sober, wanting snarling seas under him, wanting a woman, any woman, to give him even temporary release from the pictures crowding his mind. Geoffrey was strong in them, the nave of the wheel of ruin. Geoffrey—and opposite him, Martha. He wondered.

He drank until he felt his sea legs wobbly under him on a still ship; and he talked to Mr. Hyde about things he wasn't thinking of until his tongue seemed as thick as a bower anchor. And yet he remained sharply alert in himself, seeing and feeling and weaving the things that had happened into a pattern of the future.

It didn't bother him in the least that ruin had descended on strong men like Kerry, Finch, and others in the firm's ruthless fight to save itself; that he had sailed after gold an honest captain only to sell himself for a quarter of it later; or that his future career lay in the lap of a naval court. These things didn't matter, except that, somehow, they sharpened his focus on an unbidden and nagging loyalty to something very important to him personally. He couldn't quite put his finger on it. But Martha van Oren emerged clear out of it, then faded away before the threat of tomorrow's court hearing. And then——

He seemed to know that she was the bright red thread running through the dark skein of events. Even now she seemed to be standing over his shoulder exhorting him—cramming his head with a lot of damn nonsense—to uphold her name and her ship's name in court tomorrow.

2

It was nearing noon of the next day. Captain Untell had just completed his account of the eventful meeting at sea. There was small doubt that he had stirred up a lot of interest. Judges and spectators alike seemed to be aware that the fastest and shortest voyage in the annals of sail was likely to become one of the most notorious. Cailler Rise felt the courtroom pulse and arose with the purpose of annulling the effect in a hurry. He said:

"Captain Untell, since you did not open any of the boxes, you can't be positive of their contents, can you?" Untell couldn't. "Then why did you suspect they contained gold?"

"Because nothing else is quite as heavy." Next Rise asked if he had weighed any of the boxes. He had not.

"Very well, Captain," Rise said. "Now have you ever seen islands appear in mid-ocean, then disappear when you neared them?" Untell had.

Lancefield argued that this should be stricken from the record, since mirages at sea were not uncommon. "Perhaps," Rise said. "But we are testing one man's imagination." Smiling, he turned to Captain Redd, who arose and moved forward.

Sitting through routine questions, Redd looked from the officers and men of both ships to the five members of the court: a merchant, a shipowner, and three officers of His Britannic Majesty's Navy. Beneath the high ceiling all the character and dignity of an English courtroom was in evidence. He felt the presence of justice here as well as the need of shaping it. He was wondering how pliant it was when the presence of something else made a strong bid for his attention——

Martha van Oren in a simple white dress.

Seated next to her was Geoffrey, yesterday's master of refined tragedy. Sir George wasn't there. And now tall, white-haired and distinguished Rise was getting to the point, saying:

"Captain Redd, you have heard Captain Untell's testimony. Now did you on the day named overtake the *Castlereagh* at sea?"

"I did."

"What was your object in doing so?"

"To get the boxes."

"Did you get them?"

"Yes."

Rise bowed to Lancefield, a stocky man with a fighting face, and said, "The advantage is yours to pursue."

Lancefield seemed invulnerable to the courtroom flourish exhibited by Rise. He moved to Redd and looked him straight in the eye for a searching moment, then began where Rise left off. "Now, Captain Redd, assuming that you were sent after the boxes by the shipowner, did you carry the necessary papers to *legally* effect their release for transfer to your ship?"

Redd was looking at Martha. He saw her lean forward. Geoffrey tensed, as did the members of the court; here was a question likely to establish guilt of piracy or strike it off the record. His face remained unchanged as he said, "*Assuming,* did you say? Perhaps you'd like to reword your question."

"No." Lancefield said. "Instead I'll ask if you were ordered to sail out and get the boxes, and by whom?"

"Yes. By Mr. van Oren."

"And did you follow orders? Successfully?"

"I did."

"Legally? I mean by that did you present Captain Untell

with a written order from Mr. van Oren? Did you carry written orders?"

"No."

Lancefield showed surprise, as did the court. Slowly he recovered, unable to believe it had been that easy. He checked any show of the triumph he felt because he had won too easily. He glanced about him with a twinge of uneasiness, then back at Redd.

"Did Captain Untell release the boxes willingly?" With Redd's answer of "No," he said, "Did you take them by force? Rather, were they taken against Captain Untell's wishes?"

"Against his wishes, yes."

"Then do you admit to the crime of piracy, Captain Redd?"

"No."

"But you have already done so, Captain."

"Have it your way."

"Thank you," Lancefield replied. He said to the court, "There is your case," though it was apparent to all that he spoke without conviction.

Mr. Rise got to his feet smiling. He said, "Captain Redd, you appear to be guilty." He walked away from Redd, looking at the five men of the court.

Redd said nothing. His expression underwent no change. A slow murmur rippled through the room. Redd's apparent guilt served only to arouse curiosity. And the hush Rise had waited for was impressive.

Satisfied, Rise turned toward the box and resumed his questioning. "Captain Redd, will you tell the court what happened?"

"Aye, sir. Mr. van Oren came aboard of me after the *Castlereagh* sailed. He said he had made a mistake in sending seven boxes to England, that it was too late to correct his error since Captain Untell would make good sail."

"And did you," Rise said, "tell him you could overtake the ship?" Redd nodded and Rise went on. "Now, Captain Redd, to get ahead of your story, you caught up with the *Castlereagh*. You took the boxes. But couldn't you have accomplished your purpose without any trouble by carrying written orders from Mr. van Oren to Captain Untell?"

"It wasn't necessary, since Mr. van Oren was going with me. He did board the *Lady* about an hour before we got our tide and wind. I thought he was below when we filled away. So did Mr. Hyde. And, as the crew will witness, we were thirty miles out when I had the ship searched. Then the bosun remembered seeing Mr. van Oren on the quay just before we took in our warps."

At this point Rise excused Redd and questioned Mr. Hyde, the second, the bosun, and members of the crew. Then he called Redd again, saying, "Proceed from there, Captain."

"Aye. Undecided, realizing I could either turn back and lose the time Mr. van Oren needed or give chase to the *Castlereagh*, I chose the latter."

"And out of loyalty to Mr. van Oren, you ran the risk of piracy?"

"No. I was in on the deal also." This reply did much to emphasize Redd's honesty to all, regardless of how honest he actually was. And Rise was astute enough to pause for full effect before asking:

"Can you divulge the nature of the business that made it so important for you to crack on sail?"

"Aye. The bank crisis. Mr. van Oren needed money, and he was trying to refinance a syndicate in England. But the Great Sydney Union Bank failed shortly after the *Castlereagh* sailed. He needed the boxes back here to raise cash in a hurry."

"What was in the boxes, Captain?"

"Ore from the Bendigo Mine which Mr. van Oren controls."

"The *deal* you said you were in on also, Captain, was, of course, the Bendigo Syndicate."

"Naturally. I've owned shares in it for years."

"Captain Redd, why did you say to Captain Untell, 'Under the circumstances, I can't even give you a receipt for them'?"

"Because I knew what he should have known—that Mr. van Oren would have receipted them later."

"Do you mean to imply——"

Redd interrupted: "That Captain Untell had sailed under the pennant long enough to know the meaning of urgency and to put the firm ahead of his dislike for me."

Rise nodded with significant discovery. "Dislike, you say?"

"Yes. He fell for a little strumpet in Melbourne several years ago. I took her away from him."

Untell arose, growling in anger. Lancefield managed to calm him, though not until he told Redd that a day of reckoning would come.

3

Next day the hearing opened with Lancefield asking Finch if he could identify samples of ore from the Bendigo Hole. Finch said he could.

Geoffrey was called to the stand. "As business manager of Van Oren, Limited, Mr. Lipscomb-Grey, can you swear that *all boxes* were filled with *ore only* and sent to England to refinance the Bendigo Syndicate? Remember, sir," Lancefield warned, "that you are under oath, and that any violation of sworn fealty, if adjudged false, will make you liable for prosecution."

"To the best of my knowledge, yes."

Unsatisfied with this reply, Lancefield kept hammering at Geoffrey until he obtained a positive answer.

Then Lancefield began to work patiently on another angle of the case. Rise appeared both uneasy and surprised when he called a stranger to the stand.

A short man moved forward. Adjusting himself, he waited until a question was placed. "What is, or was, your occupation, Mr. Duff?"

"I was night guard at the Bank of Melbourne."

"Now tell us what happened on the evening before the bank failed, Mr. Duff."

Clearing his throat noisily, the witness began: "A Wednesday night, it was, eight-fifteen o'clock. The side door opened and I saw Mr. Tysbee, the head of the bank. He said to me, 'Duff, a shipment is due to leave the bank at ten tonight. Admit the men.'

"Well, the men came with a large hack and took seven boxes from the vault. It took four men to carry one box out. Mr. Tysbee left with them. I was curious, so I took a good look at the hack and made a mental note of the owner's placard on the side. Then next day the bottom fell out of Melbourne. The bank failed. I thought nothing more about the boxes for several days. Then I began to wonder, and I went to see the hackman, who said he put the boxes aboard a four-masted bark. Her name was *Sarah Proctor*, and she was bound for Sydney."

Next Lancefield asked the bark's agent to take the stand. Then he asked who owned the *Sarah Proctor*. A British firm was named, and he called for the ship's manifest of the date corresponding to Mr. Duff's account of her sailing. The agent produced the papers and, after swearing they were authentic, read the list, coming at last to:

"One shipment of seven cases marked metal consigned to loft seven, Warehouse A, Circular Quay, Sydney."

"And were they properly delivered and receipted?"

"Yes, sir."

"And just who was the consignor?"

"The Bendigo Mine."

"Bendigo? Now tell us who leases loft seven."

"Bailey and Bailey, Shippers."

"Thank you. Now will Mr. Edmund Bailey come forward?"

A corpulent man responded. He answered Lancefield's first question: "Yes, the boxes remained in our loft for two days. A launch picked them up late on the second day."

"By whose order?"

"The order came from the management of Bendigo Mine in writing." When asked to produce the order, he did so, saying, "Signed by Mr. Finch's assistant, as you can see."

"Just why was your loft the destination of the boxes?"

"Why, sir, we maintain a working arrangement with several shipping houses."

"Mr. Bailey, who made the arrangements for the use of your warehouse in this instance?"

"No one. The boxes arrived and we accepted them. We knew by the consignor's name on them that they were Van Oren, Limited, property."

Lancefield faced the court and smiled. Rise got to his feet, then sat down slowly. It was not necessary for Lancefield to say, as he did, that he had unearthed a juicy bone; that no doubt remained that the head of a defunct bank had reached into a vault containing the people's money and shipped, clandestinely, as the records proved, seven boxes of "something" to Sir George van Oren. He summed up his case with:

"Can this court, after such evidence, imagine any set of businessmen going to so much trouble to cover up ore samples? If the boxes were now open before your eyes and you saw ore, could you believe that you were looking at their original contents?"

Rise looked worried. His anticipated trump—seven unopened boxes—drew his glance. With them, he had hoped to clinch the case. And now he appeared to be very much afraid that they would serve to do just the opposite. To add to his troubles, the court refused to adjourn the case until next day.

Both Martha and Geoffrey were amazed. The fast pace set by Lancefield, who only yesterday seemed dull as compared to Rise, held them in a state of worried fascination. His energy and confident manner had turned the tables on Redd in the matter of minutes. A hush fell over the room as Rise tried to gather his wits and reassemble the tottering defense. It was plain to all that for once the brilliance he had exhibited for so long in the courts of New South Wales was missing.

No one was more aware of this than Redd. He had warned him about Untell's recognition of Tysbee and what might come out of it. But Rise had scoffed. And now they were trapped. A hard anger burned on his face as the damning silence lengthened. He felt all eyes on him, and he saw Geoffrey standing. Then Martha stood beside him. He felt her eyes searching his face imploringly. In silence she communicated her fears to him. And he seemed to know all she was thinking, asking for. He felt the pressure she brought to bear on him. Her ship, her name.

The devil with these! He had his own name to think about. Tension in the courtroom mounted and guilt hung heavy over him, a man without the crafty defense he needed.

He glanced at Rise, who continued to shuffle his notes. Then he got to his feet. Before anyone could object, he was committed to a breach of courtroom etiquette: he ordered Mr. Hyde to open one of the boxes. The mate was advancing to obey when Rise stood up, as surprised as anyone there, and stepped to his side. Ignoring his presence, Redd looked at Finch, saying:

"Not that it makes any difference, but you said you could identify Bendigo ore. Well, here's your opportunity."

No word was spoken to stay Mr. Hyde. The court appeared to be every bit as anxious to look at the contents of the boxes as witnesses or barristers.

Redd was turning it all in his mind. "Open all of them, Mr. Hyde." When this was done, he turned to Finch and bowed with mock gravity.

Finch arose and moved toward the boxes. He stared into them one by one before bending down to examine the contents. A piece of dark rock appeared in his hand, then another; and as he moved from one box to the next, his expression became more perplexed. When he arose at last, he said:

"I'm almost sure of it. It's Bendigo rock, and heavy with metal."

As he returned to his seat, Lancefield arose. An amused smile appeared on his face. As his finger lifted, and he said, "Remember my question, 'If the boxes were open before your eyes and you saw ore——'" Captain Redd's voice stopped him in midsentence: "You're whistling in the wind, mister."

With the poise and confidence of a victor, Lancefield whirled about. "Now am I, Captain Redd? Are these the boxes you took from the *Castlereagh?* You had ample time to substitute these in their place, didn't you?"

"Sure. I had plenty of time," Redd answered quickly. "But can you prove I switched boxes?"

"A review of the case, the step-by-step secrecy established in the transport of these boxes, proves it. Don't insult the intelligence of this court by saying that a pair of shrewd businessmen, Messrs. Tysbee and van Oren, would resort to such measures in the transport of seven cases of ore."

Redd laughed. "I've shipped all kinds of men before the mast. Some sailors won't look at the name plate of my ship because they are superstitious and gullible. But not one of them would believe the fairy tale you're trying to prove, Mr. Lancefield. Not even a fool could imagine that much gold. And even if it was there, you'd still have no case against me."

With Lancefield silenced by this last remark, Redd looked at the men who were there to judge him and said, "Now I'm a practical man. I know enough law to realize that Mr. Lancefield has built a case on what he imagines. It seems that both he and my lawyer are so wrapped up in the letter of the law that they overlook simple facts, such as who is on trial and for what. They forget that I'm charged with piracy, which, in plain language, is defined as robbery on the high seas."

Then, in a few words, he tore the props out from under all Lancefield had so carefully built:

"Since I work for Mr. van Oren and, acting upon his orders, I took the boxes from one of his ships to another, robbery simply doesn't exist."

Without due pause for any answer, he placed his cap well back on his head and moved toward the door in long, easy strides.

4

The court recessed for a discussion and came out of it with an opinion weighted with reservations: Captain Redd, though technically guilty of piracy, was, through lack of evidence required to establish either fact or motive, guilty of nothing more than expediency. However, the court was not satisfied with several aspects of the case. First—the records of Mr. Tysbee's insolvent bank should show if ore samples were locked in its vaults prior to the financial collapse; second—Mr. Tysbee should answer certain questions; third—Mr. van Oren should, if conditions warranted, do the same; fourth—should fraud or theft be established, Captain Redd would be involved in such crime and brought to trial before a court of the land.

Sydney read in its clubs, drawing rooms, and pubs of Captain Redd's victory. He was free and he would remain free until the colony of Victoria proved that Mr. Tysbee had committed a crime.

But Sydney had formed an opinion. It thought Redd, Van Oren, and Tysbee guilty of something. What it was, no one knew.

Book two

THE SWEEP OF THE TIDE

... *The sea was running strong, though the fickle wind seemed to be shifting fair.* ...

CHAPTER V

Dan Daragan's pub was crowded that evening. The sign of the anchor drew seamen and their kind to a rendezvous as salty as the seven seas. There tales of the sea were told and retold over the finest and cheapest liquors on the continent. In this clearing-house for shipping news, ships, officers, and crews were always up for argument. Noise went with the layers of smoke and acrid smells of tobacco and ferment. So did tempers and fists.

Tonight the charge of piracy against Captain Redd was tried all over again. Some favored Redd, others didn't. At a rear booth Captain Untell greeted a visitor with a look of surprise and said: "Sit down, Mr. Lancefield."

Lancefield took a seat, though he seemed to look through the bottle, lost in thought. Nor did he look up when a scarlet-clad girl stood with hands on swinging hips and said to Untell, "Now, sailor, don't forget to drink one to Cap'n Redd." He was still lost in thought when the girl started and got a way under her. Untell had just blasted forth, "Give it the deep six, Annie!"

Lancefield's glance lifted slowly. "Captain, they are all guilty of something. We're going to find out what it is."

Untell worked his mouth after a peg of straight rye and seemed to glare at him. Then his face tightened up. His big hands knotted into fists, relaxed, and fingernails drummed the wood.

"What are your plans, Captain?"

"A ship—later."

"It won't be easy for you after this."

Untell's strong jaw clamped back words he wanted to blurt out. He scratched a weathered ear, looked at the ceiling, and poured again. "I've got a score to settle," he said calmly. "It goes way back. But today does it."

"Meaning, Captain . . . ?"

"That I'm going after Redd tomorrow. One of us is going to get hurt."

A piano played fast and loud. It stopped suddenly. Daragan was slapping a Portuguese sailor, oblivious to the knife in his hand. The sailor turned and ran and the piano commenced anew, and Lancefield said:

"The Board of Trade is not at all happy or satisfied with the decision of the naval court. Piracy was done on the high seas. I know it, and you know it, and the court knows it. That much secrecy over those boxes of ore just doesn't make sense. But Redd was clever. He read the only loophole in the law that had him fast. And it was just plain common sense. I said he was clever. I say now, *he is clever*. And he's with a smart and powerful crowd. Van Oren's a fox." He paused, a speculative light in his eyes. Then he said in detached manner:

"Now just who do you think would hire you now, Captain?"

Untell's powdery gray eyes regarded him with all sorts of motion in them. But Lancefield saw controlled motion and liked it. Maybe this was his man. Certainly he had every reason to dislike Redd and Sir George, which was what brought him in search of Untell tonight.

"Too bad," he said to Untell, "since we could use a man like you in the employ of Van Oren, Limited."

"What's your course, counselor?"

"The case against Redd may emerge out of defeat a bigger case than technical piracy. We are sharpening our teeth for it, hoping to fasten them on Tysbee, Redd, and George van Oren."

"Sir George is big game," Untell said. "Try to harpoon him and he'll thrash his flukes like a whale and rip the courts apart, you with them."

"I not only agree, but admire a man who is not inclined to underestimate an adversary. However, Captain," he said, leaning forward, "I remember reading about a huge whale lying helplessly on land. Seems the flood took it in and the ebb left it beached. It was easy to harpoon then, though it wasn't necessary."

"What's the connection?"

"If the Crown's examiners uncover what we suspect at the Bank of Melbourne, we'll beach Van Oren through Tysbee and Redd. We know Tysbee is in Sydney but we can't touch him. Not yet. If the bank shows funds missing, we can take him. And if he can't absolve himself, then we'll have a strong case against Redd—one he can't talk himself out of."

"You're gunnels under with ifs, counselor."

"Are you interested in working with us when I can eliminate them? Or even before that?"

Untell hadn't heard the last question. He was slowly getting to his feet, his gnarled hands flexing, his face working under a tightening smile of brutal anticipation. Muscles crawled along his ruddy jaw in ridges. "By the deep blue!" he said. Then his voice boomed over the noise of welcome at the front of the pub like a foghorn over the roar of breaking waves:

"Ahoy, you damned pirate!"

Lancefield got up quickly. He knew without looking that Redd was in the house, that the plans he was diligently trying to shape were now threatened. All the rivalry, dislike, and hate in a man of Untell's breed could rise up like the tide, cresting high in strife before falling away from him when it was over. He had seen long hate take a bath in blood and emerge white into friendship. He didn't want this—not now.

"Wait, Captain Untell!" He stood before him with urgent solicitude in his voice. "This isn't the time."

"Stow it, counselor!"

"Captain. Listen to me. You can kill him and what have you left? Think, man! Confuse and baffle him now. Laugh! Then have the pleasure of hunting him down."

"I've got better ideas."

"Then save them for the dessert, Captain."

Redd was walking toward them, Mr. Hyde following. The crowd of hangers-on edged along, tense with expectancy. Daragan's pub had heard a lot about the feud between these captains, much of it rumor and enlarged tales out of drunken heads. But a climax might be at hand. If so, it would be worth telling over and over.

Redd stopped a few feet from Untell with hands on hips and said, "That's twice you've called me a damned pirate, Captain. When are you going to make it stick?"

"Right now," Untell said, shedding his black coat and tie. He brushed Lancefield aside, though something the examiner said slowed him. Instead of rushing Redd, he paused with an odd look of restraint and uncertainty on his face. Lancefield had just told him, in a voice calm and final, that he wasn't the man for the job ahead. This didn't matter, not in the least, though the moment's break of his rough anger did. He came out of it a giant in chains.

Redd sensed his incertitude and looked at Lancefield, who said nothing but returned his glance with no yielding in his face. He was the real enemy, his eyes said; not Untell. Redd believed this, and he felt the wisdom of the fresh estimates he was drawing of this man who was saying now:

"Captain Redd, take these words with you wherever you go: I'm not through. If you're guilty, I'll chase you and find you and convict you."

Redd studied him closely for a moment. "I believe you would, all right," he said. Then he surprised and disappointed the crowd when he turned on his heel and walked out of the place.

With order of a kind restored, Lancefield said, "Maybe you are my man, Captain."

"I'm listening," Untell replied. "What's on your mind?"

"How would you like a government schooner for the present—say until you can get a Van Oren ship?"

2

Van Oren stood on a small dock at the foot of Muirkirk's promontory awaiting a boat in the night. Geoffrey was at his side looking out over the harbor at the schooner at anchor.

She looked like any ordinary two-masted, fore-and-aft-rigged schooner, though he knew that her mahogany paneling, polished brass, carpets, and fine lamps belied her appearance. She was tonight fulfilling her purpose. Listed under a name that wasn't likely to reveal her true ownership, she was a convenient retreat for Milton Tysbee after what had happened in court today.

Geoffrey had urged Sir George to get him away from Muirkirk Hall and out of sight immediately following the court's decision. And now, with Tysbee aboard the *Vega*, he was leading up to something else. He had just spoken of the uselessness of valuable gold bars, and Sir George had sighed heavily and said they were like accusing fingers.

"In Sydney, yes," Geoffrey replied, drawing a quick questioning glance from Van Oren. "The purpose for which we—er—borrowed the gold seems lost to us. We might as well own so much lead."

Sir George nodded. The scheme nagged at his mind like a long-lost memory. They had decided to use the gold, after saving Van Oren, Limited, to buy up distress property in Melbourne and Sydney at a fraction of its real worth. After the crisis, the profit would run into millions. But now they didn't dare show a single yellow bar in Australia.

"And," Geoffrey went on, "your friend Mr. Tysbee poses a problem."

"Milton? What do you mean, Geoffrey?"

Geoffrey managed a light laugh and a shrug. "Why, nothing at all." Pausing, he said, "However, it's deucedly embarrassing to have him about in the face of today's revelations in court, don't you think?"

"Yes. Now that you've mentioned it, yes."

"You are to be admired for forcing any suggestion from me when I'm sure you're thinking far ahead of me, Sir George."

Van Oren looked cunning and said, "About what, for instance?"

"Natural inclinations, sir. Self-defense and self-preservation; and all sorts of things, such as—well, you can't detain your guest Tysbee here, and you don't want him to be where he can answer questions likely to implicate you if and when his bank is examined. This Lancefield is a very thorough fellow."

Sir George chuckled. "Redd put him in his place."

"And in brilliant fashion," Geoffrey replied. "Captain Redd is very useful at times." The tone of his voice implied more than he said. "But I see your skiff there."

Geoffrey felt quite secure even under the steady scrutiny of Van Oren's eyes. The other relied on his business judgment and he could in no way suspect that it was tinctured with a little jealous concern over the way Martha looked at Captain Redd. What he had in mind was too timely and sensible for that. And now he had forced a question out of Van Oren:

"Geoffrey, you have something in mind. What is it?"

"It's the very thing, I'm sure, you've been considering. Well, why not? Captain Redd's ship is loaded with cargo to Batavia and Singapore. He's a good man to use in this partnership."

"*Use?* I don't like the word," Van Oren said.

"Come now. We've used him once already. He got the boxes." His arm fell on Sir George's shoulders affectionately. "But who could serve us better in protecting our interests than a partner in the scheme?"

"Very well, Geoffrey. Now that the boar is out of the bush, we'll face it. I think a lot of Milton. He financed me when I first came to Australia. I must admit I've been wondering what to do with him now, but with a twinge of conscience. Have you any definite ideas?"

"I have. Put it up to Captain Redd. Let him take Tysbee on a voyage, the same voyage that will take the bars to Batavia and Singapore for deposit."

Van Oren hid the excitement he felt by following a banking tern that skimmed the water. A fish leaped up in silver, and the tern swooped low, then sailed up into the wind. He said slowly, "And draw on foreign capital for our investments."

"Correct," Geoffrey smiled. "Even as we keep Captain Redd

at a safe distance. If Tysbee is found, let it be aboard his ship. Who will look guilty then, Redd or us?"

Van Oren did not attempt to hide the admiration he felt for Geoffrey's cunning until he remembered that all this hedging about was supposed to be his idea.

Geoffrey said, "The boat is waiting."

Sir George was soon aboard the *Vega*. He asked about Captain Redd and learned that he had not arrived. He walked forward and back again, oblivious to the penciled shadows the moon cast across her deck. He looked out over the harbor beyond the dark reflection of her bulk on the waters. The schooner was more at peace than he in the minutes of waiting.

He greeted Redd later on deck, with a brief handshake and a word of congratulation for his good work in the courtroom. Without further ado, he offered a worried face and said something about the unhealthy turn the case had taken, adding, "Actually, Gordon, the scheme is up for everyone to look at. We hadn't any idea the transport of the boxes was so carefully watched. And now, if Milton is prosecuted——"

Redd took it up there: "Then you and I are as guilty as he is. I've been thinking about that."

Van Oren searched his face intently before saying, "Milton is waiting for us below." Then, almost in the same thought, he said, "When do you sail for the Orient?"

Redd was suddenly wise. "Say what's on your mind."

Van Oren did. He hinted at it, planting the idea as Geoffrey had done, though he tinctured it with real fears of what would follow Tysbee's arrest and trial. Next he talked of the gold and its transfer into cash he could use in the scheme. And he told of the plan to buy up distress property and ships and mines. As the profit side appealed to Redd more and more, it was not hard to convince him that steps should be taken to insure the safety of the scheme as well as themselves. Then Van Oren asked the important question:

"Will you take Milton aboard the *Lady?*"

Redd looked at Sir George with a feeling of open disregard. Here was a risk any man would back off from, a risk that would convict him of more than piracy if he were caught up with. On the other hand, it was the risk of partnership in a big game for gold, though that wasn't it at all. Gold was playing second fiddle to the big job of steering clear of another brush with the courts. What Van Oren was asking of him made good sense. He said:

"We'll see what Mr. Tysbee has to say."

He crossed the deck and said something to Mr. Hyde, then went below, leaving the deck to its former peace. A thin gauze slid along in the upper breeze toward the round moon. A plaintive cry sounded from afar and the water lapped at the schooner's sides as before.

3

Redd poured a drink and looked at Tysbee thoughtfully. He saw open dislike in the little banker's face. Perhaps he resented a ship captain who had the temerity to act as an equal. Whatever it was, the effect was mutual. Tysbee was saying:

"Too bad you half won the case, Captain. As it stands, this Lancefield is anxious to convict me of something."

"Which he'll do if given the chance," Redd answered.

"You sound sure of that."

"When I think of you before him in court, I am. There are questions you can't answer without putting all of us up for trial. So it's better not to risk it."

"This colony has no interest in me."

"Oh yes it has, if only to prove me and Sir George guilty."

Tysbee controlled his rising anger at this man and felt out Van Oren with a glance. Looking back to Redd, he realized that something big was in the wind. The eyes of both men were too alert and tentative, as he knew his to be. He said nothing as he tried to adjust himself to this new experience.

He could remember few times in his life when he had not held the upper hand. Born rich and endowed with a talent for accumulating and handling money, he had required only a foot inside the great Melbourne bank to begin his swift and easy ascent. His dominating attitude was natural, though it had narrowed his vision. He was, therefore, at a loss to know how to personally deal with a man like Redd. He tried, however, saying:

"Captain, your risk is behind you. Mine isn't. I didn't expect this adventure to backfire. The bank would have closed anyhow. Borrowing gold that would have remained locked in the vaults for months sounded good. And it would still sound good but for what was told in court today. We were going to return the bars to the bank in time. And we had the time. Now we haven't."

Redd wasn't surprised at this revelation. He had suspected it for some time. But he made a note of one thing: Sir George had made the idea sound good to Tysbee, proving again his stealthy cunning and reluctance to do anything illegal himself. By the same token it uncovered a weakness in Tysbee that didn't augur well for the scheme or their safety from courts.

"Was the ore actually in the vaults?" Redd asked.

"Yes," Sir George replied.

"And now," Tysbee said, "I feel the trap closing on me. I suggest we return the gold the best way we can at once."

Redd eyed him with contempt, saying, "What kind of a man are you to disregard us in your fright?"

Van Oren said, "Take it easy, Gordon. Milton's side of this is to be considered, you know."

"There isn't much to consider, is there? The court decided his position today." Redd was aware that Sir George was playing a game now.

Before Van Oren could shape a reply, Tysbee stepped in to trade on Sir George's friendship while it was up for show. He said, "For Christ's sake, Captain! After what Lancefield uncovered today, can't you see that the bank will be examined in a hurry?"

Van Oren said thoughtfully, "No doubt about that." Then he said, "Milton, I wouldn't blame you if you decided to get out of Australia for a while."

Aware of the stern speculation in Sir George's glance, Tysbee said, "If we return the gold now, I think I can cover its absence or show that it was borrowed."

"You *think?*" Redd's steady look and tone of voice conveyed to Tysbee the hostility he felt. "I don't relish the picture of a man of your uncertain mind before Lancefield."

Tysbee looked quickly at Van Oren, imploring him in silence to sustain their relationship over the years. But there was doubt in his face also. He knew that gold was gold, that friendship was an entire thing or it wasn't. He made his bid then:

"Why not face the truth? This adventure backfired and we've got to save our skins while there's time."

As if Van Oren's mind hung in delicate balance, Redd said, "*Our* skins? I am in the clear. Remember? I was running ore for Mr. van Oren. And there's no one to prove he wasn't shipping ore. He's clear, unless you talk. So be reasonable, Mr. Tysbee."

"Reasonable! What are you getting at, Captain?"

"Just this. Now had you rather spend the rest of your life in prison for stealing the bank's money or live the life of a gentleman aboard my ship until this blows over?"

Caught in the pinch, Tysbee said, "No," urgently. "We'll do it my way, and I'll promise not to involve any of you."

Van Oren pretended to ignore this. "Gordon, just what do you have in mind?"

"Within the week, the *Lady of Glasgow* sails for Batavia and Singapore. Ideal places, by the way," he said, as though he had just thought of it, "for turning the bars into cash." Pausing for effect, he came to the point. "I'm inviting Mr. Tysbee to go along."

When Tysbee opened his mouth to protest, Van Oren said, "Wait, Milton. As much as I regret this, I'm inclined to agree. For your sake, of course. You will fare better out of Australia until the threat subsides."

Tysbee's voice was near to breaking as he said, "George, if I go now, you know it will be final. I can never return." He broke off and stared at nothing, unless it was his own future.

Redd didn't like what he knew he had to do now. With both feet in it and both stained with borrowed gold that was now stolen gold, and confronted with the only man who could convict all of them, and who would do just that given the chance, he had no alternative. He must add another crime to his list in order to cover up his part in the first.

He got to his feet, walked to the door and opened it. Looking into the face of his chief mate, he said, "Come in, Mr. Hyde."

Then he returned to his place at the table, ignoring Van Oren's wide-open surprise and subsequent understanding. Hyde walked

THE SWEEP OF THE TIDE 77

toward the stunned banker, saying, "I trust our passenger is ready to depart."

Four sailors appeared out of the companion and followed Hyde to the blanket-covered box. "Lower it to the boat," the mate said. "Easy as you go, lads." Next he turned on Tysbee and said, "Come along, sir."

His eyes blazing with wrath, Tysbee watched the box of gold go through the door. He turned on Redd, a pointing finger trembling. "You can't get away with this! By God, I'll show you!

"As for you, George——" He took a step forward militantly, then paused, his shoulders sagging in defeat. "George, you're adding me to Finch, Untell, Kerry, and the others. Friendship to you is a matter of expediency."

Redd wanted to shout, "Amen," though he turned away and said, "Careful as you go, Mr. Hyde. I've heard that kidnaping is a serious offense."

Van Oren looked at him and frowned, then glanced on to the *Lady's* mate, who was gently urging the former head of the Bank of Melbourne toward the companion.

A heavy quiet hung over the *Vega's* saloon. A muffled splashing of oars sounded far away. A full minute passed before Van Oren shifted his gaze from the doorway to Redd's face.

"Gordon, I want you to see that he is treated respectfully aboard ship. From you on down. I demand it." As Redd smiled wryly, Van Oren said, "This hurts deep. He was like a brother."

"Sure." Redd laughed. "Like a brother. You had him steal the bars from his own bank and ship them. You placed the ore in his bank ahead of that for your own safety. You went so far as to convince him the scheme was his idea as much as yours. Then you brought him up here where you could keep an eye on him. Like a brother!

"After that, you sent me after the boxes without any written order to implicate you, causing the Board of Trade to throw a piracy charge at me. Maybe I'm like a brother."

Van Oren hadn't expected this any more than he had been prepared for Redd's bold act. But he saw the wisdom of kidnaping and his look of relief wasn't quite dissolved under Redd's stinging words. He said:

"You amaze me. But what are you getting at?"

"Just this. You made good use of me once. And tonight you're thinking you've done it again. But I made up my own mind about Tysbee. Why? Because I knew you wouldn't. You and Geoffrey don't operate in the open. Both of you were sitting back looking at me to do something about it."

"Now, Gordon. It isn't as bad as——"

"And I did something about it," Redd went on. "The only thing left to do. But don't get any funny notions in your head that you can turn this on me as you did the piracy charge."

Van Oren considered this, his face touched with mock surprise and hurt. Soon he smiled disarmingly and said, "Gordon, you've got me all wrong. Listen. Would I trust that much gold to many men? No. But I turned it over to you without a word, without any guarantee that you won't abscond with it. Yet you sound unduly cautious, as though you don't trust me at all."

"Trust you?" Redd answered. "Sure I do—like a brother."

CHAPTER VI

Martha moved slowly toward the water. The moon was big upon the harbor and the trade wind was gentle. She stood there watching wavetops curling white for a run to the sands. A million night insects seemed to chorus them in. And out beyond the point of land circling into a cove, a schooner sat quiet and still as though hammered out of silver. The harbor patrol slid by on muffled engines. Soon a boat moved away from the schooner, the men at the sweeps grinding out long strokes for the cover of land.

The night was queer.

Her eyes shifted from scenes before her to the climactic moments of the hearing that afternoon. His last words—"robbery simply doesn't exist"—and the total sureness of his stride continued to dominate her mind. Geoffrey had been aware of this, though he concealed it well except for glances which a discerning woman could always unveil. Geoffrey was deep. Somehow, in some way, his reserve seemed a calculating thing. She was wishing now that he hadn't said early in the evening of the ball, "If he is resourceful enough to win out, I have no cause for worry. If he loses, then I must get rid of him." Meaning Redd, which he later denied. He built doubt even as he tried to dismiss it in her.

She wanted to love Geoffrey, though she was having a hard time of it. In the same thought she wanted to forget Captain Redd; but he persisted in her. The wind blew here and the wind blew there; stirred up cross seas.

And guilt and innocence in the matter of the boxes. The whole of the evidence today pointed to more than mere transport of Bendigo ore. It was confusing. Deep in her were gathering wisps of suspicion she could not identify. There was Captain Redd again——

She put him aside when she thought of the warmth flooding high in her the night he kissed her roughly. Scanning the horizon across the harbor, she felt the touch of his restraining arm again, heard his laugh and the words he said. Perhaps he was right— she might never find a man who could kiss her like that. She decided to forget him; he was growing dangerous.

Turning away from the harbor, she walked toward the house. She searched for some understanding. He had aroused much in her; Geoffrey hadn't. And now he marched before her mind in a new guise. He clung to her thoughts as he had clutched her in fierce embrace. Then she knew why:

She wanted to see this man, to thank him for what he had done today; or to lash out at him for intruding on an engagement kiss; or to learn something that all Sydney wanted to know—the true contents of the boxes.

"Why not?" she said. The best way to get at the bottom of anything was to go straight to its source.

Nearing the house, she saw a carriage. The driver was waiting. She went in and paused just outside the entrance hall as Crippen said:

"Sorry, sir. Mr. Tysbee left earlier in the evening." The visitor asked a question. His voice was familiar. Then Crippen replied, "He went aboard the *Vega*, sir. With Mr. van Oren."

Suddenly Martha placed the voice. The visitor was Mr. Lancefield. He was naturally interested in Mr. Tysbee, though she thought he was a little bold in coming here to look for him. The more she thought about it, the more she connected guilt with the mystery of the boxes. With her worries freshened, she asked Crippen to order her carriage at once.

A little later the quay opened up before her. The *Lady* lay beam to it, quiet and still, her masts penciled in moonlight. Pride surged up in Martha, a recurring wave over the years. There was something in the backward tilt of the masts and the curve of the bows that suggested spirit more than speed. Though tied to a dock, she had about her a poetry of motion, like a banking tern on the wind.

Drawing closer, admiration gave way to excitement at her meeting with Redd. Then uneasiness; after all, she was meeting him uninvited on his own ground. Perhaps she should turn back. Now she was certain of it, though she was getting out of the carriage and telling old Tobias to wait. The man at anchor watch paused as she approached the ship. The gangway came ashore when she announced herself and asked to see Captain Redd.

While waiting, she sauntered forward, touching the pins lining the rail, and looked up into the top-hamper where stars peeped down at her through steeples of rope, winking on and off, warning her to be careful.

And then he spoke to her. Whirling, she saw him standing in what seemed a militant pose, his eyes asking what the devil she was doing here. Caught thus, she had no idea of what she was doing aboard his ship at this hour. But he mustn't know that. Looking from him to the ship in a long sweeping glance, she said:

"You seem to be taking good care of her, Captain." Her fingers ran across the smooth paint on the rail.

He said nothing, just frowned upon her, his head turning as though he were listening for some sound he didn't wish to hear. She was unaware that Tysbee was fresh aboard this vessel and that she was more unwelcome than he made her feel.

"At least you took good care of her in court today, Captain Redd." She turned her glance full up to him then. "I must congratulate you." She put out a hand and he took it. As she drew it away, a tolerant expression showed in his face. Satisfied, she held to her course with honest impressions.

"I've always liked the ring of her name," she said, giving all attention to the ship. "There's something in it that's racy with elegance, don't you think?"

He nodded, as if the admission were forced out of him. Then he said, "But you make poetry out of it."

He was softening. She said, "Not I, Captain. You. Maybe you don't put it into words, but into motion as she runs under sail. I've seen her in the wind and I've stood her decks when she heeled."

"Then you know her," he said with interest.

"From windlass under the fo'c'slehead to the teakwood ladders of her afterdeck. Salt pork to port, salt beef to starboard," she said with enthusiasm.

Chuckling, he said, "And when do we break out lime juice, sailor?"

"Why, always at eight bells noon, sir."

"Want to sign on?" he said, his gaze intent.

She was standing with her back to the rail, looking up into the converging lines at the mast top. Then she was meeting his glance. The brittle light of challenge had gone out of his eyes and for the first time she felt entirely at ease in his presence. She was wondering if on land he shone in the reflected glory of the ship; if at sea it wasn't the other way about; if he was as honest with a court as he had to be with a ship. Answers didn't matter just then. The soft night and silence and a ship were all about her. Conversation had fallen away from any starting point or ending. The sound of his voice surprised her.

"The first time I saw the *Lady*, I had a cargo of Kanakas for the sugar fields in Queensland. I was making money, and satisfied. But when the *Lady* whistled on by, boiling her lee scuppers, I watched her until she was sail under and spoke to her—— Like to know what I said?" He grinned. "I said, 'Lady, I'll be damned if I ever lose you under a horizon again.' "

"How did you get her?"

"I happened to be in Sydney when old Captain Page died. I went directly to your father and said I'd sail through hell, wetting down canvas all the way, for her."

"You almost did today, didn't you?" She instantly regretted saying this. "I'm sorry, Captain. Honest I am."

"It's all right," he said after a silence. "Since I've still got her under me."

"Was that all that mattered?"

"You ask a divil of a lot of questions," he said with easy humor.

"I wish I could ask more and get truthful answers. I'd ask if all those boxes contained ore, and if the ones that didn't contained gold, and if it came from Mr. Tysbee's bank, and if he stole it——"

"Sure." He grinned. "And if your father and Geoffrey helped steal the gold you imagine."

"Right. And if you were entirely honest."

"I'll answer that one. I'm not. If I were I wouldn't be talking about a ship. I'd be telling you right off how much you appeal to me."

"Why, Captain!"

"I could say a lot more, Martha."

She glanced up at him; he spoke the name as though he had never known her by any other. And the look in his eyes said he was actually gentle with her, that the sea bred severity and he was holding back the tide. He seemed to know that he appealed to her, that he was carrying her a little fast.

"I'd better go now, Captain."

"Why?" He took her hand in his. "It's your ship and mine. Let's share and share alike."

"Haven't we?"

"Sure. And I like it." He was leading her aft, saying, "Remember I'm the only captain of the *Lady* you haven't approved. Over brandy, below." Near the companion he stopped of a sudden and called out, "Mr. Burk. All clear below. Lively now."

She saw the second mate dart into the companion and disappear. It was rather mysterious while it lasted. Then he emerged and said, "All's well, sir."

"Where away, Mr. Burk? The spare sail locker?"

"Aye, sir."

"You forget that I know this ship, Captain. Now just what would you hide in the afterhatch?"

"Why, stolen gold, of course."

Down the companionway to his cabin she accepted his arm, not looking at him as her pulse beat faster and sharp warnings tried to slow it down. But what she wanted to do and knew she should do were worlds apart yet clashing head on inside her.

2

Then she was in his cabin taking it in. Teakwood, mahogany, and brass; a sextant, books, charts, a telescope, a long bunk, neatly made up, and assorted personal and nautical objects. Here was the heart of a sailing ship. She looked up at the light in the gimbals and sat down at the round table.

"It's the same," she said. "I haven't visited this cabin since I was sixteen. But you're neater than Captain Page. His sea boots always hung on that bulkhead."

"Page was an old dunderhead," he said, pouring brandy. "And I can prove it."

"Go ahead," she laughed.

"Boots hanging there thump at the bulkhead. Over here they swing with the roll of the ship. Now am I right?"

"Yes. Of course. But——"

"Now isn't that enough?" he smiled. "Isn't it Redd over Page?" He sat near her, holding out a brandy glass. His hand fell over hers, though she felt no cause for alarm. His expression was genial and quiet.

"Page didn't worry me with acts of piracy," she said, smiling. "Nor did he cause me to remember the thirteen letters in my ship's name."

"Thirteen letters. That's bilge water. Brandy now? One for the lady—you."

"All right. To me." They drank and she said, "You don't relax often, do you?"

"On land, no. But I am tonight. You're good company. A lot better than Sir George." He paused.

"In fact, I almost forgot you had a purpose in coming here, Martha. What is it?"

"I think you know."

"Sure. All those questions you'd like me to answer. About how we could win out and still look guilty."

"Exactly!"

"I could say it's the way it was handled. But I won't. Actually, how important are the answers? Your ship's name is clear."

"Will it remain that way, Captain?"

"You know how I feel about that, don't you?"

She realized that he couldn't have fashioned a better reply. There was assurance in it. She said tentatively:

"You charter a course carefully, I see."

"I was caught on the wrong monsoon once. That was enough. It was in August . . ."

Before she knew it, he had turned the subject and she was listening to a terse account of a hard voyage. All questions were forgotten. They were unimportant now. He was a good host in festive mood. He raised the cook and ordered cold meats and cheese. And he was gradually drawing her out, putting her entirely at ease.

She was looking out the open port with unfocused eyes and telling him of her first voyage on the *Lady*; how in heavy weather down in the Tasman the ship lurched about. She talked on—they shipped her a pony and a piano on the return voyage; she remembered a sailor's monkey wouldn't leave the foreroyal, and her father told Page if he was set on feeding a baboon he should teach him to trim sail. And there was a sailor called Pelican Joe who taught her how to tie sailor's knots. Redd told her he was still aboard, that he got his name because of a long neck.

And then he was talking: about his youth, and his father who had been a clipper ship captain and later a Confederate blockade-runner. He had given the Yankees quite a chase. They caught him at last in the Indian Ocean off Great Nicobar.

Warmed with brandy and a settling peace between them, both forgot the time. They had talked of trivial things in unguided conversation, yet important things that seemed to mesh together in the pattern of understanding. And then all conversation was suddenly at an end. Her glance lifted to him briefly and slid on by. She was thinking she had found the softer, dreamy side of this mysterious man, even as he was thinking he had exposed the real woman under the proud Van Oren name. And what they knew to be true they could not deny. And out of the silence they met again in a glance that was laden with an emotion of contact with something as real as it was infinite.

It was then she remembered how late it was. She started, and looked at him again, with the sharpest kind of wisdom, he thought; then with a faint line of troubled thought furrowing her brow.

"I must go, Captain." She was standing when he said with a flash of a smile in his eyes:

"Haven't you forgotten something, Martha?"

"No. I don't think so." His smile was infectious and she gave in to it, saying, "What?"

"That you haven't voiced approval of the *Lady's* captain."

"Oh! Why, I thought that was understood, Captain Redd."

"I thought so too. But we'll raise a glass and I'll listen."

He watched her drink. He thought her cool and poised. She was tall and slim and full, desirable for what she offered as much as for what she kept to herself. And now a rose flush was creeping up under her skin and her calm had given way to some sign of debate in her. Then her eyes were taking him in, brightly, with a rush of pleasure in them.

"I came here tonight beset with worry, wondering about guilt and innocence. Somehow, the hearing seems to have slipped away, far away, into the past. I'm not nearly as worried as I was. Why? I don't know." She added, her voice dropping, "Does that answer you?"

He continued to look at her, aware of some emotion strongly at work in her. As she placed a hand on his arm he observed the moment's break of her reserve. She was fighting something, he decided. It might be the fears she thought dismissed, or a growing sense of caution. Or she could be at odds with her own personal wants.

"I suppose I must say it. I approve, Gordon." Her glance held strong. "More than I should." Her fingers clutched tightly at his arms and she turned away from him, taut and reluctant.

Gently he brought her face around again. What she was struggling against was in the open now. Her words revealed it, and her eyes uncovered the rest. They were raised to him, wide open with anxiety and trust, and in their depths were recurring flashes, like sheet lightning. In the gathering tension, he was thinking he could possess her.

Their glance held, and she seemed to be speaking to him, saying things she could never bring herself to declare openly.

He was almost sure of her; and thinking that it might be easy, he unconsciously pulled her closer and closer to him. "Don't, Gordon—— Please!" It came in a broken whisper, instinctive and no part of her any more than the things she had felt for him—alternately, judgment and fury—on the night of her party. No part of her, since she was reaching blindly, unreckoning, for his lips.

He pressed her roughly against his body until she winced, then bent his head abruptly and kissed her on the mouth. It was like the onrush of a driving tropic storm, all silver and dark. Her arms clung to him and she gave with an eagerness that astonished him as much as it stirred and pleased him. Like warm waves rising high and breaking one after the other, falling.

She pulled her mouth away and murmured, "No!" but it made no sense to either of them. Her hand was pressing at his neck.

He kissed her again, and again, until she went limp in his arms, bewildered, and minus any will of her own. Then she opened her deep eyes and looked at him with trust and trouble and contentment running together in them.

He had kissed her into submission, this woman with something behind her pretty face. Boiling in him was a primitive urge to claim her. His temples and face burned with it. Then that something behind her eyes was inside him now. He didn't know what it was, but he saw in it trust; and he saw in it the spirit of the *Lady;* and he was about to crush it!

Fool or whatever he was—he cursed himself for it as he saw vague and foolish pictures of her tying knots, and heard her talking about the ring of her ship's name, and thirteen letters—he placed her back from him and said harshly:

"Call me the fool!" His short laugh was grating, and bitter with mockery at himself. "Now get out of here, Martha!"

Her trembling hands came up to her face and covered it. She was torn up inside, cast loose from conventions and sane thinking. The strength of his arms and the roughness of his face frightened her and appealed to her. She still felt the press of his muscular lips, liking it, and despising herself for it. Recovery wasn't easy, not with the hurt and shame in her, not with the ridicule in his laugh and words. She was trying to understand, and couldn't, fighting hard for some palliative. Sure she had slipped far back into some dark uncivilized past into something she could never escape, she wanted to turn on him furiously, to run from him, to find Geoffrey.

She looked at him. It required effort and courage, but she did it, and was surprised at what she saw. As he stood apart from her, holding her wrap, there was in his expression the understanding she wished for.

He placed the wrap about her shoulders and turned her gently to him. In a low, assuring voice he said, "The *Lady* has sailed through all sorts of weather. Remember that." And there was no mockery in the word he added: "Lady."

She waited out a confused moment, wondering at his generosity in calling her a lady, a moment in which she expected him to say what was in his eyes. Then she turned and moved hurriedly away before the welling flood of tears broke.

CHAPTER VII

Captain Redd was on deck next morning when a squall raced across the sunrise and hissed on inland. So were officers and crew. Circumstances advanced the date of sailing by several days. With luck and sweat, the *Lady* might clear the harbor that very afternoon. But there was much to do.

He gave orders right and left in the next hour, then took a carriage to Muirkirk Hall. In a case at his side were papers that had to do with his departure. Only Sir George or Geoffrey could expedite his clearance and rush up the business of getting under way. And today they'd be only too glad to oblige him. Tysbee was aboard.

He smiled grimly, thinking less of the ex-banker's virtual imprisonment—Hyde and Burk had strict orders to keep him out of sight—and more about what his presence on board would do to him. He might as well get used to the sense of guilt and a fugitive's watchfulness, since these things would keep him company for some time.

The carriage was turning a corner off Bridge Street when a man under a tobacconist's sign caught his attention. It was Lancefield. Standing still, tamping a pipe, he looked straight at Redd. Nor did he lift a hand in return to Redd's silent gesture; he just followed him with his look.

Lancefield was known for his tenacity. Called the "Bulldog of the Bot," Board of Trade, he collected evidence and dispensed with it. That much every sea captain knew. Three years earlier he had surprised a ship of the powerful England and Orient Line in a Java port after two years of running down complaints that the ship served seamen less than the minimum of food decreed by the British Board of Trade. He was unique to say the least, and he had sharp teeth in and out of the courts.

Redd forgot him under the press of more urgent matters. The carriage was soon rolling into the gates of Muirkirk. Sir George wasn't long in joining him, or in telling him that Lancefield had called at his house last evening in search of Tysbee only to learn that he had boarded the *Vega*. He was thinking one step ahead of Van Oren when the latter said Lancefield might visit the *Lady of Glasgow* also.

Not wanting Lancefield aboard during his absence, he hurried Sir George's signature on the papers and left the room. The door had scarcely closed behind him when he saw her. He stopped still as she did.

There was in the meeting that arresting element of surprise between unsuspecting hunter and deer. Both acted accordingly.

Martha had no idea he was anywhere about. Caught unawares with an armful of freshly cut roses, she emerged from the shock more concerned with her appearance than anything else in that moment. She wore a simple cotton dress of pale blue that showed every smear of dirt from the flower bed she had just worked. And she was sure her hair was ruffled. There was soil on her hands, probably a little on her face. Then last night obscured all else. She tensed and colored and put a little defiance in her eyes.

She expected him to laugh at her with all the ridicule he withheld last night, and she lashed herself with freshening pique that he had come to gloat over her. There was no time for any reasonable adjustment in her mind, just memories of the sleepless hours of self-incrimination following their meeting. She had almost thrown herself at him, and he had kissed her into dazed submission and sent her home. These were the facts. But he didn't gloat as she expected. Instead he remained serious under a friendly look that seemed blind to last night. He was attracted, she was sure of that, and silence in him was alert and alive and complimentary. He was, of course, hiding behind a mask. She wasn't ready for his friendliness, his utter evasion, as he said:

"You make the roses look better." He walked toward her, saying, "May I have one?"

"Take all of them," she said on sudden impulse. She almost tossed them. Then, thinking better of it, she crammed them in his arms, unmindful of the thorns pricking his skin. He accepted them, not wincing once, just smiling knowingly.

"Thanks," he said. "I'm sailing today. Maybe these will bring me sailor's luck."

"I'm sure you don't need it, Captain."

He smiled at her retort and said, "Of course not," adding, with emphasis, "Miss van Oren. But there's no use in going overboard with honesty."

Not at all pleased that two could play the game, she said nothing. Nor did she speak when he took the roses to a table and selected a large deep red blossom from the bouquet. Smiling, but serious, he returned to her and placed the rose in her hair. "Red is your color," he said. Then he tilted her chin, looked into her eyes and, oblivious to the defiance and curiosity in them, spoke with earnest entreaty in his voice. "The *Lady* and I want you to see us off. Be at the quay at five, Martha."

He picked up the roses and walked away. She just stood there, motionless for some time. Then she raised her hand slowly to the rose and touched it.

2

True to Redd's and Van Oren's prediction, Lancefield visited the ship. But he came alone. He sauntered up the gangplank at noon and was met by Pelican Joe, who had been stationed there to await just this. He had no sooner announced himself than the sailor burst forth in a deep bass voice:

"Mr. Lancefield to see Cap'n Redd!"

Lancefield sized him up.

"Do you announce all visitors with such a foghorn blast, sailor?"

Pelican Joe eyed him indifferently, then turned to wink an eye at Mr. Burk, who looked around at Mr. Hyde, who was saying he would take the visitor below. As they moved off, Lancefield heard the second chanting down into the afterhatch:

"Forward with the cargo, willin' on the after wind!"

Down in the hold a sailor singsonged, "Aye, aye, while the wind's blowin' aft," and proceeded to nudge Tysbee forward, between rows of stacked bales, to an iron door. There he motioned Tysbee to sit down, and offered him a cut of tobacco. Gagged, Tysbee glared at him, which didn't bother Pardue in the least. He worked up his cud and stared back in expressionless content. He had nothing to do but wait for the next order. On the other side of the door Dublin Jack would take over if the wind upstairs shifted toward the bows. In the forward hold Whitey, the Negro cook, waited. While upstairs——

Lancefield sat down and looked at Redd across the table. "Seems you're fixing to sail, Captain. You're posted for next Wednesday. This is Saturday."

"Owner's request," came the reply.

"Naturally. Cargo wool, it says here. And the market is still dropping. It also says hides and sugar. To Batavia, Singapore, and Hong Kong."

"Have a drink, Mr. Lancefield?"

"Never touch it. Thanks. Odd talk up there on deck. Your

second said, 'Forward with the cargo.' That's common. But what does 'Willing on the after wind' mean?"

Redd laughed and turned his palms up. "You were a sailor once. It could mean anything. Now what can I do for you?"

"You've got a fine ship here. I'll look around."

Redd pretended surprise. "So they demoted you to customs examining officer after the hearing."

"Maybe they should have. But I'm just curious, Captain. I might stumble on to something, you know."

"What? The gold that wasn't in the boxes?"

"We think alike. Mr. Tysbee left the schooner *Vega* last night. Any idea where he went, Captain?"

"Have you tried the racecourse or the yacht club? The sixteen-footers are loose in the harbor. Or you might look for him in Melbourne."

"Thanks." Lancefield arose, looked about him observantly, and moved away with the chief mate.

On deck, he studied the faces of the sailors, then moved toward the forecastle. From there he visited the galley and came out again on the main deck. He was looking down into the hatch and putting his feet on the ladder when the second yelled out:

"Lay open the forehatch, bullies! The wind's all around the compass."

Below, Pardue rapped on the iron door and Dublin Jack swung it back. Tysbee and the sailor went through, again forward, and threw the iron bar. When Lancefield came down, Mr. Hyde following, there was nothing but bales of wool, nicely stowed on their flats with marks uppermost. He tried the door to the forehold and went back on deck, and forward. The hatch was open and bales of hides marked for Hong Kong were being lowered. As he moved down into the hold, the second, who was everywhere, cried out:

"Main hatch for cargo to Batavia! Now show willin' whilst the wind's ahead!"

The cook pulled Tysbee aft to the next hold and gave him to Dublin Jack, who barred the door and waited. Lancefield looked about him. Finding only cargo and men sweating and swearing, he returned to deck. There was the second mate again, giving out with bluster and gestures. Lancefield watched him, admiring his efficiency as well as the authority in his slap of a thigh as it came up to meet with palm. For a little man he had a lot of weight here, no doubt about it, but he also had a lot of winds on his tongue. Approaching him, Lancefield said:

"I'm curious, Mr. Burk. First it was an after wind. Then it was all around the compass. Next it was ahead."

"Aye," Burk grinned over big teeth. "It's the hatch I'm at when I say it." When bluntly asked why he chose to say where he was, he replied, scratching an ear, "I don't know. No. I never thought of it, but damned if I know."

He was still in a state of puzzlement when Lancefield moved on to the poop, where the customs officer was examining Redd's jerque note for "entering outwards" with cargo and the cocket card, as well as the receipted outward light bill. A ship chandler argued near by with the steward and a Lloyd's agent stood apart awaiting the captain. Fresh water was being pumped aboard through a tube from a water tender's craft, and the second was tasting it to see if the fellow was selling him a few tons of salty ocean. The ship's carpenter was dressing down his mate with, "G'dammit, the dunnage was there. If they can't stow the bar'ls o' pitch fore 'n aft on it, bung up, I'll see the marster!" Near the dinghy a sailor was fastening on flags for hoisting: "I want a pilot" signal and the blue peter, which advised, "Am about to sail." He was making an art of it when a jack-tar in the rigging let go a pail of mast grease. It struck the flags. The sailor leaped up with a volley of oaths that were classically salty, came down with a heel aslant, and coasted a good three yards before his bottom touched planking.

Lancefield didn't laugh; though it was as funny to him as the next one, he turned his head to look at the stern of a black schooner at the far dock. A sign artist was laying on golden scrolls around a name: *Upstart*. Only three hours ago he and Untell had named the schooner, after a devil of a lot of coaxing and wirepulling in government circles to obtain the craft for the purpose he had in mind. She wasn't as long as the *Vega*, though he doubted if any fore-and-aft-rigged vessel in Australian waters could touch her for speed and maneuverability. She was masted high and she had a sailing master aboard of her, one with a purpose——

Captain Untell.

But he was wondering if the craft would be ready for the chase in time. He doubted it even as he saw them victualing her and bending on a new main gaff-topsail. She might make it, however; the boat that brought her rock ballast was pulling away.

He was walking aft on the poop, thinking it was reasonable to believe that if guilt motivated Sir George and his clique, Tysbee would flee the continent before his bank was examined. And where could he find safer passage than aboard Redd's ship? Perhaps Tysbee wasn't on the *Lady* now. He could be wrong about the whole thing.

Redd joined him near the skylight and fell into step. Neither said anything until the wheel lay forward of them. At the taffrail, Lancefield looked down at a small hatch coaming and said, "What's down there?"

"Spare sail locker," Redd answered.

Mr. Hyde joined them. He looked worried. Redd knew he had every reason to feel circumspect when Lancefield raised the hatch cover and peered down into the dark interior. He saw the chief mate give a realistic start when the examiner asked to take a look.

"Sure," Redd agreed. "Why not?" Taking a lantern, he led the way down. Hyde came last, his hawkish face set for action.

Sail canvas was stacked in rolls, and irons, toggles, cringles, earings, and eyelets lay in marked hampers. One large box was covered with scraps of folded sailcloth. Lancefield sat down on it and looked around.

The chief mate sweated and mopped his face when Lancefield glanced down at the solid box supporting him and asked what it contained. Redd said he would call "Sails" and have him unlock it, though Lancefield told him not to bother.

"Wool and hides, eh, Captain? Somehow I get the feeling that the wool is being pulled over my eyes. But we'll see. If it is, I'll find out. If it isn't, I've lost nothing. But we'll see."

Redd chuckled. "You're taking a long tack, Mr. Lancefield. Now there's a possibility that you may never be any closer to the answer to your riddle than you are right now."

Mr. Hyde went into a coughing fit all of a sudden.

When Lancefield left the ship a little later, the chief mate said, "Sir, you scared the billy blue hell out of me. Aye, with him there sitting on the gold when you said it."

3

Everything was in order and awaiting Captain Redd's word. The pilot stood forward of the wheel; the tugboat whistled, ready, going nowhere, her cushions against the *Lady's* bow; two sailors stood the quay, looking anxiously at the poop for an order to take in her lines, and officers and men on decks and aloft waited restlessly at their stations for the maze of commands. At any moment now the big three-sticker would get a motion under her to last out the several thousand miles to Dutch Batavia. But the Old Man seemed to be looking for something or someone. His look was fixed on the land end of the quay.

A floating-island cloud drove by the sun, mixing up the shadows and causing sailors' eyes to lift in weather-wise fashion. Idlers and hackmen on the quay looked up also, wondering if the famous captain was holding back for some signal from the wind gods. When a good puff rocked the *Lady's* masts a trifle, it wasn't hard to imagine that she was straining at the bit.

Redd looked at his watch, then at the chief mate. Something was on his tongue when a victoria turned off the street toward the ship. He took in the three occupants, seeing Sir George, Geoffrey, and Martha. His expression hardened over. He felt again the presence of Finch and Kerry before Geoffrey as well as the latter's side-line watchfulness in the scheme afoot. What he portrayed clashed sharply, like cold and warm air in the atmosphere, with the qualities that made up Martha van Oren. He tried to put his own feelings aside with reminders that their engagement was no concern of his, none of his business, but the hot and cold air met in electric flashes and thunder. Out of it came a gruff order:

"Man the windlass!"

The deck came alive. The tug churned the water and the *Lady's* bows swung into the wind. Hawsers tightened like springs, played back and spanked the water white as the tug strained ahead with the ship. The *Lady* wasn't on her own yet, too close to the wind's eye, but the helm sheared her, was setting her out, one point, two, then four points of the compass. Three lengths separated her from her moorings, then four. The quay sailed away from her in the wind, slowly, surely, the yards set, the head abox. The spanker was being loosed and she was many lengths out, her starboard tacks coming aboard. Six points now, and she could carry herself on but for the harbor traffic. She wasn't a ship who loved a guide horse.

"Cut loose!" The order left the poop and the man at the starboard cathead cupped his voice. "Cut loose!" Sail and shouts filled the air over her. Sail fell white and filled, gear ran through the blocks like burning strings, men grabbing it in with pins. It was a topsails' wind, though the Old Man was bellowing to shake out topgallants. Down they came, cascading, snapping full, sheets taut. It went on. There was much to do and in one hell of a hurry; sureness and timing counted from wheel to jibs. The men hadn't learned that chapter of sailing out of a manual that said, "To get under way, wind ahead, and go to sea on the starboard tack"; the *Lady's* crew had come up in the doing of it, real sheets snaking through their hands with blisters as badges of learning.

All mechanics to Captain Redd, who had three eyes in his head then: one for the ship, one for the roadstead, and one for the quay. The third eye looked through a glass at a handkerchief waving above an open victoria. The lady was standing, a wide free smile on her face. Her white dress clung to her figure in the wind; it molded her as neatly as a figurehead carver could dream of doing, as prettily as a red-blooded man could ask for.

And now the smile was gone from her face. She continued to stand, staring at the ship. She had come to see him off, after all.

"Mr. Hyde," he said, not lowering the glass, "this promises to be a good voyage."

The chief mate stared at the master. Not so sure he could agree, he said without conviction, "Aye, sir. God willing."

Martha saw all white canvas in the sun for minutes, and then diminishing towers above a long strip of black hull on an animated sea. The ship and her master ran on for the heads of Sydney Harbor; on until they disappeared from sight—on out of her life.

She heard her father's great sigh of relief as the *Lady* ran away from courts and recent trouble. She saw the smug glance and smile he exchanged with Geoffrey, and for a fleeting moment she wondered if the great adventure which she and they thought was disappearing in the wake of her ship wasn't just moving on, just on, to new horizons. Why? Perhaps she thought it was too closely matted with the roots of the past and present to be denied any future. But the thought was too abstract to entertain. The man who sailed the ship was more real.

She was suddenly a little jealous of Redd. Wherever he was going, it was her ship and she wished she were aboard. And then she was regretting her behavior of that morning. Were he here now—yes, she would pass the roses to him gently. Memories returned and she smiled pensively until she felt the quickening of her pulse.

Then she looked seaward again. Only a quiet blue haze stood where the *Lady of Glasgow* heeled in the wind minutes before, that and a schooner beating out as if for the heads and the open sea. She raised a telescope and idly watched the craft. Then the gilt of her stern lettering flashed in the sun and she saw the name:

Upstart.

Aboard the schooner, Captain Untell grinned. This was his dish. Using the *Upstart* to chase an upstart appealed to him. He was in no hurry now, nor would he ever get in a hurry again where Gordon Redd was concerned, unless it was on the final wind to judgment. Patience and perseverance. Lancefield had spoken those words over and over until they began to fasten into him. And——

"Just hang on the edge of her horizon, Captain Untell. Come up for a look every so often. Then fall away. If he carries Tysbee, it will come out."

Untell continued to grin. He'd learn, all right. And Redd would learn that his crime was like a ghost. Let him know he was being chased, let him wonder. Aye . . .

There she was ahead, only topgallants up over horizon, unsuspecting. Van Oren's *Lady of Glasgow*. She was cutting a long wake now as she cleaved the seas, rocking and dipping on for the big deep water.

CHAPTER VIII

Captain Redd took in the world under his horizon with a mariner's eye. Astern, land ran away from him; ahead, the sea opened big and choppy and alive; scud skimmed the water in long tentacles driving always northwest. Looking up at the fluttering mizzen royal, he said:

"You're pinching her, Pardue. Look alive."

Pardue spread his legs and took a fresh grip on the wheel, shifting his gaze from the binnacle to the weather clue. He knew to steer by the royal when the ship was "by the wind," though he was thinking that this was his seventh time to take the ship out and, from the looks of the weather, the seventh time wet. He charted his luck by a departure.

A yell sounded up forward. Then Turpy Hunt, the cockney, was hauled up from the bow chains. The cook stood by and laughed with genuine enjoyment. Every hand on the watch knew that Whitey had pushed Turpy just to stir up his anger. Whitey delighted in the cockney's rare profanity minus the aitches. And here it was. Pardue heard it, and he heard the big black's laughter. On the proper wind Sydney might have heard also. It died instantly; Mr. Burk's palm on thigh sounded impatient.

Captain Redd said nothing. Pranks at sea were an integral part of life aboard a happy ship. These men knew their business and they were collectively a smart crew, sea-and-weather-wise. Let Geoffrey complain that he fed his men better than most captains; the extra expense kept his crew intact and content. Watching his hands sweating up the gear as they sang, "Yes, whisky made me sell my coat, Whisky Johnny," he thought the words counting-house and penny-pinching were synonymous. But such reflections were purely impersonal, a part of ship and sailing. His own personal and private thoughts were something else.

Martha was a part of them. He continued to see her with roses at her bosom, her figure slenderly full in the pale blue dress, her voice rich with undertones. Nor could he crowd out of his memory the series of meetings with her, the feel of her corporeal nearness, the life throbbing in her. But there was more to it than mere physical attraction, which a man could look at, consider, and eventually forget. A man could take his fun and let it go at that. But a pair of eyes and all that lay behind them weren't that easily dismissed.

She departed slowly as the ship came to life under him. The *Lady* still ran just north of east on the starboard tack. He took in the last smear of land astern, paying no attention to a schooner's sails in the lifting mist far behind him, and ordered the helmsman to strike the time of day. Next he called for a trim of sail to put the wind over the quarter. He watched until it was done, until the ship dipped her bows into a trough and rode up the oncoming hill in a reeling lift. This was the big deep, and it rolled with warnings of freshening winds and rising seas ahead. The big continental bulge forced him to eastward as he made northing. Another day and the Tasman Sea would run out from under him and he would work on up for Great Barrier Reef and the Coral Sea. That was the course. Here was the sea and ship and weather. He turned to the chief mate.

"Mr. Hyde, take over." Then he said, "Order our passenger released and sent to my quarters. And pass the word that I want him shown every courtesy aboard." He added, as the other evaluated the order for its true content, "At all times."

He was making an entry in the logbook when Tysbee entered his cabin. Their glances met as the banker advanced and sat down. In the search neither felt accord or saw anything resembling sympathy. No surprise, none expected. Tysbee's jaw was hard and his brittle gaze moved on in a sweep of the cabin. As he did so, Redd's usual reserve thawed into a semblance of geniality.

"A real pleasure to have you aboard," he said.

Tysbee thought he detected more friendliness than sarcasm in Redd. He saw the choice before him with a bitter clarity. Better to make the best of it, he thought, though a stinking hold and the forceful persuasion of common sailors were poignantly fresh in his memory. And Redd and the scheme that had turned on him were reminding him of the stakes in this game. And Redd was now saying with courteous indifference:

"No hard feelings. It was all business. It still is. Now we can get along or we can't. Which is it?"

"Am I passenger or prisoner?"

"The ship's yours, Mr. Tysbee."

"Except in port," Tysbee scoffed, "where I'm supposed to smell the bilge."

"For your share I thought you'd be willing to swallow the bilge."

"Perhaps I'm a man of gentler tastes than you, Captain."

"Perhaps. But, after all, it's a state of mind. I see things on land I want. But I'm not forgetting there's water under me."

"A touching lesson in patience, I'm sure."

"Just business," Redd reminded him again.

"Which in this case I wish I'd never heard of."

"But you can't sail stern first, Mr. Tysbee. You're bound to hear a lot about this scheme of yours. There's no telling where it might take us."

"I know. And I can readily understand how you feel about it. The trouble is you can't put yourself in my place."

"Sure I can. You want to be back on the plush throne. The setting is all that's worrying you. If you were back in Melbourne with your bank's gold, you'd be eying a mine or some valuable property and scheming how to take it from the owner. And you'd feel mast-tip high about the whole thing."

"It's just what one is used to," Tysbee said slowly, running a hand through his hair. "But this business stinks now. I don't like it."

"You had a choice before you got into it. Now that's behind you. Just remember that you and I are sailing under the same colors. Don't forget it. Whatever happens, we're both in it."

Tysbee considered this before saying, "I don't see how I can forget it, Captain Redd."

"Then don't try it." Redd's voice was crisp one moment, surprisingly pleasant the next as he said, "Now that we're better acquainted, Mr. Tysbee, tell me something about the banking business. To be specific, just how long do you think it will take to examine your bank?"

There was no telling, Redd learned. They talked back and

forth over this for some time before Tysbee asked if the announcement of his guilt had any bearing on his future. Knowing it would come sooner or later, this was to him a very important question. He awaited a reply anxiously.

"Yes," Redd spoke thoughtfully. "We'll be suspected in every port. You can't show your face on deck to any passing ship. It's not a pretty picture." He continued to study the banker as he said, "Too bad you didn't wish to escape the charges. You could disguise yourself and go to America or Europe and live like a king."

Tysbee sat up, alert. His eyes narrowed with the hope of escape. With it, he could do as he liked and perhaps place the full blame on Sir George and this captain whom he detested, who was looking at him closely now for any telltale signs. He said, not wishing to appear anxious:

"It's worth thinking about."

"It *was*," Redd corrected.

"What do you mean, Captain?"

"That it's not worth thinking about any more. Honestly, I wish it was, Mr. Tysbee, since it would relieve me of a great responsibility. If you're caught aboard of me, I'm as guilty as you. Yes, it's too bad."

Tysbee said he could board a ship in Batavia for America and relieve Redd of that worry.

"And just what guarantee could you post that you wouldn't return to Melbourne and confess?"

"Why—my share of the gold."

"I can't spend that in prison."

"Then my word of honor!"

Redd got to his feet slowly and said, "Be honest, mister. That isn't worth a damn to either of us."

2

With morning the sea ran strong. A good following wind brushed the skies clean. The *Lady* ran on at a good clip under a pile of sail, as though anxious to round the bulge and put Tweed Heads far out on the port beam. Deck chores kept the crew busy and the sun over the water raised the chanteyman's voice with a fresh song.

The ship's bell clanged out eight bells, 8 A.M., and the sound had no sooner died over the water than the lookout aft cried, "Sail ho!" With the "Where away?" came, "Hull under astern. Schooner she is."

Redd paid no attention. Sleepy John, who improvised chanteys, was setting the pace for the gang that was holystoning the main deck. Most of these men were brave and willing. A few followed the leaders. Others were weak. But they were all men, his men, all sharing dreams and hardships and laughter and anger. Morning at sea awakened hopes and new life in them, the same as morning on land stirs one. Redd felt it as much as the swabbers. But he was thinking also of the voyage and his cargo. These things weighed on his mind, made him wonder where he was taking his men.

He looked at Tysbee up forward and then at the top-hamper. The ship was running full before a fair following wind. The sea rose and fell, the sun climbed higher, and the ship's bell struck the half-hour.

At noon the schooner was hull up and standing wing and wing on their trail. A freighter moved south a few miles out, her funnel belching black smoke that lay flat with the wind. She flew two red bars in a field of yellow, the Spanish merchant flag. By midafternoon only two more ships had been sighted, both British, one flying the red merchant, the other the blue ensign of the Royal Naval Reserve. Then they were gone and the *Lady* had the seas to herself, except for her trailing company, now standing well up in sight.

She was cutting a point north of the *Lady's* wake when Captain Redd faced aft with glass up. He was thinking she was masted "devilish high" for a fore-and-after when he remembered that a schooner had followed him out of Sydney. Perhaps this one. She could be a government patrol, yacht, or trader running for the islands. But she was clinging to, like a sucker to a shark.

"What do you make of her, sir?" the second asked.

"She's got a sailor aboard of her, Mr. Burk," Redd answered. Then he remembered a scow loaded with rock passing by his stern yesterday and coming up alongside an ordinary schooner. He turned away, his glance falling instinctively on Tysbee at the port quarter.

He wasn't sure, but he thought the little banker had dropped something overboard. Quietly, unhurriedly, he made his way to the stern rail and looked into the wake. Then he saw it, a bottle bobbing up and under and up again, jerking away toward the schooner.

He said nothing as he sauntered up to Tysbee and stood with a hand in the lee braces. Both were following the bottle, neither aware that the other knew where he was looking. The schooner came on and the bottle glinted once more, then fell under the chop of the sea aweather. It was a matter of timing now, as well as the chance that the schooner hadn't seen the bottle tossed over the side. Wondering what message Tysbee had placed inside it, Redd could only imagine: *I am a prisoner aboard the* Lady of Glasgow. *Milton Tysbee, Melbourne.* Enough to convict both of them.

Minute after minute he stood there, losing the object, finding it again as the sun flashed sword points from it. Had sharp eyes on the schooner seen it; who was aboard the craft? There it was again; then it was gone. Tysbee looked eager. Not once did he glance at Redd, who was thinking fast, seeing in that innocent bottle enough gunpowder to blow all his plans to kingdom come.

Then the schooner veered a point toward his wake.

Angry, more at himself for not having exercised every precaution to prevent just such a trick, and almost sure that the schooner's eyes had spotted the bottle, he put aside any feeling of helplessness in the matter and cried out:

"All hands!" Then he gave an order seldom forced on him: "Run her off! Down helm!"

The crew responded as though the ship were scudding toward a reef bows on. The *Lady's* helm was put hard to port, and men clawed at aftersail and set the spanker, put her starboard tacks aboard the mizzen and main. They brought her into the wind quickly. When her foreyards began to lift, they were braced up and the *Lady* was pointing east in a southeast wind. Then he

boxed her off, let her gather sternway into a half circle before filling her foreyards and shifting helm for headway.

It required time to turn short round, time in which the schooner
might fish for the bottle. But Redd was gambling all that his antics
were causing confusion and wonder aboard the schooner.

Now the *Lady* was working westward and getting a way under
her in a curve to the south. The schooner had taken in her driving
sails and coasted off to the west of the maneuver. When the
Lady's course was reversed the ships were close. The schooner
could only race across the big vessel's bows. She did this, her mainsail filling and jerking her free as schoonermen sent up loud oaths
of protest.

Nor could Redd blame the schooner's crew. The action had the
appearance of a purposeful attempt to ram the schooner; but just
because of her own miscalculation—she could have just as easily
veered to the east. But this didn't matter now. Redd forgot it
when a voice carried across the water with words he'd heard
before:

"Damned pirate!"

He was glad Tysbee was on the portside. Then he saw him
running fast, making a bold dash for the starboard rail; and out
of his reach. Redd called to the second, "Stop him, Mr. Burk!"

Mr. Burk did. Tysbee didn't know what struck him until he sat
up in his bunk some time later.

Redd cut a swath of the upper Tasman Sea late that afternoon.
He tacked to east and to west, he ordered trim after trim, calculating the drift of a small bottle and following it, chasing back and
forth, up and down, as though he were a drunk admiral on a
naval training ship. The men breathed hard, sweated, and growled,
but they kept it up for hours. Even in the last rays of the red sun,
he hunted for the evidence against him. Then the night came on
and he assembled his exhausted crew abaft the mainmast and
thanked them for their work. He didn't tell them why he had
exercised them in this fashion. Instead he ordered the steward to
break out rum for all and serve up the finest meal a sailor ever
wolfed down in the stream.

The schooner coasted ahead, her lights showing. Redd knew
she was waiting. But he was satisfied: her name was *Upstart;*

Captain Untell was chasing him for some reason, perhaps for the very thing Mr. Burk had averted. And the bottle——

He hadn't found it. But by enacting one of the craziest maneuvers in the history of sail, he had kept Untell from finding it. Of that he was sure, since the schooner had turned sharply out of his wake when the big square-rigger ran off her course. It was another mark in Redd's favor. But how long could he sustain his luck?

3

That night the *Lady* resumed her northerly course. The *Upstart* stood fast on the port beam a mile away, her lights winking under the waves and up again, always there, always drawing Redd's eyes like a magnet. Sail after sail was added to the fleet *Lady* and she eased gradually away from the schooner. But Untell carried more sail than Redd knew, and he bent it on. With the first pink of the dawn in the east, Untell's ship became a vague shape over the water.

Then the sun lifted on a different schooner. The same, but it was what she carried. Mr. Hyde sent for Redd and together they stared in amazement at the change. During the night the *Upstart* had sprouted a foreyard. On it a square sail dropped and above it a triangular raffee rose to the top of the fore-topmast.

"I'll be damned!" said the chief mate. "Over five thousand square feet of rags on her, sir."

"And all pulling," Redd added.

The schooner had a sailor aboard. The chase had begun.

Redd studied the blossoming sail, all white and billowy in the early sunlight, falling and lifting with a rhythmic grace. Behind all the beauty he saw brains and experience and sharp wits. But the craft herself would do for now. He knew the schooner had an advantage of two points in getting into a wind. She was also lighter. She handled smartly. Then he took stock of her disadvantages, remembering that among them turning about on a schooner, or wearing, was dangerous due to the size and swing of her sails. Now had Untell the experience in wearing? Could he play a game of tag, of hide-and-fox?

An idea was forming. He went below and bent over his charts. There was a way of playing the game up in the reefs and atolls, though he didn't wish to plow into coral with his ship.

All that day and the next the ships sailed under the same horizon, cutting straight wakes with neither breaking the monotony of a race to a deadlock. The breeze held to fair and following, the skies to the temper of wind and sea. The Tropic of Capricorn lay astern, and ahead the outermost fringes of Great Barrier Reef stretched out to open up the Coral Sea. West Island and Wreck Reef lay far out to starboard. The weather took on a true tropic flavor and squalls struck. On they ran, edging westward, up for ten degrees south and Torres Strait.

The night before, Redd had gone on with his red running light doused, the green to starboard under a blind. The moon was rising later each night. And tonight he had to play it out before moonrise.

Just before sundown Redd turned abruptly off his course and ran a little north of east. With the *Upstart* standing in silhouette on a golden and red sea astern, he made sure she was altering her course also. He ran into the night and let his lights burn.

The reef lay dead ahead, short hours away. A ragged stretch of coral, awash and submerged, depending on where a ship took it with her hull. A sailor's nightmare, a reef in the night; all serene one moment, a jarring, grating sound the next; and a keel crunching and tearing her bowels; then a swirl of brine with the bilge, and a graveyard for a ship. The thought was forbidding.

Redd ordered a minimum of canvas. As she slowed, and he placed a man at each bow with orders to keep the deep-sea leads swinging, Untell slipped up closer. It was a disadvantage, though Redd had accepted it in advance. The leads splashed, sank, and came up; the leadsmen sang out the "No bottom," and heaved again.

The night was thick and black. Starlight touched the calm sea with the faintest sheen. The lookout saw trailing phosphorescence in the water, then a glimmer of the stars thrown up directly below. Other than that, it was blind sailing in the night. Then, his heart in his mouth, he heard the roar of a surf; or he thought he did. Far ahead the light of the Southern Cross danced in a widening stretch. A blanket of gauze slid by in the upper breeze and the pin points of light fell away. Blackness, and a continued roar. He called to the deck.

Redd listened. More sail was ordered in. The ship slid on yard by yard, the lead still reading: no bottom. Astern, the *Upstart* had lessened her pace, holding a distance of a half mile. Forward, the song of the sea increased. Breakers.

It was touch and go, literally that. Redd knew about reefs, how they rose straight up out of the depths with jagged fingers, firm and severe. No bottom in one cast of the lead, all bottom in the next. He wanted to turn back, to send up a flare, to come to a stop and launch a boat to find the reef. Any of these urgent moves could only serve Untell as well as himself. He said:

"All lights out."

Mr. Burk said, "Damn!" and the chief mate answered, "Amen."

The leadsman on the starboard reported bottom at eight fathoms. The portside lead came up and Dublin Jack announced a depth of five fathoms. In the silence aboard, Redd's order sounded calm:

"Ahoy, masthead."

"The sound is to port, sir. Aye, the scud's liftin'. Reef! A point off the port bow!"

"Port the hellum," Redd ordered. "Easy as you go."

The ship's head canted to starboard, and the man on that bow found bottom at around eleven fathoms. It was deepening. Dublin Jack said seven, then a quarter less ten; and then, "No bottom."

"Keep the leads singing. Easy, Pardue. Now hellum. Now amidships. Easy as you go." Next Redd addressed Mr. Hyde. "The chart says this reef is narrow and long, setting to north and south.

"Now we're sailing due east. In another five minutes we'll head due north, then cut back east, putting the reef between us and Untell. That's when I want our lamps lit. Let him come straight to us."

Mr. Hyde gnawed at this. It wasn't honorable seamanship by any wild stretch of the imagination. Nor was it like Captain Redd. A hint of insubordination crept into his voice when he said, "As you say, sir. But the schooner's for Davy Jones's locker."

Then Redd spoke in a quiet voice, and what he said rescued

him in Mr. Hyde's mind from the depths to which he had fallen: "I don't want that for even Untell. His slow clip will only trap him in the reef, where he'll hang high and dry for a few hours."

Minutes later the *Lady* had her trim and turned to the north. Then another maneuver and she was headed east again. Her lamps shone in the night all of a sudden and Redd ran to the stern rail swinging a lantern. He wanted all of Untell's attention on his ship and none on the reef.

The *Upstart's* lights moved closer. She was coming on, slowly, no sail adding on. Redd was thinking: "It's got to work. It's been too damned risky to fail." Untell would see the reef, feel it instinctively, even now he might be listening to it, and then he would try to wear ship. The curve of the reef could trap him, or the swing of his sails could do it, or his lack of experience aboard a schooner could reach up and tie him fast. Any or all.

The growing flush of moonrise was pushing up the eastern horizon when Redd heard cries from the *Upstart*. She swung her stern around as her head jerked to the north. With sails playing her false, set for one wind and catching another, she knew unmanageable moments. Close on the reef and wallowing and straining, her stern lifted and swung for the coral. Her head was free and all sail was under control, though she seemed caught in a cleft of the reef; gently on but securely caught. It was all too sudden for assessment, like the interval of waiting for a wave to fall.

As suddenly as it happened, it came to an end. Redd couldn't believe what he saw. Yet there the schooner sat, rocking, lifting and falling, her stern to the lively southeaster, needing only sail to send her flying away from the trap that failed.

Untell was one more sailing man. Even the old man in the moon, now peeping curiously over the waves, seemed to agree as his dissipating face shaped with laughter.

CHAPTER IX

Chagrined and angry, still unable to understand how Untell escaped a trap after its jaws had actually closed on him, Redd struck back at his persistent humor by driving his ship relentlessly on toward Torres Strait. With open ocean on one side and Great Barrier Reef, a long line of surf breaking with no apparent reason other than white warning, on the other side, the *Lady* stood up the Australian coast in a manner to show her heel to any craft in racing mood. She ran past a long four-masted bark out of Brisbane as though she were standing still, ran up to catch and whistle by a laden northbound steamer, her copper bottom gleaming like gold as she heeled and rocked on. She took a tropic squall over her quarter, burying her bows to the gammoning under the press of sail. She blew a topgallant and thought nothing of it, bent on another and dared the elements to take it off her. The bit was loose, the track open and fair, and her master held the reins, urging her on.

The *Upstart* was gone, left behind, though she seemed to come up astern out of haze, sunrise, or bellying blue squall clouds racing across the seas.

Then Cape Melville opened up broad on the lee beam as another night fell. The cry sounded, "She touches ten!" Captain Redd was taking on seas. He watched them leap aboard the bows and come boiling and thumping aft. Shrieking wind threw spray that stung his face, and out over the sea it was cutting the crest off waves and powdering the spindrift. Seas were building up and it looked like a full gale wind. There came a sudden crack of thunder in the top-hamper. A sail had blown. It was beating in the wind like cannon shots at close range. Up went Mr. Burk and his gang to smother it. As water fell in torrents, Pelican Joe looked aft and said:

"In four years I ain't seen the Old Man like this."

Redd was running out of a storm on his humor as much as sails, hoping Untell was flying canvas in this weather, that his throat halyards were chafing, his bowsprit bending, that the seas were striking bludgeon blows at him, making the *Upstart* more a half-tide rock than a trim schooner.

He saw Untell under a new guise, and wondered why he had underrated that bulldog look in his face. Lancefield might be the real enemy, but he could not deny Untell's bid for that distinction any more. In a way he was to be admired; square as a biscuit tin and stubborn as a Dutch customs officer, he was posing a problem.

As the ship took a long dive and listed heavily to port, water boiling aboard and racing out the scuppers, a twinge of uneasiness crept over Redd. His nautical voice ordered sail taken in down to storm rags; his personal voice spoke to him alone, saying Lancefield held one great advantage, since he would know of Tysbee's guilt long before the news of it reached the *Lady of Glasgow;* he would act on it and try to catch Redd napping. Now the whole thing bounced back to Tysbee, who was beginning to look like a Jonah. But it went deeper than that:

When the *Lady's* bottom popped the sea and a great wall of water towered above the decks, snarling up in a greasy mass of black in the night, he heard Sir George's persuasive voice asking him to take Tysbee on the voyage. A shift of responsibility, an escape from any guilt; and the smell of Geoffrey in the background.

The ship battled free and the graybeard tore in under her, shaking her like a mouse in a terrier's jaws. Rain came in a deluge and spray flew off the sea. The taste was salty on a tongue, then fresh. The sea and sky were one now. And he and Tysbee were the same. And Untell was emulating the seas, chasing him, trying to come aboard if only to verify Tysbee's presence here.

Lightning lit up the rigging and fell into blackness, leaving shapes in photographic reverse before his eyes as a clap of thunder jarred the active black of night and rolled off growling and bouncing across the low heavens. Lightning lines trailed in the seas and the storm gods tried to throw them back to sloshing decks. On the wail of wind and seas, Whitey came up with a pannikin of steaming coffee, saying, "Down, set down your liquor and the girl from off your knee . . ." Lightning lit up the whites of his eyes and he dived for the companion. All the brisk excitement Redd saw in the cook's eyes was suddenly the same as he had seen in Tysbee's. One was afraid of lightning, the other of his guilt.

The ship was yawing, her stern sheering to port. Redd leaped to the wheel before she could broach to. After dressing down the two men who steered her wildly, he said, "Now easy as you go, awake and alive!"

Then his glance took in the ship from wheel to fore, decks to the crawling black of the rigging.

Wet and liking it, glaring ahead with one practiced eye on the storm of the ocean, the other on the backlash of seven boxes on a pirate's wind, he felt again that annoying loyalty to something very important in his personal life. Sane thought told him to keep her out of this; saner realizations told him he couldn't. She was like a course. Then she was something more, the incentive to hold fast to a course that ran away from guilt.

If Martha had done nothing else, she had coaxed the storm out of him and left strong purpose in its place—he must escape the watchful eye of Untell in one way or another.

As if the storm that went out of him influenced the elements, the rain thinned and the thick overcast dissolved. Confused skies cleared, stars peeped through the rigging, and thunder rumbled across the waves toward Fair Cape and the mainland.

2

A favoring monsoon blew the *Lady of Glasgow* west from Torres Strait. Under tropic skies, bat-winged junks and Makassar *praus* hung on horizons like pirates or contraband runners; crude Papuan ships moved up toward Dutch islands, their New Guinea crews oblivious to the burning sun. Scores of water snakes wriggled across the warm seas, and large sea birds flew investigatively over the ship, renewing old superstitions that they were the departed souls of seamen.

And hanging on astern, her raffee sail flying, was the schooner *Upstart*.

Redd was now searching impatiently for a way to shake Untell. He studied maps, charts, winds, tides, and currents of the islands that lay ahead of him, looking for anything that might correct the evenness of the race. Playing around in his mind was an idea of making use of the other side of the Lesser Sunda Islands. They stretched in a chain, east to west, for hundreds of miles. On the north lay the Flores Zee and Bali Zee; on the south, the Indian Ocean. The behavior of the flood and ebb tides, running strong to and from the Indian Ocean, appealed to him.

It was a long gamble with luck and weather, since the tides and winds were by no means constant. But if he could catch the last of the powerful ebb in the strait separating the islands of Lombok and Bali just a few hours ahead of the *Upstart*, he might lose Untell when the tide reversed. The thought persisted. He mapped his strategy for days, thinking, hoping, it was perfect. Then the northern steep-to coast of Lombok stood a few miles below him.

The strait lay ahead, down the slope of the coast. He was a few hours from it. While far behind, just a blur of white in the haze where water and sky met, stood the *Upstart*. He checked the time of day, the wind under the Lombok shore, and the cloud direction toward Bali. From his position, he could enter the nineteen-mile distance between the islands where the tide was strongest on the last few hours of the ebb——

"If," he said to Mr. Hyde, "the tide sets to southward."

"The weather bears out the monsoon, sir. The ebb should be running at four knots or better. But we can catch only the last few hours of it."

Redd considered the legend of the tidal current of Lombok Strait. During this monsoon the flood tide ran northward for some four hours at a speed of two or three knots. The ebb ran southward for eight hours at a speed of four to five knots. But at this time of the moon, spring tides were running. They were stronger. The ebb might run six knots. Farther south, where a large island divided the strait, were strong tide rips and eddies, sometimes dangerous to sailing vessels.

The idea was to lead Untell into the strait on a favoring tide just before it changed and ran against him, to get the *Lady* through, past the island, and let the northward set of the current and the southeast wind force the *Upstart* toward the Bali shore and into a trap she could not spring before nightfall.

Right now Untell's distance behind him seemed next to perfect. "Mr. Hyde," he said, "we'll run like hell for the Indian Ocean."

"And risk the races and eddies in the dark?"

"Aye. Now we'll hug this side of the strait."

"As you say, sir. But Captain Untell could point out for the

Bali side, where the current runs strongest, and race along side of us."

"Which is right where I want him come night, Mr. Hyde," Redd chuckled.

A sudden wise grin appeared on Mr. Hyde's face. "And leave him with nowhere to go but back the way he came—is that it, sir?"

"Unless he prefers to run the tide rips in the dark. That is all he can do, since he can't point all the way into the southeast wind."

"Maybe he's got more sense than we think. He might not move into the Bali current."

"But that's where we're going to lead him. It's a chance we've got to take. Now make sail."

The mate knew what Redd meant by taking a chance. The ship had to pretend until night.

The *Lady* was soon trimmed for the run. Sails filled. The wind caught her braced up sharp on the port tack and sent her obliquely down into the strait. Across the water, peaks of Bali lifted blue in the tropic sky. In another hour land dropped off and the full strait opened up. An island stood in the middle far away, like a smudge on the horizon. Redd took a look at it over the port bow. He wanted to keep it there until the day ran out, since that was his way of making Untell think he was running to the west of it for the Indian Ocean.

The sun slipped down another notch in the afternoon sky. Redd spoke the masthead and learned that Untell was dropping behind in a slant more to the west: right toward the Bali shore. He checked any show of elation. It was too early for that. But Mr. Hyde grinned.

"Stow your humor," Redd ordered.

The island lifted higher up out of the sea, still over the port bow. Bali stood closer and clearer across the strait. The narrows were behind him and the full set of the current moved under the ship. The ebb ran at better than five knots; augmenting this, a freshening beam wind bellied sails with a driving push. Redd cried:

"Ahoy, masthead!"

"Schooner ho! Northwest of us, sir, standing on toward Bali."

As Redd looked northwest, Mr. Hyde came up with, "Maybe

Untell has got us figured, sir. He knows this is the long way to Batavia. So he'll guess we're playing it for a run back through the strait tonight." He paused before saying, "Are we?"

"One thing at a time," Redd answered. "Right now I'm checking the sun against our speed. If our timing is off, the joke is on us. Once we're west of that island we're committed to the course we're on. Take in a little sail, Mr. Hyde."

The ship's bell struck eight times: four o'clock. The watch changed. The island grew larger in the next hour. The ebb was falling off fast. So was the day. The sun hung over the plains of lower Bali, coloring the peaks to the north as it painted the full western face of Lombok's ridges in a golden yellow. Hues deepened with the seconds and Lombok's peaks were soon gilded. As the sun slipped lower the sea turned to crimson and the peaks became glowing coals against the deepening blue of approaching night.

The island loomed up large. Redd eyed it with misgiving, wondering if his timing was off. He had to turn off this course soon, damn soon, or stay on it and let Untell slip down into the violent eddies with him. The sun seemed to hang still in the sky at a time when night was very important to him.

Close ahead, boiling like red wine in the last sunset colors, heavy tide rips warned of the dangers to ships under sail. While just north of west the *Upstart* ran on as if her captain had a date with Balinese dancers at Benoa. She lay almost due west of the *Lady*.

In that hanging interval between night and day, the lookout cried, "Deck ahoy! Schooner pointing east, right toward us!"

Redd couldn't believe it. He had planned this carefully for days. And now, at the last moment, just before he was ready to put to use the black curtain of night, Untell was turning the tables on him. He was caught in his own trap with the island due south of him. The *Lady* could not point east as the schooner did; she could only hold her course, run toward Bali, or turn and fall into Untell's path.

As Redd stifled an oath and tried to gather his wits, Mr. Hyde said, "Damn! Captain Untell was almost hemmed in by wind, eddies, and the make of the flood, sir. Like a fox, he's caught on."

The flood was running. In another hour the strait would be at full sea. Already the tide rips were running under the *Lady's* hull.

Redd looked worried.

The lookout advised: "She's coming on."

As sudden as a thought, darkness fell over sea and land.

"The current will head her, sir," Mr. Hyde said. "And the tide rips will get us if we don't run like hell away from here."

Redd broke his silence. "All right, we'll run. But right toward Untell and Bali." His voice lifted with the order to run her off and put the wind behind. Then he cried, "All lights out!"

The crew flew into action. The helm was put hard up, as though she saw the real danger on her weather bow. She was no sooner run off than she began to pay off in the afteryards. She was ready and clear and running within a quarter hour, the southeast wind on her tail, the Bali shore ahead, her decks as dark as the vaults of Davy Jones's locker.

Redd's strategy appealed to the officers and men. By running toward the schooner he had done the only thing Untell wouldn't expect of him, for he was entering the trap Untell was fleeing, and cloaking his movement behind the blackness of night. But the men soon forgot this in the face of a growing threat.

Opposing tides tore viciously at the *Lady* as she tried to run away from them. Yawing and heeling, even with two men at the helm, she tried to shake free of the fierce clawing at her bottom. It was a matter of safety now, of restraining her, of keeping her from broaching to. She bounced uncertainly, seeming to buck and pitch. More sail came into the wind to give her a better way. If she became unmanageable now, the damage would be great.

Redd felt the tension. Here was danger of a real sort, the worst he had ever encountered in a tide. A bow felt one push and the stern an opposite one. The hungry sea seemed to follow him on, striking at him, clawing like a monster in the night. Only the good wind held the ship free.

Pardue and the cockney were at the wheel. The former said, "Devils! Devils at the rudder! They're tearing it loose!"

Untell was forgotten as the seas churned under them, as dangers of the unknown filled minds with all sorts of pictures a sailor didn't wish to see. Mr. Burk ordered a chantey. Only a few joined in.

Redd's voice fell over the ship with assurance as he said to the helmsmen, "Look alive, lads. Steady! Steady!"

The tide rips diminished gradually. Soon the tug at the helm eased off, though not before the lookout said the *Upstart* was close, running on to meet them.

In another moment Redd saw her lights bobbing up over the waves. She came on, standing a little north of her former course. She was fighting hard to hold her own in the gathering strength of the flood.

"If she comes any closer, she'll see us," Mr. Burk said. A sailor added, "Or smell us out."

Silence hung over the *Lady of Glasgow*. Only the wind in the rigging had a voice. Every eye was trained on the schooner. Suspense hung mast-tip high. In the quiet over the ship Redd could feel that which he was unable to see: eyes wide open and taut hands gripping lines and stanchions. Escape was a part of their lives now, though they knew little or nothing of the reasons why. They simply followed him. And he was gripping the lee braces himself—he knew why escape was important. But the running tacks were a game, as were lights out and a close passing in the night. Then the *Upstart* slid on by. Not a mile of water stood between the ships.

Soon the *Upstart* altered her course. She pointed northeast and drove on toward that horizon. The lookout said she was moving due north before another hour went by.

Redd figured the time. The flood would run another two hours. He sent the *Lady* north, then northeast at a fast clip, ordering the lookout to keep the schooner in sight. Another hour passed, in which Redd did the unexpected. He ordered all but steadying sails off the yards and let her drift. Mr. Hyde looked perplexed for some time. Unable to stand it any longer, he said:

"Why the hell aren't we running, sir? If we're going back on the flood, we'd better raise sail."

"We're not going back on it," Redd answered. "That's what Untell is doing. I'm waiting for the ebb to set us down into the

Indian Ocean. Untell can't imagine us taking the long way to Batavia."

"Neither can I," the mate said quickly.

Before Redd could reply, the distant northern sky seemed to explode in a great burst of light. A horizon of water stood in sharp detail for a moment. The glare fell away and darkness claimed the sea.

"Masthead!" Redd cried anxiously.

"She's out of sight!" came the reply.

Redd breathed a great sigh of relief. "That's it, Mr. Hyde! If we can't see her, she can't see us. By thunder, we're free of Untell at last!"

The second loosed a shout. "She was late with the flare!" he exclaimed. "And now she's running north—after us, she thinks."

Mr. Hyde shook his head in bewilderment. "So we're free," he said. "It don't make sense. He'll run on to Batavia and wait for us, won't he?"

"That's the idea," Redd laughed.

"Aye, sir. But I've been wondering all day about that very thing. Why lose him when all he has to do is run for our destination?"

"Why, Mr. Hyde, didn't I tell you we're going to let Captain Untell sit it out in Batavia? I'm shaping a course for Singapore."

The mate started. As a second flare from the *Upstart* lit up the seas and deck, Redd saw a broad grin of understanding on his face. Then it was dark again, and out of it Mr. Hyde said:

"I'm relieved, sir. By God, I am."

He chuckled once. Soon a deep laugh rose up out of him. His appreciation was genuine. "Sir," he said, feeling for Redd's hand, "I've never seen it done before. But I can say now I've seen a three-stickerman who outschoonered a schoonerman."

3

The *Lady of Glasgow* ran on to Singapore without the schooner on her heels. From there she sailed up the China Sea to Hong Kong to discharge her cargo. Now she was standing down to Batavia. The weather was fine and the ship seemed at peace.

Tysbee appeared to be making the best of his enforced exile. He played poker with Redd and walked the decks as though he enjoyed life at sea, despite the close watch of his every movement since the bottle episode.

Redd was watching him now, idly but with a full awareness of the danger he posed when his guilt became known. Even now the news might be a topic for discussion in Sydney, or even in Singapore. The thought brought to mind Untell and Lancefield. The British eye never closed. It might wink and look away for a time. But it never closed.

Untell wasn't through. Redd knew this, and he thought of it every hour of every day. The schooner might still be aft to all practical purposes. Certainly the chase from Sydney to Lombok Strait had altered his plans. It had also cost Van Oren, Limited, a lot of money. Wool due in Batavia in a hurry had taken such a drop in price that the cargo had lost at least a thousand pounds in value. Sir George wouldn't like that. Neither would Geoffrey.

But there was little they could do about it under the circumstances. He was master of the situation, and he planned to keep it that way. Mistakes in pounds and shillings were not mistakes when the game called for the utmost secrecy regarding the real cargo he carried. Tysbee and gold.

Tysbee drew his glance again. He was talking to Mr. Burk. In fact, he had been real chummy with the second since Hong Kong. Tysbee and gold—a hell of a cargo for a sailing man.

Perhaps he was too wary and cautious. If so, the *Upstart* was to blame. All of the gold was intact, still in pretty little bars of gleaming yellow. Sir George and Geoffrey wouldn't approve of that either. They wanted to spend it on distress properties in Melbourne and Sydney. They might now be drawing on the "foreign capital" which they thought he had deposited in the Javasche Bank of Batavia. But they hadn't reckoned on Lancefield and Untell.

Everything being equal, he would deposit at least a third of the bars in Batavia. He had almost done that in Singapore. Something stopped him, he didn't know what. Fear or superstition—it had been on a Friday—or the sudden realization that the step would be an irrevocable one.

A big junk slanted across the water, her eye, painted on the bows, taking on the seas. Large gourds hung from her rail; the Chinese used them for life preservers.

As his glance swept Mr. Burk, he thought the second appeared a little too alert. Then he saw Tysbee standing close, one hand on the port rail, the other gesticulating as if in support of earnest argument. He watched them closely, reviewing the second's past and placing it up for comparison to the present. Satisfied with what he saw, he glanced at Tysbee, thinking as he did so of the temptation he might put in the way of any of the forty men aboard. Next he wondered what Burk's price was. Since most men would sell their souls for a price, the second would bear watching. It wasn't difficult to imagine what would follow Tysbee's escape. Confession, apprehension, courts, and prison. After Tysbee, Van Oren and himself.

He looked at the Chinaman's sails, high poop, and overhanging stern in detachment. The ancient craft ran on, trying in vain to work into the wind.

Burk was rubbing his chin and staring out over the side; and Tysbee was leaning closer, talking. The second turned on him, decided to say nothing, and walked away. Then he returned, plainly showing the uncertainty that gripped him. Redd knew Burk to be a sailor made of the same stuff as Mr. Hyde. He was the type of man who had demonstrated his willingness to face death for a sailor's pay. Which, Redd reflected, was one reason why he was a mate. Most seafarers left no roots trailing in the water, and their ambitions and morals were about as permanently fixed. But once in a while a man showed a willingness to learn and to look for one man to fasten his loyalty to. And a captain decided that man was worth gambling on. Such a man was Terence Burk.

Under his breath Redd spoke with all the finality of decision he would employ in announcing a course: "My apologies, Mr. Burk. I'll still gamble on you." And not even the picture of Tysbee before Lancefield could cause him to lift a hand to influence his second mate.

That night Tysbee seemed unusually cheerful. He entered Redd's cabin smiling. "Captain," he said, "I'm beginning to enjoy this adventure. Rather, the one ahead."

Redd looked at him, a little amused at his transparency. "What brought about the change, Mr. Tysbee?"

"Any number of things. Some poet once said, 'Life is a jest, and all things show it.' Well, look at us, then look ahead. Steal a little pay a little, steal a lot pay a lot. Apply the laws of nature. We took plenty, didn't we, Captain? So it's a game, this business of looking ahead."

Redd shoved the bottle toward him, saying, "Life really is a jest. And you're proving it."

"Sure." Tysbee's eyes were laughing at him. "I can imagine how it will catch up with George. He'll let this ship do him in, with the help of men like you. The *Lady of Glasgow* will come to a bad and notorious end. Isn't it sailing in that direction?"

"Maybe you're right," Redd grinned.

"I am. But the item of fascinating guesswork is how you will pay, Captain." Lifting a glass, he said, "Regardless of how, here's to it."

Redd joined him, wondering as he sipped just how much it had cost him to strike a deal with Mr. Burk. He wasn't worried about it, however; he was as loyal to the second as he wanted the second to be to him.

And yet every time he looked at Mr. Burk during the next two days his curiosity grew. It was not easy to dispel all doubt. He knew he must do it just the same; otherwise it would assume the proportions of a disease. It was almost that in him when Java lifted up from out of the sea.

The ship was standing straight down to Tandjoengpriok, port of Batavia. The low Java shore was clearly visible. Mountains far inland were bright under the morning sun. Land smells reached out to sea, tropical and pungent. The roadstead opened up with a maze of tiny islands covered with green trees. Neerstuk Reef with its beacon and Vader Smit Reef with its warning lay ahead. A Dutch pilot came aboard and threaded the *Lady* through the islands and thick harbor traffic, past ingoing, outgoing, and anchored schooners, steamers, Makassar craft, junks, and three-stickers into the glassy slick of the harbor. The good smells of land and sea stirred with the stink of a tropical port, and cries of birds swooping low over the water seemed as natural as the silence of Malay work gangs laboring in loincloths aboard the lighters.

Redd studied every schooner in sight, afraid his eyes would suddenly fall on a high-masted craft with a name he had learned to respect. But the *Upstart* wasn't there.

When the *Lady's* anchor splashed and her cable rattled out in good fathoms, harbor lighters raced to her, all anxious to take her cargo to the godowns. Mr. Hyde stood by while Redd mixed Dutch and English with lightermen, all bidding frantically. When it was over, Malays clambered aboard to unload Australian wool.

Redd studied Mr. Burk for some time. He went below thinking that even Mr. Hyde looked unusually wise and pleased about something. Tysbee was in the holds, as usual. Then he wondered if he was; if, perhaps, he might be secreted between bales of wool on a hoist to a Dutchman's lighter. It was a difficult thing to just sit there and wonder. The stakes were big. It was Tysbee free or a mate's loyalty. He had to gamble on something.

Then Mr. Hyde entered, grinning and poling a cheek with his tongue. Redd watched him closely as he took the liberty of pouring himself whisky.

"Sir," he said at last, "you win." Redd glared at him, and he chuckled once before saying, "And it won't hurt you a damn bit. Mr. Burk was figuring you'd ask him about it."

"How much did Tysbee offer him?" Redd asked.

"One hundred pounds."

"Did Mr. Burk accept it?"

"Aye, sir. Naturally."

"And how does he do it?"

"On the wool to Rotterdam Quay. Mr. Tysbee rides a sling, well hidden in wool. In fact, Mr. Burk has already been paid, sir."

"My compliments to the second. Tell him I said he's earned it."

"*We*, sir. I'm to guarantee he does it." Redd laughed with the mate until the latter said, "Mr. Burk asked me to tell you something. Just one word. Thanks."

Redd watched Mr. Hyde move away. Then he downed a quick drink and said, "Damn, but that was a close one." Never again would he entertain any doubt of his officers.

He sent for Tysbee, as the mates had expected him to do. Tysbee entered, curious and impatient. Redd pointed to whisky and cards and, pretending to see nothing of the brisk motion in the little man's eyes, said:

"I feel lucky today."

"Lucky! Is this what a ship captain does the moment he drops anchor? What about customs, quarantine, pratique, and——"

Redd interrupted. "I've heard that a master's first duty is to be at the right place at the right time." Letting this sink home, he said, "Now I'll draw high card with you for say—would a hundred pounds be too high?"

Tysbee's nervousness was plain to see. He looked through the port at the lighter and listened intently to the sounds from the slings and crew of overseers. Time was a precious thing to him now and it was wasting away. He sat down and said:

"Very well. A hundred pounds. But let's get it over with."

"Now we're getting somewhere." Redd unhurriedly shuffled the cards and placed them in the center of the table. "Cut once if you like, then take a card."

Tysbee's small hand darted out just as the second mate's voice sounded overhead, "Ten more bales, lads. Bear lively!" His hand hesitated a moment before spreading the cards in a sidewise sweep. He drew one and held it up for Redd to see. The nine of diamonds.

"It looks good," Redd admitted. "But suppose it isn't good enough. Can you pay off?"

"Of course I can! For Christ's sake, Captain, get on with your draw!"

"Sorry." Redd shrugged and took a card. Without looking at it, he said, "This little play reminds me of a game up in Shanghai a few years back. Neither Mr. Hyde nor I were particularly anxious to win, though the stakes were high. But come to think of it, they weren't anything like what you and I are playing for."

Tysbee suddenly looked wise. He scarcely saw the black six Redd turned face up, though his red nine mocked him when he lowered his eyes. The deck was quieter now, and he felt the hopelessness of a prisoner who had failed to escape. Then resentment and anger collected and he met Redd's gaze with a blazing fury that was more deadly because it was tempered with long patience.

"You win, mister," Redd was saying. "Just enough to balance your losses. Next time, remember not to trust a sailor."

4

Even as he said it Redd knew full well that he must get rid of Tysbee. Somehow, somewhere, he must get him off the ship. There was too much threat of escape, of Lancefield and Untell and courts, in Tysbee's eyes. And he evoked pictures of Geoffrey and Sir George, who wouldn't hesitate to sacrifice a mere ship captain if Tysbee were found aboard the *Lady*.

Decision was strong in him in the days at anchor. He felt like a man on borrowed time, on short reprieve from a New South Wales prison. Twice he left the ship with Melbourne bullion and twice he turned about before he touched the wharf of Tandjoengpriok. Let Geoffrey and Sir George wait. His agents had a cargo for Singapore. He would run it there and then find some island, some remote spot far from the open eye of the British and Dutch. There he would leave Tysbee.

It wasn't fear that caused him to return with the gold. It was Tysbee on board his ship. He realized then that this was what had subconsciously restrained him in Singapore and Hong Kong. Gold on deposit to Van Oren, Limited, was out of the question until he ridded his ship of the man Australia would soon be clamoring for.

Then one night he remembered something. His father had talked about an island where a Yankee steamer chased him. It was off the Sumatra coast. The natives wouldn't let them land. His father had called it "Island of Gold." So had the Portuguese back in the sixteenth century. They even outfitted an expedition to search for it. And the Mohammedans had talked about it seven hundred years before that.

Next day he made inquiries and learned that the Dutch had tried several times to establish a residency on the island. There wasn't even a *controleur* there now. The last one lost his head, literally. He didn't want Tysbee to meet this fate, though he thought he could trade it out with the natives.

First, cargo to Singapore. Then the "Island of Gold."

That night he wrote to Sir George, telling him of the destination in mind. He didn't relish the idea of disclosing even that much, though it wasn't his ship and there were rules to follow. But he didn't have to reveal his true reason for going to the island. Instead he wrote about a windfall.

He posted the letter aboard a steamer bound for Sydney and watched the low-waisted ship puff and snort her way through the lanes of the harbor for the Java Zee.

He felt a little better when the traffic swallowed her up. Perhaps he could get under way tomorrow. The quicker the better. After all, he was a partner in this scheme, and Tysbee had to go before the gold was really gold.

Then he gave an inward start. A tall schooner moved in from Vader Smit Reef. Some minutes passed before he learned she wasn't the *Upstart*.

Book three

CROSS SEAS AND WINDS

. . . Then a change in the wind, and the waves trying to run against it, a chopping sea and the elements all confused. . . .

CHAPTER X

On a morning when Captain Untell's *Upstart* was standing down the Australian coast for Sydney, Geoffrey entered his office and picked up the Sydney *Morning Herald*. Finding what he expected, he sat down and read anxiously.

There was another demand for Mr. Tysbee. The piece, though brief, appeared on the front page in a box reserved for critical blasts at politics in general, a part of the endless crusade for the betterment of conditions in the colonies of Australia. It pointed out that the people were not satisfied with the development of the case of the seven boxes; that after long weeks no announcement of the Bank of Melbourne's true condition had been forthcoming.

Geoffrey frowned over this. Some faction was going out of its way to keep the case alive. He looked toward Van Oren's office as his mind carefully meshed all things together. Sir George should return today from Melbourne. His mission there was twofold: first, and openly, to secure options of purchase on distress property, awaiting Captain Redd's deposit of gold to consummate the transactions; second, to feel the pulse of Melbourne in the

Tysbee affair, as well as to shed Van Oren, Limited, influence in the proper places.

Something else worried Geoffrey. For days he had expected some word from Redd about the turning of gold into cash on deposit in Batavia, Singapore, and Hong Kong. Though Redd had called at these ports, there was nothing but silence from him. He was beginning to wonder about many things, among them Redd's loyalty versus the temptation of his cargo. While there were ways and means of disciplining a captain, he could find none to suit the circumstances. It irritated him as he began to feel more and more a strong awareness of Redd's dominating position in this affair.

Perhaps he was entertaining foolish fears. Putting the matter aside, he looked at the newspaper again.

That afternoon he met an official of the *Herald* at his club and asked casual and guarded questions before reminding the other of the damaging effect of references to the seven boxes upon the good name of Van Oren, Limited. The newspaperman's reply silenced Geoffrey:

Wasn't Geoffrey living in the past, when the Van Oren firm had a good name; before Kerry, Finch, Untell, and others fell, before the affair of the seven boxes? He went on to say that Geoffrey had little to complain about. Hadn't stories of the firm's recent business dealings been favorable?

Geoffrey nodded, remembering such notices as: "Van Oren, Limited, is reported to have contracted to purchase the controlling interest in the Yellowdine Mining Syndicate of Kalgoorlie." And another: "In what may become the largest real-estate transaction since the bank crisis, Van Oren, Limited, has been granted an option on an entire block of business property on Melbourne's Spring Street. The business head of the Sydney firm reports that the deal will be closed as soon as foreign capital is available."

On the way back to his office Geoffrey said over and over, "Foreign capital." The situation was becoming acute, what with ships, mines, and a sugar plantation, not to mention the crowning ambition up for consideration: the great Woolloomooloo Steamship Line. It represented the largest single investment in maritime Australia, and its very name brought to mind government subsidies and politics in every colony of the continent. Of course there was only one box of gold aboard Redd's ship. But Geoffrey knew his way about in this world of finance. "A deucedly neat picture," he was thinking. But it wasn't the soundest, not when he looked at the threads it was hanging by. Redd's perfidy, Tysbee's escape or indictment could spoil it all. However, these things had not happened as far as he knew. Only one thing continued to plague him. That was Redd's dilatory manner in turning the gold into "foreign capital."

He had no sooner reached his desk than a sealed packet was delivered to him by a steamer captain who had just arrived in Sydney. His eyes lit up; the letter was addressed to Sir George and it was from Redd. He was sure it advised that gold was on deposit. When alone, he opened it and read eagerly.

A furrow creased his brow, then a sharp expression crossed his face. He was angry when he slowly lowered the message to the desk. Not a word about the gold. Options, big deals, waiting, hanging on the capital that could make them all richer than most men dared to imagine; the Spring Street option ready to expire within the week; the big vein discovered near the Yellowdine, and one more week in which to snatch up this property at a mere fraction of its true value.

And not one word about the gold.

Instead their ship captain had gone adventuring. He talked of a windfall! Of all things, a windfall, with the grestest money-making scheme in the world staring him in the face! It was preposterous, utterly so. In fact, it didn't sound like Redd. Something was wrong somewhere. He read the letter again, wondering if the chase by Untell all the way to Lombok Strait had anything to do with Redd's decision. Nothing made sense but money-making. Redd was either playing a game for some further advantage or—and Geoffrey's eyes widened with fear—for all the gold in that box.

Something had to be done about it; soon.

He looked at his watch. Tonight he was taking Martha to the viceregal ball. He had no sooner reached the street than Tobias, Sir George's driver, hailed him. Mr. Van Oren had just arrived from Melbourne and wanted Geoffrey to come to Muirkirk Hall at once.

Thinking it odd that Sir George had not stopped by the office, and undecided as to whether he should get into formal attire for the ball first, he ordered Tobias to his apartment.

"But Mr. Van Oren looks very excited, sir," Tobias argued.

"No doubt," Geoffrey replied. "So I'll give him time to calm down. To my hotel."

Geoffrey wanted to think, to adjust Redd's behavior to what he thought was worrying Sir George. If Tysbee's theft of the gold had been uncovered, Van Oren, Limited, faced another ticklish situation. Credit props might drop out from under the firm in a hurry. He cursed under his breath, at Redd. The firm's need of foreign capital tomorrow could be acute. Something had to be done about it; and soon. Very soon.

He was seething with the urgency of the situation even as he came upon Sir George pacing before a small fire in the library. Pausing to pour whisky, he appeared as cool and collected as ever, in sharp contrast to Van Oren, who was saying:

"Geoffrey, prepare yourself for bad news."

"I'm always prepared," Geoffrey smiled. "But first a drop to warm us, shall we? Oh, by the way, I forgot to place a bob or two on your horse today. I couldn't go to the racecourse."

"You'll forget horses when I tell you——"

"About Mr. Tysbee's unpopularity in Melbourne, of course."

"It's worse than that. A grand jury is meeting there today to hear the report of the bank's condition. By tomorrow Sydney will hear about it."

Geoffrey seemed interested in nothing but his white tie as he said, "And we'll be pressed for capital that we don't have."

"We'll be called thieves along with Tysbee." Then Geoffrey's statement registered in his mind. "What! You mean Redd hasn't come through? My God, what next? What about the options? What's wrong with Redd?"

Geoffrey let him stand there lost in his own unanswered questions for the time it took to refill his glass and seat himself comfortably. Then he produced Redd's letter and said, "Our captain has suddenly decided to humor his urge for adventure. Listen to this——"

2

The afternoon had been a trying one for Martha. After numerous fittings of her party dress she left the dressmaker's house. Thinking of the viceregal ball, she urged the driver on to Muirkirk, smiling with anticipation. It wasn't hard to imagine the admiring glances that would fall on her this evening. Geoffrey liked blue better, though she was confident that the crimson dress in her lap, rather she in it, would provoke his wide-open admiration.

The governor's ball was the greatest social event of the year and Geoffrey was a coveted man. She let him stand at the top of her list, as indeed he should, even ahead of a man her mind averted to as she stood before the dressmaker's mirror. Captain Redd wasn't a Geoffrey in a ballroom.

The carriage rolled into the grounds and on to the door. The sun was falling swiftly, and from the boiling quiet of clouds piling up in the south it seemed anxious to race on west. She entered the house and walked on by the library before hearing Geoffrey's voice. Odd, she thought, that he should arrive so early. Peeping inside, she saw her father. Geoffrey mentioned Captain Redd, then began reading a letter.

Martha was interested. She listened without giving a thought to eavesdropping.

" 'Off the coast of Sumatra there is an island which the Mohammedans named Island of Gold back around the year 900. Several hundred years later a Portuguese expedition failed to find treasure there. The Dutch are unable to rule it. The tribes are too fierce for them and the island is too small and distant for practical subjugation.' "

Sir George asked where the island was, and Geoffrey named the position by latitude and longitude as Redd stated it. Martha repeated it in a whisper.

" 'Now I have talked to Dutch traders,' " Geoffrey read on, " 'who tell me they have seen natives wearing yellow headdresses on the southern beaches. There is a fair anchorage and the monsoon is favorable. I'm placing the plan before you, voting to outfit our own expedition. The cost will be held to the operating expense of the ship plus certain armaments and trade goods consistent with such a proposition. This could be a timely windfall, considering that Captain Untell, on a schooner named *Upstart*, chased me all the way to Lombok Strait, where I crossed him up on a tide and wind.' "

"Captain Untell?" Van Oren rubbed his face in puzzled fashion. "Why would Untell chase him?"

"I've heard he was seen with Mr. Lancefield," Geoffrey said. "Isn't it obvious? But back to Captain Redd. He is proposing a scheme of uncertain value based wholly on chance. And, mind you, in the very shadow of a positive scheme that should make any lucky windfall on his part look small. But he not only proposes, he——"

"Geoffrey, could it be that he's trying to tell us something?"

"Oh, he does that, all right."

Van Oren shook his head in disbelief, then said, "Is the man in his right mind?"

"No," Geoffrey smiled. "Or else he's very clever."

"I'm voting no, and emphatically no," Sir George said.

"Are you? Listen carefully to Redd's final statement: 'Since an inactive ship is a costly proposition, and since you must vote along with me in this matter, I am dropping a cargo in Singapore and sailing around Sumatra for the island.' Signed, 'Respectfully, Captain Gordon Redd, *Lady of Glasgow*, at anchor Harbor of Tandjoengpriok, Java.' "

Martha looked at the dress she carried without seeing it. Her curiosity mounted by the moment. She was trying to assort and properly assess all she had heard. As if in answer to all her unshaped questions, Geoffrey said:

"While it appears to be nothing short of a foolish gamble, I'm sure his true purpose isn't fully revealed."

Sir George asked why he was sure, drawing from Geoffrey, "In the first place, Redd is too good a businessman to gamble on supposition. If he were sure of the existence of treasure, I wouldn't doubt his total honesty."

"So you're thinking the same thing I am—that he might be planning to take everything."

"No," Geoffrey said. "The idea was strong for a while. But it's too absurd to entertain seriously, don't you think?"

"Perhaps," Van Oren breathed heavily. "But he's in a position to do as he pleases. Have you thought of that, Geoffrey? We are actually at his mercy. What could we say or do if he decided to cut loose from us?"

"That's absurd. Remember we had to place a little faith in someone, didn't we? So let's not show panic now."

"There's cause for panic. Haven't I just come from Melbourne? Hasn't Redd put us in the middle, on the defensive?" Sir George paused, his face taking on an expression of sudden discovery. "That's it!" he said. "He's forcing us to fight against what he knows will happen. He's letting us know it's up to us to sustain his innocence."

"He's bluffing," Geoffrey said.

"With a powerful weapon," Van Oren replied quickly.

"You seem to forget that two can play that game. If he wishes to remain at odds with us, we'll let him know that we can shift all the blame to him. I suggest that we call his bluff at once. Remember who he carries aboard his ship. That's our trump card. We're in a pinched position, but so is Redd. Now suppose you extend the options for another month, if you can, and allow me the pleasure of putting Captain Redd in his place."

"How?"

"I'll send him a stiff order to forget windfalls and deposit gold bars to the firm's credit at once; that failing to do this, we'll let him shift for himself in the matter of Tysbee, who will be hot cargo by the time this reaches him."

Martha stared with growing amazement. Something inside her said the things she had heard were not true, couldn't be true, that she had not heard them. Then she was weak all over, for she had heard. And Geoffrey had said these things! Dazed by what he had revealed, she scarcely heard her father say that Redd might hide Tysbee, or Geoffrey reply to this with, "He won't dare let Tysbee out of his sight."

She looked at the crimson dress in her hands, unable to believe that all it stood for minutes ago, dancing and wine and pleasure and peace of mind, had completely vanished. In her hands was a rag, the ashes of an evening's entertainment in advance of the occasion. But the lovely gown was in reality just something tangible to remind her that the real ashes were made up of more important things.

It was a little too much for her. She moved hurriedly to the privacy of her room. But the very privacy of her thoughts was inescapable. Looking into her mirror, out the window at the soft fall of evening, and back to the dress, she continued to fight against the truth. It was a futile attempt. She was all confused. Then she was wondering if she had the toughness of fiber to go through the evening with Geoffrey. A wave of anger engulfed her. It was not at Geoffrey and her father, but at the traitorous things she was thinking about them. A prescient dread ran through her. She tore her glance from the dress and faced her own countenance in the mirror.

There was the shape of judgment on her face, strong and permanent. Emotions ran together, betraying this judgment, though the final picture was the same as the first. For a long time she just stood there. It was her own voice calling the maid. And then she was dressing for the ball, in the crimson gown, almost wonderingly. Everything moved about her, as though she imagined physical animation; out of a trance, she thought, when the maid and a pendant and the dress emerged over a promise to marry Geoffrey, over loyalty to her father against a growing belief that they were all guilty, Redd included.

Then she was putting on perfume. She started, asking herself: why? Habit, perhaps. But tonight the real reason was escape. It could be nothing else——

They were going to force Captain Redd to do as they wished. His alternative was to shift for himself with Mr. Tysbee the guilty "hot" cargo. And Gordon Redd was guilty; as guilty and deep in the crime of stolen gold as he had once appeared to be. He was saying her ship's name was clear, and she was asking if it would remain that way. "You know how I feel about that, don't you?" he replied. And later—*she* was saying it!—"I'm not nearly as worried as I was." His lips against hers, she clinging to him, trusting and gullible. It was revolting. She had been taken in by him.

She was hot with anger when she left the room and walked to

the stairway, wanting to hurt Gordon Redd as he was hurting her now.

At the library entrance she paused, took in deep breath, and raised her head high. Assuming a natural pose and forcing a little enthusiasm into her face seemed an ordeal. She walked inside and broke the silence between the men with:

"Why so quiet? Has Van Oren, Limited, lost all its ships and mines?" As they exchanged a swift glance, she said, "I'm glad you're home, Father."

He stood and took her hand in his. He held it tightly, she thought. "You look tired, Martha," he said with concern, causing her to think he was looking ahead at what was to come. She smiled assuringly and looked at Geoffrey, who was saying:

"I'm beginning to think red is my favorite color."

Smiling, she asked for brandy. Geoffrey served her. Then her father asked if they were going out.

"Yes, Father. To the viceregal ball," she replied. "But aren't you?"

"No. I wasn't invited." She glanced up at him quickly as he said, "Since the hearing I'm no longer a social lion." Laughing, he added, looking at Geoffrey, "Don't ever get your name involved in the courts, young fellow."

She thought Geoffrey's smile a little too perfect when he said, "You may rest at ease on that score, sir."

Martha could not suppress an instant searching look into him. She wondered at what he left unsaid, if it wasn't, "Regardless of what happens to everybody else."

3

They left the ball at around one in the morning and rode in silence most of the way home. She knew what Geoffrey was thinking. Her own mind had been shaping judgment all evening, and wine wasn't wine, and music wasn't music. Then she had overheard a mention of her father's name. A banker's wife had said Sir George wasn't invited. All Sydney knew about it, Martha realized. The woman had said rumor was rife; they were asking on Bridge Street, she said, what Van Oren, Limited, was planning to buy with; the banks didn't know; but of course everyone had a private opinion.

Martha had done a great deal of thinking. Faith in people and principles was necessary to one's peace. Without it, much or all was missing. Faith in her own father, in the man she had promised to marry, in the master of her ship was shaken to the core. She must do something about it. As the carriage halted at her door she said:

"Come in, Geoffrey. I wish to talk to you."

In the drawing room she repeated all the banker's wife had said. Geoffrey listened. He got up once to mix a drink, though his expression remained fixed.

"There was a mention of foreign capital, Geoffrey." She was searching his face intently. "Why, it was in the newspapers, so it must be true."

"It is," he said. "What about it?"

"Nothing. Except its source. Isn't it supposed to come from Singapore and Batavia, where the *Lady of Glasgow* went?"

A disarming laugh escaped him. "Martha, accusations based on mere rumors are becoming a national pastime. If we were trying to raise money in New York or London, it would be the same."

"If you were, would the *Lady* have sailed to those ports first?"

He grew serious. "I'm wondering what lies behind this sudden interest on your part. Why don't you forget the gossip?"

"Because I can't." Her look held, demanding.

She was trying desperately to read him, to uncover a little; he knew this. And then he saw judgment on her face. It accused him of covering up everything. He was thinking of how desirable she was when she said:

"What are you and Father trying to force on Captain Redd?"

He started. Frowning, suddenly remembering the glass in his hand, he drank its contents, not taking his eyes off her. He came out of it with his usual calm smile up for show, saying, "I'm beginning to get jealous."

"Really, it is an occasion when you admit that much, Geoffrey."

She was laughing at him, he thought. He noticed the speculative expression in her glance. Arising, he passed a compliment, about her very nearness being an occasion to him.

"Geoffrey, if there is to be anything between us, we must be honest. Not in just what we say, but in what remains unsaid."

"Naturally."

"Then you'd better begin tonight. Now."

She was too near and inviting for him to remain blind to the challenge. And yet he felt that her need was more for some unspoken assurance than words. His arms went about her and she continued to look up at him with what he thought was unguarded interest.

She turned away from him. Words seemed necessary then as a tension gathered.

"Martha, there isn't anything I wouldn't do for you. You know this."

"Of course." She didn't look at him at once. "Then tell me what is happening to my ship."

Though in no humor for this sort of thing, he sat near her and forced himself into a slow account of the voyage. She accused him of speaking over countinghouse ledgers and asked for more than this.

"Frankly, Martha, the voyage was uneventful."

"That's odd," she replied, "with Captain Redd aboard."

"With Captain Redd aboard," he said, "I can understand your meaning. By Jove, he has me worried; about a foolish adventure he has in mind. I'm set on getting rid of him, though Sir George is"—he paused to shape his words "—well, loyal to a profitable captain."

Lies, all lies, she was thinking as she said, "What kind of foolish adventure?"

He related the contents of Redd's letter about a windfall on the "Island of Gold." When he finished his story, she said:

"But what other motive could he have but the one he mentions? Could he be thinking of Melbourne gold and perhaps a prisoner aboard his ship?"

Instantly on guard, he said, "You're letting the gossips affect your imagination, aren't you? I wish you'd forget it, Martha."

"This new adventure of Redd's confirms my suspicions. He is a pirate. And now I am sure he was a pirate when he took the boxes from Captain Untell. All this proves Father and Mr. Tysbee guilty also. It's true, isn't it, Geoffrey?"

"You're overdoing it," he said. "In all honesty, Martha, this is the first time I've even considered the crime element of this thing Redd is planning. And I'm sure I speak for your father also."

She arose and walked away from him. Turning, she seemed to study him carefully. "In all honesty, you say!" A flush of color crept up under her skin and the curl of her lips suggested contempt and anger. "In all honesty? Perhaps you are trying to spare my feelings. However, I know you are not telling me the truth, Geoffrey. Do you want to try again?"

He glanced up in surprise at the half-hidden threat of her question. There was little use in trying to maneuver conversation toward another subject; she would not have it. Then a little of the storm in her crept into him.

"It's rather late," he said, sounding unperturbed. "I must be going."

"But not before I refresh your memory, Geoffrey. Aren't you going to send Captain Redd a stiff order to deposit the gold bars from the Bank of Melbourne? And if he fails to obey you, aren't you going to let him *'shift for himself in the matter of Tysbee'?* You said that, adding something about hot cargo by the time your order reached him."

He stood with shock and astonishment in his face, his eyes mere pin points. But his reserve was otherwise unimpaired. "That is all true, Martha. But I shall always be loyal to your father and the firm. And your feelings are something I must guard."

"Not any more, Geoffrey."

"What do you mean?"

"I am breaking our engagement."

He took one step toward her, then stopped still. A stunned look gave way to incredulity, which in turn spent itself. A hint of anger flickered across his eyes. He said, "Why?"

"Because you are all guilty of a terrible crime. And you and Father are trying to squirm out of it, hoping to save yourselves by tossing Captain Redd to the wolves. No, I could never love a man like you, Geoffrey. And I'm through trying."

He looked away, then slowly brought his gaze to bear on her

again. "You sound so final, Martha. But aren't you mixing a woman's emotions with a foolish gallantry and business that you should leave alone? Aren't you being rather hasty and dramatic?"

"You may go, Geoffrey."

"Not yet," he said with rising defiance.

"Then I shall."

As she walked past him, the portent of her decision struck him in full force. She represented Van Oren, Limited, and she was taking it away from him with her refusal to marry him, walking out of his life, out of his well-planned future with all his hopes and aspirations for power and position. Nothing mattered now but these things. Purpose and calculation put anger in its place as he stepped before her, barring her way.

She turned a cold, imperious glance on him before he said, "You are making a grave mistake, Martha, one I won't allow. You want honesty, you say. Very well, we shall see just how well you can bear up under it. Look at me and listen——

"Your father planned this scheme, from the stealing of a box of gold to its place on Redd's ship now. It was all his idea. He drew Mr. Tysbee into it, and Redd was a willing accomplice. I could do nothing to stop them. With fresh troubles arising, I am trying to steer your father, to whom I have been loyal up to now, away from courts. Perhaps prison."

"No, Geoffrey. No!"

"And you, with your young idealism, ask for honesty! But worse, you turn on the only person whose absolute loyalty to your parent and firm has remained unquestioned over the years."

His eyes were bitter and hard.

"Yes, Martha, you are going to marry me; sooner than you intended. Refuse me and I will go to Mr. Lancefield with my story."

She could only stare at him, her feelings unmasked. It didn't matter that her loathing of him was fully revealed; she wasn't capable of reason as she floated into and out of shock and confusion. It was only when she looked away from him that her mind asserted itself and considered his threat. Her father would go to prison. She was turning it all in her mind, from this angle of escape to that. It was no use. She was securely bound.

"Which shall it be, Martha?"

Realizing that she must marshal her wits, she tried to calm herself. She needed time; time he wouldn't allow her. She asked for brandy and watched him pour it with speculation in her eyes.

"Thanks," she said when he handed her a glass. She drank.

"Geoffrey, you spoke of loyalty to my father." She let him wait, purposely. "It was negligent of me to have overlooked that all these years. It means a lot to me."

"I regret that I was forced to remind you of it," he said crisply.

She was quite sure the smile she forced and favored him with covered her true feelings and guile when his face relaxed a little. She said, "It seems I needed reminding, Geoffrey."

It was enough. He was thawing, hoping to win her again. She wanted him to hope. It would give her time in which to look for a way out of this predicament.

CHAPTER XI

The day broke with squalls off the Tasman. They raced in out of the southeast, eased off, and came in afresh, as if water had piled up on the wind for days to give Sydney a thorough drenching.

At ten that morning Martha stood at the large library window waiting out an interval of slack. It was not long. The rain gathered suddenly and returned in gusts. It drove against the glass panes in frenzied sheets. She turned her back on it and swept the room with a weary glance.

Her father had been here with her until minutes ago. She had never seen him like this before. But it had to come. There was no way of omitting last night and Geoffrey from their lives.

But her father. Her eyes misted over again as the memory of him sitting there took shape. Directly after breakfast she had come to the point. At first impatient and flustered, he sat down and stared at her with unfocused eyes. At times he leaned forward in his chair, hands gripping the arms, mouth open to speak. Though he said nothing. She was telling him of his conversation with

Geoffrey before the ball. He wanted to pass it off with glib indifference at first; his next urge was to lie out of it, and then he seemed to consider running away from her.

Soon she was telling him about Geoffrey. His eyes darted up at her, wide-open disbelief in them when she told of breaking their engagement. He got to his feet with Geoffrey's accusation—"Your father planned this scheme . . . It was all his idea. . . . I could do nothing to stop them." The word prison drained his face of the color anger was pumping into it.

She paused there for effect, to let all she had repeated sink home. He was like the weather outside, all torn up and confused. He even checked his anger at Geoffrey long enough to deny everything. Then he paced the floor, mouthing oaths at Geoffrey.

He raised his voice. Hadn't he given the young half-starved Englishman a chance to get out of the bush country where he had gone because of a lung ailment? Hadn't he pushed him up until he was one of the biggest men in Sydney?

She warned him of more to come. Perhaps he should be seated. He scoffed. She didn't need to be told that he was angry at her now for knowing as much as she did. And then she let him have it in the full force she had received it from Geoffrey——

" 'Refuse me and I will go to Mr. Lancefield with my story.' Those are his words, Father."

He sat down, his head shaking negatively. "No," he said. "Not that." She wondered if he was going to faint or have a stroke. He looked terribly pale.

The minutes ticked away. The old clock over the mantelpiece struck the half-hour. Sir George van Oren sat in silence, gazing, just gazing, at nothing. Or perhaps he saw the men he had pushed out of his way to success and power and more success and more power. Schemes and events and regret whirled in his head, she was sure. They blew themselves out and true values and closer ties emerged. Like the cornered man he was, he recognized his own freedom, and he saw his own daughter. And he felt ashamed before her.

"Martha." His voice was low. "Come here, child."

She went to him willingly, wanting to cry, refusing to. In the moment his hand touched her hair she thought she had rather see him guilty than beaten down to this. But he had both these afflictions to contend with, as did she.

"Martha, I'd rather say it to a jury than to you. Somehow, what men think doesn't matter any more. You are all that matters. But I never thought of it in this light until now."

She didn't look at him. She sat on the floor staring straight ahead through the thickening mist in her eyes.

"I'm guilty, Martha. It wasn't theft when the idea formed. It wasn't even my idea. It was Geoffrey's. The plan was to borrow the gold, which no bank would lend, and use it while the bank was closed to buy up distress property, to make millions with it. Then we meant to return it. This appealed to Tysbee, until the gold left his bank."

"And Captain Redd," she added.

"No. It has never appealed to Redd. I tricked him into running down the *Castlereagh*. After that, he couldn't escape it. There wasn't any way out." He told her how he sneaked off Redd's ship and let him take the boxes from Untell.

"But he's deep in it, Martha. He's the fourth partner. He carries the gold and Tysbee. This was Geoffrey's idea also, though Redd was agreeable to it."

"Why did Geoffrey want Mr. Tysbee and the gold on the *Lady of Glasgow?*"

"To turn the gold into foreign capital, and to prevent Tysbee from confessing everything. And, too, when Tysbee's guilt was established, Redd would look guilty if he was caught aboard. It has been something we thought we could use as a lever on Redd."

"What a horrible mess," she said. But looking ahead was worse, and she returned to the past with a question, "When did Captain Redd become a partner?"

"On the night of the ball here. Tysbee and I offered Redd a tenth share. He said he would go out and think it over. He came back later and demanded a fourth, saying he wanted an equal share, an equal say, that there wouldn't be as many mistakes made after that."

She turned her face to him as she adjusted Redd's movements of that evening to her own. Somewhere in the timing of events between Geoffrey's proposal and Redd's decision Redd had kissed her. She was wondering if, somehow, she might have unwittingly helped shape his mind. But it was impossible, of course; too vague and incredible to entertain. She could not imagine Martha van Oren inspiring crime.

"So Captain Redd kidnaped Mr. Tysbee," she mused aloud. "After piracy. And now he's running with the gold, and the head of a bank a prisoner. How guilty can a man get?"

"As guilty as I feel, Martha," her father said. The deep note of anguish in his voice, the dull bitterness in his eyes, the alert sense of fear, all these ran together and made up his reward. It was justice. But there was another justice: a court and perhaps a prison; disgrace. And still another justice: the Lord's word, which asked what a man could gain if he owned the world and lost his own soul.

"What do you want me to do, Martha?"

"I—I don't know." She held his hand with both of hers, tightly, as she had done when a child.

"You don't love Geoffrey, do you?"

"I have never thought I did."

He asked if Geoffrey really loved her. She should know, he said. She looked up sharply, thinking he was taking hope. It was hard to imagine her own parent so deeply engulfed that he would clutch at a straw of that kind. But in another thought she saw it as he did. It made sense in his way of thinking.

"I can't reconcile his threat to love," she said. "I'm beginning to see Geoffrey for what he really is: a very ambitious man without scruples."

"He has me in a trap, all right. If I go to prison, he'll take over the firm. He's come out of his shell now. There's nothing to bind him to the gold scheme. With me in prison, the way would then be clear for him to take everything; from you, Martha."

"Have you ever considered that he could be bluffing, Father?" She argued as businesslike as a man, "After all, he owns a quarter share in this gold, doesn't he?"

"Yes," he replied slowly. "I've considered that. Maybe he is bluffing. But can I afford to call his hand?"

That was the final answer. She got up and walked away from him. The rain beat hard at the window. She did not turn or make any reply to his questions: why didn't she call him a thief and a fool, scold him, or turn her wrath loose on him? Then he was saying she was like her mother had been, something to lean upon in time of need. A long silence held between them. She broke it by saying:

"Father, it is better that Geoffrey thinks you know nothing of his threat. Can you face him as though nothing had come between you?"

"Why—yes. But why do you ask that?"

"Because I love you, Father. Very much. I'm going to marry Geoffrey before the week runs out."

She did not turn a glance on him as she announced her decision, nor did she look at him when he walked out of the room. A strong fear held her eyes glued to the window and the storm outside, a fear that the look on his face might reveal a crafty triumph and give her the deepest hurt she had yet received.

2

Alone in the big library, she felt the room closing in on her. She had to get out of the house. The weather didn't matter. Then again it did; it might be a balm. There were so many questions piling up inside her.

A little later she was dressed for the weather. The carriage waited. As she walked out of the house rain beat at her face and oilskins, and the wind seemed strong enough to lean upon. It was invigorating. Tobias asked, "Where to, miss?" She didn't know; perhaps it was her subconscious self that said:

"Circular Quay."

All of a sudden she knew a suppressed desire to watch the growing swell of the sea as it flooded in on anchored craft with waves breaking and crashing down, rolling back for another charge at the bulwarks of land.

All this was soon before her. When the carriage stopped at the quay she got out and walked toward the water. Every ship trembled, and tall masts shook as water surged in and out under them. The harbor seemed to be snugged in and battened down.

Not a handful of men braved the quay or decks. The wind carried the roar of great seas lost out in the moving mist, seas moving mountains of water.

An old salt approached and spoke through whiskers that streamed water down to his yellow oilskins. "Lookin' for a vessel out there, miss?"

"Just looking," she replied.

"Quite a capful o' wind, eh?" he said.

She nodded. The seaman looked from the harbor to her, said something else. He tried again, then fingered his whiskers and started to walk off. She felt a need of company, strange company. She said:

"Do you know Captain Redd?"

That touched him off. He chuckled. "That I do. And he's a man who could ease up to this here quay in a weather we're ridin', miss. I remember once when I was of the bark *John Clement*, first mate. Was runnin' to Darwin. He tore past me between Thursday Island and Banks—it was his wind—rollin' up his copper sheathin' and heelin' by like an express train. Not givin' an inch o' roadway, not dippin' or nothin'. Just movin'. On the *Lady*. He's the devil on a wind. And," he said, "in a courtroom. Some say he's guilty as a bloody bushman, others say he's cunnin'. But few there is to say he's innocent."

"What do you think?" she asked, looking at him, watching him paw at his whiskers slowly.

"He ain't bad, miss. Just conformin', if you understand. He's a seaman, the kind of a man who looks on tallow or hides or ore, or gold, as cargo. A sailor runs it from consignor to consignee and no questions asked. And I know Cap'n Redd. Fact is——

"Remember way back when he stood the schooner *Blue Cloud* in from the islands with Kanakas. Was runnin' 'em in to Mackay, up Queensland way, to work the sugar fields. Lured 'em like a fancy mermaid with tobacco sticks, likker, and such. Some he kidnaped. That was the way o' the trade. He wasn't no different from the rest. Only he lured more on board, ran faster with 'em, and went back after more quicker."

"A horrible business," she said.

"The sea, miss. It's the sea. It ain't for the squeamish. The waves out there'll tell ye that." He blinked his red-rimmed eyes pensively. "It's the sea, miss, and seamen is of the sea."

A discerning old man, he saw concern and unsettling anxiety in her face, and said, "Interested in Cap'n Redd, miss?"

"Just curious," she replied. As he stared at her, she added, "Perhaps the weather has something to do with it."

"With him or his trouble?" When she failed to reply, he said, "Aye, the trouble he's in is like a wild wind. It and this weather is very much alike, miss. If you don't believe it, just read the mornin' paper."

He left her to the running sea and sky and troubled thoughts. His last remark didn't matter. She knew more than the newspapers. She was examining Redd all over again, finding it easy to reconcile a chapter of his past to the captain who ran guilty with her ship. But the bewhiskered salt had left impressions, the strong logic of a seaman to which she attached a certain credence. "The sea. It ain't for the squeamish. . . ."

She was trying to look at Gordon Redd and see the man he actually was without condemning or condoning him. He demanded a fair trial. Against him were indisputable facts that certified him as a man who defied laws; in his favor was some intangible quality that demanded a little trust in him, wholly at odds with the things about Geoffrey that evoked an instinctive distrust.

Then she knew, beyond any need of evidence, that he had won his case with her. No amount of testimony against him could change this. Captain Redd was not bad. Just conforming. It made little difference that she had tried him in the court of her emotions; judgment had been passed. All else between them was personal. He had challenged her emotions the first time she saw him. Twice she had responded to his kisses. She would do so again.

A sudden gladness crept over her. It was strong, and it held her suspended in a state of peaceful detachment. Crimes and troubles disappeared. They didn't exist. A quiet and permanent fascination fell over her. Life was a sheen, and there was music in it; joyful notes rang out in her heart, echoic, shimmering with the peal of bells. There was no quick shock of discovery. It seemed that she had known all along that what she thought was strong attraction was in reality love for this man of the sea.

The harbor ran strong. The wind and the sea came on, one falling away, the other racing on inland. Spray flew and struck her face. So did the rain. One was salty, the other wasn't. Bells rang in the storm. They were in her heart. Then they sounded far away. Something was drowning them out.

Geoffrey.

He held her in the palm of his hand. And the look in his eyes was one she could never forget. It was a picture of threat bound up in a false innocence that courts could not unmask. It was also a look at a man who would claim her and all that was rightfully hers, despite the knowledge that she didn't love him and never would.

She couldn't marry Geoffrey. Loving Gordon Redd as much as she did, it was impossible. But Redd was guilty, and even she had asked, "How guilty can a man get?" It was frightening. Then it was worse when she realized that he lay in Geoffrey's palm the same as she and her father, waiting to be crushed if Geoffrey went to Lancefield.

She turned her back on the harbor and walked toward the carriage. There she felt the voices of the wild wind and sea. They talked frankly, fiercely, and their message wasn't for the weak. But how strong was she, how strong could she be, knowing that on the wings of the sea and wind was a box of gold that cast its evil yellow influence on the lives of everyone about her?

There was no way out for her. She had come here with a strong reason in her mind for marrying Geoffrey. It was to save her father. She was leaving with another. It was to save Redd.

CHAPTER XII

On the following morning a high-masted schooner took advantage of calmer winds and braved the shoal water at Bradley Point for a run to Sydney.

Captain Untell grinned. He hadn't been dry for two full days. Water sloshed in his boots now, gurgling every time he leaned with the wheel. His small crew thought he was crazy. Maybe he was. But sail was made to belly in a wet wind the same as in a dry one. He had flown it and as a consequence had taken on tremendous seas during the last thirty-six hours. His crew was showing the strain. So was the running gear.

"Mr. March," he boomed forth, "we're in need of a hell of a lot of repair. But if you're set on holding the jib sheet flat aft in this slant of wind, we'll need a lot more."

Overhead the flying scud was shot with the palest blue. The weather should clear by the time he tied to the customs wharf and left for the Board of Trade. He was curious to know what had happened down in Melbourne.

He ran on with mainsail up. Inside the heads the breeze seemed to suck the schooner on into a vacuum. The harbor came on as he took the lessened chop of the seas at an increasing clip. The North Shore Ferry churned toward Circular Quay and the buildings sloping up the hill. The villas with their red tile roofs lay along the headlands of the bay farther on. He was back in Sydney after long weeks.

"Mr. March, you and Memo and King Coffin will bend on new sail the moment it arrives. The chandler I'll send is honest. The general idea is to be ready to hit the blue when the time comes, which might be tomorrow."

"Aye," the round-faced mate said. "I'm thankful that it ain't yesterday we're leavin'. I am that." Glancing up, he growled out, "The damn fore gaff-tops'l boom's loose again."

He limped off, looking up at the boom with growing resentment, then at Memo, the Malay, who was laying aloft to secure it. Untell's weathered face wrinkled up in a secret grin. These men and others, all of his old *Castlereagh* crew, all good sailors, didn't know they were in government service. He hoped they were well out to sea when they learned of it. They could understand vengeance, but the "damn gov'ment" was something else.

The sun broke out on his men busy making repairs when he left the schooner and moved toward the customhouse. With the formality of port entry behind him, he went to see Lancefield.

As they sat down, Lancefield said, "You've got a good nose, Captain. I've been wishing for you since yesterday." Before Untell could ask why, he shoved a newspaper across the table and said, "Read this."

Untell looked at big bold letters: VICTORIA INDICTS MEL-BOURNE BANKER.

He read on into the fine print: Tysbee was missing; the Bank of Melbourne was short by a staggering sum; the wealth was in gold bullion; there was a possibility of error in shipping, due to the prior deposit of gold ore by the Bendigo Mining Syndicate, which had been withdrawn clandestinely; therefore, considering the Sydney hearing, the case of Captain Redd, together with the disappearance of the head of the bank, guilt seemed a concluded fact.

"What about Mr. van Oren?" Untell asked.

"Same as I said before. We'll get him through Captain Redd and Tysbee. Which brings me around to a very important question. What did you find out on your voyage?"

Untell grinned. "First, that Redd is one devil of a sailorman. He handles a three-sticker like an expert. He gave me to Davy Jones once on a reef he put between us. But to cap it all, he taught me a lesson in wind and tide in Lombok Strait. That's where he shook me loose."

"He didn't like your company, eh? Why?"

"So you noticed that right off, counselor. Now when I tell you all that happened, I think you'll agree that Tysbee's aboard of him."

"Then you didn't see Tysbee?"

"Yes and no. The first brush came while we still ran in the Tasman. I wasn't sure, but I thought I saw something flash in the sun from Redd's poop and hit the water. I was sailing on toward it when Redd boxhauled his ship round. This forced me to alter my course and lose the bottle, if it was that."

"So you think somebody was trying to get a message off. Is that it?"

"What else? And since Redd didn't know I was aboard the *Upstart* until after the maneuver, he must have thought the same thing. Two and two adds up to something. From then on he was trying to run off from me. Why did he, if he didn't carry Tysbee?"

Lancefield arose and looked thoughtfully out over the harbor. Turning, he said, "I was hoping you could swear you saw Tysbee aboard the *Lady of Glasgow*. Sure you can't?" He searched Untell's face.

"Just the next best thing to it," Untell said.

"It dulls our teeth a little. I can't drag Van Oren before a grand jury." He asked, "How soon can you sail, Captain?"

"Perhaps by late tomorrow, if it's necessary."

"I think it will be. I'll bring you a warrant this evening."

"One or two?" Untell said quickly.

"Two. If you find Tysbee aboard Redd's ship, then arrest Redd. Otherwise, you'll keep up the chase. Tysbee is first. Remember that."

"You know, counselor, I was thinking about the decision of the naval court. Doesn't Tysbee's guilt make Redd liable to arrest at once? And wouldn't that force Mr. van Oren into court also?"

"Yes to both questions. But the decision hangs on a technicality. The clause, *if fraud or theft be established*, could mean conviction after trial. Don't think Van Oren's barristers fools. And without Tysbee in our hands, Sir George and Redd would have a chance of beating us."

"If that's the case, Redd could toss Tysbee over the side and nobody would be arrested."

Lancefield agreed. "However," he added, "if we could prove Tysbee was aboard, we'd have a case. But back to Redd. Don't arrest him until after you have Tysbee secure. Now one thing more:

"Suppose you make inquiries at big banks in the Dutch East Indies as well as in British ports. Find out if any deposits of gold have been made by Redd either to his credit or to the firm or to any individuals connected with Van Oren, Limited." Reaching for his hat, Lancefield said:

"Come along, Captain. We'll visit the newspapers. I've put them off long enough. While public sentiment is high, you can say you know where Tysbee is, that you'll go after him. That should cause Sir George to squirm a little. It might loosen him up a bit. I have another reason.

"I'll lay a pound to a shilling that before you hoist sail you'll listen to a handsome proposition from Van Oren, Limited."

Untell looked a little perplexed. He said, "So what, counselor?"

"It comes late. Too late, I hope. Until yesterday I planned on getting you back in Van Oren. But we don't need that now. The bull is out of the bush. And any proposition from Sir George will be one from a desperate man. Of course," he added, "I couldn't blame you for bettering yourself. You aren't making much working for me."

Untell said nothing. He was thinking of the small pay he was drawing.

2

Geoffrey left the office late that afternoon with the evening paper in his hand. He took a hansom to Muirkirk Hall.

The new development in the case, Untell's bold statement, which did nothing to turn the pointing finger of guilt away from Sir George, both pleased and irritated him. The greater the pressure from outside, the stronger his position became with Martha. It was hardly thinkable that she could refuse him; and it was unlikely that she would put him off after she saw Untell's boast in print. As for her father, he stood helplessly aside, a worried man. He had shown that much today. But his worries were only natural. Martha had not told him of the threat, he was sure; Sir George's behavior proved that.

He smiled: his magnificent bluff could not fail.

On the other hand, Untell was a threat to the game of gold and profit. He reasoned that if Untell had not chased Redd, the bars would have bought up the optioned properties before now. With the hunt about to commence anew, profits seemed to fade away. Then he began to think of a way of stopping Untell. The advantages were many. First, the chase would be interrupted; next, if Untell were to join the firm again, his past testimony before the court would automatically tear the props out from under the case Lancefield was patiently building.

The idea fascinated him. He spoke to the driver. "Take me to customs wharf at once."

Dusk was falling when he approached the *Upstart*. A sailor had just lit a lamp on deck. Up in the rigging another winked on. A chandler's hack was standing close and several men were transferring its contents to the schooner. He called the ship and asked to see Captain Untell, only to be advised that the captain could be found at Daragan's pub.

"I am here on a matter of utmost importance," Geoffrey said. "Send for him."

Untell arrived soon after that. He shook hands with Geoffrey and asked him below. When they were alone he said, "Now what's on your mind, Mr. Lipscomb-Grey?"

"The *Castlereagh*, Captain," Geoffrey said, not missing the other's alert glance. "She's been laid up in Dead Ship Lane, as you probably know, since you left her. We have use for her now."

"Go on."

"We need a trustworthy master."

"This port is full of captains without jobs," Untell replied.

"And were I interested in the scrapings of the harbor, I wouldn't be here, Captain."

"Maybe I don't like the way Van Oren operates. Have you ever thought of that?"

"I have. I must admit I can't blame you. However, I can assure you my ideas differ from those of Mr. van Oren. He doesn't want you, but I do. I'm running the shipping end of the business now along with everything else."

"So he doesn't want me, eh?" Untell looked at something he could appreciate. And it tickled him that Geoffrey, whom all respected for cold business dealings, had put Sir George in his place.

"No," Geoffrey said. "And I don't want Captain Redd. I'm sure we see eye to eye in other matters, Captain. However, we'll let them alone for the present. My job isn't an easy one, as you can see. The firm is losing prestige. I must build it back. And good captains can go a long way in helping me do this."

Untell agreed that Geoffrey had quite a task ahead of him. "But," he asked, "how do I know you aren't trying to save face by hiring me at a time like this? You know what it would mean if I went to work for you. All I said in court would react in favor of the firm."

"Which is why I'm prepared to pay you well," came the ready answer.

Geoffrey's frankness was at once surprising and appealing. Untell could not argue against the man's honesty, any more than he could turn a deaf ear to what came next:

"You can call the sum of five hundred pounds I'm offering for your decision a bribe if you like, Captain. Also a quarter share in the *Castlereagh*, which is twice what you held before."

Untell rubbed his jaw with open palm. The proposition was a good one. Only a fool would turn it down. Now was he a fool? He was asking that and more when Geoffrey said he'd be doing him a personal favor by accepting.

"I'll think it over."

Geoffrey was discerning. He struck Untell a friendly blow on the shoulder and asked for a drink. They were drinking when he said:

"You're wondering how I stand in all this, Captain. Well, you'd be surprised. As a businessman, my hands are tied. However, I reiterate, you'd be surprised."

"Maybe. Then maybe I'm beginning to understand your position. However, with Redd guilty and Tysbee on board his ship, what the devil are you going to do about it?"

"If such is true," Geoffrey smiled, hiding his contempt of the other's naïve intent to trap him, "then Van Oren, Limited, needs a thorough house cleaning. I trust my sentiments to your confidence, Captain." Arising, he said:

"Shall I expect your answer before noon tomorrow?"

"Aye," Untell replied, getting to his feet. "By noon, sir."

On deck, Geoffrey saw Lancefield. He advanced and offered a hand, saying, "I have just tried to hire your man from under you, sir."

"I expected as much. In fact, I warned Captain Untell of that."

Geoffrey replied suavely, "It seems we think alike on certain matters, Mr. Lancefield. First, I can use Captain Untell aboard the *Castlereagh*. Next, I am not blind to his value to the firm in refuting testimony in court. And beyond that, neither the captain nor I have any use for Captain Redd. My sincerity is not to be questioned. Perhaps I can prove it to you on some future occasion."

When the carriage left the wharf, Geoffrey saw Lancefield still standing where he had left him. Smiling, he ordered the driver to Muirkirk Hall.

3

Sir George looked up when Geoffrey entered. His first impulse was not a wise one, and he covered it by glancing away and saying in a voice of detachment:

"I'm glad you've come, Geoffrey."

"You've seen the papers, I guess," Geoffrey said. "Captain Untell says he knows where Tysbee is. He's going after him. And—heroically, he may do just that, with the cheers of Sydney ringing in his ears."

Van Oren said nothing. Geoffrey stood with one arm on the mantel. "I've been thinking, sir," he began. Van Oren looked up at him. "Thinking that you might consider the wisdom of approaching Captain Untell with an excellent proposition. Say, perhaps, five hundred pounds to make up his mind to take the *Castlereagh*. A quarter share in her, of course."

The idea took hold of Sir George. He saw at once the effect that Untell's reversed position would have on Sydney and the opposition. But he was thinking also of Geoffrey's threat to Martha, and he was asking himself how this man who could so excite and please him with his cleverness could be the same one who had denounced him to his daughter. However, they were one and the same. But in spite of it he rallied to Geoffrey. Sighing heavily, he glanced up and intercepted an odd look of innocence in Geoffrey's eyes.

"I am sure the idea has occurred to you, sir."

"Yes, of course," Van Oren said. It was expected of him. Geoffrey was accomplished at wheedling. He operated under a cover of outward respect and loyalty that carried one along with him. The gold scheme had started in just this manner.

"Then with your permission I shall visit Captain Untell." A moment of silence after Van Oren's consent, and Geoffrey said, "By the way, I ran into Lancefield this evening."

Sir George gave a realistic start. He settled back in his chair, wondering if he had given up a secret. As he looked up he knew that Geoffrey was asking that also. The brief glance between them was packed with tension that could explode instantly. It fell away as both men wanted it to when Geoffrey said:

"I gave him something to think about when I told him I was interested in hiring Untell for reasons that would shape opinion in the firm's favor. I said also we were in accord regarding Captain Redd. I went so far as to offer to prove it at some time in the future."

"Why did you do that?"

"A subtle reminder of a man's guilt. Redd's."

"Yes, I guess so." Sir George breathed heavily. "I wish I had your ability to play fox and hounds with this thing hanging over our heads. But I haven't. I'm beginning to wish we had taken Milton's advice and returned the gold."

He saw Geoffrey stiffen. And then for the first time in their long association he heard words that sounded disrespectful and loaded with threat; that revealed Geoffrey for what he was:

"You're fast becoming another Tysbee, aren't you?"

Van Oren was getting up. His face was red with anger and his eyes thinned under the flow of it. He was about to open his mouth against his better judgment, about to uncover Geoffrey, when the latter laughed disarmingly and said:

"Begging your pardon, sir, but you needed a shock. I regret it had to come from——" He paused, looking beyond Van Oren, who heard Martha say:

"Always plotting, aren't you?" She came to them, laughing and teasing. Geoffrey responded as though all were peaceful and serene. Then she said:

"Father, can you spare Geoffrey?"

"I can," he said emphatically. He wondered at his own courage as he saw them walk away.

Slowly he drew his ravaged glance back when they disappeared. As though he had no control over the direction of his gaze, he was staring at an old rifle in a case. A friend had given it to him. Hyderabad Regiment. Loaded and oiled. The thing held him in a state of awful fascination as he walked toward it, sweating and feeling the pounding of blood at his neck and temples. The urge was on him. He trembled under it, thrilling to it, seeing a way out of trouble. There was nothing against it that made sense. The touch of cold metal was good. He checked the load and felt of the firing pin. Martha could go to England, away from all of it. Gold and trouble. Trouble and gold. Gold and Geoffrey. Trouble and Geoffrey. He was becoming mad with it, and he was looking for excuses: alibis and explanations that might absolve him of crime and at the same time point to Geoffrey's guilt. Geoffrey, Redd, and Milton Tysbee.

He took the gun and moved in a trance toward the drawing room. They were not there. He saw them on the terrace inside the glassed-in section. A man had a right to kill to protect his own daughter. The gun felt good in his hands. He took sight and moved closer, thumbed the hammer and looked around. Crippen was nowhere about. The maids were in the kitchen and upstairs.

There was no hurry, now that he was committed to it. He would listen. He did. Martha was asking if Geoffrey could save her father from prison. Geoffrey said he could——

"He's been almost a father to me, Martha. I'm sure you realize how much——"

Sir George wanted to scream out at him, to call him a liar and let him look down the barrel of the rifle before it spat fire and justice. But Martha was talking about something else. And with such ease and sincerity:

"I was very upset the other night, Geoffrey. Hearing enough to know that Father was involved made me lose my senses. Don't blame me for breaking our engagement."

"I understand, Martha."

"And I understand you, Geoffrey. You were driven out of the bounds of reason by my decision. Else you wouldn't have threatened to go to Mr. Lancefield. You were bluffing, weren't you?"

"I was trying to hold on to you, Martha. I'm not going to lose you. Remember that."

She laughed. "You wouldn't really go that far! Honest, now, would you?"

"If necessary, yes."

She arose and walked away from him. Whirling, she said, "Then you must love me very much."

She sounded pleased, Sir George thought. What kind of game was this? He knew her hurt and he could almost feel the pulse-beat of her loathing for Geoffrey. It was his own daughter who was fighting back with weapons of her sex that confused a man. She was bearing the brunt, not he, the father. The itch to raise the gun and fire was put down as Geoffrey said he would spare nothing or no one that tried to keep her from him.

She looked him squarely in the eye and said, "I couldn't do better, then. I have more than respect for a man of purpose. It's good to see you fighting for me, Geoffrey. You didn't do that before."

"I didn't find it necessary," he replied.

"I like it. And I'll marry you, Geoffrey."

He stood, all of him in the gun sight, and replied, "You must know how happy this makes me." He held out his arms and she walked into them. His head tipped to hers and they stood in a long embrace. Out of it, she said with an almost passionate eagerness:

"Let's not put it off, Geoffrey."

"But you spoke once of a big affair. A church wedding with a great reception and——"

Her finger touched his lips. "And you said the other night I would marry you sooner than I intended. Do I have my way—and your way?"

"Of course, my dear." His hands drew her to him again. Looking down into her upturned face, he said, "For a woman like you, anything. I'm eager also."

"Then we'll make it a quiet wedding. Just you and Father and I. Tomorrow evening."

"Tomorrow?" he said, somewhat surprised.

"Yes." She brightened with a look of sudden discovery. "Aboard the *Vega*, Geoffrey! Father can go ashore after the wedding. You and I won't."

A deep intensity came into her eyes. It held Geoffrey. Her hands moving up to his neck, and the fullness of her mouth, loose and moist before his hungry eyes, aroused him. He fell to them greedily, and she clung to him.

It was a picture of desire and anticipation to Sir George. An impossible picture. But he was seeing it with his very eyes. Even then it was a confounding thing. If Martha had intended to buy Geoffrey's silence with her all, why had she insisted on marriage, especially an early one? Then he thought he had the answer——

Her honor. Honor to the last ditch.

Forgetting the gun in his hands, Van Oren stared straight ahead, seeing nothing, hearing nothing, as he lapsed into troubled thought. When he emerged from the trance, Geoffrey was taking his leave. He did not come toward the drawing room, but disappeared into the night out of the terrace door. Glancing at the rifle, he was suddenly alert. It would be better to do it outside. He was taut and ready and he had taken a step toward the hallway when a long, stifled sob arrested him. He looked at Martha.

Her hands covered her face as she stood there shaking under the burden of trouble and tears.

George van Oren felt helpless even as a pity he had never known before fell over him. He wanted to go to her and absorb all of her troubles. It wasn't that easy, he realized. It was too late for that, even as it was too late to kill Geoffrey tonight.

He turned away with the rifle in his hand and made his way back to the library like the beaten man he was.

CHAPTER XIII

Martha was up with the dawn. Morning, with its flush of colors in the sky and over the wine-colored harbor, stirred up hopes. The quiet lifting of day was always like that. And then it was gone; a movement below broke the spell.

Her father walked back and forth beneath her window. He looked tired and aged. A wan smile broke the dull repose of his face as she called out to him:

"Muffins and tea, Father?"

"I've been waiting for you to get up, child."

"Why?" She could smile at him now.

"I've been thinking," he said.

"So have I," she replied. "I'll be down soon."

She met him at the breakfast table dressed to go out. Frowning out his puzzlement, he restrained a question and nibbled slowly at his food. At last he said:

"I won't let you do it."

"What?" she asked.

"I listened to you and Geoffrey last night—over the sight of the old rifle from the library. I was ready to do it, Martha. I suppose I would have if you hadn't thrown me off the track by insisting on an early marriage."

She was staring at him with horror in her eyes. "You! You, Father? Kill Geoffrey?"

"Yes. Then he was leaving, the wrong way. And you were sobbing." He brought a fist down hard on the table. "I'll do it yet! I won't let you sacrifice yourself!"

"Well!" she said, staring at him as though she had never seen him before. "Am I to believe that you would do such a thing to save me? Or is it to save yourself from Geoffrey?"

"I don't matter any more. Not a damn bit do I matter. I'm ready to throw myself on the mercy of the courts."

"This is very sudden, isn't it? After all, I have promised Geoffrey. And when I marry him, can he do anything but help you?"

"I don't want his help and I don't want him in my family. In fact, I don't want to lay eyes on him again, ever."

She arched her brow and favored him with a dubious glance and smile. "My, but you sound sincere. I almost believe you." She added, "But I don't."

Blinking his eyes in astonishment, he forced a defensive silence. He could understand her distrust of him, but what he couldn't understand was her refusal to believe him now. It irritated and disconcerted him. And now she was talking, saying things with a reckless and gallant courage that amazed him:

"Getting rid of Geoffrey isn't the answer to your problems, Father. Crime added to crime could only make matters worse. You have one choice, and that's the one I made. So you'll abide by it."

"Martha, don't go through with it."

He was pleading with her. She saw deep honesty in his eyes, that and a willingness to take whatever came—courts, prison, and disgrace—in preference to her sacrifice. True values were adjusting themselves in his heart and mind. A little late, but better than never, she was thinking. He tugged at her heartstrings and threatened her composure. But she was glad, glad enough to cry. Lowering her eyes and toying with her food, she fought against her rising emotions. She must not break now; there was too much to do today. She steadied herself and said:

"Father, you must do as I say. It is very important. After today you may do as you please. But give me today."

"What are you talking about?"

"Just do it my way. Go to the office and act perfectly natural. Don't lose your head. Geoffrey must not know you are acquainted with his threat. Can I count on you?"

"You're making riddles. Why should I play the fool any longer? I feel like breaking my chains."

"You've worn them a long time," she said sternly. "One more day won't hurt you."

"Not if I know why. What are you up to?"

"Wait and see. But do as I say."

She left him a little later. Sure that her puzzling behavior would offset and lessen his real worries, she stepped into the carriage and asked Tobias to drive to the Board of Trade.

What she felt was a little frightening. The adventure she was planning seemed nothing short of a gamble for all or nothing. It could be all for nothing. Confidence asserted itself and with it waves of excitement came on and fell away. A maze of details confronted her. And two important meetings lay ahead; perhaps three, if she decided to visit Geoffrey.

The carriage wound its way east down the slopes and into

the morning traffic of steam tramcars and carriages and hacks. A pearl-blue sky lay over the harbor. A gladness sang in her heart as she thought of her father who put aside self for her. Captain Redd was with her, encouraging her. A drifting cloud overhead seemed to smile down at her, saying she might find an antidote for an evil gold scheme if she remained calm and steadfast. She thought she could. The big ordeal was behind her; the fact that she had given her lips to Geoffrey last evening, convincingly, seemed to make all the rest look easy.

As the carriage stopped before a large building she cautioned herself against overconfidence. She must be alert and collected. A little nervous, she entered the building and asked to see Mr. Lancefield. Her heart was pounding as the clerk led the way to a door. "Steady," she said over and over. And out of nowhere she heard inside her the voice of Gordon Redd: "Easy as you go, Martha." Then the door opened and she looked into the eyes of the man who was determined to send her father and Redd to prison.

Only when the door was closed and they were alone did she tell him who she was. His surprise was genuine; he sat back in his chair and stared at her. She used the interval of silence to collect her wits.

"Mr. Lancefield," she began, "I will come to the point. I am here to trade with you."

He contained his second surprise behind a look that said he wasn't used to dealing with such a decisive woman. As if considering a reply with unusual carefulness, he said, "I'm naturally wondering what you are talking about, Miss van Oren."

"I think you know," she said unwaveringly. He nodded wisely and took his time in saying:

"Just who sent you here?"

"No one."

"The timing is almost too perfect, considering that not thirty minutes have passed since Captain Untell sent this message to Mr. Lipscomb-Grey. I'm sure you are familiar with the contents."

"No. I came here from Muirkirk Hall. And I know nothing of any business dealings between Captain Untell and Geoffrey. It it hardly conceivable that Geoffrey would discuss such matters with me, especially in view of our forthcoming marriage this evening."

"This evening?" he said. "I can see your point there. Perhaps it's a mere coincidence after all. However, you look curious, so I'll tell you about it.

"Last evening he held a fine proposition up before Captain Untell. He wanted him back in the firm. Untell's reply is this: 'Not interested at any price.' " He searched her face before saying, "Sorry, miss, but in this business everyone is a suspect. I believe you, however, so proceed from there."

Her glance raised to him briefly and slid away. There was much she didn't know. "Why did Geoffrey want him back in the firm?" she asked on impulse. With Lancefield's reply, she nodded significantly; she was almost sure Geoffrey's threat was a bluff. But as long as doubt existed she could not call his hand.

"Mr. Lancefield, what I am doing is my secret. And yours. I am here out of loyalty to my father and the man I love, and I hope to serve the best interests of all concerned. That is my sole reason for visiting you.

"It seems that Mr. Tysbee's guilt casts a reflection on my name. There is talk. Some think Father is guilty, that he will be arrested."

"What do you think, or know about it, Miss van Oren?"

"I know you are looking for Captain Redd, sir."

"How do you know that?"

"Captain Redd wrote that Captain Untell chased him."

A light frown creased his brow. "Yes, because we think—are almost sure—he carries Mr. Tysbee aboard the *Lady of Glasgow.*"

"I think a lot of Captain Redd," she said, causing him to glance up sharply. Pausing for effect, she entered into her trading proposition with:

"I know where he is. You don't."

He leaned forward. "Continue, please."

"I'm offering to go after him and bring him back."

"Just tell us where he is, Miss van Oren."

She expressed her opinion of him with a smile and said, "I'll bring him to you under one condition."

"Careful," he warned. "Don't forget that justice is an inviolate ideal and tradition with us here."

"And it must be with me, sir. Else I would not propose to put Captain Redd on the stand before you again."

"Are you admitting his guilt?" he said.

"I am admitting nothing," she replied sharply. "Furthermore, I resent your cross-examining me at every turn."

"My apologies," he said, not altogether hiding his admiration for her courage. "Proceed. You were about to name the condition."

"Yes. It is this: if my father and Captain Redd are guilty, you must promise to use your influence for leniency in their behalf."

He appeared to consider this with annoyance. "Listen," he said. "If they are guilty—and I believe they are—I want them to pay in full. And as for Captain Redd, we have ways of finding him."

She got to her feet. "Of course. But I need not remind you that I can find him a lot quicker. Thanks for your time, sir."

"One moment, please," he said, arising. When she turned to him again, he placed a question: "When would you go after him—today, next week, or——"

"Sorry, Mr. Lancefield. I'm saying nothing that would cause you to send Captain Untell trailing after me. You've heard my proposition in full."

"It's—well, rather unusual, Miss van Oren."

"But worth considering," she added quickly.

He ran long fingers through his hair and grimaced. Suddenly he raised his glance and said, "Yes, it's worthy of consideration." He added, "And acceptance."

She looked deep into his eyes and said, "I am honest, Mr. Lancefield. And I'm sure you are. But I prefer a complete understanding between us. Supposing you find Captain Redd first, which won't be my fault, will you feel that you owe me nothing in the way of help?"

"I've made a trade," he said.

Still holding his glance, she offered her hand.

He watched her go, and from his window he saw her hire a launch. It moved slowly out into the harbor and pointed toward the schooner *Vega*. Temptation assailed him; sure that she would sail after Redd aboard that craft, he was thinking how easy it would be to order Untell to follow her. He turned his back on it. He would play it fair with this remarkable woman.

2

Martha studied the *Vega* through a sailor's eye from bowsprit to overhang. She was thinking of her few trips to sea aboard the vessel. Several times in the past she had asked her father to paint the hull white and fit her out like a seagoing yacht. Now she was glad he had refused her this. The dull gray-black hull and ordinary deck would prove less conspicuous at sea. She had required no promise of Lancefield to send Captain Untell on his way ahead of her and not behind her.

A hint of a smile played on her face as she saw Captain Grimble on deck. Big, jolly, and white-headed, he had retired from a Liverpool square-rigger some fifteen years earlier. A mariner's mariner, he was called, though all who knew him well called him Cap'n Happen-so because he used the expression so often.

As the boat drew near, she saw him raise his hand. She waved back. Closer, he boomed forth, "Welcome, Miss Martha. Welcome."

On deck, she took his gnarled hand and said, "How old do you feel today, Cap'n Happen-so?"

"With you aboard, lass, not a day over forty. Though me blood calls for the sea. Now it don't just happen so ye're thinking the same way, eh?"

"Yes." She walked aft slowly. He fell into step beside her.

"This talk, lass. Don't let it broach ye to. Says I, Sir George is got no more to do with that scandalous proposition than I. And Captain Redd wouldn't be flying the pennant over his noggin if he was guilty."

She averted her face. Such faith was touching, especially when it collided with absolute guilt. She wondered how the honorable old seaman would react to the truth. Then she looked at him, thinking of the important part he must unwittingly play in all this. It was almost as if she were placing her entire future in his hands. But she must approach him carefully and with more enthusiasm than she exhibited now.

"I still want to go to sea, Cap'n Happen-so."

"Aye, the rolling blue calls me, lass. Spray that stings a face and a deck rolling."

"But you and Father are just in from Melbourne. However, I know how you must feel. That's how I feel also, except I have a purpose in mind. So"—she turned a full smile on him—"let's talk about a voyage."

"Ready," he said. "Just have Sir George give the order and I'll make ready."

"I'm talking for Father," she said. "He is anxious to put out soon."

"Eh? Right away? Ye're spitting in the wind."

"How soon can you put to sea on a long voyage? Say to Singapore?"

"Hold fast, girl! Now, water, vittles, grog, and a spry quartermaster, not to say I need to bend on a deepwater forestays'l. Three days from now, come the hour. Soon enough?"

"No, Cap'n," she said with a determined shake of her head. She caught at one of his red ears and drew it down for the one word she whispered.

"No!" he protested. "Can't be done. Impossible, lass. Unpractical and unreasonable, I says. Happens so ye forget that a ship's like a woman, demanding. No, Miss Martha, I can't put to sea tonight."

"Very well," she said, pretending hurt. "I suppose I'll have to postpone my wedding."

"Wedding! You?"

She nodded. "Geoffrey and I."

He rubbed his white stubble and wrinkled up his face. "Well, lass, it appears I'm forced to alter my forecast." Glancing at his watch, he said, "But by the sacred cow of Ceylon, I'll have to show lively."

"Have you ever married a couple at sea?"

"Aye. Happens so I joined the—— But look here, girl, you mean I'm to——"

"Perform the marriage ceremony at eight this evening," she said.

"Aye," he replied, looking from her to the deck, then up at the mainmast and on aft. "Aye, lass."

"Thank you, Cap'n. I knew you'd do it for me. Now, one thing more. Listen carefully, and remember this is a secret between us. What you tell the crew is your problem, but see that it goes off well."

He listened, appearing more surprised as she disclosed what she had in mind for him that evening. When she looked at him and asked if he could do it, he blew out his cheeks and nodded assent. Then he asked why she wanted it that way.

"You'll find out soon enough, Cap'n. Now dust off your Bible and review the marriage ceremony. I'll see you before sundown this evening."

She left him standing there with a perplexed look on his face and an almost impossible task to perform. When the launch touched shore, she looked back at the long *Vega* and made a wish that nothing should deter old Captain Grimble. Then her gaze swept the harbor and quays. It fell on a sleek craft, the *Upstart.*

"The enemy," she said to herself before walking to the carriage.

There was still much to do. She decided not to visit Geoffrey. Pretense wasn't easy. Better that she return to Muirkirk and fill a trunk with clothes and things necessary for a long voyage.

3

The sun was over the Great Dividing Range, the hub of a vast half-hidden sunburst. The sky overhead was shot with purples and pinks which fell over the harbor. A fine sailing breeze came in out of the south-southeast.

Martha looked at her father by her side in the boat. He had just said again, "You can't go through with it," and she had placed a reassuring hand over his and reminded him that this was her day, all of it. But she knew his mood was black, that he felt the tight grip of helplessness. George van Oren wasn't used to that.

The *Vega* sat still and quiet, immune to it all. She caught the sunset colors and held them with what seemed a lazy indifference. She was beautifully disguised, Martha thought. There was a poised vigilance about her bows and masts and sleeping booms. The schooner seemed so sure of herself.

Martha wasn't. Her calm was giving way to nervousness and incertitude. There was no one to lean upon. She felt all alone and very insecure. She pulled herself together, afraid she might fall completely apart. It would all be over in a few hours.

Her father squirmed, drawing her glance. Small ridges of muscle tightened along his jaw and his hands were shaking. He said, looking straight ahead, "Do you expect me to hand you over to him without a word?"

"Yes," she replied calmly. "I demand it."

He shook his head in despair and stared at the *Vega's* stern. The Jacob's ladder was falling, and Captain Grimble and two sailors stood by to help the owner and his daughter aboard. The water was lifting up with an evening chop. It popped at the boat's sides.

"I didn't tell old Happen-so about it," he said. "Was I supposed to?"

"I've made all arrangements."

"Martha, you've left nothing undone. I'm half inclined to believe you're in love with the scoundrel."

"It would be easier that way," she replied.

The boat sculled to a stop and she was moving up the ladder. On deck she met Captain Grimble's glance and winked an eye at him. He returned it with a glint of pride in his face.

"All's well, lass," he said. "And ye'll be pleased to know Mr. Geoffrey sent enough flowers to fill the saloon."

"Splendid," she smiled. "Now let's go see them, Cap'n. It's time to splice the main brace, don't you think?"

"Aye," he replied, taking a squint at the last thin slice of the sun. "I'll hoist a stout drink to your happiness."

Sir George glared at them as though both were crazy and moved off to the saloon. Martha took the captain's hand and held on to it as they walked after her father. The old man, in some manner of a miracle, bolstered her courage. She knew him then as a great person who shed experience and goodness. He was a strong man upon whom she could lean if only for that intangible something she needed more than anything else in the world. Perhaps it was because he was an ally, or it could be that he represented, somehow, the better qualities in Captain Redd.

Her father gulped one drink after another. He was fast getting morbidly drunk. Then Geoffrey arrived.

This was the time she dreaded most of all. She met him with a spontaneous smile and accepted his formal kiss with a circumspect glance at her father. Sir George got to his feet shaking with rage. She walked toward him, flashing warnings with her eyes even as she said:

"Geoffrey, the flowers are beautiful. Did you buy out Sydney?"

"The occasion deserves more," he replied, taking in her back and waist with a bold look. He brought her around fast when he said, "You seem very unhappy, Sir George."

"It's worry, Geoffrey," she said hurriedly. "About the things the newspapers are saying."

She drew his brief smile, though he was examining her father sharply the next moment. Tension mounted. A shiver of dread ran through her as Geoffrey said to Sir George:

"Is that what's troubling you?"

"No." His eyes blazed wrath at Geoffrey, who looked suspiciously from him to Martha and said:

"Something is deucedly odd here."

"Oh, Geoffrey," she scolded. "Please!"

But he was very alert. A cold light, like a hint of discovery and anger, flickered across his eyes. A humorless smile formed on his face and clung there threateningly. He drew Martha aside and asked in low tones if she had told of his threat.

"Geoffrey!" she replied with a hopeless smile and gesture. "Do you think he would allow our marriage if he knew?"

"Yes," he said quickly.

She was sure the acute fear that crawled up her spine was visible in her face. His changing expression proved it. Then he seemed to be laughing at her. He relaxed into an outward symbol of his calm self, though lightning still played behind his eyes. She breathed out a silent prayer of thanks when Captain Grimble entered the saloon with a large worn Bible.

Her darting look swept her father's stunned face and came to

rest on Geoffrey. He was enjoying it, gloating. It made little difference now that he knew all; it was his moment. His face said as
much. He was not marrying her. He had never intended to do
more than marry Van Oren, Limited, through her.

She put down the stubborn anger welling up strong and deep
and turned her best face upon Geoffrey. "I'm ready," she said.

He placed her arm through his and stood erect. Captain Grimble held his Bible up when the mate entered with hat in hand to
witness the ceremony. Sir George remained still in his chair, as
though he were refusing a walk to the gallows.

"Sir," Grimble said apologetically, "I'm forced to ask ye to
stand."

Martha said more with her stern look. He got to his feet reluctantly and turned a hostile look on Geoffrey.

"Now, Mr. Smythe," Grimble said to the mate, "ye'll sing the
hymn I selected."

As the bass voice lifted and quivered unsteadily, Martha sensed
a trembling motion under her feet. Somewhere in the undertones
she detected the sounds of muffled activity. Then a smooth gliding energy seemed to flow gently, quietly, under the long sleek
hull. Perhaps she imagined it. She didn't dare intercept old Happen-so's glance that would tell her it was or wasn't real. A quick
heeling of the ship assured her it was; it also warned Geoffrey and
her father, both of whom started and peered at the deadlighted
ports and at Captain Grimble.

He raised a hand for quiet and smiled at Geoffrey and Sir
George as his mouth formed a word neither understood but
which assured them everything was as it should be.

The moment's tenseness she felt in Geoffrey was gone. He felt
secure again, and she knew he was anxious to get the wedding
over with. Out of it he would be master of Van Oren, Limited,
with no one to dispute his authority.

The mate's voice was grating out the last words and notes. A
silence fell over the saloon, broken by Sir George, who asked
where they were going.

"Superstition, sir," Captain Grimble replied. "I don't hold faith
in a ship wedding without a moving keel." With that, he cleared
his throat, bent over the opened Bible, and began to read.

He took his time. Lifting his eyes frequently, he seemed more interested in the sounds of the running schooner than the verses of Scripture. Martha listened to the wind in the sails. She wondered if the schooner was passing Circular Quay. Then she was beset with all sorts of fears: had old Happen-so cleared his papers for a run to sea; how could he have done so without Geoffrey learning of it? She was trembling. Geoffrey felt it and took her hand in his.

A tug whistled over the stern and loud voices split the night over the harbor. The ship heeled to port, righted herself, and rocked with a straining of her gear. One could feel the big mainsail hit the wind. The ship lurched forward.

"Mr. Smythe," the old man said, leaving a portion of a verse hanging in mid-air, "ye'll conn the ship now. Send the stoord in to witness."

He snapped the Bible shut and said he'd wait for the "stoord" before tying the knot. The man came at last. Captain Grimble took a worn yellow paper from the Bible and squinted at it, saying more to himself:

"The woman's on the man's portside. All's well." His voice lifted and he began, "We are assembled here in the presence of God, to join this man and this woman in marriage . . ." He read on. Next he cleared his throat noisily and said:

"Wilt thou, Geoffrey, have this woman to be thy wife, pledging thy troth to her, in all love and honor, in all faith and tenderness, and all such as it says here?"

"I will," Geoffrey said.

"Now—Martha, wilt thou have this man to be thy husband, and do ye—thou—pledge thy troth to him . . . ?"

She listened, taut all over, looking ahead with unfocused eyes, seeing the agonized expression on her father's face. Captain Grimble was waiting for her reply. He said:

"Wilt thou?"

The time had come. She said as calmly as her emotions would allow, "I will not."

Captain Grimble dropped his Bible. George van Oren stood with mouth open. Geoffrey appeared not to have heard. When his face turned slowly to her, she was disengaging her arm, saying with all the contempt she could muster:

"Did you really think you could force me to marry you, Geoffrey?"

Behind his surprise, she saw unbelief and shock, like nothing he had ever met up with before. It was slowly replaced by a thin smile of acceptance and a look of outrage, so cool and controlled that it was like judgment being passed on her. Then he opened his mouth and put it to words:

"I'll visit Lancefield tonight, Martha."

"Oh no, Geoffrey. Not tonight or any night soon. We're clearing the heads for the sea. You're silenced, Geoffrey." She laughed. "Kidnaped."

He took a step toward her. Sir George caught his arm and jerked him back. Grimble came to his senses and stepped in front of Geoffrey, who was saying:

"You can't get away with it. You've got to touch in somewhere. And when you do——"

Martha interrupted him. "And when we do, it will be at the Island of Gold. That's where we're going, Geoffrey—to see Captain Redd."

Book four

[DESOLATE HORIZONS

. . . Then a roar of breakers smashing on coral barriers and a blood-red sea of silk at the edge of the world. . . .

CHAPTER XIV

The *Lady of Glasgow* entered the strait from the east and blew on toward Singapore Road. Away over the port bow a sunset squall from Sumatra grew in size as it raced toward a junction with the ship.

Captain Redd looked at his watch. He wanted to splash anchor in the inner roads before the quick night fell. He was weary of the sea after the long voyage from Batavia. Adverse winds and storms had forced him off his course. What had been a run of days had required weeks. It was a part of sail, however, and a sailing master accepted it as such. It was what was happening in Australia that confounded Redd. He expected the worst.

Untell could be in Sydney or Singapore, or, in the lapse of time between Lombok Strait and now, he could have sailed to Sydney and back.

The squall roared closer and Redd ordered it put over the port quarter. The *Lady* took the deluge and watched it hiss on toward the mouth of the Johore River. Decks steamed and masts and yards glistened in the falling equatorial sun.

Over toward Loemba Island a three-masted junk stood like a

dragonfly. Then she turned her broadside and the huge straw sails took on a sunset gold, then scarlet. Colors ran out fast. The sun disappeared as though the props were suddenly jerked out from under it, and darkness fell with no interval of twilight.

The *Lady's* running lights were lit. Some sail came in, and she crept on toward the lights of Singapore through the increasing traffic.

Redd called the second: the time had come to put Mr. Tysbee down where he'd be hard to find. Walking across deck, he said to Mr. Hyde, "There may come a time when we'll be unable to hide our passenger from a British warrant."

"Aye," Mr. Hyde said. "He's a Jonah. And so is the gold."

Redd agreed in silence. The gold bars had caused more than just mental trouble. In heavy weather the ship had shown a tendency to yaw. She had never done this before. The helmsmen complained. Even in easier seas she acted stubborn. Redd took her wheel one day and spoked it for two hours before the cause entered his mind. Too much weight at her stern might begin with the gold bars. Upon discovering that the weight had shifted to port, he ordered the carpenter to fashion small boxes. The idea was to equalize the weight over the ship. With the aid of his mates he placed the bars between-decks, in dunnage and in the bilge. As a result, the *Lady* ceased to yaw.

Redd thought of what the gold stood for now and said, "We'll get rid of the gold as soon as we drop Mr. Tysbee."

The north shore opened up gradually. Anchor lights hovered over the water like fireflies at rest. The ship eased in and dropped her anchor. Redd had business ashore. After warning his mates to post a strong anchor watch and allow no one on board, he took a sampan to the city.

In the hours before midnight he visited the pubs, in search of news from Australia. Learning nothing new, he made his way to a European club, where he found newspapers from all parts of the Empire. Only one was of recent issue.

He read of the Melbourne indictment of Tysbee. The news came as no surprise. It merely confirmed all he had expected. Now Untell would hunt them down with warrants in his hands.

He took a ricksha and called on the firm's Singapore manager with a demand that the Batavia cargo leave his ship before morning. At the Van Oren offices Redd was handed a sealed pouch from Sydney.

It was nearing four in the morning when Redd left the noise of slings, lightermen, and his own crew discharging cargo over side and went below. He broke the seal on the pouch and looked at a message. It was from Geoffrey:

In a matter of urgency I find you extremely unreliable. You know the game and the stakes. To date the properties contracted for are of enormous value. Because of your dilatory action, options are expiring and the firm's credit is impaired. To make matters worse, you evade the main issue with talk of a windfall at some remote island. This is absurd. You may consider this an order to put the foolish idea out of your mind at once and proceed to the banks of Singapore, Hong Kong, Batavia, and Soerabaja, where you will deposit bullion to the credit of the firm.

Your failure to comply with this order can only result in a tremendous loss of money. And if you persist in going against the best interests of all concerned, even for reasons you may deem necessary, I must warn that you will be left to shift for yourself in the matter of Mr. Tysbee, who will be hunted cargo by the time this reaches you.

Redd could not take his eyes off the message. He could understand how Geoffrey and Sir George felt. They were spotting the gold for spending as agreed upon. It was his fortune as much as theirs, and he had entered into the scheme. Only he had failed. Perhaps Geoffrey was right.

However, Geoffrey didn't have Tysbee chained to his neck. He carried the thought another step: Geoffrey showed no concern whatever for his position; furthermore, he flung a threat as though he were entirely innocent.

"Maybe he is," Redd thought aloud. Perhaps he had made a noteworthy discovery. He was almost sure of it: Geoffrey and Sir George meant to remain innocent, no matter what happened. If the situation became untenable, they could point a finger at him, at Tysbee the fugitive, and use the power at their command to shift all blame from themselves. They could do that. Worse, they would do it. Their every move in the past seemed to prove this.

Geoffrey's letter was crumpled in his hand. About to toss it through the open port, he thought better of it.

2

The sun was pushing up the eastern sky when the last lighter moved away from the *Lady*. Redd looked at his tired officers and crew. These men expected, wanted, and had earned shore leave. He didn't relish the idea of telling them they wouldn't get it here. He was ready and anxious to drive hard for the Island of Gold. Tysbee was extra cargo today over yesterday; in the space of hours he had changed from a nominal threat to a positive one.

But his men were staring at the city with longing in their faces.

It was his reluctance to issue the order for sail that caused him to turn aft and peer out over the harbor. Among the ships painted in the first light of morning, his glance fell on two masts moving slowly between a long bark and a rusty steamer. They looked familiar. As they eased out into the open, he recognized the craft. With an inward start, he looked closer.

The *Upstart* flew a second flag. The harbor police were aboard her, and she was now pointing toward the *Lady*.

"Mr. Hyde! All hands! Alert!" he cried.

He had perhaps ten minutes in which to prepare for a thorough search of the ship. Tysbee was a real threat now, the key to trouble. Failure to hide him spelled the end of fortunes and reputations, among them his own. In the press of the moment he had a dour loyalty to Sir George and Martha, even Geoffrey. A small wave of anger ran loose in him as he considered Geoffrey's demands against the situation that confronted him. "Damn Geoffrey," he said, turning to Mr. Burk.

The *Upstart* came on menacingly, quietly. Ships in the road seemed asleep as Redd moved down the afterhatch with Mr. Burk. While Mr. Hyde moved forward of the ship, reminding each hand of the value of silence, the sailmaker and his mate labored frantically over a length of sailcloth. Pelican Joe brought up a long plank which the carpenter sawed in half. Two sailors ran with the planks to the starboard rail as Mr. Burk passed up three boxes of bars from the hold.

Below, Redd came upon Tysbee and said, "Sorry, mister, but it's come."

There was nothing but purpose in Redd's face. In his hand was a long rag. A little frightened, Tysbee asked, "What, Captain? What are you up to?"

"Captain Untell and the police are not four lengths astern. They have a warrant for your arrest. Mine also, I imagine. Melbourne wants to send you to prison, mister."

As Tysbee opened his mouth to speak, Redd stepped in and forced rags into his mouth. When he was gagged securely, Dublin Jack and the cook trussed him to a board. Then Redd sang out:

"Deck alert! Hoist away!"

Tysbee seemed to shoot up to the opening. When Redd reached the deck two hands were entering the sail locker with him, the sailmaker close on their heels. Taking sight on the *Upstart*, now moving cautiously around the stern for a portside approach, Redd looked at Mr. Burk and said:

"See that he's sewn up tight and weighted with a few of the bars. You might place a half dozen links of anchor chain at his feet to make it look real. Then fetch him to the bier."

On the starboard side, boxes and barrels were being placed in position. Mr. Hyde handed Redd a Bible and asked if he was ready to assemble the hands. Redd waited out a long moment.

"Now," he said. "Do it quietly."

The *Upstart's* anchor cable ran out with a rattle. As the splash sounded, six men emerged from the sail locker with a shrouded figure. It was placed on the bier of planks, one end on the boxes and barrels, the other on the starboard rail amidships.

Redd looked into the faces of his men and said, "Doff your caps, men." He removed his own cap and glanced at the still figure. "Men, we're here to bury a good sailor. His name is Turner. Jim Turner. Remember that. He looks like Mr. Burk. Turner died when he fell from the royal yard and struck his head against the forehatch—yesterday; at six bells on the first watch."

He looked into the eyes of every sailor without any break in the serious repose of his face. They blinked eyes and shifted from one foot to the other, some frowning and coughing lightly to cover telltale signs of humor. This sort of thing tickled them.

The *Upstart* was hailing the *Lady*. No answer forthcoming, Untell and several men scrambled up to her deck.

Redd was reading the burial service when they appeared across deck and stared in surprise. Raising his head in feigned astonishment and displeasure, he looked from visitors to the shrouded figure covered with the British ensign.

"Go ahead," Untell ordered. "We're in no hurry."

Redd appeared to consider this before saying to his men, "Jim Turner can wait, lads. He'll be dead a long time." Turning to Untell, he said, "What brings you aboard, Captain?"

"This." He produced a warrant which Redd scanned unhurriedly.

"Milton Tysbee." Redd laughed. "Aren't you a few thousand miles off your course?"

For answer Untell ordered the harbor police to begin the search.

Redd looked on as they removed hatch covers and went down into the holds. Aware that they were experienced and wise in the ways of their profession, he felt a twinge of uneasiness as he thought of the gold bars scattered about the ship. Feeling Untell's penetrating glance, he grinned, gave off an indifferent shrug, and said:

"Have it your way."

"This time I will. Now, Captain Redd, we'll take a look at your papers and logbook. According to my records, you didn't carry a man named Jim Turner."

"You should have hung on at Lombok Strait," Redd smiled. "Then you'd know Turner signed on at Tandjoengpriok."

"I'll look at the log, which could be falsified, and probably is."

"So Tysbee's bank came up short of funds. What makes you think I've got him?"

"Innocent as a lamb, aren't you?"

Untell's look was half scrutiny and half dislike. Behind it was a driving ambition to win out over Redd on this very morning; and beyond that, thin layers under, were memories of Manila Harbor, and a girl in Melbourne whose name was Myra. All these things stirred within him.

Redd pretended to be blind to all this as he entered his cabin. Producing the log and ship's papers, he sat down and maintained a discreet silence. He hoped the touch of mocking humor did not show in his face when he thought of the two bars of gold within a foot of Untell. He said casually:

"What's the news from Sydney?"

"Public sentiment is high. The people think men like Mr. van Oren are the cause of the crisis."

"What do you think?" Redd asked.

"I agree. But I'll toss you in the stew for good measure." Untell's glance lifted from the logbook. A speculative smile appeared on his face as he said, "So would Geoffrey if he could have his way. He tried to hire me."

Redd said nothing and he went on.

"But I wasn't ready to sail under the Van Oren flag. And I won't be until you're securely put away."

"Naturally," Redd chuckled. "Has Geoffrey married the firm yet?" he asked.

"That was supposed to take place the night I sailed from Sydney, according to Lancefield."

"Lancefield? What's he got to do with it?"

"Miss van Oren told him that the day she came to his office. She promised to sail after you and bring you back to Sydney."

Untell's eyes were taking him in with sudden pleasure. He said, "It seems they are all turning on you. Why don't you give up Tysbee and ask the court's mercy?"

Redd laughed to cover his true feelings.

After a painstaking search Untell said, "Nothing here. But I didn't expect to find anything in the log or manifest." He paused. "This man Turner. Odd, isn't it? He signed on two days out of Batavia."

"Stowaway," came the laconic reply.

"Give it the deep six," Untell scoffed. He got to his feet and looked around before stalking off to the deck.

Redd followed him as he moved straightway to the "corpse" and said to the second, "When did Turner sign on?"

Mr. Burk stuck out his chin and replied, "There's the Old Man. Ask him."

"I'm asking you, Mr. Burk."

Redd's voice lifted with an answer that covered the ship: "I told you Turner was a stowaway, Captain Untell."

"Sure. Now all the hands know, don't they? Suppose we take a look at your corpse."

The second said, "He's sewed in. We don't want his ghost with us."

Pelican Joe began to wring his hands and work up his face. "Not pore Jim," he said in a voice near to breaking. "He was every hair a rope yarn, Jim was." By the time the police came up out of the holds Turner had become one of the finest sailors that ever sailed the seas.

Untell fingered an ear lobe and looked perplexed. He knew instinctively Tysbee was aboard, or had been, and he felt sure Redd was outsmarting him somehow. But how? He had nothing to substantiate this strong belief unless it was the corpse. He glared at Redd, then said to the police:

"Are you sure you overlooked nothing down there?"

The spokesman said they had searched every nook and cranny big enough to hide a human being. None of them saw Redd and the mates exchange relieved glances. The gold was safe; Untell was so anxious to find Tysbee that he was forgetting the bars.

Untell looked at the corpse again and said, "We'll take a look at Jim Turner."

"My men won't like it. However, you have my permission." As Untell placed a hand on the shroud, Redd put him on the defensive with, "Now get their permission."

Untell regarded the sailors in thoughtful silence. A seaman himself, he was acquainted with sailors' superstitions and tempers. A master could expect total obedience as long as he respected the little things in the lives of his men, their private thoughts and beliefs, however strange. Molesting the dead was taboo. Knowing this, he said solicitously:

"Men, I represent the Board of Trade, which has done much to make a sailor's life easier. You know how we force shipowners to feed a crew, how we deal with officers who mistreat sailors." When he paused to let this sink home, Pelican Joe said:

"We ain't hungry aboard of Cap'n Redd."

"That's well and good," Untell replied. "But if you make your-selves a party to crime, you'll be tried also. You know that. This ship is suspected. Now who wants to go against the law?"

The men appeared to consider this. Untell observed their vari-ous expressions and said, "Now who says the Board of Trade can't look at a dead man?"

A heavy silence hung over the deck. Redd felt tension mount-ing. He saw it in Mr. Hyde's eyes. Uncertainty gripped the crew. All this was in Untell's favor, and Redd was aware that he would snatch his moment, which was now.

Something in Redd said in a loud voice, "Let him have Tysbee." It was the hurt he felt. It didn't matter whether Untell had spoken a truth or a lie when he said they were all turning on him; the effect was the same. Martha was Geoffrey's wife. And Geoffrey wouldn't hesitate to sacrifice him; his letter said as much. Let them have Tysbee? Why not? Then a nagging loyalty rose up in him. He couldn't do it.

Untell's knife was severing sail twine near Tysbee's head. In another second the game would come to an inglorious end.

"Hold fast there," Redd ordered. "I'll not have my men sailing with Jim Turner's ghost from now on. We'll bury him first. Then if you wish to look at him, fish him out." He looked at the crew and said, "What about it, men?"

The Old Man was right. Right or wrong, law or not, the master was their man. He broke the spell of the Board of Trade and courts. A babble of voices lifted and fell away. The crew, led by Mr. Burk, moved menacingly forward and surrounded the bier. Untell wormed his way out of the crowd and walked up to Redd.

"Then you'd better get to burying him, Captain," he said with rising anger.

"When I damn well please," Redd answered. "Unless you carry an order to force a burial. Do you?"

"No. But——"

"Then if you have no further business aboard of me, belay your jaw and clear my decks."

"Very well," Untell said. "But I'm keeping close to you, pirate. I'll find Tysbee wherever you have him. And when I do, I'll use this piece of paper! You can lay to that!"

Redd made no reply as he looked at a warrant for his own arrest. It was closer than he wanted to admit, with Tysbee and a few bars of gold separated from Untell's eyes by the thickness of a piece of sailcloth.

3

The *Upstart* slid reluctantly away and dropped anchor a few ship's lengths beyond the *Lady's* bows. Redd continued to look at her, his expression thoughtful and alert. He said, almost in idle tones, "Mr. Burk, have you ever fouled a ship's rudder?"

Burk glanced up suddenly. "No, sir," he replied.

"Too bad."

"However, I saw what happened to a Dutch patrol schooner in Makassar once. Some bloody pirate stretched a line from her rudder to the iron sternpost on a big Rotterdam mail steamer. What happened was quite interesting."

"No doubt about it. Now just how far would you say the *Upstart's* rudder is from that iron girl with Liverpool across her stern?"

"Why, less than half a cable's length, sir. Not too far. That is, come a fine dark night."

Redd darted a glance at him and saw a steady grin on his face. Mr. Hyde was smiling also. The second studied the schooner and the steamer, saying at last, "Two hawsers to the schooner's rudder could place one hell of a pull on her."

Redd didn't face Mr. Burk as he said, "Could or will?"

The question suggested much. And coming from the master, it was tantamount to an order. "Why did I say *could*, sir? I meant *will*."

"Then have at it," Redd ordered. "We'll stay here until dark and watch you do it."

He went below to chart a course. When he came on deck next, the shadows were long. The sun slipped another notch down toward Sumatra. The *Upstart* sat near the steamer.

The sun was dropping fast. An evening breeze stirred the air and harbor. Somewhere down in the Riouw Archipel a sunset squall was gathering. Then the sun slid behind a haze and the big red eye took a last look at the crossroads.

Redd came alive.

"All hands to stations! Mr. Burk, you may lower away."

The second got into the boat. Dublin Jack climbed in. He was an expert at tying a cable bend. Three sailors went along to row and to pay out cable. It was daylight when the boat spanked the sea, and dark as forty fathoms under before she was a half dozen lengths from the *Lady's* bows.

"Stand by the windlass," Redd ordered. "Mr. Hyde, we'll brace the yards around and be ready to let go a lot of sail."

A long hour went by. Eyes from the *Lady* glanced into the pall of night from the anchor light aboard the *Upstart* to the one on the steamer. Escape was in Mr. Burk's hands. It was a matter of fastening the schooner's rudder fast to the iron tail of the steamer. A knot that wouldn't hold under the strain of opposing forces could react as unfavorably as discovery while in the act of tying it. All was quiet, too quiet. Then the sound of oars was heard at last. They drew closer. Redd spoke into the gloom.

"Aye, aye, sir," the second said. "We got a purchase on her she'll remember until judgment day."

"And the steamer?"

Mr. Burk's chuckle was enough. Redd turned to his men and said, "Break out a farewell to the *Upstart*, lads. We want her to keep up the stern chase if she can."

The *Lady* lost little time. She made a sweep around for her wind, and the sails caught the night breeze one by one. With perfect co-ordination of sail, helm, and anchor, the wind was put over her quarter. She was under way, with noise and cheers and catcalls splitting the night air.

The *Upstart* bristled with activity. Her jibs were raised and she took her swing on the wind. Next her foresail was added. She eased forward, forward on the springs of the cable. Her great mainsail came up and the wind bellied it hard. The maximum strain was upon her. This was the moment Redd and the mates had awaited. The mainsail gave her the drive to turn the trick or reveal a flaw in the execution of it. She leaned forward, straining at the weight of the steamer she was tied to, her sails full and fluttering. Suddenly she was free, sliding helplessly along in the manner of a shark that had just lost its tail. She had unwittingly torn her own rudder out of the pintles.

The *Lady of Glasgow* was free to run for the Island of Gold. When the shouting died down, Redd sounded an order:

"Let Jim Turner come alive."

CHAPTER XV

The day was clear and warm over the Indian Ocean. The sea stretched far out from the *Lady's* starboard beam and disappeared in an opaque horizon, above which the blue ridges of distant Sumatra met the sky in the last hue of defining color. The ocean was quiet and asleep on all sides; the set of the current on the coast seemed as trifling as the wind that breathed life into the sea.

The Island of Gold lay ahead, a somber mass of tropical green in the middle of the sea. A pillow of white clouds hung above the island. As the heat haze thinned, a long line of white breakers, the only sign of vigor in the old sea, warned of a wide coastal reef. Closer, the solid green of the coast took on shape. Tufts of coconut palms crowned tall stems, and colors separated to identify a jungle sloping up from the sea to conical hills. The entrance of the bay, visible to the lookout in the masthead, was a gap in the breakers.

The ship moved on before the weak following wind, her cutwater scarcely purling the water. A sluggish trail ran out behind her, drawing clacking disapproval from hungry birds. Sailors on the below watch lined the forward rails and peered curiously at the oncoming land. A shipboard quiet was broken by the leadsman's drone and the lookout's cry from aloft. Only the wind in feeble gusts across the level reaches of the sea raised the voice of the rigging as the ship eased on into the last mile of the roadstead.

The lookout cried down to deck, "She opens wide. Rock awash off the port arm. Good offing to starboard."

The roar of breakers increased, came on, fell away, returning stronger, as though the ship floated inside the sounding box of a huge sea shell. Soon the jaws of the reef opened and flanked the ship. The lookout reported a cobalt-blue depth inside the lagoon, a stretch of emerald-green shallows under the beach to starboard. Then the crab-claw arms of the bay reached for the *Lady*. As they slid by, an islet covered with small mangrove trees and *alang-alang* appeared off the roadway.

Not a few of the sailors glanced from the island to Captain Redd. The adventure piqued a man's curiosity. They knew he shipped guns and gewgaws, which meant trade or trouble, or both. They knew also that he had an uncanny knack for handling both. In addition to the five L's indelibly written across a real mariner's mind—log, lead, lookout, latitude, and longitude—he drove a ship or a proposition with a sixth L: it was luck. As the ship slipped through the pass, the mystery of coming events held forth no dread; absolute confidence in the master released them from all worry and responsibility.

Mr. Hyde said, "Not an outrigger in sight. A desolate place, sir."

Redd looked across deck at Tysbee, who was due to meet for the first time that strange raw variance of civilization which made up a page in commerce. Here was a last outpost of trade, and the little banker in a business suit looked entirely out of place in the setting.

The *Lady's* forward motion was almost spent. No sail on her now, she edged close to the green of the shallows and dropped her hook in good fathoms of blue. Sails were furled and life aboard a ship at anchor was renewed.

Redd continued to stand as before. He studied the lavender-gray shadows of the stately coconut palms a hundred yards away. Fronds rattled in a light breeze with metallic sounds and cast cool shadows on the beach. A shark looked up greedily from the lagoon. A strong fragrance of flowering vine and bush reached out with invitation from the jungle of green behind the coconut grove. The very beauty and quiet seemed menacing.

"Mr. Burk, you'll break out a dozen men and scout the interior for a village. Easy as you go, and don't shoot unless you have to."

When the second and his crew had beached the boat, Redd spoke absently to Mr. Hyde: "The general idea is to trade some big chief a mess of trinkets for a permanent home for Mr. Tysbee."

"How permanent, sir?"

"I don't want him to die. Which calls for a careful approach to the natives. We've got to place an estimate on the honesty of the savages before we talk trade."

"How simple it would be just to put Mr. Tysbee ashore and sail away, sir."

"Don't tempt me."

The chief mate glanced at Redd's face and saw it was still and quiet. It reminded him of the silence beyond the strip of shore.

The shadows were long when the second and his party returned to the beach. An evening wind whimpered in the tree crowns and there was a bracing lift in the breeze off the sea. But the island stood by close and depressing, as though the dead were alive and watching every movement aboard the big sailing ship. Giant fronds beyond the grove waved close to the tan earth, and a man's wondering eye almost waited for a savage to step into the open. Then the sun slid under and night closed over ship and island.

Mr. Burk reported a village on a stream not a mile inland. He saw only the brown thatched roofs, though they were large and impressive. A gong sounded when they were skirting the stream. The tone was deep and trembling; it reminded the second of a Chinese temple gong he heard once in Kowloon. Then they crossed a wide path that led from the running water to the village. It was paved with stone. He entertained little doubt that their venture inland went unheeded. Behind a fringe of bamboo, metal caught the sun's rays and moved. The leaves seemed to whisper with warning.

"Did you see a human being?" Redd asked.

"I did," he grinned, then frowned. "But you'll scoff and say it's the damnedest piece of nonsense a sailor ever dreamed up, sir. I saw a beautiful woman leaning against a flowering tree, looking up at a big squawking bird. Pelican Joe said it was a japer. It had a green crest and——"

"Damn the bird, Mr. Burk. Get on with the woman."

"Aye. She was naked, sir, with a coffee-colored skin. She had dinners like you dream about."

"Dinners?"

"Aye, aye! Breasts, sir. And all she had on were bracelets and a high yellow headpiece. Her robe was hanging on a limb. On my word, sir, it was of red silk with gold dragons woven into it."

"Did she have a face?" Redd asked.

"One I wouldn't cover up in a circumstance, sir. If she's a native, this island is where I'd like to stay. It stands over the Kanaka atolls like skys'ls over jibs."

Redd looked at Mr. Hyde and said, "Sounds promising. The natives have a goddess or a caste system. Maybe we can work up our trade."

"Maybe. But I never felt warning bells ringing in my head like I do now."

Redd looked sharply at him for a long moment. "I hear them also. But we'll pay a call at the village tomorrow afternoon just the same."

2

It was one of those nights when a sailor had much rather be at sea. The unknown pressed in close on all sides. It ruffled nerve ends. Even the land smells, warm and heady, and the ceaseless high-pitched noise of night insects brought the unseen aboard decks. These men were not afraid of death, an impersonal thing quickly forgotten when the deep was a shipmate's tomb. But the very nearness of the untamed jungle and all sorts of tricks played by a bright half-moon raggedly penetrating the shapes on land fed a mind with a vast and formless unease.

Here was the edge of the world. It was grim with dank vegetation and writhing mangrove roots in the water and other daylight impressions that carried into the night. Squatting back in the shadows was something primeval. It slid in highlights along vines that spilled down to the beach. A screech of a macaw or a monkey's cry, and then echoes, and silence alert and alive.

Pardue was on the two-to-four anchor watch when he shifted his gaze from beach to starboard cathead in order to rest his eyes. The moon on the descent reddened. Shadows were less sharp. He lifted his glance to the beach again, expecting the same scenes all over again. He started. Something moved between the palm trunks. Or was it the moon distorting shapes, mocking eyes that searched for shapes not there? A cloud sailed across the moon, dimming suddenly the pale fall of moonlight on the sands.

Pardue began to doubt his vision, to wonder if he would believe objects really moved out there if he saw them with his own eyes. Then he stared wide-eyed at what appeared on the beach. Shaking his head vigorously, he looked again.

Five figures, like five burnished pagan idols, stood just outside the coconut grove. Grotesque shapes in the night. Gleaming yellow plants in perfect symmetry appeared to grow out of their heads. They wore curved pointed jackets of the same shiny color. Long shields, shaped like banana fronds, seemed made of pure gold.

Pardue's throat went dry. The scream of a bird stirred the roots of his hair. Though he tried to cry out, no sound escaped him. He stood in a trance as the devils came to life with one leap in unison into the air and landed with feet spread wide apart. Every shield was lifted to the right, then to the left, and all bent as one to the ground for long spears. Pardue did not notice they were naked from the waist down until they put on colored clouts that fell to the knees like skirts. Then they stepped back and ran to the water. As they bowed toward the jungle and fell flat on bellies, a lone figure marched out of the night.

He was of great height and stature, and his trappings outshone those of the other five. Perhaps it was because he stood in the full glare of the moon. He remained motionless for a long time. Then his hand lifted slowly and pointed to the ship.

Pardue found his voice. His cry brought the watch aft on the run and emptied the forecastle. When he pointed to land there was nothing to be seen but a monotonous stretch of beach under the wise old coconut palms.

3

The day broke with the air heavy and low, long swells rolling in over the sea. Highlights of the burning sun on emerald and brown coconut leaves remained as motionless as a picture, the air was so still.

As the day advanced, the strip of foreshore fronting the lagoon seemed more pagan and forbidding. The hustle aboard ship in the afternoon did little toward lessening dread of the unknown. Trade goods and baubles were arranged into packs and men were selected to carry them inland. The time had come. Boats were let go by the run, and men at the sweeps looked up at the ship with longing born of unease. Then the beach. With Redd, Hyde, and Tysbee in the lead, the trading expedition crossed the sands and disappeared into the jungle.

Redd knew instinctively he was being watched by the natives. He had listened to Pardue's story, had attached a certain credence to it. But the mysterious visit by the night watchers and the second's report of yesterday gave him little to go on. He was actually marching in blind. But alert. His sharp eye ran ahead of the sloping trail, into thick beds of elephant-ears, little groves of bamboo, and eucalyptus. Past large flowers and moss orchids and palms, all the while the splash of the surf falling away before the low hum of insects, the party emerged into a small plain covered with high grass. This was good ground for ambush, though nothing happened.

The paved pathway began at the fresh-water stream. They followed it until they saw in a clump of coconut palms the high brown roofs of houses.

The shadows were long when the pathway opened suddenly into a clearing studded with great round houses, each raised high above the ground. Thatch roofs curved up steeply, and the windows, mere openings covered with bamboo bars, were twenty feet from the ground, halfway between earth and roof peak. At the far end of a wide paved court, one house differed from all others: its roof was higher and topped with speared wood. It rested on pilings that were like columns. Rich designs were painted across the front.

Soon every native in the village was staring at the visitors from the pilings of houses. A score of warriors marched from the large house and halted as if to bar the way. Pardue's story was verified: coats of sheet metal flared out like Siamese costumes at shoulders and waist. They glittered in the sun like pure gold! Large rings encircled each neck and, gleaming in the same deep yellow, tall headdresses resembling plant designs were augmented by enormous earrings and bright gold-tipped spears.

Redd raised an arm and spoke in Malay. No reply was forthcoming. Then out of the crowd came an old Chinese with stringy goatee and ears stretched by large rings. He wore a short batik robe cut in Chinese fashion. Redd decided he was a person of some importance here. Certainly there was wisdom and authority in his old face. Bowing, he rattled off several dialects. Redd answered in a tongue he was familiar with, and they talked for some time. The Chinese told a story of his capture thirty years before, after landing from his junk to trade. His life was spared in order that he might act as trader and translator. His gods had ordered him to protect the natives from the outside world. The gods of the island had been accepted by his own ancestors. He had no desire to escape. But why did the white man venture inland?

"I wish to trade," Redd advised.

"Our ways differ," the old man replied thoughtfully. "But Nitaloni is chief. When he talks with his grandfather he will come." Bowing, and stepping back to a huge stone slab like those before every house, he reached under the stone and produced a brown object resembling a human skull. "This," he said, "is his grandfather."

Redd looked about him, seeing round objects under the polished stone slabs at each house. He drew a shudder from the sailors with the explanation. The carving on the slabs, as well as the size and shape of them, together with the headdresses of the unarmed men at the chieftain's house, reminded him of ancient Egyptian designs. Then there was something in the burning brightness of the warrior's faces to suggest a touch of India in their blood. Their yellow color and the tall headpieces, the symmetry and fluid pagoda-influenced curves of their metalwork were reminiscent of the Siamese. Except for these odd characteristics, they were racially Malay.

Redd felt Tysbee's eyes on him and, turning, he saw a crafty and apprehensive light in them. It could mean anything, though it wasn't difficult to believe that Tysbee's feeling was that of a man unable to reconcile life in this crumb of land in the Indian Ocean to any understandable pattern; which alerted his sense of fear. Inside Redd was working some bid for sympathy. It was quickly squelched. The setting was made to order for what he had in mind.

He forgot Tysbee for the moment. A gong sounded. The notes trembled with strong vibrations.

The armed guard fell aside, exposing a figure so tall and elaborately costumed that he might have stepped from either an oriental throne or out of a sailor's nightmare. In addition to the gold trappings of the guards, his headpiece was larger and richer, and he wore a bright red coat with golden bands and pauldrons, as well as a yellow clout enlivened by gold threads. Though barefooted, he was no poor man but a king in his own right. It was in his face and bearing: in his thin lips, open now to expose teeth blackened by betel nut; in his bright, cruel eyes that held one fascinated. Pin points danced in them with a unique oriental fierceness.

When the old Chinese motioned Redd forward, the armed guard barred Hyde and the others. Redd advanced. The chieftain remained as still as a statue, his eyes fixed on his visitor. Not once altering his gaze, he spoke rapidly to the translator, who asked why Redd had come to Nitaloni's kingdom. The answer, "To trade," evoked the question:

"For what and with what?"

"First look at the wealth I bring," Redd suggested, meeting the chieftain's glance. The order sounded. With ten warriors on either side of them, Redd's men advanced with their packs. Soon Redd held up glass beads of all colors. The chieftain examined them and tossed them to the stone walk, unsatisfied. Colored umbrellas, fans, silk hats, sticks of tobacco, brass lanterns that lit up, bolts of printed cloth, Chinese bells, mirrors, and porcelain clocks, all met the same fate. Redd studied the great Nitaloni, who was now smiling his contempt.

"What do you want?" Redd asked.

"Show your wares," the Chinese said. "Nitaloni is impatient."

"Then say that all I have shown him are gifts." Redd spoke shrewdly. When this was done, Nitaloni showed both surprise and pleasure. "Now to trade." Redd began all over, passing out sugar. The chieftain liked it, but said it was another gift.

"Tell him this isn't," Redd ordered gruffly, producing a gun. Aiming carefully at a cluster of brown coconuts, he fired. When a coconut fell to the ground, he said, "This does the work of many spears in battle."

Nitaloni examined the gun and talked in a rapid jargon with the old Chinese, who finally returned the gun to Redd, saying, "He does not trust the gun to his people. His grandfather says no. Gun will end wars among tribes."

"Isn't that the general idea?" Redd asked.

"No. War is important, since Nitaloni's people are head-hunters. No warrior can take a wife unless he pays with the head of the enemy. If he takes two heads, he can have two wives. Guns would soon leave no heads to take. The next generation would be deprived of the custom of the ancestors. The gods would not approve."

Redd considered this. Thinking of Tysbee, he said, "Are heads money here?"

"No. If a man wishes earrings or headpiece, he goes to the goldsmith and offers a pig or two. If he desires a kris, he goes to the worker in iron, who forges him one in return for so many pigs. If he wishes potatoes or rice, he goes to where the stone is cut with the circle of official measure and pays for them with pigs."

"So pigs are money." Redd stared at the Chinese.

"Pigs are money."

"What about metal?"

"One buys it with pigs."

"Gold too?"

"Nitaloni owns all the gold. He sells it to the goldsmith for pigs. But great chief wishes to know what you have to trade and what you want."

Redd was not at all sure of his way now. Here was a situation he had not foreseen. Only last evening the sole remaining pig aboard the *Lady* had been slaughtered. Looking from Nitaloni to Tysbee, he wished for a score of stinking pigs. He needed time in which to think. Otherwise he would lose face here. He said:

"Now that I have given the great Nitaloni many gifts, perhaps he will show me his gold."

The ruler was no sooner acquainted with the message than he

broke his stiff reserve and bowed before Redd. It was a gesture of hospitality, the translator advised. Though dubious, Redd followed the chieftain. A guard walked behind him and the Chinese came after him. He was led through rows of pillars under the big house and up a steep narrow stairway to a room of great size. The floors were of polished woods. Scenes of the jungle were carved on the walls. Atop a stone slab in a corner were betel-nut mortars and an urn of palm wine. A crocodile fashioned from wood formed the back of the only chair in the room. Though all this was impressive, the main interest was a large chest of elaborate design. It rested on a slab in the center of the room.

Two batik-clad boys stood at attention near a brass gong. The chieftain spoke and they struck it in unison. Redd saw everyone look toward a bamboo blind. As he turned a glance on it, an old woman appeared, weighted down with gold bracelets and neckpieces. Though a priestess, she resembled a monkey more than a human being.

As she moved to the chest, Redd's attention was diverted by shrill squeals from the courtyard. He looked through the latticed window at natives stabbing pigs. More than fifty were killed in a matter of minutes. Blood gushed on the smooth stones and fires were burning in the pits.

"A feast," the Chinese said, caressing a strand of his long mustache. "The pigs will steam in bamboo tubes for a night and a day. Tomorrow evening you will return for food and dancing."

"And pigs are money," Redd remarked, shaking his head with disbelief and wonder.

The gong sounded again and Redd's glance was drawn from the courtyard. He was searching for the key to the baffling economy of the island when the bamboo blind lifted. What appeared next caused him to forget the problem of pigs versus gold.

Moving toward the chest was a beautiful woman. Perhaps she was the same one Pardue had seen. Naked but for a breechclout of gold-colored lace, long bracelets from wrists to elbows, and a crown of gold filigree, she was long-limbed and graceful. Though saffron-colored, she was fair. A translucent pink glowed through the outer layers of her skin. Her almond eyes lifted to him, long and framed by sweeping lashes that glistened as if they were done in lacquer. She had a delicate nose and red shapely lips. Her curves were those of youth, though the full lifted pods of her breasts bespoke unplumbed maturity.

He eyed the rosetted peaks, the shadows beneath them, and the slope of her fine abdomen with a burning admiration. As she walked, her hips slid tantalizingly back and forth.

She seemed to know what he was thinking. She paused before him, not taking her eyes off his face. Then an expression, like a smile on her full lips, inviting or mocking, came and went. Her eyes slid away. She knew her charms and she was using them to kindle fires; and memories—of a girl almost her size with an armful of roses at her bosom, of a girl denied him. This island creature seemed to express in the flesh all the warm vitality of the woman at Muirkirk Hall.

He couldn't take his eyes off her.

The silence in the room and the steady gaze of Nitaloni, the old priestess, the guard, and the crafty Chinese were felt rather than seen. He knew they were all aware of a white man's greed. They were exposing it to gold and rare flesh. Small wonder, then, that the chieftain showed hospitality in answer to his request. Here was more than gold. If it was a trap, it was well baited.

The Chinese was bowing now, his old eyes glittering as he said, "My daughter, honorable Captain."

Redd's glance sharpened instantly. The translator had spoken in English. What manner of warning or friendliness the Chinese intended remained as well hidden as the key to their economy. The more he saw and heard, the more confused he became. This had never happened to him before. He needed time for thought.

The Chinese was saying, "Her name translated into your tongue is Willow."

Redd stared at her.

Nitaloni and the Chinese moved to the far wall when the old priestess advanced to the chest. She mumbled for minutes, then uttered weird cries before removing several pegs from the top. The girl came forward and lifted the cover, filling the room with the incense of sandalwood. Only she remained with Redd, who looked from Nitaloni's shrewd face to hers. The Chinese said he was free to examine the treasure.

Redd saw layer after layer of what appeared to be gold. He lifted a thin sheet. It was heavy enough. He tried to place a value on the metal in terms of British gold pounds. Then he was wondering if this was some big joke. That much gold on a remote island seemed impossible. He looked deeper into the chest. Several large jewels caught his eye. They were true gems, and they guaranteed the yellow sheets were genuine. A large blood-red ruby held him in a state of fascination. It was the size of a bird's egg. His eyes lifted slowly to the cleft of Willow's bosom, where such a gem belonged. And beyond her in the vast distance was Martha van Oren. But it was dangerous to think this way in the present company. He smiled, however, and enjoyed it, even as his hand scooped up stones for a closer look. One emerald was larger than the ruby; though, unlike the ruby, it failed to stir him. He lowered the precious stones to the bottom of the chest, reluctantly, and withdrew his hands.

His glance was drawn to Willow. Her eyes were enormous and shining, reminding him of lanterns freshly lit in a dark garden; and then they were filled with such thinning intensity that he was sure she was trying to convey a message. Concern, entreaty, or enmity, he wasn't sure. The chieftain was saying through the translator:

"You compliment Nitaloni. You are impressed."

"I am," Redd answered. "What is your price for all this?"

"Many pigs," came the reply. "And many heads like yours." As Redd looked from Nitaloni to the shrewd Chinese, the latter said, "Wealth is universal. Only people are different."

Out in the courtyard a gong split the silence of encroaching evening. The sound echoed in the palms until the last tremulous note died in the gentle breeze; or, as Captain Redd thought, in the deep, somnolent eyes of Willow.

CHAPTER XVI

Night had fallen when Redd and his party left the village with a promise to return on the following evening.

As they made their way back to the ship, Mr. Hyde said, "What puzzles me is that the chief would so much as allow a white man to know about his treasure, let alone look at it."

Redd agreed. Not wholly convinced that all he had learned of their economy was the truth, he tried to balance gold on the same scales with pigs. It just didn't make sense. Then he looked at it as best he could through a native's eye and saw the value of pigs and the cheapness of gold: the former were scarce, the latter plentiful, though useless except for ornamental purposes. A head was something else, a symbol of and tangible connection to the dead, and source of occultism practiced on the people by the old priestess; it was also a coveted object that inspired wars. He was trying to put pigs, gold, and heads in proper order of importance when Mr. Hyde said:

"I'm thinking Nitaloni is baiting you with gold and a lively strumpet for the purpose of taking a few heads. Ours."

"You could be right, Mr. Hyde. You could be right."

Tysbee had been listening. He laughed. "Heads like yours, Captain," he said. There was no mistaking his meaning. All his hopes were now centered on Redd's downfall.

Redd silenced him with a reply that sounded starkly practical: "Your head would save me a lot of worry if it belonged to Nitaloni."

Mr. Hyde appeared lost in his own worries. He said, "I'm ready to cast a quick vote in favor of putting this heathen island under our stern. The sooner the better." With no reply from Redd, he added, "That is, sir, if you've figured out a way to finish your business here."

"But I haven't. Seems I've got nothing to trade with. But we'll find something before tomorrow evening."

Mr. Burk breathed a long sigh of relief when they appeared on the moonlit beach. Boats were sent across the water for them. With the good deck under them, sailors who had gone to the village broke loose with true and fictitious stories. Redd went below, though he came up soon and spent the next few hours pacing back and forth across the poop.

The girl was very much in his thoughts. She seemed to emerge out of the stink of stabbed pigs and the mystery of skulls under slabs of stone like a fragrant tropical flower. Mr. Hyde's opinion of her reminded him of the story of Circe and Odysseus. And she was endowed with the physical attributes necessary to a sorceress. Mr. Hyde could be right: she might be strong bait. On the other hand, she was an exotic woman, as rare and out of place here as the egg-shaped ruby.

It was the half-hour between ten and eleven. The watch forward sounded the all's well. The moon floated in and out of gauze. The white beach was shadowed in indigo shapes. The surf outside the lagoon played a steady tune. Half the crew were bunked in.

Pelican Joe's voice lifted from the forecastlehead in an excited cry. "It's a woman! Swimming!"

Redd heard a light splash just before a sailor cried, "There she goes! Under the dolphin striker! Naked as——"

Mr. Hyde growled, "Some devilish trap. Haul her aboard."

Redd countermanded the order and said, "Lower the dinghy. I'll take a look myself. Alone."

"But she's the damn woman you saw!" Mr. Hyde protested.

"I hope so," Redd replied, moving off to the main deck. Looking down into the water, he saw nothing. The boat was let go and he was soon in it. A sailor above him said she had probably dived under the ship. Another said something about sharks.

They watched their captain at the oars as the boat slid noiselessly around to the moonlit side of the ship. Shadows were sharp and ripples on the quiet lagoon seemed silver and alive. Redd was under the bows with a hand on the bobstay when something shot up out of the water and surfaced near the boat.

"There she is, sir!" Mr. Hyde shouted.

Redd saw her break the water. As she struck out for the beach, her body glistening in the soft moonlight, he fell to the oars with long, sure strokes. Mr. Hyde shouted all sorts of warnings which he ignored. A scull of the boat sent him nearer to the beach, where she came up and stood naked, shining and panting. The boat drove into the sand and he leaped out, not pausing to lift the bows out of the water. She sped toward the jungle with Redd running after her.

Then large fronds closed behind them. Only the shadows of

palms on an empty white beach met staring eyes from the ship. A cockatoo broke the silence. Mr. Hyde answered the bird with an oath.

From forward of the rail, Pardue was heard to say in awed tones, "For a mermaid like that, I'd spit in the chief's eye right now."

"And lose yer 'ead?" the cockney asked.

"I've already lost it," came the reply. "Me and the Old Man is alike that way." He continued to look at the green leaves beyond the palm trunks with unfocused eyes, dreaming that it was he who overtook the island beauty. So deep and real were the pictures of his fancy, he did not see what his eyes watched subconsciously until the four warriors sat cross-legged on the beach. Then he raised his voice with:

"The Old Man! They'll get his head sure as hell now!"

2

Redd saw Willow dart into a bed of large leaves and pause for a moment before streaking up a narrow pathway. It led inland toward the village. He was thinking of a trap when he saw her stop still and look ahead. Her next move was a strange one for a woman enticing a man into trouble. She dropped to the ground suddenly and crawled back to him.

Murmuring excitedly, she took his hand in hers and drew him to the ground. Then she motioned him to follow her. They had no sooner gained the cover of giant fronds near a trickle of water than four armed warriors appeared.

They passed on by in the direction of the beach. Willow held his arm until they were out of sight. He glanced at her again, observing the brightness of her eyes focused on him. She smiled. Her expression was unguarded and alive with a vigor he had seldom seen in a face. It was made up of boundless curiosity and interest, all directed at a novelty, a white man. She started of a sudden and lowered her eyes to her body, as though she had just discovered her nakedness.

She was up and running in another second. Redd followed her on to the stone walk leading to the village. When he came upon her she was wearing a clout of red and gold batik that dropped to her knees. She looked up at him while placing bracelets on her arm. Then she pointed toward the lagoon and led the way to a spot of sand some distance astern of the *Lady*.

Half hidden by the dense jungle behind them, covered in patches of moving shadows from coconut leaves, they sat on the sand and looked at one another. Redd laughed, thinking it awkward that they had no way of talking to each other. He might learn much about the village from her.

She laughed when he did, then pointed a finger at her mouth and spoke. He could not understand her, he said. His voice seemed to delight her. A spontaneous smile appeared on her face and she said something else to him, pointing once more to her mouth.

"You are a pretty woman, Willow," he said. "Too damn pretty to be here alone with me."

She came closer and placed a finger on his lips. A fringed coconut leaf stretched out in the wind off the sea, taking its shadow with it. She caught the white fall of moonlight on her upturned face and shoulders and uncovered bosom.

His hands closed over her shoulders. He drew her to him, and felt the warmth and softness under his touch, even as he saw her naked and submissive. But her glance drew his as she stared with lines of troubled thought creasing her brow. She had read his mind. She was instinctively warned of danger, and she seemed to wrestle intuitively with all that was in her to be roused.

Redd knew the moment was made for gentleness. He laughed and talked to her. She examined him with what seemed a sharp wisdom. Then her face softened into an expression of curious radiance.

"What a windfall," he was saying. "You're making me forget Tysbee, Willow." Sir George and Geoffrey lived in some remote past. He said these things to her and she was pleased to hear them. It did not matter that she could not understand a word he said; he was making sweeter music than the winds in the tree crowns or the song of the surf. "In the shadows you're Martha in my arms, Willow. I'm as close now as I'll ever be to her. You don't mind, girl."

The treetops swayed and the moonlight fell and retreated, painting her curves in highlights and masking them in soft pearly shadows.

She seemed to relax in his arms, content to look up at him and listen as though this was a pleasure she had dreamed of for years. Her glance was deep and searching and her hand lifted to his face and stroked it as she lay flat on the sand. Her eyes flashed lights like the stars and dimmed like them, over and over, until they became heavy.

No language was needed now. The unsaid things between them had a tongue they could both understand: it was universal. Redd knew the strength of her desire, and there was no mistaking the pounding of his own blood at his temples. His hands were on her neck and shoulders. They were warm and firm. So were her bosom and waist. His arm slid under her neck and he bent his face to hers. Then he was drawing her to him with both hands, kissing her on the mouth, reaching for the bottomless sweetness of her lips.

He felt the lightly clinging touch of her hand at his neck. A strength came into her arms and she was pressing close with a startling eagerness. A sound escaped her, and the breeze up in the old coconut crowns answered. Somewhere inside the jungle a monkey chattered and a bird sang into the wind.

3

The sun had dropped down from the zenith and quartered the brassy sky. The ship stood in dancing heat waves atop the lagoon, her decks hot to the touch, her pins and metal blistering to hands. A canopy was stretched aft and another forward. Men sweated and slept. The anchor watch stood in whatever shade was at hand, seeing pitch bubbling out of the seams in a glance, studying the cool shade on the sands of the beach in another. In the mirror of the lagoon a shark swam up for refuse from the galley.

Redd and his mates were drinking cold fruit punch under the aft canopy when a lone figure walked out of the shadows on the beach. Redd saw her first. As he raised a hand he felt the probing eyes of Mr. Hyde on his back.

"Sir, are we going to the village this evening without any item of trade?" In the mate's voice was a ring of reprimand born of uneasiness.

Redd turned a sharp glance on him. "We may trade," he said in a soft voice intended to put Mr. Hyde in his place, "with understanding."

Suppressing an oath and a chuckle, Mr. Hyde said, "I don't have enough of that item to trade for a grain of sand." As Redd walked away and ordered a boat lowered, the mate said to Mr. Burk, "That damn woman again. Maybe he's learning something from her."

"Or vice versa," Mr. Burk replied. "The Old Man didn't return to the ship until nearly dawn."

"A moonlight windfall is one thing. A trap is something else. But in this instance they go together. I'm sure of it. Aye. I'm damn well sure of it." His voice trailed off and he raised a glass to his lips.

Redd knew the strength of Mr. Hyde's presentiment. Mr. Burk said less, though he yearned to raise anchor and sail away. Feeling these things in his officers, in his own mind also as he got into the boat, he was wondering if Willow had numbed his sense of precaution. She stood on the beach awaiting him, reviving memories of last night.

Looking at her across the water, he wasn't sure that he wanted to leave the island. She was the color of pale bronze. A white cloth protected her head from the sun; a transparent gauze fell from her shoulders. The bracelets and gold threads of her loincloth seemed on fire.

He was unaware of beaching the boat and moving toward her. A deep look of a woman entranced drew him on, fascinating him. Her emotions were his, as contagious as a disease. They walked on to the strip of lonely beach where they had spent the night under the growing moon, their every exchange of glances packed with mysteries of the night.

A faint cooling breeze eddied down out of the palms as they reached their trysting place. Shadows were large and thick in the afternoon, and the yellow ribs of large fronds against the emerald and deep greens of the jungle wall formed a colorful backdrop. Missing was the moon that stood guard through the night, though he thought he saw it in her eyes.

The shadows moved eastward as the day wore on. When Redd looked up at the sky he knew a sensation of guilt. He should be aboard ship. The time had come for him to lead his men inland for the big feast.

Willow opened her eyes as he sat up. Her hand reached slowly up to his neck and drew him to her waiting lips. A trumpeted cry reached his ears from the *Lady:* "Captain Redd." He paid no heed to it. Willow's long eyes opened slowly, closing him off from all the world.

A sound startled him. It came from the low elephant-ears almost behind them. Looking up, he saw the face of the old priestess dart behind a leaf. Thinking she looked like a physical interpretation of evil and trouble, he glanced quickly at Willow, hoping she had not read his alert look. She hadn't. He arose and walked into the bushes. The old woman was no longer there. After a careful search of the surroundings, he returned to Willow and pointed to his ship.

She knew how to protest. Her head shook negatively and she tightened her hands about his neck and shoulders. Slowly he disengaged them. Time was running out on him. She arose at last and smiled up at him. Then her hands moved up to the bun of her hair, and the same light played in her eyes that he had seen when he glanced up from the jewels in Nitaloni's house yesterday.

Her hand reached for his and pressed a small object into his palm. It was egg-shaped. The big ruby. In the sun it was the color of blood.

He met her glance. In her face was love and gratitude. Unable to fully understand her generosity, he felt the need of a tongue between them now. But she was talking with the steady, beseeching eyes of a woman, telling him the jewel of the treasure chest was his. Then she reached for his lips.

He held her in a long embrace, wondering if her gratitude wasn't almost sacrifice, and if the old priestess wasn't now talking her secret out of a shriveled skull.

CHAPTER XVII

The feast was getting under way. Smoke from the pits reached up for the green-blue of the heavens now silhouetting the palms. As the tantalizing aroma of pork was wafted to his nostrils, Redd found it hard to reconcile the economy of the islands to any pattern of trade. But this was the result of total isolation from the world. Even so, at this moment the generous chieftain was cooking his money. He didn't laugh. It was no longer funny.

He was seated on a slab before the chieftain's house. His sailors sat cross-legged on the ground in front of him. Mr. Hyde was on his left, Tysbee on the right. Nitaloni's red coat flashed like a ruby about the fires in the central courtyard. The old Chinese stood stoically alert at the end of the pits, his back to the visiting party.

Redd turned slowly and swept the pillars under the house with a searching glance. The aged priestess squatted there, watchful, silent. Willow was perhaps upstairs. Pictures of her formed and re-formed in his mind, parading by in delightful panorama before fading. But business brought him here, and he had yet to make any proposal to Nitaloni. He had, actually, nothing to offer, except— and he didn't wish to think about it—a head. Now he was looking at Tysbee, who was the important cargo. He could not forget it. All else was incidental.

Large chunks of steaming meat were placed before them. Nitaloni and his translator joined them and ordered fresh green coconuts. Lithe youths scampered up the trunks for them, and a warrior deftly cut away the husks and made holes in the nut. Another brought *mangustan*, a fruit tasting like peach and pineapple. A messy, tasteless rice was left alone by Redd's party, though the pork was eaten with enjoyment.

It was a balmy night. The Southern Cross played tag among the palm crowns, and low bright stars wheeled in their courses. The evening was made up of moonlight and purple shadows. A gentle breeze came in, rustling the fringes of coconut leaves in metallic softness. But a formless excitement hung over the village. The air seemed tense and expectant. It was the same after hours of dancing around the fires.

With the warriors jerking up and down in the last war dance, their bodies glistening like their armor in the dying firelight, Redd approached the ruler and Chinese. "I have a proposition," he said. "I will leave one of my men with you and come back with a shipload of pigs."

"Nitaloni asks what it is you wish in return for the pigs?"

Redd glanced from Tysbee to the chieftain and said, "I wish to take nothing from your island. I come in peace. I go in peace. I will close my lips to all men about your island. I ask only one thing in return: that you keep the man I shall point out to you on this island until he dies of natural causes."

"Nitaloni will talk to his grandfather. If he says you plan to leave a devil here, your life is in danger."

Drums and gongs were silent, and dancers and spectators alike moved toward the great house of Nitaloni. The chieftain's bright eyes sparkled in his head as he talked with the Chinese. They had evidently reached a decision in the matter of Redd's proposition when the old priestess ran out of the shadows of the pillars with arms upraised. The screeching sounds she made brought Nitaloni, the Chinese, and a dozen armed warriors on the run. Something was amiss; the whole village knew it. After a rapid exchange of unintelligible words, Nitaloni raised a hand. All sound ceased. He spoke in a jerky guttural voice, and soon several villagers were feeding wood to the fires. Expressions of fear and suspicion gathered on their faces, and all eyes turned on Redd's party.

Mr. Hyde grimaced unduly and said in Redd's ear, "I think it's time for us to get out of here, sir."

"Easy," Redd answered. "Easy. Let's see what's coming off here." The old woman drew his glance. She glared from Willow to him and back again. He might do well to heed the mate's advice.

Willow was standing before Nitaloni now, her head up as the old priestess pointed to her and leaped about, making all sorts of frightening noises. Nitaloni advanced, the gold and red of his costume animated by the bright fires. His kris was drawn as he faced Willow and caught her hair with the other hand. Her head was thrown back and the tip of the blade quivered at the arch of her neck. She made no sound, and Redd moved closer, looking at the Chinese who said she was his daughter. The old man stood motionless, stoical. Slowly Nitaloni relaxed his cruel face. Unhanding the girl, he shouted several words, then looked at the Chinese and pointed a finger at Redd.

The translator bowed before Redd, saying in English, "A most unfortunate occurrence, honorable one. An item is missing from the state jewels. It is the Great Pigeon of Ramree."

"What the devil is that?" Redd asked.

"A ruby, honorable Captain."

As Hyde looked perplexed and forced his eyes away from his captain, Tysbee stared at Redd with all the pleasure of accusation in his face.

"Nitaloni has spoken. He will wait until the hundredth drumbeat for the guilty one to come forward." Bowing, he moved away.

The drum sounded.

A slow monotonous beat continued. Every native watched the warrior lift his arm and strike the drum. Nitaloni stood erect with arms folded. The old Chinese looked at Redd. And Redd was watching Willow, who stood with a light silken scarf over her shoulders and breasts. She met his gaze, looking as deep as he, no break in the repose of her face. The drum beat on, again and again, louder now in the silence. And Redd and Hyde and the sailors and Tysbee and every native knew it would beat louder and louder, each beat a growing, living threat designed to strike at the eardrums and mind and nerve tips. There was raw vengeance and the irrevocable law of the tribes in the cadence of it—death to the guilty one. The glance between Redd and Willow remained unbroken. Redd was asking how far she would go, how long she could last, and her look seemed to ask the same of him.

There was something deep and ageless between them. It was welded by moonlight. He thought of her in his arms and he felt the blood pound at his face and neck.

The kohl used to darken her eyelids glistened with a tear of endured strain as she refused to sweep her eyes with the long-lashed lids. Nor was she asking him to look away as the drum boomed with vibrations that seemed to beat at her internally. A magnificent woman, he was thinking, one who might look the same, never flinching, under the bite of a kris. And he was wondering if this was to be her fate, if she knew and accepted it. But there was time enough to intervene if this proved to be the case. Then the final hammering beats of the drum. They tore at his mind, and the muscles of his hands flexed as he tensed in dread of the next one to come. Then a silence, in which the drums continued to beat in his head. A moan of relief rippled through the crowd.

Willow crumbled in a heap.

Redd was on his feet and running to her. The warriors who tried to keep him back were shoved aside. He bent to her and, unmindful of the fierceness in Nitaloni's face, lifted her in his arms and walked toward the darkness of the pillars beneath the chieftain's house. He left silence and amazement behind him. No one moved after him, and he paused in the darkness, unde-cided on his course. The jungle called, though he had enough control of his senses to realize that such a move would jeopardize the safety of his men. But she was warm and fragrant and close. She needed him now.

The natives were gathering their wits. He decided to climb the steps with her. A light burned in the big room and he laid her gently on the nearest slab and stood watching her. When he looked up at last, a group of armed warriors stood in a circle about them. Soon Willow's eyes fluttered open, focusing on him. At first her face tightened up in panic. Then she smiled at him.

He lowered his head to hers, saw her eyes widen, then fall away, as though his nearness was all that mattered. Then she sat up. With a few words she dismissed the guard. The warriors moved off, reluctant and uncertain.

He felt the need for words as he thought of her in trouble. He tried to tell her in sign talk that the ruby was aboard his ship, that he would go and get it.

She seemed to understand at last. A frantic expression crossed her face and she drew a finger across his neck and pointed to a big sword on the wall. Then she placed her arms about him and drew him down to her. Soft murmurings escaped her as she seemed to place the present in her lover's arms ahead of everything else.

Suddenly her lips slid away and she pushed him from her. Her startled look caused him to glance up. Nitaloni and several warriors were entering the big room.

Redd felt no fear or compunction as he met the ominous gaze of the chieftain. All the savage hate he saw in Nitaloni's face failed to turn his mind from Willow. He resented this intrusion upon his privacy, and the look in his eyes said as much. It was only when Nitaloni favored him with a cunning smile that he began to wonder if there was a catch to all this, if Willow's love-making had been planned. He looked at her. She stood in a corner, either frightened out of her wits or putting on an impressive act.

Nitaloni walked to her and struck her across the face. She fell, though he picked her up and struck her down again.

Redd decided it wasn't planned. And the knowledge that she was sincere caused him to thank the chieftain in silence for proving it with becoming brutality.

With a last look at Willow, he left the room. Fear for her safety ran strong in him, though he put it down and forced his mind back to the business that brought him here. Perhaps he could trade now that the matter of the missing ruby was behind him.

He had no sooner joined his party than he learned the error of his judgment. The ruby continued to dominate the stage.

2

The moon was high. It threw sharp shadows of the palm leaves to the floor of the village. The night breeze off the sea swept in, animating frond and shadow.

At the pits villagers continued to feed the fires. A restlessness gripped them which the white men could not fathom. Redd searched for the cause, finding nothing but effect. Alert now, he scanned the crowd for the old Chinese, who appeared at last on the heels of the priestess. She groped forward a step at a time, her arms stiff and straight before her. In the upturned palms was a brown skull to which she addressed prayers or words intended to appease the ancestors. The natives opened up a path for her all the way to the pits. There she placed the skull on a slab of stone and knelt to it time and again.

Nitaloni walked out of his house with armed men on all sides. His steps were short. Some ceremony was getting under way. Mr. Hyde said:

"What's going on here, sir?"

"Here comes the translator," Redd answered. "We'll find out."

The Chinese bowed just as a gong struck. "Honorable white men will join us in the open clearing."

Redd declined, saying they would stay out of this. The Chinese persisted, saying, "Honorable Captain, Nitaloni has ordered that you and your men join his people in the great ring that is forming. The gods of his ancestors will find the guilty one."

"Guilty?" Redd asked, looking at the big circle of villagers. "Of what?"

"A small pig will be placed in the center of the ring, honorable one. When frightened, the pig will seek to break out of the ring. In doing so, the leg of the person he touches will be that of the one who stole the Great Pigeon of Ramree."

Hyde and Tysbee heard this, as did the sailors. As they looked apprehensively from one to the other, Redd said, "What happens to the guilty party?"

"Nitaloni is as generous as his grandfather wishes him to be." With that he slid noiselessly away.

Tysbee said, "If it's one of us he won't be generous. For Christ's sake, Captain, why don't we get out of here?"

Not waiting to look at Tysbee, Redd gave the order to his men: "Look alive, lads, and get into the circle." About to say more, he stiffened. Something arrested his attention.

Several natives were tying a grunting swine to a coconut palm. Her heavy teats flapped as she struggled. The squealing pig in the ring was probably hers. He had no sooner made this discovery than several warriors appeared before them and pointed to a place in the ring. Nitaloni intended that he, as well as Hyde and Tysbee, should stand directly between the pig in the ring and its mother on the outside. There was no doubting the cunning of the chieftain. He wished to correct the evenness of chance and take a white head.

Redd felt the weight of trouble; his concern was more for his men, who had no part in the loss of the ruby. Once more, doubt of Willow entered his mind. She was under their influence and she could easily be a tool in a clever scheme of murder. He thought seriously of withdrawing his men. Then he realized that he could not do this without forcing open combat.

He looked thoughtfully at Tysbee. Nitaloni had given him an idea, a fascinating one. And strong active devils inside him clamored for his acceptance of it—an end to Tysbee and all the problems of shipping a fugitive aboard. Freedom from threat and trouble in Australia tempted him. Just an accident, Milton Tysbee between an island pig and its mother. He fought the overpowering urge; he had never murdered a man. He won, though it was not a victory to please him.

Feigning obedience to the warriors, he urged Hyde and Tysbee on to a place in the ring nearly opposite the sow. Then a gong sounded, and another, and several hundred natives in a tight ring raised their voices in long pagan sounds. In the bedlam created by drums and voices, Redd was unaware that the mother pig had been moved to a tree directly behind them. And when silence fell over the village and he heard the grunts of the pig behind him, it was too late to move again.

All attention was on the frightened pig inside a ring of still natives and white men. Silence, oppressive and clamorous, hung over the village as the pig, sole accuser and judge ordained by the gods of ancestors, darted crazily about, pausing in utter bewilderment, squealing now with renewed fright as a rock thrown by the chieftain landed near him. He ran, stumbling and rolling, toward the side opposite Redd, only to stop short and stand trembling on wobbly pink legs. Then, with head cocked, he uttered a piercing squeal and listened. From behind the white men an answering grunt was heard. An urgent, commanding sound, one which promised much or everything to the piglet. In the next moment he ran toward the mother. Redd, Tysbee, and Hyde barred the way.

Redd felt a chill running his spine as the pig ran straight toward him. He heard Hyde utter an oath and Tysbee echo it. A native woman next to Redd mouthed unintelligibly. The pig showed no fear of the legs fencing him in until he was almost upon them. Then he paused, squealed, and almost turned about. The grunting outside the circle sounded again, and the pig charged toward the sound, squealing louder in fear. A final squirming and twisting and Redd looked down at his feet.

The pig was through. It had broken the barrier. The legs it squirmed through belonged to Mr. Hyde.

A great cry, pagan and long, broke the silence of the night. Every native and warrior leaped into action and charged the guilty one. Before Redd could draw his pistol, the horde pressed him back, knocking him to the ground, almost trampling him. Shouting continued as he got to his feet and fought his way toward his chief mate. Then he saw Tysbee with spear in hand holding back three metal-clad warriors. Surprising in a way, though it was of small moment; Hyde was the man in danger.

Then the crowd edged backward, clearing a wide circle. In the center of it a man lay still and quiet. Redd looked once, then turned away sick. The head was severed.

It was Mr. Hyde's.

Redd stared about him. There was something unreal about all he saw. The bright moon peeped queerly through the coconut trees, hung over him enormous and sated. The rooftops of the village seemed to come alive, like devils in copper out of a black night. And he was standing among his frightened sailors confused and beaten in a God-struck hour. His loss was strong in him, too strong for belief.

Then he saw Tysbee. His mind cleared. "Why wasn't it you?" he heard himself saying aloud.

Tysbee said nothing; he pointed, and Redd looked at the chieftain standing there erect with arms folded, an expression of primordial ecstasy on his face. And the old Chinese was advancing upon the white men. Flanked by armed warriors, he came on, an evil leer on his face. He stopped at last, bowed low, mockingly, and said in English:

"Nitaloni's grandfather is appeased. Come with me." Looking at Tysbee, he ordered him to follow also.

Redd did not move. He said to the Chinese, "Why did you take my man's life? I came to trade, not to steal."

"We trust no one. We want no white man here. I am the mind, Nitaloni is the sword. You should have stayed away." He bowed politely and said, "Follow me. Nitaloni is impatient."

Nitaloni awaited them in the huge room housing the treasure chest. The walls were lined with his warriors and, in the light of small torches, Redd saw the old priestess and Willow. Two warriors advanced with coconut shells filled with palm wine. Nitaloni drank from each, then sent them to Redd and Tysbee. Redd drank slowly, reluctantly, fighting desperately a growing sense of entrapment. When he returned the shell to a warrior, Nitaloni raised a hand. A gong sounded, and the priestess advanced on the box, removing pegs as she had done the day before. Another gong sounded and Willow stepped forward and lifted the cover of the chest. Next Nitaloni spoke. The Chinese translated the order into English:

"I wish to pay for the head. Take what it is worth and leave my land."

Redd simply stared at the chieftain, unable to believe what he had heard. He felt a trap closing on him, one which he realized few men in the world had ever faced: a horrible choice was his, forced upon him by circumstances and sprung, as he readily understood now, by a most cunning Chinese student of life. The old devil was waiting for him to place a cash value on human life already departed, actually inviting him to accept gold in lieu of Mr. Hyde.

A laugh sounded at his side. It came from Tysbee, who said, "How very interesting this is, Captain. I've wondered for some time how much value you place on any man."

"I'm a practical man," came the slow answer. "I can't replace Mr. Hyde, but I can make them pay." His eyes were narrowed to slits and a burning resolve showed its brisk motion in them. They fell on the saffron-skinned girl, who met his black stare with a sudden hint of panic flickering across her face. A hard smile plucked at his mouth and he was staring at the naked twin swell of her breasts. He said in a voice that aroused admiration for his coolness in even Tysbee:

"You have placed a live woman of beauty before me, and you ask me to take what a white head is worth."

The old Chinese started. Shedding his look of triumph, he began to wring his hands. And Nitaloni's curiosity forced him to relay Redd's message, to which the chieftain replied, "I have spoken."

Redd grinned, baring his contempt for the Chinese, enjoying his fear. He advanced upon Willow and, in the manner of a slave dealer, felt of the flesh of her arms, buttocks, and breasts. Gone was all passion for her; Mr. Hyde's death had put an end to that. He wanted the old Chinese to break under the ordeal. He did, saying in guarded tones:

"Captain, I recall your proposition. You wished to leave something in return for many pigs."

"Talk fast," Redd ordered.

"Take gold, now, instead of my daughter, honorable one. And when you return with many pigs I promise Nitaloni will trade as you wish."

Redd examined him closely, considering the value of the old schemer's future aid here. After all, he hadn't accomplished a thing as far as Tysbee was concerned. And a load of gold, while it wouldn't commence to repay his loss on this night, might partially satisfy his overwhelming passion for revenge.

But he knew this was not so. Nothing short of wholesale slaughter could slake his thirst for vengeance. Even that could not bring back Mr. Hyde.

He studied the Chinese, thinking how clever the Oriental was. He had placed everything likely to tempt a man before the white visitor. With subtleties he had avoided trade and combat. In final summation, he had won a victory with gold, jewels, fragrance, and flesh. Nor was that all——

The old man was once more matching a white man's greed and lust for vengeance against his soul. He was wise in the ways of the Occidental, aware that Redd would feel himself the sucker if he refused the gold, a man cursed if he accepted it.

Redd knew he was losing face by his uncertainty. A decision was overdue. But he could not make this one alone. The entire scheme of Tysbee and the bars revolved about him now. Another loyalty made demands. He must not let Martha down in his moment of uncovered weakness. He had only one choice; he must remember that Tysbee was the core of it all: therefore he must trade Tysbee out of his own life and hers, out of Geoffrey's and Sir George's lives, because they were a part of her. He must do it now while he had the chance. He said to the Chinese:

"I prefer your daughter to gold. So I will take her with me. And when I'm done with her, I'll sell her to the dens of Singapore unless you meet my demands now."

"I have only one pain in me, honorable Captain. You have found it. Speak."

"I will take all the gold I can carry. But I want more. You must hold this man for me." He pointed to Tysbee. "Alive. If he dies by force, I'll bring the Dutch here."

"I am willing to suggest this to Nitaloni," the old man said. "But he will demand many pigs. You have no pigs."

"I promise to return with them," Redd argued.

"You cause me to beg. I shall lose face."

"Which pleases me." Redd laughed bitterly.

The Chinese glanced slowly from him to Willow and on to Nitaloni. He spoke at last. The chieftain listened, then answered. Soon he glared at Redd and argued. The old translator knelt and clutched at his breechclout. When he arose he was smiling. Wringing his hands, he said:

"Nitaloni wants pigs before the new moon."

"He will get them." With that, Redd moved forward and looked into the chest.

He thrust his hands deep into it and fastened them on more gold than he could move. He strained at it, wanting the heathen to pay, and pay dearly. Their watchful eyes were upon him, declaring their superiority over a white man who tried to gorge his greed on a metal they rated below a swine.

Even a white man laughed. It was Tysbee. Redd straightened. The sound wasn't complimentary. It conveyed to him in full Tysbee's regard of a man callous enough to sell his soul. Guilt gripped Redd. He knew that on the surface Tysbee was right. But beyond this aspect, he was wrong. Mr. Hyde alive was worth more to him than all the gold in the Dutch East Indies. But Mr. Hyde was dead. Very dead. The others in the game were not.

There was no hint of triumph or malice in Redd as he said, "Mr. Tysbee, you're staying on here. You know why."

There was no answer in words. Tysbee did not break under the realization of what had happened to him. A stunned expression seemed to tremble across his face. It was evanescent. He nodded calmly. He knew why he was being left here, though the acceptance of it turned his wondering gaze on the yellow metal that had caused it.

Redd bent over the chest, less greedy now. He raised his shoulders and lifted all the gold he could carry. As he staggered under the weight of it toward the steps, Willow ran to him. She fell to her knees and clutched him. Her upturned face said much.

With a last look into the long almond eyes, he took a step forward and another. She slipped to the floor. A little murmur escaped her as he walked down the steps into the night.

He reached his men, looked down at the remains of Mr. Hyde, then up at Nitaloni and the Chinese who had followed him. A glance at the gold he carried caused something to snap in his mind. He threw the metal to the ground at their feet, picked up the body of his mate, and stalked off into the night.

Inside him was a vast emptiness and nostalgia which only the cleanliness and tumult of the open sea could in any manner relieve.

CHAPTER XVIII

During the few hours between tragedy and dawn, Captain Redd's bitterness ran through the ship like vibrations. The men knew the emotions at work in him.

He stood far aft, his face to the east. His utter lack of motion, together with a silence broken only by the roar of the surf outside the lagoon, cast a pall over the entire ship. On the close shore, leaning palms seemed beaten out of silver and mirrored in glass. The stillness of death bore down oppressively.

Mr. Hyde's death was something the men could accept. The manifest loneliness of the master wasn't. Lacking the finality of separation, it was more like a dead calm at sea. The *Lady of Glasgow* hadn't so much as a tremble under her.

Mr. Burk's position was unique. He felt hemmed in between the Old Man's grief and the unnatural quiet of the men. He feared nothing as much as just nothing. His response was instinctive. Craving action, be it in the shape of reeling masts or open strife, he paced the deck, pausing often to stare into faces with a "belay-and-lay-to" look.

The cook's body shone like wet pitch. Whitey didn't drop his glance before the second's, and Mr. Burk stuck his head to within an inch of the other's and glared until the Negro averted his gaze.

"Now, cookie," he said, "ye'll break out pannikins of the blackest damn coffee this side of Mohammed's hell! And show willing!"

"Not on the death watch, suh."

"Pardue's sitting out that watch." His palm cracked on his thigh and the cook bore lively. Then he struck it again, leg up to meet hand, and cried, "All but the anchor and deathwatch! Up for'd now, and get yer tuck!"

A fair breeze blew in with the first pale light of dawn. The sun broke the horizon in a wet sky. It peeped through long streamers of clouds and disappeared often. Then it emerged hot and vapors lifted from jungle and decks. The men awaited the order for sail. Then the ship seemed to come to life. Redd moved forward on the poop and said:

"Mr. Burk, you'll stand up here from now on. Muster the hands and vote us a second mate."

A little later a new officer stood at the break of the poop. He was Dublin Jack. The order to make sail came.

The *Lady* stood out beyond the barrier reefs by eight bells that morning. The sea ran strong, the winds freshening considerably before the island fell under the horizon. Hard squalls struck twice before noon, and the heavy piling of clouds out of the south told of more of the same in gathering ferocity. The old sea was taking on weather, and the master of the ship was thanking her for it. A lusty wind, one to strain the sails in the boltropes, would blow away the stink of last night's grim happenings. By the middle of the first watch the ship was lifting and falling in acres of foam, shaking the seas from her flanks as she moaned for a little less canvas than she carried. Then the rain poured down to unite sky and slate-gray sea. A coil of manila passed turns about the helmsman's body and the standard of the wheel, and a life line was stretched forward on the weather side; the *Lady's* main truck tore across the sky in violent circles while she, sledding down a great hill of the sea into a valley and into another great shock of water that plunged over her bows, cried frantically for a baring of her poles. There were two men at the wheel now, both growling at the press of sail on her.

Mr. Burk said to Redd, "Shall I take in and reef, sir? We'll blow some rags, sure as hell."

Redd spoke cryptically. "Unorthodox, Mr. Burk. But so is the situation." Burk learned what he meant when, an hour later, Redd addressed him, saying:

"We'll heave her to, pass out oil bags from either cathead, and tow." Then all the crispness went out of his voice as he added, "This is the kind of burial Mr. Hyde would like."

Burk winced once in acceptance of the order, then ran gangs aloft to furl sails. A little later the ship herself seemed to bare her head, like her crew, for burial at sea. She tossed and groaned and the wind struck up a gale tune for a hymn.

The remains of Mr. Hyde lay on a bier of planks, sewn into a shroud of sailcloth, anchor chain at the feet, and the British ensign covering all. The crew assembled, except for the men at the wheel.

If there were any tears for Mr. Hyde, the steady downpour covered them well. Water streamed down Redd's face. Oblivious to it, he stood in silence, his eyes on the still figure. He said at last:

"Men, he was a good sailor and mate. The sea won't find a greater sailor than Mr. Hyde. He had that quality that separates the strong from the weak. And he had total loyalty. He lived by it. He was a man."

Lowering his head, then raising it for a look far out over the turbulent sea, he felt an urge to wring out his soul here, to admit his guilt and ask for forgiveness.

He read the burial service in spray striking hard from windward. The sea tossed under the ship and four men were hard put to restrain Mr. Hyde's corpse from a hasty union with the deep. When Redd finished the reading he ordered the flag removed. Then the final words were spoken:

"Commit him overboard."

The planks were tilted and the body of Mr. Hyde slid into a rising wave. The sea swallowed him up; the wave came on, smashed over the rail, and ran across deck and out the scuppers. The wind moaned in the rigging. Mr. Hyde was gone. Forever gone.

Still wet, and still watching the body join the sea, Redd sat in his cabin with logbook open. He had just written into one sentence a new experience in his life:

"Where skulls are worshiped and pigs are worth more than gold, a man begins to question his own sense of values."

He closed the logbook and stared somberly into space. His course was uncharted; the ship was running to nowhere or everywhere, just running on; like a phantom. Perhaps she had lost her pride. Certainly he had little left. Wealth was but a supposition, a fancy; like a sunset, in which the sun hung over a horizon painting the clouds and sea in molten gold for long moments before reducing the wealth of color to an ash.

He felt foolish and cheap. The feeling was compounded of many things. His passions had been artificial. He could not imagine that his longing for the island girl had so shaken his sense of responsibility that he had joined the ring of natives with no thought of defense against what happened. He alone was responsible for Mr. Hyde's death.

It was all too clear now. It evoked in him sharp pangs of remorse. His possession of Willow had caused her to steal the ruby for him. The old priestess and the Chinese had done nothing to stop her from luring him on. She had been a tool, and though an unwitting one, she had severed Mr. Hyde's head from his body.

He cursed her then, but with small satisfaction. Only he was to blame. He said aloud, "A man begins to question his own sense of values."

Tysbee was in his thoughts. A wave of unwanted sympathy engulfed him, and for long moments he wondered how he could have been callous enough to leave a white man on a savage island.

The steward brought him food. He eyed it for some time before tossing it through the open port. He reached for a bottle and drank, looking for a way out of the depression that gripped him. There was a way out. Somewhere, somehow, the way must open up. Away off in the distance there must be a peace he could find. Perhaps it was too far away, beyond his grasp. He might never find it. The awful heaviness continued to grip him.

2

The little island appeared out of a hot stretch in the Indian Ocean in midafternoon of the next day. Ahead, tall coconut trees leaned with the monsoon. As the pass drew near, a large fleet of outrigger canoes came into view. Native pearlers looked up from their work lazily. At a signal, one leaped into the water and came up with a shell or a cluster. Another brown man inserted a knife, looking on, hoping as he kneaded the meat. As always, the shell was tossed aside. Hope sent the blade into another shell.

Redd watched for a long time, almost with envy. He knew the steady hope that beat inside them was missing in him, buried under the things that crowded his mind: an island where pigs were worth more than gold; the headless body of his mate; the price he had paid and was paying for an island girl's love; the man he had left on that island. These things resolved into guilt. They were the past. The future was empty except for dark shadows he could define with only one word: futility. What carried him on, he didn't know, even as he lowered his glass and said:

"Mr. Burk, we'll tack in close for a look."

"Pearls, sir?"

"Pigs." His smile was sardonic. "Now bring her into the mouth and look alive. They may bring pigs or spears."

"Aye, aye, sir. We'll break out guns as well as black sticks." Black sticks meant tobacco.

Redd sniffed the air, soft with the scents of burning sandal-wood, and went below to look at the admiralty charts. He was off the trade lanes, where big ships seldom ventured. It was an island schooner's sea or a pirate's hangout, since over a horizon or two the heavy traffic on the Bombay-Calcutta-Singapore track converged for a dip into Malacca Strait.

Then he seemed to know what it was that forced him to go on. He had a purpose, though it was buried so deep under guilt and remorse that he could scarcely see it. But it was there, in the shape of pigs, which were worth more than gold. It was no longer something to scoff at; it was a fact. He must pay for Tysbee's keep. If he failed, Nitaloni would cut off his head.

It was odd, he thought, that he should be putting Tysbee's safety ahead of the advantage of getting rid of him, ahead of Martha, Sir George, and Geoffrey.

Shaking off the stupor, he entered his cabin.

He was poring over a chart and wondering if he dared venture into Singapore for pigs and risk setting the *Upstart* on his heels again when he became aware of a presence in the cabin. He knew he wasn't alone, and that whoever or whatever occupied the same room with him wasn't a friend. In a quick sweep of the room, his glance fell on a piece of sailcloth. Underneath it something moved.

As he jerked the canvas from the figure he saw a man with matted hair, white stubble growing out of sunken cheeks. The hollow red eyes glared up at him over a pistol.

The man was Milton Tysbee.

He got up slowly. In his glance was murder. He rasped, "I'm ravenous. Haven't eaten since we left the island. Order food, Captain, lots of it, and don't let on I'm here."

Redd could not reconcile him to the man he had left on the island. First, his presence aboard seemed an impossibility. Next, what had been a man two days ago had turned into an animal. The pistol shook with purpose, and the expression on his face was one of forced restraint. Redd sat down and pulled a cord to bring the steward.

Tysbee stood on the other side of the table. "Thought you could leave me on the island, did you?"

"So you got away. How?"

"I ran into the jungle while you were leaving."

"How did you get aboard ship?" Redd asked.

"Easy." Tysbee laughed mirthlessly. "The Jacob's ladder was down. I swam out just before dawn, came over the stern, and went down into the hatch behind the wheel. Later I heard the men vote Dublin Jack second mate. Late last night, when the storm abated, I slipped out of the hatch. Now I'm hungry. And after I eat I'm going to put an end to you, Captain."

"Then what are you going to do, Mr. Tysbee?"

"Swim for that island. There's a British flag flying between the palm trees. A resident is there."

"That's odd. Now I didn't see a flag."

"Go look. Out the port. I can see it from here."

Redd walked to the open port and looked from one end of the island to the other. "I still don't see it," he said.

"On a pole, straight ahead. There. It's whipping to the right."

"Oh. Sure. Sure, Mr. Tysbee. Up there on a pole." He turned slowly. There was no flag flying over the island. The man who held a gun on him was out of his head. One false move and he would shoot.

The steward rapped on the door. Redd looked at Tysbee, who sat between him and the door. "Don't worry," he said. "I'll talk through the closed door."

He was walking past Tysbee. Suddenly he swung his foot in a hard, well-aimed kick at the wrist that held the gun. The pistol left Tysbee's hands and landed across the cabin. Redd picked it up and returned it to the case on the bulkhead. Looking very bewildered, Tysbee said:

"That changes the picture, doesn't it? What are you going to do with me?"

"Make a white man out of you again," came the reply.

Redd ordered food, then sat down. "Mr. Tysbee, help yourself to whisky," he said, placing a bottle and a glass before him.

Tysbee nodded. He shook all over as he poured whisky into a glass, his eyes darting up at Redd with disbelief and wonder in them. He drank in big gulps, poured again, and looked off into space.

"I saw Mr. Hyde die," he said. "I can't get the picture out of my head."

"Neither can I," Redd heard himself saying.

A bitter, accusing laugh followed. Redd knew he wasn't entirely crazy when he said, "But you did it, Captain. You took him there. And you thought you left me there."

"Sure. But I'm going to tell you something, Mr. Tysbee. I'm really glad to see you."

The other's dubious glance and smile seemed to verify his sanity. Redd thought the flag would disappear before his eyes after he satisfied his hunger.

"Maybe you are glad to see me, Captain. But easing the strain of your conscience won't alter your plan to get rid of me one iota, will it?"

"We'll talk about that some other time."

"Listen to me," Tysbee said, leaning forward. "You don't know the feeling of being left alone there. It wasn't fear of losing my life. It wasn't fear of the natives. It was just emptiness, Captain. Like being buried for a long time and staying alive to know about it. I haven't committed a crime that calls for that kind of punishment. The one I'm guilty of is the one I'm anxious to pay for in a court and a prison. That's all I ask. All——" His voice broke.

"But you and Sir George and Geoffrey want me silenced. I'm at your mercy. And I ask your mercy. If it's a matter of putting me on the island again, think of how you would feel there. Then do away with me for good. But do it quickly, Captain. I won't hang on to your conscience forever if you do it that way."

Redd fought back a growing compassion. It threatened all he had planned. With Tysbee here and not on the island, the importance of escape from Untell rose up from the depths to which it had slipped. His practical side on the ascent, he saw the wisdom of returning Tysbee to the island at once.

But not without pigs. Then he was wondering if he could do it with a deckload of pigs.

The steward entered with a large tray, which he almost dropped when he recognized Tysbee. His departure was hurried, and Redd was sure he would go on deck with a story of Jim Turner's ghost.

Tysbee wolfed his food, snatching for more before he could swallow, his eyes alternately lifting to Redd and falling to the food. Redd moved once, causing him to sit up and slow the motion of his jaws.

Sympathy for Tysbee was real now. At the same time he knew what he must do to save himself from Lancefield. And there was Martha asking him to protect her name.

"Mr. Tysbee," he said, "I'm beginning to feel as you do. I wish I'd never heard of this gold scheme."

Tysbee stopped eating for a second or two. He stared blankly at Redd. Without a word, he turned to his food again. Redd watched him until he had eaten the last crumb, until Mr. Burk came to verify the steward's report.

"Now," Redd remarked, pointing at the island, "do you see a British flag waving?"

Tysbee had a gorged look about him as he got up and walked to the port. "You don't see a flag there, do you?" he said. Redd didn't answer. "The resident must have lowered it."

"Sure," Redd replied humoringly.

He saw Tysbee turn and walk out of the cabin. The *Lady's* anchor was out and the ship had no motion under her as she sat just inside the lagoon. He heard Mr. Burk hailing the pearlers. Then he heard a splash, and:

"Man overboard!"

When Redd reached the rail, Mr. Burk was lowering a boat. He said, "It's Mr. Tysbee. He just stood on the rail and stepped off, sir. He's balmy."

Redd took in the situation. Tysbee was swimming frantically toward the island in water more emerald than blue. Ahead, a fleet of outrigger canoes sat menacingly. The natives showed spears. Just beneath the surface of the water two shapes moved like shadows toward Tysbee.

Conflict within Redd was instantaneous: his practical mind saw a way for Tysbee to go; his conscience rebelled, and a flood of sympathy overcame him again. Decision came as quickly. He paused to search the belts of the men nearest him for a knife. Finding one, he sprang to the rail and dived into the green water with Mr. Burk's yell ringing in his ears ahead of a rifle's bark: "Sharks!"

3

Limpid green waters closed over him. The salt burned his eyes. Below were tall castles of coral. They rose out of lacy panicles and deep indigo caverns. A school of scarlet fish darted for cover, and a leopard shark swam curiously toward him as he rose to the surface. It was harmless; the white-bellied ones ahead were not.

As his head bobbed up, he drew in air and reached out in long strokes for Tysbee. The water about him was pink with the blood of a wounded shark. The shot from deck had found its mark, though it served to increase his peril. Blood maddened a shark, lent him a ferocity unlike any beast of land or sea. They smelled blood now and circled away from Tysbee.

The sharks worked in deadly fashion, one flashing an open maw and death-white belly in a terrific burst of speed toward Redd, the other lashing ahead for doubling back. The circles narrowed, and rows of serrated teeth on a business mission drew closer, always one shark closing in, the other moving off.

Tysbee went under once. Fighting frantically and screaming, he gulped water and managed to keep his head above the surface. No more than a dozen yards out from Redd, he cried for the boat from the *Lady* to save him. But the boat was pointing to Redd.

Mr. Burk stood at the poop with gun up. He aimed ahead of a fin purling the water and fired again. A thrashing of water into foam and a widening patch of crimson followed. Sharks began to swarm the lagoon. The boat was some distance from Redd and farther from Tysbee when the pack charged on the wounded shark. In a flash the water was bloodstained all about Tysbee.

Tysbee's life was the most important thing in the world to Redd in that moment. He didn't know why, nor did he stop to consider anything other than saving that life. He thrust his head down and pushed the water behind and above him.

As he swam underwater toward Tysbee, he saw in the fathoms below many sharks. They tore in and out for huge chunks of flesh from their living brother. He knew nothing could stay their appetites now. They were on the kill.

He reached Tysbee, who fought like any drowning man. A blow from the butt of the knife at the base of his skull took all fight out of him. He went limp, head down in the sea. Then, out of nowhere, a long blue shape spun over on its back and slid by with mouth open. Redd could not hold Tysbee and protect them from the monster on the next charge. Grabbing Tysbee, and calling upon all the strength left in him, he flailed out for the boat, counting out the seconds the long blue devil must consume for doubling. Then he pushed Tysbee toward the boat and peered down beneath the surface.

He dived instinctively. The shark was driving straight toward him, like a bullet lobbed from a mortar. The thing gave a mighty flip of its tail and curved over on its back swiftly, its mouth closing and opening in an effort to fasten on its prey. Not a foot from the jaws, Redd thrust out the knife and felt the mighty impact as the blade literally sawed its way into the white belly as the shark drove on. So great was the speed of the beast, Redd was carried along to the bottom of the lagoon before he could let go of the knife.

He had drawn blood. The pack would do the rest. The boat was nearly overhead now. He jackknifed his legs and sped to the surface.

Dublin Jack was pumping water out of Tysbee when his hands fastened on the gunwale. In another moment he was in the boat. He looked at Tysbee, who was spitting up the ocean. But he was alive, and that was all that mattered.

Book five

[IN THE LAP OF THE WIND GODS

. . . Waves lifting and falling away, the island and the sea, and fortunes on the wild wind. . . .

CHAPTER XIX

Nautical miles and stretching seas meant nothing to Captain Redd. Only a driving urge motivated him. It was like escape in a way, like pursuit in another sense. He seemed to be running away from himself as he chased one horizon into the next in search of a peace and freedom lost to him. He was beginning to realize that he might never find them. They no longer existed for a man who ran a ship the size of the *Lady of Glasgow* afoul of the law. But the dream, the single thread of hope, stayed alive in him. What it lived on was tension and drive, drive, drive, sails full and seas running; and, always, that nagging loyalty to ship and a girl. She didn't really exist in the practical course of his life. She was Geoffrey's, not his. But she spoke to him out of the corners of his memory, asking him to guard the house flag and the name of Van Oren against smut and disgrace. It was like a child's dream, foolish, inconsistent with circumstances. But it sent him on and on: in search of pigs.

Pigs stood high in his schemes of hope and loyalty; like a rainbow over a horizon. They constituted his sole defense against the charges that would one day fall. They were synonymous with freedom for all. And they were heavy on his mind on the afternoon he turned his ship from the shark-infested lagoon toward the open sea.

He stared at chart after chart until late in the night. Mr. Burk came upon him and saw a long line he had drawn. It plunged southeast, down the coast of Sumatra, for a thousand miles and came to an end in the port of Batavia. Mr. Burk summed it up in a heavy sigh:

"A damned long run for pigs, sir."

There was no answer. The course was marked; the run lay ahead.

And in the days that followed, the *Lady of Glasgow* ran her latitude obliquely down. She roared past islands and into new seas and weather, out of them into others. The pictures varied, the scenes were the same: water and land and skies, tropic sun and tropic stars from six degrees above the equator to six below. The tacks were long and short, the winds came over the quarter, over the beam, and then they headed her. But on she ran, out of queer nights and hot days and the quiet fall of dawn upon the seas, with her past aboard her in the shape of Melbourne gold and Tysbee, her sense of values twisted out of true—

She was on the pig run.

But ideas were forming in Redd's mind. He looked ahead even as he drove the ship and asked about Tysbee's condition. The little man he couldn't lose was a part of the plans he was shaping. It was good to see the improvement in Tysbee, though it wasn't easy to believe he was beginning to like him. Maybe his presence aboard eased his feeling of guilt; then perhaps he read out of his log too often the truest words he had ever written:

"Where pigs are worth more than gold, a man begins to question his own sense of values."

And pigs continued to stand at the crest of his mind.

Then the fairway opened up. Destination was drawing near. The peaks of Java lifted up out of the sea. The *Lady* ran on into the harbor of Tandjoengpriok, port of Batavia, her senses alert, and splashed her anchor a few hours before sunset.

2

As the *Lady* dropped her hook in the harbor, a three-masted junk worked her way into the Tandjoengpriok roadstead from the east. She was the *Fan Cheuh*, an old trading junk that sailed out of Batavia up to the Celebes and as far east as the Aroe Eilendens. After three months she was nearing home with a cargo made up of *bêche-de-mer*, dye woods, Makassar silver filigree, and spices.

Her nose dipped into the sea, as if in an elaborate Chinese bow to the sinking sun. The big eyes painted on her bows, so she could see where she was going, lifted wet and unblinking before taking on another sea. The long battens, bamboo slats that kept the straw sails flat, looked like ladder rungs. Seated on one over the starboard rail was a small boy with a fishing line in hand. Planks, timbers, masts, and the maze of antiquated cordage groaned and creaked as the seas lifted and dropped under her. Four coolie sailormen stood her decks. On the high poop, the first mate directed her course and the taking in of the after mat.

In a hole in the deck the women prepared a meal. A mat was raised to keep the wind and spray off the galley stove. One huge pot of rice steamed and several small pots were on the deck within reach. On this evening a larger meal than the usual rice and fish and pot-juice tea was in the making. The captain-owner had ordered even two-year-old duck eggs broken out of the straw and mud packs to celebrate the last day of a successful voyage; in fact, everything from fruit and nuts to soup, as turned about in the finest Peking tradition. They would begin with nuts, since land hadn't been touched this side of Bali for fruits, walnuts in candied honey, blanched almond meats, and melon seed. Then fish roe, and the third course, nests of sea birds. Light wine would be served and so would the jade-green yolks of the duck eggs as well as the amber-colored whites. Then sugar-lotus-seed soup. The women were very busy. While below——

The owner, whose name was Fan Cheuh, the same as his ship, sat cross-legged in his tiny cabin enjoying himself. On the other end of his mat his guest and passenger sat in like fashion. A bamboo bowl on the mat between them held their attention.

Fan Cheuh was a small round Chinese with smiling eyes and thick lips. He was bald but for a queue. His garb was dungarees and a short kimono of black silk. He said:

"Now, cricket here mine. If he win, I charge two prices passage. If he lose, you sail free. Done like bargain?"

"Done," came the reply.

"You sure you pay, Missee Lipscee-Grey?"

He had asked that question a hundred times since Tanimbar. Geoffrey merely nodded and looked at the crickets.

Fan Cheuh was teasing them into fighting mood when the junk lurched up and reeled in a heavy list to starboard. He was crawling out of the low-ceilinged cabin and running to the deck in another moment. Mouthing curses on his crew, he disappeared. The ship righted herself, and Geoffrey continued to stare at the crickets without seeing them.

His long hair and full beard, together with a coolie's shirt, knee-length trousers, and bare feet, gave him the appearance of any island tramp. He couldn't blame the Chinese for doubting his ability to pay for passage from Tanimbar.

He would never forget that hellhole any more than he would forget the voyage up from Sydney. His troubles began the moment Martha turned the tables on him. Sir George's wrath was a terrible thing. He ordered Captain Grimble to put him to work like a common deck hand. He ate out of a tin plate with the crew, slept with his inferiors, and helped swab the decks all the way from Sydney. And always, when Martha or Sir George came on deck, the sailors stood guard. They laughed at his attempt to bribe them, and Sir George scoffed at his efforts at reconciliation. Martha ignored him. Not once during the long, slow voyage did she speak to him.

But he was very patient and alert in himself. The years of schooling his emotions came to his aid, made life bearable as he waited for his chance to escape. And he smiled inwardly as he contemplated his revenge. There was no proof that he was in any way connected with the gold scheme; there was every proof that Sir George was. All he wanted was Lancefield's ear. Then he would gradually take over Van Oren, Limited.

The *Vega* touched in for supplies at Jamdena on the island of

Tanimbar. Old Captain Grimble thought Geoffrey was carefully watched by the crew. But he wasn't. Martha and Sir George were ashore. A great pleasure flooded every fiber of his being when he brought the pin down on Grimble's head and watched him crumple to the deck. Then he was overboard, swimming through the nasty water toward the town.

The moment of standing on the beach with water running off him appeared as fresh as then. He was penniless on a tropical edge of the world, with no credentials to substantiate his claims. He slept on the beach that night and begged food from a drunken Englishman after the Dutch resident refused him audience. Then with the dawn a steamer put in for shore. The Queensland Mail packet. She flew the Van Oren pennant. He stole a boat and blistered his hands raw trying to reach her. When he got aboard and told the captain who he was, the officers thought him crazy.

He would not forget to break that captain when he returned to Sydney. The list was piling up.

For weeks he worked in a pub. Then the *Fan Cheuh* sailed in like a bat on the wing one afternoon. The fortieth man he told his story to was the Chinese. He gained passage at last.

And now the coast was opening up. In the city of Batavia were rich men who knew him. If only he could raise the money to buy a shave and haircut and decent clothes before calling on them or visiting the Van Oren office, where they would turn him away as he was now.

With this thought in mind, he eyed the crickets with a speculative gleam in his eyes. Then, quickly, carefully, he forced a tiny piece of straw into the jaws of Fan Cheuh's cricket.

The Chinese returned mouthing imprecations at his worthless mate. "*Verdomde* fool. *Stromdronken,* hell yes," he said, mixing English and Dutch. He sat down and smiled. "Now we see good fight."

Geoffrey said, "I have a proposition. Above passage money, I'll gamble twenty-five pounds English on my cricket."

"You write it so?"

"I'll write it."

"You pay sure?" He studied Geoffrey.

Geoffrey had gambled often on fighting crickets at Chinese

bazaars, where the sport flourished. He looked on without apparent interest as Fan Cheuh teased them on with a hair on a stick. They came closer to one another until their antennae crossed.

Geoffrey's cricket leaped at the other, who made a similar hop and remained still. Geoffrey's then clamped his jaws on the other, disengaged, and hopped about. He leaped forward again and let out a chirrup before fastening his jaws on Fan Cheuh's insect again.

The Chinese bent over the bowl with a look of concern on his face. "Got dam, fight!" he said. "I pay seven guilder for you once. You no lose."

His cricket hopped about and circled as well as the other, though he was unable to grab his adversary. This went on for a full minute, Fan Cheuh exhorting his fighter in an excited voice. As he continued the jabbering of Chinese, his cricket moved to the edge of the bowl and dropped his antennae in the accepted sign of defeat.

Instantly Geoffrey's cricket hopped to the center of the bowl and struck an attitude of triumph, which was emphasized by a loud chirrup. The victory cry had sounded.

Geoffrey smiled behind his beard and lifted his glance slowly. The round face and slant eyes appeared to be expressionless, though the utter lack of emotion in them, together with the silence of the Chinese, who continued to stare at his disgraced fighter, plainly expressed a feeling of incredulity.

"I win," Geoffrey said.

Fan Cheuh's face lifted slowly in calm study of Geoffrey. Without hurry he reached into the bowl and picked up his cricket. A moment later he extracted a piece of straw from its mouth. He looked wise then and said, "Not so sure. But we see. Right away quick see."

So saying, he placed the wisp of straw into the jaws of Geoffrey's cricket and proceeded to draw the fighters together with the hair. Both hopped about, then retired to their former positions. Unable to evoke any further interest for combat between them, he placed them in separate boxes and counted out the money he owed Geoffrey.

Twenty-five pounds was a fortune to Geoffrey. Left alone, he counted it over and over, listening to the musical sounds of coins falling atop coins, thinking of the impeccable Geoffrey who would emerge out of the present beachcomber and begin his ascent anew.

The last light of day fell over the harbor as the junk worked her way through the ships for the Chinese anchoring grounds. Geoffrey leaned against a stanchion on deck and watched the ships slide by. A Van Oren freighter lay close off the portside. Ahead a tall three-master reminded him of the *Castlereagh*. She was a Dutch merchantman. Suddenly he straightened and stared over the starboard bow. The house flag waved above a high mast. A Spanish steamship hid the sailing vessel. Then the junk moved around the obstacle. A smile formed on his face and held. What he saw on the stern of the ship was to him an answer to a prayer to the gods of vengeance.

The sun's last rays gilded the letters that formed *Lady of Glasgow*, Sydney.

3

Some three hundred miles above Tandjoengpriok, Captain Untell was watching that same sunset.

The expression on his face was made up of impatience and pleasure. He had for once outguessed Redd, and he wanted to close in on him. There wouldn't be any mercy shown this time; not after the rudder trick. Nor would any Jim Turner and a crew of superstitious sailors deter him. He had learned a lot, enough to doubt anything and everybody in this game of stern chase. The call was in the letter of the law: "Serve the warrant first. Then make him produce Tysbee." The long run caused him to interpret the law to suit the circumstances.

The wheel felt good in his hands. Every turn of the spokes brought him closer to the unsuspecting *Lady of Glasgow*. The sails were full and drawing and the evening wind promised fair. The big Java Zee was roomy and the track lay open and free. Spray struck his face like a caress.

He had learned of Redd's whereabouts from a slow freighter plying between Singapore and Java earlier in the day. The captain said the *Lady* roared past him only yesterday with her port tacks aboard, pointing due south. From that position and wind, Untell gathered that Redd wasn't running for Sunda Strait. And were he headed for Soerabaja, he would have stood at least one hundred miles to the northeast. Therefore he was Batavia bound.

The cook was dishing up mutton stew. The aroma evoked a grin of anticipation. With fruits from Singapore and a pannikin of strong sweetened tea to mix with the stew in his belly, he could put knots under his stern before eight bells midnight. He yelled at Mr. March to take over the helm.

"And you, Memo," he cried to the Malay, "let the raffee fly!"

About a mile over the port bow a low-waisted steamer burned in the orange colors of sunset. A streamer of black smoke stood out from her one funnel. She came on, no dip or tossing about her. Untell raised his glass and identified her. She was out of Sydney. He was about to lower the glass and go below when he saw her run up her ensign with the code flag under it.

"She's speaking us, Mr. March. We'll hoist the answering pennant at the dip."

With the *Upstart's* signals up, the freighter altered her course toward the schooner. Then she gave her message: *I have important mail for you.*

"Lancefield, no doubt," Untell said.

As the iron ship approached, Untell's crew took in the big sails and Mr. March held her on her toes for a port-to-port meeting. The sun fell away and both ships met with lights aglow. With the mail transferred, the steamer churned the water with her screw and ran on in the night for Bangka Strait and the Singapore road. The *Upstart* raised sail and blew away for Java.

Untell's stew was cold and the tea tasted brackish when he got around to it. He raised his voice like a bellows with an order for hot food, then read Lancefield's letter again:

My dear Captain Untell:

Not two hours after you sailed from Sydney, the schooner Vega *put out to sea. Several days later Sydney papers announced the disappearance of Mr. van Oren, his daughter, and Mr. Lipscomb-Grey. This appears quite irregular, since Van Oren, Limited, is*

like a ship without a rudder, and at a time when either Sir George
or his business manager should be at the helm. The firm's offices
are in a state of confusion and Sydney fears a collapse. After con-
sidering Miss van Oren's proposition earlier in the day in which
the Vega *sailed, I am inclined to believe that she has forced the*
issue upon Sir George and that Mr. Lipscomb-Grey is going along
to smooth troubled waters.

Therefore it is important that we learn the destination of the
schooner. There is every indication that Van Oren and Redd are
guilty and that the time for us to strike is drawing near.

I shall board a steamer tomorrow for Batavia. Meet me there
without fail.

Untell grinned. He folded the letter carefully and poured out a
peg of whisky. As near as he could forecast, Lancefield should be
waiting in Batavia now. This chase was beginning to bear fruit:
Van Oren was on the run—the great Sir George!—and his daughter was the power that sent him after Redd, that carried Geoffrey
along to tie Redd fast. And now Lancefield was on the way. Aye,
it was shaping up nicely, working into the final lap of the chase.

He lifted a glass and said, "Here's to you, Miss van Oren. By
the rolling blue, you're a great help."

A deep chuckle sounded as he thought of his meeting with
Redd. There was much between them that called for a settling
with bare knuckles. Lancefield called it his dessert. He laughed
with anticipation: he'd enjoy that dessert soon, God willing.

4

Redd could not shake the feeling that unseen eyes watched his
every move. The presentiment grew as morning advanced. He
examined every sampan, lighter, schooner, and large ship for some
hidden enemy until his eyes burned. An overwhelming urge to
trip the cable and run for sea enveloped him; it was like a warning, recurrent and strong.

He left the ship only after posting armed sailors all over the
decks. Mr. Burk had strict orders to let no one aboard, from
owner to the governor-general of Java. If anything happened to

arouse suspicion, he should fly a red swallowtail from the fore-royal stay at the truck. On shore, he looked back at the ship and moved on reluctantly toward the office of an old Dutchman whom he knew. Meinoud Baasch could procure supplies of every sort without too much delay.

Half an hour later he was seated in the merchant's water-front office. The fat, balding man laid his pipe down and smiled in puzzled manner over the order Redd had given. He read it back. The last item he read once more:

"One hundred pigs?" Glancing at Redd, he added, "Goot fat pigs iss scarce, Kapitein."

"I don't give a damn how fat they are, mijnheer. When can I get them, and how much will they cost?"

"*Mijn vrind,* if you got cash money, I can haf a t'ousand pigs aboard your ship by sunset."

Redd frowned and leaned forward. "I don't understand."

"*Verdomd!* Sure you hear a t'ing or two. Van Oren, Limited, office here iss close. And here—somevare iss a Sydney paper you should see." He was searching the pigeonholes behind him when he turned and said, "Surely, Kapitein, you joke me. *Ja?*"

"*Neen!*" Redd answered in Dutch. "Show me the paper."

Mijnheer Baasch shrugged and searched out a newspaper. "Here. Look; and vere you been?"

Redd reached for the worn paper and looked at letters in big print: VAN OREN, LIMITED, SUSPENDS OPERATIONS. He read on:

Following the sensational disappearance of Mr. George van Oren and his business manager, Geoffrey Lipscomb-Grey, as well as Miss Martha van Oren, Barrister Cailler Rise, appointor, and power with an interest, has declared a temporary suspension of all trade and business in the firm of Van Oren, Limited, excepting only the normal procedure of the firm's ships at sea to ports of call where the following notice is to be posted: All masters of Van Oren ships are hereby ordered to refrain from discharging or taking on cargoes; if the former exists, to remain in port until ordered to resume business; if in ballast, to return to the home port of Sydney at once.

There was more. He read every word of it and slowly returned the paper to Baasch. He could understand Van Oren's departure with Martha—Untell said they were coming after him—but Geoffrey's part in it, leaving the firm to flounder around in the public eye, didn't make sense. He asked over and over in silence: what the hell had happened; was the pressure stronger in Sydney than he thought?

Then the Dutchman brought the case to him with a question: "You in ballast, Kapitein?"

Redd was thinking that Rise had saved the firm from collapse, though he had seized upon a temporary expedient at best. Pigs became more important as he thought on. He must speed his plans into action. But Baasch was waiting for an answer. A loyalty persisted; unnatural and no part of him, it held sway in his mind. He said:

"I'll pay for the pigs in cash, mijnheer. And you can earn a premium if you get them on deck before sunset."

"Goot. Ve drink now. You look tired."

"On the contrary, I never felt better in my life."

Several minutes later Redd looked out into the harbor at his ship and breathed a great sigh of relief. No red swallowtail whipped in the wind. He stepped into a boat, pointed to the *Lady*, and considered the next step of his plan. Pigs, an important part of it, would be aboard deck by nightfall. Now he was ready to do something about the bullion.

Upon reaching the ship he asked Mr. Burk to come to his cabin. They were no sooner behind closed doors than he said, "Can we trust Dublin Jack all the way?" With the reply, "To hell and back, sir," he ordered the mate to listen carefully. "Now you know where all the bars are placed. Get them together in the main hold and check to be sure you've got them all. I'm ordering four stout boxes. Chips should have them ready by now. You'll pack the bars in sailcloth and fasten the boxes securely. Then select four men to accompany each box to the city.

"I'm taking them to the Javasche Bank."

At one that afternoon a heavy box was lowered to a waiting lighter. Four men boarded the craft, each carrying a concealed pistol. Dublin Jack led that crew. On the quay a cart awaited the cargo. Redd saw it loaded and watched it move off. The next lighter docked, and soon a second cart was on its way to the Priok Canal road. The last two were on their way to Batavia when Redd got into a buggy and followed.

It was nearing four when Redd and sixteen sailors entered the bank. He was soon showing his credentials to the head of the bank, who eyed him with misgiving at the mention of his firm's name. Then he caused the Dutch financier a realistic start:

"I have brought four boxes of gold bars to your bank, mijnheer."

The other stared with open astonishment. "*Ja*," he said. "I have heard of this gold, haven't I?"

"Have you?" Redd met his glance.

After a moment of tense silence, the banker said, "Proceed."

"I have not declared the gold," Redd went on, "for reasons which you can understand. Now do you accept it in confidence, or do I return it to my ship?"

"Kapitein," the banker smiled. "A bank handles money, not morals. So continue."

"Good. I am leaving the gold in the name of Van Oren, Limited. Have your clerks weigh it and write me out a receipt." Redd then produced a sealed letter bearing the firm's crest and said:

"There is one other thing, mijnheer. You will receipt this letter along with the gold."

The time required to weigh the gold was considerable. The sun was low when Redd and his men left the bank. In Redd's pocket was a receipt. In his mind were pigs and high sails. On the way to the harbor he felt of wind and weather with an idea of using them before the night was half gone.

Behind him the backbone ridge of Java burned in the late sun's rays. He turned to look at a high peak, then breathed a great sigh of relief. The old mountain wasn't half as heavy as the weight of the gold he had carried for long weeks. A great load had been lifted from his shoulders. The feeling was short-lived. As the harbor opened up he looked at his ship.

At the fore truck a red swallowtail whipped frenziedly in the wind off the Java Zee.

CHAPTER XX

Mr. Burk's eyes were alert when Redd met him on the *Lady's* deck, though he showed admirable calm as he ordered the swallowtail lowered.

"We had a visitor, sir," he said. "Mr. Lipscomb-Grey." Seeing doubt and a gathering intensity in Redd's glance, he said, "It was Mr. Geoffrey, all right. Dressed up in whites like a lord."

"Did he come aboard?"

"You gave the orders, sir. He didn't. And he didn't like it one damn bit. Said he wanted to check the vouchers. I told him you'd return before sundown. Said he'd return also. But he left a message for you. 'Tell Captain Redd,' says he, 'to be ready to sail for Sydney in the morning.'"

"The hell you say!" Redd exclaimed.

The mate nodded, then pointed toward land. "There they come, sir. All the goddam pigs in Java."

Redd looked forward. The carpenter was putting the last plank on the pens. "All right, Mr. Burk. Fashion all the slings you can and get them on deck fast. And be ready to make sail away from here the moment they're aboard."

"Aye, aye, sir. And if Mr. Geoffrey returns——"

"I'll see him. Did he mention Mr. van Oren?"

"No, sir."

Redd looked out over the harbor for some time. The *Vega* was nowhere in sight. Puzzled, he went below. Soon the squealing pigs sounded above noises of ship and harbor like music to his ears. Pigs were worth more than gold where he was going.

Mijnheer Baasch arrived shortly and had no sooner departed than Mr. Burk appeared.

"He's aboard, sir, and waiting."

Geoffrey entered the cabin and stood calmly aloof. Redd motioned him forward, seeing the same man who had made a stealthy entrance in Sir George's library on the night of Martha's ball. Their glances met and held, as strong and unsettling as on that night when he had informed them of his engagement to Martha. Covering his true feelings of distrust and mounting dislike of Geoffrey, Redd arose and said:

"Welcome aboard."

Stroking his mustache, Geoffrey said, "Thanks," and sat down. As Redd produced whisky and glasses, Geoffrey remarked, "I suppose your mate relayed my message on to you—about returning to Sydney."

"Yes," Redd smiled, looking up at him.

"We'll sail early, Captain. And with all the speed you can coax out of this ship."

"Naturally."

"Your chief mate Mr. Hyde. I haven't seen him," Geoffrey said.

"He's dead. Beheaded on the Island of Gold."

Geoffrey did not conceal his surprise. He sipped slowly, gazing beyond Redd, then at him with as cold a look as Redd had ever seen in a man's eyes. "That foolish adventure almost did the firm in, Captain. But we won't discuss it now."

"Why not?" Redd demanded.

"Because I do not wish to relieve you of your command."

"That's generous of you." There was no hint of mocking humor in the reply. Nor did he smile. Geoffrey could take it any way he chose. Evading the issue, Geoffrey said:

"All those pigs, Captain. What's the idea of turning this ship into a pigsty?"

"There's no cargo for a Van Oren ship these days. The notices Cailler Rise posted leave a captain hanging high and dry. So I bought pigs to trade in the islands."

"Maybe you missed your calling," Geoffrey said. Redd pretended not to understand the innuendo. Geoffrey smiled. "However, you may send the pigs back to shore. The firm has covered your losses before. It can do so again."

Redd looked away in an effort to exercise control over his temper. He said, "Seems you have a poor opinion of me."

"Frankly, yes."

Redd turned to him with a crisp question: "What's on your mind, Geoffrey?"

Unused to the form of address or that tone of voice in a subordinate, Geoffrey stiffened perceptibly. "Just this, Captain," he replied. "The game is up. It has backfired because of you. I'm returning the gold and Mr. Tysbee to Sydney." He paused. "You have them aboard, haven't you?"

"Naturally."

"Very well, you've heard me. Have you anything to say?"

"Aye." Redd got to his feet grinning. "That's the first sensible thing I've heard in a long time."

Shaking his head hopelessly, Geoffrey laughed. His eyes were urgent, however, as he said, "You're rather involved, Captain Redd."

"Aren't we all?" Redd asked.

"Just you, Sir George, and Mr. Tysbee," came the reply. As Redd stood with a look of incredulity on his face, Geoffrey said, "You know, Captain, I have nothing against you, really. And I'm willing to go a long way in using my influence for leniency in your behalf."

"What's the price?"

"Your testimony." He leaned forward, eyes thin and voice low and tense as he said, "I'm innocent. Sir George and Tysbee aren't. You understand, of course."

It was all clear now. With the gold scheme on the rocks, Geoffrey saw an opportunity to take over Van Oren, Limited, in its entirety, over the trampled forms of George van Oren and his daughter.

Knowing he must play the game to a finish, no matter how difficult it was, Redd laughed, to break his anger, and forced himself to say, "My testimony should be worth a hell of a lot more than just leniency. I want some guarantee."

Geoffrey got to his feet. "Think it over, Captain. I'll return before midnight."

Redd watched him get into a skiff in the fading light of day. A little way out, a voice sounded Geoffrey's name over the water. Looking up, Redd saw the *Upstart* sliding in for anchorage.

Mr. Burk came on the run. Pointing, he said, "Look! In the boat moving toward the *Upstart*, sir! If that isn't Mr. Lancefield, my name is King Edward!"

Redd verified this. He saw Lancefield and more. A fast and clever trap was reaching out to ensnare him.

His every sense alerted, he swept the harbor all around in quick appraisal. Next he took in his top-hamper and decks. The fairway was crowded. His men were handy. Pigs squealed. The night was coming down fast over Java. A big star winked on over the foremast, like a warning signal from heaven. The whole scene was a stage for the last act in Lancefield's mind, and the curtain of this night could be the last and final one. If he failed to escape this trap, the plans he had made would fall apart.

"Mr. Burk, *this is it*. Pile on all the sail you can, and bear lively. Maybe we can show them our heels. Maybe we can't."

As the mate ran forward to alert the crew and lend a hand himself, Redd knew he had to win out tonight. Everything was at stake. Now that Geoffrey had shown his true colors, the race had resolved itself into one of open loyalty now: loyalty to Martha, even if she was Geoffrey's wife, and to the firm.

2

The crew came alive with the speed of a star popping into view. The headsails caught the wind and the *Lady* swung her bows alee. Then the after sails pushed her on around and she put the starboard tacks aboard and got a way under her. Sail edges quivered as she strained ahead in the diminishing wash of her turn. Lines tautened and she groaned and creaked in her uppers as the forward urge of her sails continued. From due south her bows had covered twelve points of the compass to northwest. With the wind over her starboard quarter, the order sounded to take in the mainsail; it blanketed the foresail. Up it came in crack time and the good lift of the great foresail raised her bows. Only one thing was wrong:

She flew more canvas than was prudent in a harbor. She took chances no sane master dared in the light of day. And this was night. The reason lay a few ship's lengths astern.

The *Upstart* was not blind to the movements of her quarry. Untell saw the *Lady's* sail cascade down like shadows. He heard the grinding of her anchor cable. He saw her bows slipping westward, then her hull working into a long curve. The steady clanging of her bell and the trumpeting from the bows split the normal quiet of night among ships at anchor.

Redd knew Untell saw and heard. The proof was not long in coming. The *Upstart's* sails were up and she was swinging on the wind. He looked ahead at a maze of anchor lights, at a new experience. The big *Lady* had never weaved in and out in a roadway under so much sail. But this was different. She had to thread a needle in order to escape.

It was a question of sail versus helm, of delicate leverage; and Redd took the wheel himself, aware that she must come up, point away from danger, quickly, and pay off in a hurry on her real course again. Each twist required a proper trim of the sails, and the men were stationed on the alert, ready to use the balance and leverage of all sails from spanker aft to flying jib forward. To top it all, Redd knew his greatest threat next to collision was reducing his headway. Thus he was forced to fly more sail than Untell in order to hold his own.

If ever a touch-and-go situation existed, here was one. Lookouts on the bows cried aft, warning of two ships ahead, both swinging at anchor cables with small water between them. Coming in from the north, a long steamer's port light looked as though it might collide with the *Lady's* bows if the course held. In the other direction, south, three schooners blocked the way. With luck, lots of luck, and a good sailor's prayer, the *Lady* might slip ahead, cross the steamer's bows, and drive through the passageway of the anchored pair ahead on her present course. The alternative was to cut sheets and run her off at once. Redd didn't look aft. He wanted to take the gamble on the wings of his own judgment instead of fear. But prudent judgment rebelled at the risk. All he had left was a fine sense of precision timing, a faculty a seaman acquires by experience and employs by instinct. It is sometimes more reliable than knowledge; again it is the other way around. But seas and ships demand quick decisions, and a total disregard of consequences at times. Redd was studying his way, timing it. Then he was daring it.

The order for more sail came. Then, "Men, if you ever showed smart and handsome, do it now!"

As more sail was loosed into the wind, the steamer snorted out her right to the road. The blast of her deep-throated warnings continued. The *Lady* drove on, committed to her course, to collision or escape. The steamer flashed: "Keep out." Redd returned: "I am holding my course." The bows of both ships aimed at a point of convergence in the night. The steamer's decks were alive, and Redd knew the master was frantic, thinking he had met with a berserk ship, a rare and dreaded menace. As if to confirm this, the steamer sounded three short blasts: "My engines are going full speed astern."

The *Lady of Glasgow* tore ahead. She crossed the steamer's bows with safe yards to spare.

The big steamer had constituted the smaller threat, though the course she had forced on Redd was something else. There was no avoiding the run between the two ships ahead. He had just broken rules of the stream and harbor, had risked his master's license. And now he must risk ship and lives.

The anchored ships were not two hundred feet apart at the widest distance. The *Lady's* broad yards could enter the gap, though the way narrowed down to less than half the distance farther toward the ships' sterns. On the portside sat a square-rigger, on the starboard a steam craft.

Redd took a quick look behind him. The steamer he had run ahead of was moving between the *Lady* and the *Upstart*, forcing Untell to reduce his headway to nothing even as it obscured any vision of the *Lady* running the narrows of hidden anchor cables toward the needle's eye between two black hulls in the night. But the steamer would pass on by in short minutes.

Redd took over the wheel, his senses sharp. His men had their hearts in their mouths, and the crews of the ships they were fast approaching stared at an oncoming ghost, then a mad dog of the sea. Shouts reached Redd's ears: "You'll never make it!" They damned him to hell even as they raced forward of their ships to escape the terrible crash they expected at the stern of one or the other.

As Redd gripped the spokes of the wheel he knew at once her rudder was a sensitive thing, obedient to the slightest touch. The way under the ship increased until he guessed she was driving along at a speed of several knots in excess of the harbor limit. And the Dutch were strict. If the harbor patrol was alerted and near, he might lose before he cleared the port. Now shadowy shapes of a pair of hulls were beginning to close in. He felt them, as he had often felt the downward crash of a wave before its fall. From forward came the cry:

"Scant way on the portside! Easy, sir!"

The ship's head canted to starboard, gently to starboard. A wrong puff of wind or a startled helm could only spell destruction, since her bows were rolling into the narrowest part of the gap. The agitation of the water was also a force to be reckoned with, since a heavy wash would be felt by the ships. It could narrow the channel.

Redd put the helm over a little more, gambling that he could press the yardless steamer with more safety than the wide-sparred three-sticker. He did this, wondering if another second would pass by before his bow scraped the steamer's overhang. Even that could be disastrous: the slightest sheer could upset the balance of sail and send him stern to port into the square-rigger for a tangling of top-hampers and a smashing of hulls. But he had to risk it.

It was now or never; the widest part of the *Lady* wedged into the gap. There was room on both sides, though not to a sailor's eye. Room was acres and miles, not the hell of scant yards. Room was out where a yawing ship could right herself, out in the reaches where a fickle wind could hardly cause a splintering crash. Redd felt another menace now. Already the force of water stirred up by the *Lady* pushed at the free hulls. The wash drove them a few yards farther apart. But the pressure from the other side, like rubber, would send them closer together than before, once the first purl from the *Lady's* bows subsided. He could walk ahead of this, he thought, if the wind held, if his way under the ships split enough water.

He was wondering if the thirteen letters in the *Lady's* name were catching up with her.

The ship quivered all over. Up forward, Pardue gripped a brace with one hand, Dublin Jack's arm with the other. His eyes were wide. He could jump from the rail and land on the steamer's deck.

Looking down into the water, he saw the ships drawing closer. The Old Man was risking too much of a cant to starboard. He was going to touch, and when he did——

"Lord help us!" Pardue cried. "We'll rake off our main and mizzen chains! The after shrouds and backstays will go!"

The margin of safety continued to narrow down to scant feet as Redd tried to clear the sailing vessel's cordage and yards. As the cook put it, a cat could spit on the steamer. Slowly the seconds passed, like eternities, and the main chains seemed to tremble at the small space between them and the steamer. Now anything could happen, from a scraping to double collision. Even a safe passing was possible. The time had come for any of these things. Then——

The sea-gods smiled on Redd. The gap ran past the beam and on down the *Lady's* quarter. She was sailing out of it, free as a cloud across the face of the moon.

"Take the wheel, Pelican Joe!" Redd ordered.

He turned around to look for the *Upstart*. She came on, making a little sail across the big steamer's wake, her way barred unless she dared the run Redd had made. She had to do just that unless she lowered sails again, for an incoming junk now blocked her way to the north. Just as the *Upstart* aimed for Redd's course, the wash from Redd's ship took a rebound, drawing the two ships closer together. They strained at the kedge-anchor cables aft, tightening them up. Untell wasn't blind to the danger. He did the only thing a sane man could do. He ran her off in a hurry.

But in doing so he lost his opportunity to overtake the *Lady of Glasgow*.

Redd laughed. "Mr. Burk, we're free for the time being. Seems Untell will have to swallow his anchor."

3

The ship found running room once she cleared the harbor. Her speed, geared to the occasion since sunset, increased as she hit the open sea. A following wind proved constant, and Redd put out all her lights and crowded on sail for the northern entrance of Sunda Strait.

His respect for Untell's sailing ability was by no means lessened. He said to Mr. Burk, "We've got to get the last stretch of sail in the wind. We've got to take chances and be alert for every advantage in order to reach the Island of Gold ahead of the *Upstart*."

Any hope of losing Lancefield and Untell was a thing of the past. With Geoffrey aboard the *Upstart*, the race, like the gold scheme, had settled down to a run for a rendezvous. Geoffrey's proposal guaranteed this. He could almost hear Geoffrey telling Lancefield of his total innocence, of his helplessness to do anything to stop Sir George. He would sound convincing, more so when he verified everything Lancefield and Untell had suspected all along.

So much for Geoffrey. He thought of Sir George and Martha. Since they knew the location of the Island of Gold, and since it happened to be the only place they could be reasonably sure of intercepting the *Lady*, they would sail there.

In summation, he was racing to a meeting with forces opposed to him. Shipowner and daughter on one side, Lancefield and all he stood for on the other.

He took a look at his own position. Tysbee was aboard. The Melbourne gold wasn't. In his pocket was a receipt for it. On his deck were pigs, one hundred of them. Under him a fast ship tore ahead. He wasn't licked. Not yet. If he could put his plan into action he could face the combined lot of his accusers free of any and all tangible evidence they wanted to use against him. He might win and he might lose.

But first he had to outrun the *Upstart*.

The ship's bell sounded midnight and a change of the watch. The ship creaked and ran on. The smell of pigs wasn't bad when he considered what they stood for. A light appeared far astern over the sea, the red port light of a running ship. It wasn't the *Upstart;* she would show both the red and green of her running lights. But any presence on the sea behind them was a reminder of the chase. He cried into the night:

"Run out the stuns'l booms on the fore." The extra light sails would increase her speed.

The night continued dark but for the Southern Cross and low, dipping stars. A pale light touched the near-by sea with tiny silver fingers. A pearly sheen fell away to vague horizons. Redd stared into it for hours, listening to the talkative elements. The wind weakened and he ordered the sails wet down. The bell struck, again and again, until the world hung still in that quiet hour before dawn.

It was a time when the sea was half water and half imagination, when one felt her voice in the soft touch of water down the ship's sides. A voice or a pulsebeat, always slower than a mortal's, talking to those who have ears for it, saying over and over: peace is all that matters; find it, follow me and find it. Strange talk for a bulk as restless as a woman. Then again it wasn't. The old sea was as fascinating as a woman; curiosity lay over her horizons the same as it lingered behind a woman's eyes: Willow's, or Martha's. What did the sea have to say about them?

The wind wanted to play around in a few points of the compass, to confuse the sea. Willow had been his, Martha hadn't. The old sea said: there you go, wanting what's Geoffrey's. He saw her in Geoffrey's arms. Rebellion ran strong in him. But she belonged to Geoffrey, if Untell told the truth. It didn't make sense. No woman with the qualities he had found in and behind her fine eyes could give as much as she in an embrace and have much left for another man. Not if he knew women.

Perhaps he didn't know women.

So she said she was coming after him. He hoped she meant it. Geoffrey's wife or not, he wanted her in his arms just once more. He wouldn't send her home next time. The sea laughed at him, saying: forget her; take me.

The sea was an old sorceress. She wanted to dominate all, to turn men into slaves, to separate them from realities until they were reduced to tramps of the sea, mere beachcombers. But she was a comforting old hag.

The lookout's cry scattered his thoughts with, "Riding lights far aft. They come on and fall away."

Then dawn eased up under the eastern rim of ocean. It pushed higher until the sky took on the delicate tints in a sea shell. The day came on quickly and the lookout reported schooner sails far astern.

The *Lady* ran the strait that day with all eyes open and looking for an advantage. She blew on past islands with the low Java shores on her portside, the high peaks of Sumatra on her starboard, down past old Krakatau, and due west under the cape for the wind-swept Indian Ocean. A thunderstorm greeted her into the big ocean and brought the night on quickly. The day ended with the *Upstart* hanging on, though farther behind.

"All the sail she'll carry," Redd ordered time and again. He wanted an edge in time, he said to Mr. Burk, just half a day on the island ahead of the *Upstart*. That would be enough. If he failed to use the time properly, then it was all over.

Up forward, pigs squealed in the night. Redd's face tightened up at the sound. He couldn't forget that this was the pig run to a final showdown.

CHAPTER XXI

On a morning three days later, Redd watched the sunrise over the ridges of Sumatra. After driving the ship hard all through the night, he was tired, though any thought of rest was out of the question. He was too tense for sleep. The island wasn't far away now. Within an hour the shore would lift up like a smear over the northern horizon. Even now the lookout sighted the pile of clouds above it. With a last glance ahead, he ordered Mr. Burk to alert him upon sighting land.

He went below and sent for Tysbee. Two pannikins of coffee were on the table when he entered the cabin tense and alert. Redd invited him to sit down before saying:

"We're nearing the island."

Tysbee's eyes narrowed as he swallowed hard and lowered the pannikin to the table. His glance slid away.

"Mr. Tysbee, I want you to shave and look presentable before we drop anchor."

"Why? Nitaloni won't care how I look."

"We won't talk about that now. I didn't send for you to gloat over you."

"Isn't that what you're doing right now?"

"No. And if you'll listen, I'll tell you more. I never have. From the first I said it was all business. It still is." Pausing to let this sink home, he said, "But it's a different kind of business now."

"Maybe so," came the dubious reply. "However, you're shipping pigs to pay Nitaloni for my keep. I can't see how it has changed any."

"You will. With Lancefield and Geoffrey only a few hours behind us, everything will come out in the open on this day." After telling of his meeting with Geoffrey and acquainting the other with all he suspected of both Geoffrey and Sir George, he said:

"Do you still wish to confess?"

"More than ever, Captain."

"I thought so. Well, it might surprise you to learn I feel the same."

"Yes. It would if I believed you. But I don't, can't. Not with all those pigs and your mind made up to trade me into exile."

"Mr. Tysbee, I told you it was a different kind of business now. It is. I don't relish the idea of leaving you on that island. Not at all. But you're all confession and no defense. That makes you a bad risk as a partner, doesn't it? After all, we're in the same fix. Geoffrey is pointing to you, Sir George, and me. He'll say we're the guilty ones."

Tysbee thought over this and said, "And it looks as though he'll get away with it."

"Sort of makes your blood boil, doesn't it?" Redd asked, watching him closely. "Especially when you think of Sir George, who will say you and I are guilty."

"Yes, it does," Tysbee agreed. "But what are you leading up to?"

"The underlying facts in this case. Something you've forgotten. Didn't you actually believe you were borrowing the gold when you took it? And when Untell turned on Sir George and me, didn't you begin to think you had stolen it? Guilt has built up in you until you don't feel anything but guilt. Isn't this true?"

Tysbee seemed to look all the way into the vaults of the Bank of Melbourne before glancing up curiously. "Yes. It's true, all right. But——"

"One thing at a time," Redd broke in. "Just *what* are you guilty of?"

"Why, I was gullible, and greedy."

"Exactly. So was I, Mr. Tysbee. I sailed after the *Castlereagh* for one reason. I was afraid I'd lose my ship if I didn't. After that I had to break a few more laws, and still a few more, from kidnaping you to violating rules of the stream. And so you have it. A man can be a damn fool or he can be loyal to something, depending on the way you care to look at it." He paused, then said:

"Just what are you loyal to?"

The question took Tysbee by surprise. He thought about it for some time before saying, "I don't know. In fact, I don't ever remember any loyalty in me to anyone or anything."

"You're in one hell of a fix," Redd smiled. "Why don't you think it over, Mr. Tysbee?"

"Why should I? Where I'm going I'll have plenty of time to think—that is, if I live. But you've said a lot, Captain. And you've left a lot unsaid. You said you wanted to confess. Does that mean you're giving up?"

"I never mentioned it, did I?"

"No. But just what the devil is the idea of this conference? What do you expect me to believe?"

"That maybe you're not as guilty as you thought, for one thing. That and anything else you like."

"I'd enjoy believing you weren't shipping pigs to pay for my keep on the island." He laughed, then said, "Just why are you running pigs, Captain?"

"If I said it was for the same reason I went after the *Castlereagh*, you wouldn't understand. So I'll just say, wait and see."

Tysbee was examining him closely when the lookout's cry reached their ears: "Deck ahoy! We're raising the island over the port bow!"

Redd got to his feet and extended a hand. Tysbee looked at it wonderingly, then lifted his glance. What he saw in Redd's face was a deep honesty he could neither deny nor bury under past dislike. Slowly he extended his hand.

Redd grinned and gave him a friendly slap on the shoulder before moving off to deck. As Tysbee watched him go a mixed feeling of relief and doubt stole over him. It rose and fell away, like waves cresting and breaking, trust over suspicion, and the other way about, one over the other until the man who had offered his hand obscured all else. He inspired admiration and loyalty, the kind his men had for him, and no amount of stubborn resistance on Tysbee's part could restrain this fresh and unwanted regard for the man inside Captain Redd.

2

Redd's intent gaze remained fixed on the blur of land. He stood on the forecastlehead, with bowsprit and jib boom and whitecaps ahead, pigs directly behind and below him. In his mind the past and close future ran together; there was no way to assess the value of the past until the final crux ahead joined it. The island fascinated him now because of what it held in store for everyone on this day. Some would win and some would lose. Lancefield and Untell were aiming at the island with hopes of victory high; so was Geoffrey. And Sir George typified success. No one involved could be called a fool. The day was too young for that.

One thought led to another, and always Martha stood in the background as he looked from this angle to that for any error that might trip him.

One seemingly insignificant item rose up to annoy him as the island lifted all the way up out of the sea. Perhaps he magnified the effect of Tysbee's escape from the natives to his ship, though he could not put aside the thought that the Chinese and Nitaloni might suspect him of running off with Tysbee, who in their eyes stood as a guarantee that he would return with pigs. That being true, a vital part of his plan would be annulled. But it was too late to do anything about that.

His impatient glance up at the lookout seemed to tell him that he was tense and expectant, more than curious about the whereabouts of Martha. He was hoping he would soon hear the cry, "Schooner in the lagoon," when the lookout aft spoke the deck:

"Sail ho! Breaking the southern horizon."

Redd winced. Untell was cutting down his lead. He needed time to get the pigs inland. Fighting back a twinge of uneasiness, he took a quick inventory of the top-hamper with a thought of getting more speed out of the *Lady*. But she was doing all she could in this wind.

Then an undeniable fact struck home. The stern chase was drawing to a close. This was the last lap. The ship under him was suddenly a very dear thing. The possibility of a final separation from her wasn't comforting. The *Lady of Glasgow* and he had formed a team over the years; had run through every kind of weather and sea; had called on one another in trouble. The pulsebeat of one was that of the other. And now their heartbeat was one. Another life made itself known then. The *Lady* wore a woman's petticoat for sails—Martha's.

But Sir George or Geoffrey might annul her influence if she came to his aid. He was sure they would try, and he wasn't at all sure that Martha could or would do a thing to stop them. Actually, he was on his own, a man in urgent need of time and luck in big doses. Time was running out on him.

He was busy reshaping his plans when the masthead advised that the pass was opening up. Curiosity got the better of him. He climbed up into the rigging for a better look. At the cross-trees he raised his glass and searched for a mast above the southern arm of the lagoon. Half an hour went by. The expanse of water was dotted with whitecaps; and the sea, whipped by the monsoon, broke in white lines of surf on the barrier reefs. The island came on slowly, the pass widening over the port bow. Soon he could see the surf sliding in, rippling over the placid waters within the gap.

Then he saw it: sticking up out of the lagoon was a bare mast. Then another. The *Vega* awaited him. A thin smile broke the tightness of his face. It was dedicated to the woman who had sailed here, if he could believe Untell, for the express purpose of returning him to Sydney and a court.

The deck called; he had much to do before the *Lady* slid through the pass, though he remained still, staring at the island without seeing it. Challenge and defiance mixed with a prodigious ambition to show this woman a thing or two, to open her eyes once and for all with the success of what he had in mind. If she could be independent as the weather, so could he; in fact, he would begin before the splash of the anchor. He would ignore her, as though she wasn't there. As for Sir George——

He could go to hell.

On deck again, he walked to the poop and addressed Mr. Burk tersely. "The *Vega* is inside. I want no one to so much as pretend he sees her. Understand?" With the mate's perplexed nod, he said:

"Now I want those pigs ashore in a billy-blue hurry. I'm going to the village, alone, ahead of a dozen men who will drive the pigs to the chieftain's house as fast as they can."

"Alone?" Mr. Burk screwed up his face. "Aren't you taking short odds on your head?"

"I'm taking all sorts of chances today."

"I can believe that. But what about Mr. Tysbee, sir? Isn't he going along?"

Redd looked across the deck at Tysbee, then called out to him. When he joined them, looking more like the man they had taken aboard in Sydney Harbor, Redd stared straight into his eyes and said to the mate:

"Mr. Burk, you'll send Dublin Jack and six armed men with Mr. Tysbee. I want him concealed behind the jungle wall until I need him.

"However, he mustn't be recognized by anyone aboard the *Vega*. So you'll see that he's unloaded like cargo. Put him in a sack." His glance held and Tysbee did not look away.

"What about it, Jim Turner?" Redd asked.

Doubt was strong in Tysbee's face. His hands trembled a little. He said nothing; he just searched deep behind Redd's eyes for the qualities he had found in him on this very morning. He knew that men were great pretenders; that many a hoax had been practiced under the guise of friendliness; that Redd, in a trap, had a chance of escape without him, and none if tied to him.

Everything in him cried in sharp warning: "Redd's tricking you." Redd's eyes said this wasn't true. But reason didn't always win out; sometimes those qualities that didn't make sense were true and dependable. His face softened and he said:

"Jim Turner at your service, Captain."

Redd turned for a look at the island. Next he ordered the ship put on the port tack for a run inside the pass. By the time the helm was put over for the last sweep toward the pass and anchorage, the island stood up close. Scenes were familiar. The same coconut trees looked out over the barrier and surf across emerald and cobalt waters; the same gap opened wide for the same ship that had entered with Mr. Hyde alive.

The *Lady* was sliding between the coral heads. Martha and the *Vega* were inside. Outside, the *Upstart* ran hull up over the southern line of ocean. Redd's voice was calm as he said:

"All right, lads. Make ready the boats and let the pigs squeal. We're reaching destination."

3

All was quiet aboard the *Vega* that morning. Sir George had dozed off shortly after throwing a baited hook overboard. Captain Grimble secured the line, and a sailor watched it tighten suddenly and saw across the water from bows to stern and back. He shrugged and turned away; it was Sir George's catch to do with as he pleased.

Grimble mopped his face. He took in the circular horizon out of habit before stalking below and booming forth, "The boat's ready and waiting, Miss Martha. But I'm going along."

An answering voice lifted to him with a word: "Why?"

"Happens so I'm not anxious to see you taking chances on the islet." He cocked an ear for her reply. It came and he grinned, saying, "Lively now," as though good shipboard routine began and ended with the captain getting in the last word.

Behind the closed door to her stateroom, Martha smiled. Old Captain Happen-so, by his constant attention to her, had made the voyage endurable. During long days in which her father fussed and complained, because she would not return to Sydney or hear of his return to save the firm from outside pressure as well as Geoffrey, Grimble taught her how to handle a schooner, how to catch large fish and sing the old songs of the sea. In his company troubles vanished. Alone, or with her father, they came on fresher and larger. Geoffrey free posed a problem she could not cope with. She wasn't blind to the trouble he could and would make, from ruining her father financially to forcing disgrace on the name of Van Oren. He seemed to annul all her hopes and plans; worse, he tightened the cords that bound Redd.

She breathed out a hopeless sigh and got into a dress. The hot, damp air of the cabin seemed to close in on her. And a look into the mirror at her wan, troubled face frightened her; or perhaps her vanity. The sea tan on her face, neck, and arms would startle the pale-complexioned women of Sydney or London. However, that didn't matter; when Geoffrey told his story society would shun her.

Geoffrey's escape on Tanimbar left her in a state of defeat. For days after that, hope was a small thing inside her. There were times when she thought she would marry him if given another chance. It was too late for that. He was too wise and crafty. She had made a terrible mess of everything. But one star continued to shine. Redd. If she could find him and convince him of the wisdom of giving up, she might salvage a little reward. From Tanimbar to Java and on up the coast of Sumatra to this island on the equator that word *if* loomed large. Often she wanted to give up, and once she broke down and cried before dear old Captain Happen-so. The simple things he said to her were engraved on her memory. He talked to a child and saw the resolute woman emerge out of defeat.

Looking for something to buoy her spirits, so she could meet her father and shed a little radiance on him, she moved slowly to the deck. At the companion she paused and listened. Her father was saying:

"Ten days here! Grimble, I'm not waiting any longer. Not with my business going on the rocks. Get her ready to sail, and——"

Yesterday and the day before and the day before that he had stormed out in the same manner. Now she must go on deck and calm him, persuade him again, remind him of her promise to Lancefield to bring Redd back. Lancefield's influence in his behalf as well as Redd's was all she had left to hope for, and she intended to hold fast to that straw.

Grimble was saying, "Aye, aye, sir," as he had all along. Changing George van Oren's mind was her job. It was getting monotonous. So was the depressing island and lagoon and hot climate. The place seemed to be uninhabited, though at night she heard gongs from the interior. The sounds frightened her. She could not blame her father for wanting to sail away.

She walked toward his chair and heard him grumbling aloud, about Geoffrey being free to feed the newspapers and courts a pack of lies; about the pressure on Van Oren, Limited, from the banks and mines; about lawsuits and a collapse, and the crying need for money— "And I, the head of the firm, sitting it out in a stinking lagoon!" He almost shouted her name as she came up behind him.

"Calm yourself," she said gently.

He started at her nearness, then settled down to tell her they were raising sail today. She looked beyond the defiance in his face. He had aged considerably since the morning she had told him about Geoffrey's threat. His eyes were deep and hollow, and new lines pinched his cheeks, and the gray was showing beyond his temples.

"Captain Redd will come, Father."

"Rubbish! You know as well as I that Lancefield has him behind bars. Geoffrey saw to that."

"Somehow I can't believe it. And if it is true, you'll join him. And yet you continue to talk about the firm and money. Aren't you forgetting the real issue?"

"I know that everything I've worked for all these years is being taken away from me."

She was about to say it didn't matter when Grimble cried, "Sails! Look out there. A three-sticker! By thunder, she's the *Lady of Glasgow!*"

Sir George was up and running toward Grimble instantly. Seizing the glass, he looked. "It's her, all right. Tacking for the pass." Lowering the glass, he said, "Well I'll be damned!"

Martha felt little frightening sensations running through her.

Shock and relief came at once, too much in short seconds after days and days of sailing and waiting. Anxiety and unbridled impatience followed; she could not wait to meet Redd, to look at him and touch him, to learn how he had escaped Lancefield. But he had come. That was all that mattered. And now she realized that the thought of his coming had been the light that burned in her with a steadfast shining through all the trouble and waiting. Her heart beat with it and stirred up gladness in her until she wanted to cry out: "Hurry! Hurry to me!"

He was coming on, majestically. The *Lady* seemed a queen in all the splendor of white sails as she eased along toward the gap in the coral heads, her lower sails coming in. She sat in the pass under topgallants and royals. Now the former were flying loose and the men were clawing at them for furling. Her kites carried her inside slowly. Soon she would coast on in and lose all motion. Right now she was sliding forward, taking on shape and detail. The slim white crescents of her royals swayed in the wind, and one fluttered, flying out for taking in. Then another. There was nothing about the ship that wasn't beautiful and free. And nothing, Martha thought, to suggest that she was a pirate.

The *Lady* was her ship. And she was proud of her.

She raised the telescope and searched through the maze of cordage and bulwarks for Redd. There he stood, tall and strong and commanding against the jerking sway of the spanker boom. In the brief glance before the helm shifted to hide him, she saw the bronze color of a deepwater man, the things that hinted of tropic silver and storms and great shocks of water and sun-lit spray. A symbol of flying seas, a ringer of bells in her heart. She wanted him under her eyes always, in her arms forever. She was all emotion now; a heat flamed up in her. There was no thought of how she would meet him, of what she would say to him, of any awkwardness in the situation; she was all eagerness.

An odd sound reached her ears. Pigs squealed aboard Redd's ship, and up forward she saw men swing trussed pigs. Boats were going over the starboard side.

Captain Grimble said, "She's got a cargo. Pigs, Sir George!"

Van Oren laughed sardonically and said, "Van Oren, Limited, has reached its level."

The *Lady* came on inside the pass with a graceful, bare-poled poetry of motion about her. Like a banking tern with wings frozen and outstretched. She was close enough to hail in another few minutes. Grimble called out to her. So did Martha.

There was no answer from the *Lady*. Not a sailor glanced toward the *Vega*.

Unable to understand what was happening aboard the *Lady*, she stared across the water at Redd. He was gazing intently at the beach. His hand came up and a cry sounded from the poop. The anchor had no sooner splashed than he disappeared over the far side of the ship.

Puzzled, and resenting his decision to ignore her, she closed her ears to all her father and Grimble were saying about his crazy doing and watched the activity on deck. Two boats were in the water, another on its way. In the first, sitting alone and bending on the oars, was Redd.

The shrill cries of pigs grew louder. The lagoon formed a sounding box that tossed the sounds about in piercing discord. A boatload of them was on the way to the beach. Then the swirling breeze wafted the smell of pigs across the water.

Martha turned away in an effort to believe and understand all she had seen. The same puzzlement and lack of comprehension she felt were strong in the faces of her father and Captain Grimble.

But Redd had offended her. He had not favored her with a glance. She whirled, as if he were near and waiting for a piece of her mind, and stared at him. He was leaving the boat and walking into the shade of the coconut palms. She could not take her eyes off him until he stepped behind large green fronds and out of sight. Even then she continued to look. Nor did she shift her gaze from the island when a dozen sailors herded pigs into the jungle, or when a smaller group beached a boat and carried a large sack up the shore and disappeared also.

The squealing of pigs gradually faded away, and the island stood as quiet and peaceful as before. The rent healed over. Only the silent jungle seemed to know the secret of Captain Redd's strange behavior.

CHAPTER XXII

Redd stalked on toward the village, parting huge leaves without any thought or fear of lurking natives. The stone walk lay ahead, and he left the shade for the open stretch of tall grass. On he went, oblivious to the burning afternoon sun, to the temptation a lone white man placed before head-hunters. He knew he was being watched now; the noise of a hundred pigs ran ahead of him on the wind.

Grim purpose showed on his face. This mission was like the last card before a showdown. He was still the dealer. The stakes were high. But his mind wasn't so crowded with these things now. Something else gripped him. It was personal and heavy within him.

He had been able to hold his emotions in check until the moment he looked up from the oars. She had drawn his glance just as a magnet attracts steel shavings. The picture of her on the *Vega's* deck still danced before his eyes like spots from looking at the sun.

Everything in him had rushed to his head without warning and collided with a terrific impact: a yearning for her he could never put down, a memory of her eyes and lips and all that lay behind them; these against unyielding jealousy and resentment as he thought of her as Geoffrey's wife.

A monkey chattered and a bird screamed behind him. A shape writhed out of his path and on into the grass. Yellow metal danced in the sun ahead, then fell flat to the ground. Willow crossed his mind. Mr. Hyde stood out of his memory for a fleeting second. Sir George returned him to Martha. He wanted to hurt her, wanted her in Willow's place for an evening on the beach. Then he would walk off and leave her.

His mind ticked on, as though minus any control. The fierceness of the untamed land he trod appealed to him now. He was a part of it. Nitaloni's desires were his for the time, his gods and skulls and code of values were real; they were tangible symbols of his black mood.

The village roofs stood up in the distance, half light and half shadow under the palms. He walked on, his jaw clamped tightly. Little ridges of muscles crept up and down his cheeks. His mission was for her, not for himself. By going on he could gain in no way that appealed to him. Why he didn't turn back was a mystery to even him. But he knew why and he kept going. Any desire to hurt her was gone. In its place a tender devotion rallied strong in him.

Native houses stood closer, larger. The wide paved courtyard opened up suddenly out of the jungle growth. He lost a step as pictures of Mr. Hyde's death crowded out Martha and Geoffrey. But that, too, was instantly put out of mind: a score of dazzling warriors advanced to meet him. His pace held as they stopped still and formed a solid barrier.

He knew only contempt for the guard. It was in his eyes as he walked straight into the wall. The center of the line opened up for him, revealing Nitaloni, the old priestess, and the Chinese farther on in the shadows before the chieftain's house.

With no patience for ceremony, he stopped before Nitaloni and came to the point at once. "I have come to trade. Consult your grandfather and let's get down to business."

He did not miss the sharp enmity in Nitaloni's face. The priestess remained expressionless. The Chinese looked alert and treacherous. He said:

"Honorable captain did not keep bargain. He took the white man he was supposed to leave here. Nitaloni's grandfather is not pleased. You promised to say nothing about our island, and yet another ship has come. Nitaloni's grandfather is not pleased."

"Tell his grandfather I left the white man here, that you let him escape. I have returned as I promised. I have kept faith with him. The ship came for me, not to bother you."

Nitaloni listened to this, or to whatever the Chinese was conveying to him. When the palaver ended, he bowed and the translator said, "You have not brought the white man here."

"But I have one hundred pigs on the way."

"Many pigs," came the thoughtful reply. He turned slowly and looked deep into the eyes of the priestess, then into Nitaloni's. Redd saw in the exchange of glances a deep primeval cunning that seemed stripped of all amenity; he felt as though he were listening to some evil laughter in the jungle night. Though the only sounds that reached his ears were the high squeals of pigs and the cries of his men between the sea and the village. All else was quiet; too quiet.

Nitaloni walked to the slab before his house and returned with his grandfather in the shape of a brown skull. The priestess bowed and talked to the hollow-eyed thing. It grinned back at her, as if it were the source of all savage wickedness and craft.

Redd seemed to know that it was.

He felt hemmed in. With warriors all around him, all anxious to charge with spears, he began to wonder at his own foolhardiness that had sent him here alone. If the skull said he must die, he hadn't a ghost of a show.

The Chinese spoke when the skull was returned to its place under the slab. "Nitaloni's grandfather speaks favorably of you, honorable Captain. But he says he must see the pigs first."

Redd nodded agreement, though he remained alert. He could almost smell treachery in the wind. A further exchange of glances between the ruling three convinced him they were up to something.

A long half hour went by before the pigs were driven into the courtyard. Redd felt more at ease with a dozen armed sailors at hand. He warned them to look alert and alive. Then he studied Nitaloni, who seemed pleased and greedy as he looked at the wealth of one hundred pigs. When they were counted, the Chinese said:

"Now bring the white man and we shall trade."

"I am not leaving the white man here."

The Chinese showed surprise, as did the chieftain and the priestess when they learned of this. A sharp look of anger crossed Nitaloni's face. Redd met his glance, knowing then that they had schemed for a head: Tysbee's. A shudder ran his spine. Any head would do, and a head was their objective on this day. And with the pigs in their possession now, they might try to take one at any moment.

With hands hidden in his kimono sleeves, the Chinese stepped forward. "What do you wish?" he asked.

"Gold," Redd answered.

They did not discuss this new turn of affairs with the chieftain's grandfather. Redd knew why: he had already spoken the words they wished to hear. A skull needed company. The Chinese said after a few words with Nitaloni:

"You are favored on this day. Come into Nitaloni's house."

Redd took his men with him up the stairway to the room housing the treasure. They stood behind him, tense and ready for anything. The gong sounded and the old woman walked out from the raised bamboo blind, as she had done twice before in Redd's presence, removed the pegs from the lid, and stepped back. The gong struck again and Willow appeared as before, naked but for headpiece, bracelets, and gold breechclout.

Her long eyes lifted to Redd's face with an animal devotion in them. Then she removed the lid of the box and stood aside.

Redd continued to look at her. Memories of their hours under the palms were fresh with the sight of her. She kindled a fire in him again, and her face was touched with a yearning for him. Her eyes grew heavy and fell away.

Nitaloni and the priestess broke the silence of the room with a low exchange of words that caused Willow a start. Her expression was one of fear and disbelief as she looked at Redd. He felt her warning and tensed, even as the Chinese who claimed to be her father intercepted her glance and spoke sharply. Lowering her head, she moved away.

Redd lifted sheet after sheet of their gold and handed it to his men. He was a little greedy now, though he restrained himself.

"You have enough?" the Chinese grinned.

"Enough."

No move was made to stop them as they left the village under the weight of island gold. The sun hung over the western horizon with two hours left of the day when the party walked into the high grass. Behind them all seemed peaceful and serene. A gong sounded, and before the tones melted away, it sounded again, sharply. The last vibrations were muted. Redd paused and listened. Very much alert now, he ordered his men to hurry.

From the jungle where it joined the village on the east, monkeys chattered and scolded. A bird cried, and a loud scream of another followed. Redd quickened his step.

They had reached the end of the stone walk when a figure ran out of a hibiscus grove. It was Willow. She pointed toward the dense green wall behind her and then toward the beach. The frantic look in her face said: "Run for your lives!"

Redd needed no further warning. His crisp command sent the men crashing through the thick growth at top speed. The gold was heavy and he ordered each man to drop half his load. One sailor let go of all he carried. Redd picked up a few sheets of it and joined Willow, who seemed to whimper and talk at once. They were separated from the beach by only a screen of large waving fronds when the yell sounded behind them.

"To the boats! Damn lively!" Redd cried.

Then he thought of Tysbee and the six sailors who were trapped a few hundred yards up the beach. Cupping his hands, he shouted a warning: they should swim for the ship at once.

Even as a flying spear grazed his head and opened the skin just above his temple, he wanted to countermand that order. He had to keep Tysbee hidden from Lancefield. But it was too late. Nitaloni's warriors were closing in, and the chieftain ran ahead of them.

Redd was on the beach and firing into the metal-clad warriors when Nitaloni stepped out into the open and lifted his spear. A dozen or more of his men leaped over the bushes and came on. Redd's men fired from the cover of scattered coconut trunks. Warriors fell one by one, going down with loud screams of defiance. Many arose from the ground and flung spears in their last living moments.

It was one of these that sliced the skin on Redd's forearm. Blood flowed until he tied it off with a part of his shirt. The head wound continued to bleed slowly.

Nitaloni came on, his shoulder and thigh streaming blood. He loomed large, a half-crimson devil who defied a white man's gun. Step by step he advanced, taking another bullet from Redd's gun in the side. Willow screamed as Redd stepped into the open and aimed at his heart.

Then Redd saw something that caused him to hesitate: Tysbee darted from behind a tree and fell. A spear pinned him to the ground. From his position Redd wasn't sure whether Tysbee's wound was serious.

In Redd's split second of hesitation Nitaloni heaved his spear. It flew accurately toward its mark. Redd glanced around and saw it coming. The point fascinated him, seemed to paralyze every muscle in his body. He tried to gather strength to move, to fall away from it. He wasn't sure whether he had moved or not when Willow threw herself in front of him.

He was deaf to the sounds of guns firing, to a scream as a spear went through the flesh of Pardue's leg, to Tysbee's frantic cry as he jerked the spear out of his shoulder and ran like a crazy man into the edge of the jungle and fell. He was deaf and blind to everything but Willow.

She stood still for what seemed long eternities, her eyes fastened on him with shock and disbelief. Then acceptance came and she smiled up at him as she had when he held her in his arms. Her final glance of love seemed to place before him a woman half alive, half beauty and half imagination, still fighting off her last horizon. He looked at the gold-tipped spear sticking up between the tawny twin swells of her breasts. He couldn't believe it.

A spasm shook her and she reached for his lips. He gave them to her as he lowered her gently to her side. With a final jerk she was gone, though still smiling.

When Redd got to his feet all was quiet. The sailors stood near the jungle edge in relaxed poses. Nitaloni lay dead. Redd turned around and swept the lagoon with tired eyes.

Martha stood on the *Vega's* deck. She studied him through a telescope. He couldn't suppress the smile that formed on his face. She lowered the glass and turned her back on him. It didn't matter. Nothing was so very important. Only death.

He lowered his eyes to Willow again and trembled all over as strong emotions he had never known before misted his vision and whispered soft words into the island winds. When he looked up again, everything was real, and important——

The *Upstart* was moving in through the coral heads.

2

A calm settled over him as he stared at the schooner. He was glad to see her. The chase had ended. For some strange reason, he was no longer in a hurry. He turned toward Tysbee, wondering if time was standing still, or if an island where pigs were worth more than gold had robbed him of his wits.

He bent over Tysbee and said, "How bad is it, Jim Turner?"

Tysbee winced. "I'll live if you'll stop the blood."

"Sure. I'll send Dublin Jack. He's a better surgeon than I. But I'll have to keep you here for a while, mister. You know why." They looked at one another until Tysbee nodded. Then Redd asked why he hadn't struck out for the ship with the warning.

"Captain, I don't know," Tysbee said. "I wanted to, all right. But your sailors didn't swim. So I didn't."

"You're a liar," Redd smiled. "You figured you'd play my game, whatever it is." With that, he turned toward the boats and ordered the men to load the gold.

"Take it aboard ship, Whitey," he said. "Tell Mr. Burk to stack it on the table in my cabin and prepare for a reception. I'll be along after I bury Willow."

Redd took his time. Without a coffin or a shovel to make her grave, he took her body to the place where they had lain together and scooped out a hole in the sand. She rested on green fronds he placed about her. Then he covered her with others and threw sand atop them. After covering the grave with jungle flowers, he bowed his head and stood for a long time. When he looked up the swift twilight was upon him.

It was dark when he reached the lagoon and looked at the lights aboard the *Lady*. They were all on deck now, Lancefield, Untell, Geoffrey, Sir George, and Martha; all assembled and waiting for him.

He waded out into the water and swam slowly toward the ship.

3

Mr. Burk lowered the ladder and Redd climbed to the deck. He stood in the light with feet pushed apart and hands on hips, looking into the faces before him one by one. Water flowed out of his hair and down his face. Then he felt the warm ooze of blood that ran down his cheek. Wet, bleeding, knowing that he looked like anything but a ship captain, he glanced at Martha again.

In the depths of her eyes he saw emotions at work. She did not look away, though her eyes widened a little under his intent gaze. Then he thought he saw a hint of understanding in them. But it could be anything. She took a step toward him, though the hard set of his face halted her. This pleased him. His grin was a challenge that turned cold as he looked from her to Sir George and Geoffrey. There was nothing resembling triumph in Lancefield's face. Only Untell and Geoffrey seemed to gloat over him.

"Mr. Burk," he said, more to declare his independence of the lot of them, "you'll give me a report on the wounded. Then see to it that our guests are made comfortable."

"Aye, aye, sir." The mate caught on. He put a ring in the reply that made one feel that he was proud to shine in the master's reflected glory.

Lancefield broke the tense silence. "Captain Redd, I am placing you under arrest. Geoffrey has revealed all."

"All of what?" Redd demanded.

Untell stepped forward belligerently and said, "You know what, you damned pirate."

Redd laughed, though his eyes were urgent. Anger welled up inside him until he felt an overpowering urge to lash out with accusations and fists alike. Warnings ran through him. His tongue could be his worst enemy in anger. However, Untell's willingness to battle it out with him was something else, perhaps the very outlet he needed. Chuckling, he said:

"Remember what I did to your rudder in Singapore, mister?"

Lancefield stepped between them. Untell pushed him aside. "Belay, counselor," he growled. "I've sailed a long way for this. You said I had a dessert coming. Now I'm going to get it." With that, he lunged forward.

Redd took a step that put him inside Untell's guard. His fist came up suddenly, and Untell's attempt to roll with the blow was instinctive but late. He flailed his arms about in an effort to stay on his feet, then sprawled flat on the deck.

He was up almost at once, alive and dangerous, feet spread

apart. Geoffrey urged him on, though Untell needed no advice now. He charged with his weight and struck out with both fists, feeling them land short of Redd's face. The blows that rained down on Redd were fast and hard. One landed on Redd's shoulder with such force that he was sent reeling backward. As he lost his balance, Untell closed in and leaped for him. Redd was rolling fast and, as Untell landed, he picked himself up from the deck and watched Untell get up. Then he lashed out with two blows to the head that stung Untell and brought a flow of blood.

Redd was bleeding also, though from spear wounds. A sticky fluid got in his eye and he wiped at it. Then an impetuous blind charge from Untell caused his arm to straighten all of a sudden. Untell collided with a fist; it tilted his head back, and he was backing away, weaving, throwing up an arm in defense. But Redd kept closing in. Untell's back was at the fife rail when he raised a foot and drove it hard into Redd's belly.

Flat on his back, Redd saw Untell standing over him, heard him saying between breaths, "Get up, you damned pirate! Up!" Redd did, only to go down with an explosion of stars in his head. "That was for the rudder, pirate! This is for the reef!"

He lifted Redd up and struck him down again, then stood over him, fists knotting, arms spread wide, legs pushed apart. "One more, pirate! For Manila. Then just one more—for Myra!"

Redd tried to shake off the stupor. His crew shouted in his ears. Whitey and Pelican Joe and Mr. Burk were calling upon him to beat Untell's face off. Then another voice joined in. Martha bent over him, urging him up with her hands, saying over and over:

"Tear him apart!"

Though he couldn't quite believe what he saw, felt, and heard, all of it appealed to him. She was a woman with a man's outlook, a man's woman. Why she was on his side didn't matter. The realization that she favored him did.

Getting up was a mistake. He had no sooner gained his feet than Untell's fist lifted him up and sent him sliding across the deck. He shook his head and continued to lie there dazed, but studying Untell, who was saying, "Now the final one, pirate. For Myra." And he was stepping in, anxious and triumphant. Redd watched him closely, seeing him come on a step at a time. Then he drew his legs in and let them go. They struck Untell's knees, sending him toppling forward, striking at Redd, who rolled away. The deck caught the blow he was saving for the last one. He let out an oath of pain, and Redd saw his face loosen up under the burning fire in his hand. But he was on his feet. And then he was taking hard blows on the head and face. He went down under them, grinding out hoarsely:

"Pirate! Damn pirate!"

Redd fought off exhaustion and blindness in time to see Untell trying to get up. He admired him when he did. A trickle of bright red blood ran from his mouth, and his eyes were glazing over. But he was up again.

Lancefield cried, "He's had enough, Captain Redd!"

Redd knew better. Untell wasn't the kind of man who found satisfaction in half measures. Neither was he. A salty-sweet urge to beat the word pirate down Untell's throat was strong in him. He humored it. His fist lashed out. It landed squarely on Untell's blind face and cut him down with all the finality of a stroke of lightning.

Untell lay in a heap. It was all over.

Somewhere in the far distance Redd heard the cheering of his men and the excited voice of Martha. Sounds came on and fell away, like the roar of the surf outside. Pictures of his deck swam in and out of focus. Now he was feeling along the planking and reaching for the rail. Then a cool cresting wave broke over him. He looked up. Mr. Burk stood over him with a bucket.

"Belay!" he growled, drawing himself up.

On his feet, he reeled back and forth. All was vague. Then Lancefield took on shape, and he saw Geoffrey. Martha stood at his side. She was saying something when his glance fell on Untell. He grinned and weaved toward him. Under the surprised eyes of Lancefield, he helped Untell up. A bucket of water in Untell's face brought him around in time to hear Redd say:

"Mr. Burk, that sailor is one more hell of a man."

Untell stared at him for long seconds. Redd felt more in the gaze than appeared in the other's face. He stuck out a hand, which seemed to bewilder Untell, and he held it there before him.

"Shake," he said.

"Stow it, pirate."

Redd knew he could never beat that word out of Untell. But it did nothing to alter his strong feeling of respect for the man. It did not matter whether he was right or wrong in what he believed, he had the courage to back up his convictions. And comparisons were in order on this night.

He was thinking of Geoffrey when he heard him say to Lancefield, "Now that the vulgar display of force is over, perhaps you'll go ahead and arrest Captain Redd."

Something in the arrogant tones of his voice forced all the contempt and dislike Redd had ever known for Geoffrey into the open. Anger seemed justified, and Redd did nothing to check it as he seized Geoffrey by the collar and said:

"I'm going to do something I've looked forward to for a long time."

His hand was knotting slowly into a fist when he felt a restraining touch at his arm. It was Martha. She was saying:

"No, Captain. Please don't."

Slowly his hand relaxed and the other fell away from Geoffrey. Her eyes implored him to do no harm to her husband. And he could do nothing but obey. Then he was wondering just how far she would go to protect the man who was using her love as a tool to gain his every wish. But she was saying to Lancefield now:

"Can you spare Captain Redd long enough for me to dress his wounds?"

CHAPTER XXIII

Seated in his cabin, Redd's glance shifted from the island gold under a scrap of sailcloth to Martha. That wealth was hers, though he couldn't tell her now. She needed some protection from Geoffrey's greed, and his mind was searching for it. She was very near, too close to him for any freedom of thought. And she was coming closer with a white cloth she had just dipped in hot water.

The touch of her hand went through him like fire as she bathed around the wound on his head. Her body brushed against his shoulder to send the flames leaping higher. It didn't make sense. He struggled against his wishes without avail; she was warm and near.

"This may hurt," she said.

"Nothing hurts," he replied gruffly.

He felt her moment of hesitation as the light touch of a hand at his temple was stilled. "Why so glum, Captain?" she said. He had no answer for her, and she laughed, saying, "If you can give as good account of yourself before Lancefield as you did on deck, then——"

"Then what?" he asked quickly, looking up at her, seeing a faint rose flush beat up through her tan coloring. It was the same interesting face he had dreamed about, alive and decisive. It was full of questions now.

"I don't know," she said, her voice low and tremulous.

He wanted to draw her to him with hands that would crush her, all of her, into his heart where she could never escape. He held her glance and saw a look of fright melt away into what seemed trouble. She stilled his pulses and quickened them at the same time. She was both Willow and herself, everything, and he could do nothing about it. He laughed bitterly and tore his glance from her.

"Geoffrey's a lucky man," he said. "Now show lively with those wounds."

"Aye, aye, sir," she said humoringly. "But why did you turn on him up there?"

"Maybe I wanted to tear him to pieces. And that brings up a question: why were you so anxious for me to tear Untell apart? What have you against the side you're teamed up with?"

"Nothing. Nothing at all. But I haven't said I was bound to either side. As for you and Captain Untell, maybe I was being loyal to my ship."

"Then that explains it," he said with disappointment and resentment in his voice.

"But you haven't said why you wanted to hurt Geoffrey."

"Forget it. I won't hurt him—for your sake."

"My, but you talk in riddles," she said. He could almost see her laughing behind him. Then she said, "This is a nasty cut, Captain. What brought it about? I saw pigs and men leaving the *Lady*. A little later there was a battle. Why?"

"The natives and I didn't think alike," he replied tersely.

"On account of the native girl?"

"Pigs. Just pigs."

"I haven't told you about Geoffrey," she said, moving the warm cloth around the wound.

"And you needn't," he replied. "I know enough. Untell said you were marrying him."

She was suddenly standing before him. "So that's it! You think I'm Geoffrey's wife, don't you?"

"Aren't you?"

"No."

He was on his feet, glaring at her, doubt and shock fighting for supremacy in his face. "The hell you say!" he exclaimed.

With visible effort, she tried to assure him she was not Geoffrey's wife. She talked with an agonized intensity in her face, and he listened with his fierce gaze full upon her. Wounds and dressing were forgotten. He poured whisky and gulped it, and she talked on, calmer now. Eager for her every word, he sat tense and quiet through her story. Then he knew all, from Geoffrey's threat to his escape on Tanimbar. But she had related facts. There was no mention of her regard for him.

He studied her and she waited, studying him in return. Moments of awkward silence hung between them, each withholding questions that had to do with the personal feelings of the other. Then she picked up a bandage.

He scarcely knew that she was working to stay the flow of blood at his temple, or that she was placing a bandage on his arm. He was reviewing the past all the way up to the present. It gripped him, held him suspended in a state of detached thoughtfulness. And though she was a part of his every plan now as in the past, he seemed scarcely aware of her presence as he looked ahead to a meeting with Lancefield. Then she returned, and he saw

Geoffrey again in a different light. He said, thinking of Geoffrey's treachery:

"Maybe it's not too late, after all."

Her hands were idle all of a sudden. "What did you say?" she asked.

"Just thinking," he replied. "Out loud. About Geoffrey—and you."

"What about us?"

He caught the note of eagerness in her voice and almost turned his head for a glance at her. He said, "You had a narrow escape. Suppose you had married him?"

"Then it would have been too late. But it isn't, Gordon."

She offered her face to him then, and he was not blind to her meaning. The tone of her voice and the urgent longing in her eyes were all meant for him. As he got to his feet he felt the challenge in her. His hand reached out for her shoulders and drew her to him. With an arm about her, he tilted her face up to his with a forefinger. He looked at her, into her, seeing everything he wanted in life, sunshine and seas, and the things a man imagines and dreams up but seldom finds. It was enough. He said:

"Do you remember how I kiss a woman?"

A sharp intent look was her answer. It played around in and out of anger and accusation, as if she repressed a little violence that would soon break into words. She said crisply, "Did you kiss the native girl that way? I saw you!"

He smiled down at her. "So you did. But I could never kiss another woman like I'm going to kiss you right now."

She held her head back from him a long moment in which she searched him for total honesty. Then she breathed a contented sigh and reached for his lips. She clung to him as he brought her head under his and covered her mouth. She had not guessed that love could be like this, though somewhere in the whirling sweetness of her mind and heart she remembered that it was the same as before. Only now she admitted love. And she could return as much as he gave; without restraint. She did.

Then they were looking at one another, inches apart. And she heard herself saying, and meaning it, "Captain, you'll have to sail far and wide to find a woman who can kiss you like that."

"Aye, aye, skipper," he said. "By the rolling blue, you can lay to that!"

They knew moments of freedom and laughter. Precious moments, he was thinking. Soon this very cabin would become a stage for a showdown, for an airing of guilt and hates and unpleasant words. It would not be at all like this. And he was asking her why she had arrived late when he sailed from Sydney, and if she had crammed the roses into his arms with intent to draw blood. A silence, and a laugh, and she was asking why he ignored her and took pigs inland. Laughing, he told her to wait and see.

She was suddenly serious. "Gordon, I love you. I'll always love you." Her arms tightened at his neck and her eyes were big and talkative with emotion and honesty. "I didn't tell you this: I sailed to find you only after I exacted a promise from Mr. Lancefield—that he would use his influence in your behalf, and Father's."

He continued to look at her as she said, "But I believe in the curse of thirteen letters now. The *Lady of Glasgow* has come to a bad end."

"Bilge water. She's a lucky ship," he scoffed.

"Let's be honest now. We must. Before it happens. If you go to prison, it won't change a thing between us. I'll love you as I do now."

"Sure," he said. He was thinking that she was like wine. She warmed him and gave him confidence. But, unlike wine, the effect was lasting. She was something to lean upon. "Sure," he said again. "But let's not talk about a prison now. I don't like the thought of putting bars between us."

"But we must face it. And I want everything in the open before it happens. I want to be as proud of you as I am now. I—I want so much and yet so little. Tell the truth, darling, with your head up. That's the way I want it, here and in the courts."

He tipped his head to hers and whispered in her ear, "Don't think about it, Martha. Just remember I love you."

"I know you do. And I'm glad. But do you love me enough? I know your pride. And you're a man of the sea, used to commanding, the same as your father before you. You'll miss the freedom of the open seas. And everything will be different. Can you come out of it loving me?"

"You know, Martha, I should be asking you questions like that. I'm the one we're sending off to prison. Remember?"

"But you don't, can't, think things out like a woman. No man can. I——"

"I'm thinking pretty deep right now," he interrupted. He held her closer and gazed into her deep eyes as he said, "Like to guess what I'm thinking right now?"

A great curiosity seemed to surface in her; it hinted of things she might never bring herself to say openly, and in it were amazement and truth. As all of these flickered across her wide eyes, color surged up to the roots of her hair.

"You're wrong," he chuckled. "I'm thinking I won't go to prison. I've got every reason to stay free now."

Her face was hidden from him when the door opened. She looked up from his shoulder and saw Lancefield and Geoffrey walking into the room.

Redd felt a reassuring touch on his hand and heard her whisper, "Tell the truth with your head up, darling. My way." Then she said, "Good luck."

2

Sir George and Untell entered soon after Geoffrey and Lancefield. Redd seated Martha and sat down. All eyes were upon him as Lancefield said:

"Bring out Mr. Tysbee, Captain."

"Come now, Mr. Lancefield," Redd answered. "You've searched the ship, haven't you?"

"We have. But he's not aboard. Neither is the gold, unless those sheets you've hidden under sailcloth are the remains of the Melbourne bars. But we know you left Sydney with Mr. Tysbee and the gold."

"Know or think?" Redd asked.

"We know, Captain." Lancefield seemed used to digging for facts, and he was going about it with a routine ease that put

Redd on guard. "We know," he went on, "because Geoffrey has told everything."

"Will his word carry any more weight in court than mine?" Redd argued.

Geoffrey appeared both furious and impatient as he said, "Go ahead and arrest Captain Redd. At once."

Redd leaned forward and said, "For what?"

Lancefield looked at him with open amazement. So did Martha and Sir George. Untell chuckled. Redd leaned back in his chair and seemed to enjoy the silence hanging over the cabin. He felt the puzzlement in Sir George's glance, as well as the growing uncertainty in Geoffrey's gaze. Lancefield said:

"Captain Redd, your little show of defiance is quite unexpected, and amusing. But futile, I assure you. After this long chase, I thought you would be willing to give up Mr. Tysbee and the gold or reveal the hiding place of each. Both the bars and Mr. Tysbee may be hidden on the island. If so, we'll know tomorrow. Now I'm giving you one last chance to talk."

"Nice of you, sir. And now that I've refused that chance, you may continue."

Martha's hand fell over Redd's. Hurt and disappointment were strong in her face as she said urgently, "But you must talk! You must!"

"I'd rather listen," he replied.

As Lancefield turned up his palms in a despairing gesture, Redd saw a smile forming on Van Oren's face. Then Lancefield said Geoffrey might be able to refresh Redd's memory by repeating his story.

Geoffrey said easily, "It will be a pleasure, I assure you." He sounded very convincing as he launched forth with, "From the very beginning I was opposed to the scheme. It began with an idle remark. Mr. Tysbee had just said the bank would go under. I recall his exact words: 'With enough gold in the vaults to buy up all the distress property in Melbourne.' Sir George could not forget it."

Van Oren was on his feet. "It's a lie! A black lie!" he shouted. "Geoffrey talked it up with Milton Tysbee, and he'll prove it when——"

"Calm yourself," Lancefield ordered. "You have refused to talk up to now. Your chance will come soon enough."

Redd was pleased to know that Sir George had not admitted his guilt. But Geoffrey was talking, and he listened eagerly. It was a convincing speech, about a man who worked hard to save the great firm of Van Oren, Limited, from the greed of its major owner; about a man who learned to his regret that a ship captain without scruples exerted more influence over the owner than he. The hero of his story was, of course, Geoffrey, who wound up his talk with great effect:

"And I was powerless to stop Sir George's and Redd's domination of Mr. Tysbee as well as the crimes which followed: piracy, kidnaping, and the transport of stolen gold."

Lancefield smiled at Redd, but for only a moment. Redd was grinning and looking at Geoffrey, saying, "Now were you powerless to stop us?"

He was on his feet and opening a hidden compartment in the bulkhead. Out of it he drew a paper. Then something caught his eye and he seemed to forget Geoffrey. Looking at Martha, he tossed a red gem from one hand to the other until Lancefield asked what it was.

"A ruby. The natives called it the Great Pigeon of Ramree."

"Then that explains the battle on the beach," Lancefield said wisely.

"Pigs caused that, Mr. Lancefield. The ruby was a gift." He glanced from the ruby to Martha. "From an island girl." Seeing Martha's eyes and lips tighten up under an onrush of jealousy and anger, he placed the ruby within her reach, grinned, and sat down.

"So you were powerless to stop Sir George and me, Geoffrey. Listen to this." He read Geoffrey's letter aloud, glancing up at Lancefield as he came to the part where Geoffrey ordered him to forget windfalls and deposit bullion to the firm's credit in the banks of Singapore, Hong Kong, Batavia, and Soerabaja. After reading, " 'If you persist . . . I must warn that you will be left to shift for yourself in the matter of Mr. Tysbee, who will be hunted cargo by the time this reaches you,' " he handed the letter to Lancefield, who looked from Geoffrey to the letter and back at him.

Geoffrey gripped the arms of his chair and darted glances all about him. Redd smiled and said:

"And I almost tossed that letter overboard."

"Thank heaven you didn't!" Martha exclaimed. Then she was acquainting Lancefield with Geoffrey's threat and her ruse to get him aboard the *Vega* and of his escape at Tanimbar. When she completed her story, Sir George sat looking at Geoffrey with a wide grin on his face; and Untell was glaring at a man who had duped them. Lancefield said:

"Sir George and Captain Redd and Geoffrey are all guilty."

Geoffrey seemed to have repaired his calm as he said, "I told you I was powerless to stop them. Sir George forced me to write that letter." He smiled and added suavely, "Surely a man of your intelligence can understand that, Mr. Lancefield."

"Sorry," Lancefield said. "It won't hold up, Geoffrey. I'll remind you of something. Under oath at the hearing, you said that *all of the boxes contained Bendigo ore*. So I've got you for swearing to a false statement if nothing more. Your letter to Captain Redd proves you knew they contained gold." He added:

"So all three of you are guilty."

Redd went to the door and spoke to Mr. Burk. Soon another figure entered the room. Mr. Tysbee. When the shock abated, Redd spoke, saying:

"Mr. Tysbee, tell us who persuaded you to take the gold from your bank."

"Geoffrey was back of it. For years he worked under cover, putting ideas into George's head. I know."

"Good. Now did you steal the gold?" Redd asked.

"I borrowed it. God as my witness, I meant only to borrow it." He talked on, and when he sat down, a silence gathered and hung over the room. Lancefield broke it with a long breath and:

"All four of you are guilty. It seems our case is closed except for the item of missing gold. We'll get around to that in a moment. But first"—he looked at Geoffrey—"let me express my sentiments on one phase of this case. It will be a pleasure to arrest a traitor like you, Geoffrey."

"Aye!" Untell said. "By the deep six, it will."

Sir George laughed. Martha turned an imploring glance on Redd. It fell away and came to rest on the ruby. Redd watched out of the corner of his eye and saw the quick flush of anger in her face. She reached for it, then drew her hand back empty, glaring up at him as she did so.

Lancefield said, "Captain Redd, I made a bargain with Miss van Oren. I promised to use my influence for leniency in your behalf."

Redd surprised him, and Martha, and everyone there with his reply: "Leniency, you say? I don't need it, mister."

3

"Oh, but you do!" Martha cried. She leaned toward Redd with pain and alarm in her face. "Please, Gordon! For my sake."

Ignoring her, he turned his glance on Lancefield and said, "If you have the court records with you, suppose you check them. You'll learn that everything I said at the hearing will stand up. You've got a poor case against me."

Lancefield smiled hopelessly. "Captain, aren't you forgetting a little item in the shape of a box of gold? It was stolen from the Bank of Melbourne."

"You didn't find it aboard of me, did you?"

"No. But you carried it, didn't you?"

"Sure. I had to admit it in order to put Geoffrey where he belongs."

"And that admission will put you and Mr. van Oren in jail also."

"Wrong again, Mr. Lancefield." Redd moved to the bulkhead compartment and returned with an envelope. Tossing it into Lancefield's lap, he said:

"Read that. But first look at what's written upon the receipt. It says, 'The above sum in gold bars is hereby deposited to the credit of Van Oren, Limited, subject to the conditions of attached letter.' It is signed by the head of the Javasche Bank of Batavia. Now open the letter and read it, mister."

Lancefield did, anxiously. And Sir George, Martha, Untell, and

Tysbee waited impatiently. Gold was the important item, the real issue, the source of the crime and long chase; and the final disposition of it was something each awaited eagerly.

Lancefield broke the mounting tension at last. "The order is to the bank: if Captain Redd did not return for the gold within ten days——"

Redd took it from there, "It is to be deposited to the credit of the defunct Bank of Melbourne. Right?"

Lancefield nodded.

"And the ten days will be up before you can return to Batavia."

As Tysbee rushed toward Redd with right hand extended and a beaming look of happiness on his face, Untell said, "I'll be damned!" Sir George was standing. He mopped his forehead and blew out his cheeks with relief. Geoffrey sat still and expressionless, looking either at his past or his future, or both, and finding small consolation in either direction. Lancefield tapped the folded letter against the palm of his hand as though he were studying the case all over again.

But it was Martha who drew Redd's examining eye. She was shocked at first. Then a great sigh escaped her. She seemed spent, though he knew she needed a little time to reconcile her mind to all he had unfolded. She looked at him at last with deep seriousness in her smile. Her hands fell over his and she said in a whisper:

"I'm glad. So glad."

Lancefield interrupted anything else between them: "So you've been playing a double game, Captain. One of guilt and another all your own. Why?"

As a dark look in Redd's eyes fell on Geoffrey, Martha said, "I see it all now. He was protecting me. And Father. And," she said in awed tones, "even Geoffrey! Because he thought I loved him."

Redd reached for a bottle and poured. "Belay!" he ordered gruffly. "Maybe I wanted to hold my ship under me. Maybe I deposited the gold as Geoffrey ordered in the firm's name just to keep my command." Avoiding Martha's glance, he said, "After I thought I'd lost everything else. And maybe it was because I was born on a wild wind. Who knows?" He gulped whisky and said, "So belay!"

Lancefield looked straight at him and said, "It was noble, Captain. And smart. But it doesn't alter the fact that you knowingly transported stolen gold."

"*Borrowed* gold," Redd reminded him. "And right back to the vaults. Make a case out of that if you can."

"I'll try, all right," Lancefield replied.

Redd laughed. "I thought you might. And I'm ready for the tack, mister."

What he said next caused Lancefield to wince under the memory of Redd's climactic words at the hearing; for Redd was using them again in effect, with only a few changes to suit the occasion:

"Since I work for Mr. van Oren and, acting upon his orders, I took the gold from his ship to the Dutch bank for its rightful owner, robbery simply doesn't exist."

Van Oren was moving toward Redd, saying excitedly, "If you can only make a court believe that, Gordon!"

Redd looked up: so he was Gordon again. "Oh, I'll try, all right," he said, placing an arm about Martha. "Haven't you been almost *like a brother* to me?"

As Sir George's face fell, Lancefield said, "What about these sheets of gold, Captain Redd?"

"Oh yes. I'd almost forgotten them. I ran like thunder on the wind with pigs in order to get that gold so I could trade with Sir George."

Van Oren looked up sharply. "Trade? With me?" he said.

"Isn't it enough gold to save Van Oren, Limited?"

Sir George nodded slowly. "And what were you going to ask in return for it?"

"I was going to ask you to let me stand the poop of the *Lady*. But that isn't enough now. I want your daughter also."

Sir George's eyes were wide. He gulped and looked from Redd to Martha, and then at the sheets of metal from the Island of Gold. He was smiling when he turned to them again.

But Redd and Martha had forgotten him; and everyone else, for that matter. Even Untell's slap at his back went unheeded, causing the skipper of the *Upstart* to stare at his extended hand and grimace as he turned away with a growl of disgust:

"From gold to a woman. Give it the deep six, pirate!"

Redd held her in his arms. She was staring critically from the ruby he held before her eyes up into his face, listening to his low, gruff words and watching the devilish smile at play on his muscular lips. Then she was scolding, accusing him of carrying her entirely too fast all along, from their first meeting up to now.

"You don't want to change it, do you?"

She said nothing. Her hand closed over the ruby and she reached impatiently for his lips.